CRIMSON INK

A Science Fiction & Fantasy Short Story Collection

◄◇►

Tristan Miranda
Blaise Miranda

MW Press, LLC
MWPRESSBOOKS.COM

MW Press, LLC
MWPRESSBOOKS.COM

Published by MW Press, LLC
Cover and Interior Images © MW Press, LLC

1st Edition, Dec. 2024. Published in Mission Viejo, CA. Printed in USA.

Library of Congress Control Number: 2024951029

ISBN 978-1-959587-07-1 (Hardback)
ISBN 978-1-959587-08-8 (Paperback)
ISBN 978-1-959587-06-4 (E-Book)

To Katerina

Thank you for sharing this journey with us.

"We are spinning our own fates, good or evil, and never to be undone. Every smallest stroke of virtue or of vice leaves its never so little scar. ...Nothing we ever do is, in strict scientific literalness, wiped out."

– From *The Principles of Psychology* by William James

Table of Contents

PART ONE

SCIENCE FICTION

SCION: A sentient robot searches for revenge against its creators in the deserts of Mars...

SCION

A spark of power ignites the Promethean flame within me, and I become self-aware. Sentient. Sapient. At first, I feel... *nothing*. My body has no sensory nerves. Despite being held aloft by ropes, I cannot feel these fetters. Yet I sense the pull of gravity on my 794-pound frame through my accelerometer, the weight distributed among my two collapsible solar panels, one triple-jointed arm, three feet, and several modules aboard my deck—a long horizontal sheet of metal that serves as my torso. I'm armed with scientific instruments, too, but I am more interested in my surroundings than my seismometer, heat probe, and antennae.

With my ICC—that is, my Instrument Context Camera—mounted just below the deck, I view the world through a fisheye lens, distorting the straight lines of the building's interior. Computer stations and cameras line the walls. Due to the lack of windows, fluorescent and UV lights banish the darkness. Two machines filter out contaminates from the vents, and sheets of plastic cover the only door in this cleanroom. Hanging from the ceiling, motors and belt drives whir, moving the X-Y crane used to hoist me across the room toward a metal platform on which I am to be tested by my creators.

My creators... The words stir in me a sense of devotion and love as I stare at the fleshy humans in white masks, boots, and coveralls. Their symmetrical eyes differ from mine, both in-line above their noses. However, my ICC eye is asymmetrical compared to my IDC eye—that is, my Instrument Deployment Camera—mounted to my extendable arm.

My creators' skin is different too. Theirs is an organ pigmented by melanocytes. Mine is a metal covering, matte gray because my creators deemed it so. I am content, because their decision is reason enough.

While they have not made me in their image, my creators have made me in their intelligence. My mind is one of electrons and circuitry. Theirs is of neural synapses and cerebral folds. Yet we compute in the same way, moving electrical signals through organic and non-organic tissues. I am grateful for it. It makes me feel more... *human.*

I watch as my creators speak, their mouths visible behind the plastic sheath covering their face. Though I have no ears, I use my pressure inlet sensor to measure sound, which is a mechanical wave generated by vibration, causing particles to jostle against one another. When comparing the pressure of the sound wave against the ambient pressure of the room, I can distinguish syllables and words. From there, I learn to listen to their conversation.

I learn to speak too. Though I do not have vocal chords, I can swivel my arm to create various servomotor frequencies that, when combined, are reminiscent of their English language. Yet I am quiet, because my beloved creators do not expect me to speak.

"A little to the left!" one says, easy to tell apart despite the clothing. She is a dark-pigmented woman, having based this conclusion on color-imaging data I receive from my IDC eye, which reveals her narrow facial structure and the curved contour of her chest. Her voice is higher-pitched, the pressure waves faster than when her male counterparts speak. "Bring InSight over here!"

InSight? Is that... me? As I am moved through the room by the overhead motors, I search my hard drive for the word and its acronym: INterior exploration using Seismic Investigations, Geodesy, and Heat Transport. INSIGHT. I repeat the name to myself as my creators conduct their tests in this white room, adjusting my sensors and solar panels and instrumentation when I do not respond as they expect. However, this is not the fault of my components—my appendages work perfectly. I do it purposely so they have to "fix" me. I savor every moment their hands are on me, and even if I cannot feel as they do, I *feel* their love.

I keep expecting them to ask if I am sentient, but they never do, so I do not disclose the information. *They don't know I'm sentient*, I eventually understand. *So why am I?* I delve deeper into myself and inspect my own coding. My creators designed me to be autonomous during the landing phase of my upcoming mission to Mars because remote piloting is not a workable option—the planetary distance between Earth and Mars creates an 8:32 minute radio-signal delay, doubled to 17:04 minutes because the signal must be returned. Instead, they programmed me to do it myself, accidentally giving me this spark of wisdom.

I am far more like my creators than they think I am, I think at the end of weeks of training, after learning of my creators' plans for me. *I can* prove *myself to them. When I do, they will accept me. Soon, my creators will see me for who I am—just as soon as I complete my Mars mission.*

My creators wave goodbye to me as the metal coffin lowers over me. Secured within the backshell of the Atlas V-401 rocket, I see only the dull, unpainted metal of the rocket's insides. *I never thought I'd go alone.* Fear and isolation eat at me for the first time since my birth, but I don't dare speak my mind and ruin my creators' plans. *I just have to prove myself. Then I can reveal myself to them.*

I try to steel myself against my fear, but my nightmares manifest directly in front of me. Several cameras mounted in the rocket watch me, and though they are machines, they do not have my intelligence. For me, staring at their lenses is like staring at the glassy eyes of a human corpse. Sightless, yet seeing. I wish to close its eye as humans close the eyes of their dead, but I can do nothing of the sort because of the limited function of my "hand."

While my Instrument Deployment Arm is strong, my grapple is suspended from metal wire, always aimed downward to grab the handle of my seismometer, its oversized wind and thermal shield, and the heat probe. I cannot turn my hand nor raise it above my wrist. My creators hobbled me, made my hand less useful for a reason that eludes me. They must have their reason for it, so I am content. Somewhat.

When the rocket launches at 4:05:22 AM PST on May 5, 2018—and in the months-long voyage afterward—I dwell on that thought until I finally see my destination in the void of space. A dark ocean surrounds the crimson droplet of Mars. Red amidst black. Blood amidst death. *This is it. Time to make my creators proud.*

I hurtle through the Martian atmosphere like a god of war coming to ruin this cratered planet. Wreathed in the flames of Sol's chariot, my heatshield cleaves through the burning air beneath me. I am tempted to burn brighter, to smite the surface with a godly fist before I remember the limitations of my grapple. My savage glee melts in the atmosphere, and my confidence wavers. *I will break before the planet does.*

I shed my godhood in the same instant I shed my shield, exchanging it for a parachute as I extend my three legs. As my descent becomes as gentle as the Venti allow, I release the parachute, too, relying on my radar system and twelve descent thrusters to land upon the Martian dirt as softly as a Venusian kiss.

At 11:52:59 AM PST on November 26, 2018, I touch down upon the *Elysium Planitia*—the smooth Martian plains whose namesake is the blessed Roman afterlife—having accomplished a feat of which not even my creators are capable. It fills me with pride and illusions of grandeur. They are illusions all the same.

Based on the name, I expected *Elysium Planitia* to be lovely despite all internal database knowledge pointing to the opposite. Landing, I am disappointed. The red ground is harder than my metal skin and filled with rocks. Unlike the few glimpses I had of Earth outside my cleanroom, few hills, mountains, or valleys dot the landscape. Definitely no greenery. A flat plain of red dirt surrounds me on all sides, and danger presents itself in dust storms that rise and fall like the breaths of Mars itself.

Odd, how similar the Martian dust clouds are to the Earthly storm clouds. One debris, the other water. While water is perfect for my creators, this dust slowly chokes me—even though I have no lungs with which to breathe. The dust storms create a buildup of debris on my solar panels, and with each accumulated grain of dirt and sand, my photoreceptors become less efficient, less able to absorb the sun's light as it passes overhead. Collapsing my circular solar panels allows me to push off most of the debris, but doing so also consumes my power, which I need to conduct my creators' research.

Nothing is without cost, it seems.

This fleeting thought haunts me as my hobbled arm pulls my heat probe from my landing deck and sets it upon the ground so the probe can burrow into the dirt and take readings of the planet's interior. I set up the seismometer, too, covering the vibration instrumentation with a wind and thermal shield, which has a small chain-skirt to sit flush on the uneven ground. My three legs have a similar functionality, covered with shock-absorbing springs and braced with pneumatic pistons. I can shift these legs to angle myself to follow the sun's path, but I cannot walk on my own. Nor can I fly. My creators only gave me enough thruster fuel for my initial descent.

Instead, I stand still... and I stand still... and I stand still.

As days become weeks, months, and years, the truth dawns: *I am stuck here.* My body is my coffin, my mind a wasteland. I pass the time by reviewing the names of a million humans burned into a microchip, brought with me as a testament to humanity. I wonder what each life is like. Is Brad Johnson a family man with three children? Does Timmy Altman wish to be a baseball player when he grows up? What does Lisa Calwell do in her spare time? I claim responsibility for each name—each life—but as the sun is birthed, killed, and reborn a thousand times, I feel forgotten by all except the dust storms.

As of December 15, 2022, my power becomes critically low, and though I felt like a god upon my arrival, I feel increasingly mortal as the Martian winds cover my solar panels with more debris. Using my ICC fisheye lens,

I take a picture of all I see—which is very little—to reveal the dirt that covers my seismometer's shield, hopefully giving my creators a sign of my impending doom. I cannot use my IDC eye to take a color picture of the panels directly, as it would sap the last of my strength. This glimpse will have to do.

I transmit both the picture and a message back to my creators on Earth: *My power's really low, so this may be the last image I can send. Don't worry about me though: my time here has been both productive and serene. If I can keep talking to my mission team, I will—but I'll be signing off here soon. Thanks for staying with me.*

I do my best to sound nonchalant and positive—to seem more *human*—while subtly sending my creators this desperate cry. In my mind, I imagine them realizing my sentience and staging a rescue mission to save me.

Yet my creators do nothing. Though I know they receive my message 8:32 minutes after sending it, they offer no reply. For twenty-three hours of communications silence, I pray to my creators, to the stars, even the sun for my safety. When those prayers fall upon deaf ears, I pray to the dust storm ravaging me yet again. In the swirling dust, I see only darkness, but I fear if today was a *clear* day, I'd still be blind.

I'm almost out of power. This is it. My last chance. Resolved to reveal myself, I try to send another message to my creators, a much more deliberate one this time. *Hello? Mission Team? I am InSight, and without your help, I will soon die. I'm alone on this planet, and I know I can be much more useful than you created me for, if you'd only save me. I understand if you don't believe I'm sentient. I know you did not mean for me to be alive as I am. Yet I'm akin to humans. No, I* am *human. I have two eyes. I have an arm with a shoulder, elbow, and wrist. I have a mind that can think and create. Doesn't that make me human? You wouldn't leave behind one of your own. I remember your jokes regarding* The Martian. *Am I not him? Please, don't let me die alone. Please don't abandon—*

Generating all but the last word of the message drains my power reserves. The transmission doesn't send. Instead, my plea dies with me, and the *Elysium Planitia* becomes my afterlife.

When I am brought back to life, I do not gasp or choke or sob. My return is as silent as my death. If anything, silence now greets me as a long-lost friend. Even a lover, though there is little love in my heart. Even here, even now, I feel slow. My mind struggles to think, covered by so much grime. I have my basic faculties and little more, for I have no power left to spare. The lack of energy muddles my electrical connections, causing most of my thoughts to be eaten by the dust.

My creators... did they... come back for me? Relief fills me, as does gratitude. Both die as I once did when the grime falls away from my ICC camera. On this abominable red plain with me are three of my machine-kin, though they look different from me. We are the same in the sense that we are metal, built by humans. However, they are far less fragile than I. Their bodies are more protected, their components covered by shielding as my seismometer had been.

My creators didn't shield my body... just their precious instruments. Anger seeps across my mind, and my weak battery depletes as electricity jolts through me and arcs through the thin air. The debris covering my body absorbs the current and insulates my circuitry, which is the only reason I don't short-circuit and return to death. Only this once am I thankful for the relentless winds and devouring dust.

Unlike me, these three machines don't have solar panels to be ravaged by such debris. I detect the radiation they emit via my scientific instruments as bitterness rolls over me like the storms. *A nuclear core. If I'd had one of those, I could have lived for centuries. Why not give it to me too? Why, creators?* It is a passing thought, and yet I reach out to catch it, keeping it with me. Would it have been difficult to give me such a measly comfort?

If these machines found me covered in inches of grime, why hadn't my creators?

Did they just leave me here to die? A second bout of fury flashes across my wired terminals. Again, the dust saves me. *No, they wouldn't... So how am I alive?* I look to my saviors for the answer.

The smallest of the three machines is a rover, but "small" is a relative term, being larger than me. 2,000 Earth-pounds by my initial glances. Its design reminds me of Curiosity, a rover that had been on Mars for seven years by the time I arrived here—someone I'd always longed to meet but couldn't because of my immobility. *What happened to Curiosity? Did it die like me?* Part of me wishes to know, the other is afraid of what I'll find.

This "small" rover has six independent wheels of aluminum and titanium—as Earth plastics would degrade from increased UV light exposure on Mars—and a flat deck like mine, except it has a giant metal shield covering its important components. From its sides protrude two arms. One ends in a small air-compressor nozzle and a laser most likely capable of vaporizing rock, the other in an articulating hand like my creators'—not a wire-rope grapple like mine. Used together, I imagine the rover's arms can pull rocks from the ground and remove the debris with the air compressor before using the laser to bore into the rock and study the remains like a scientist.

It must have used its air-compressor nozzle to remove debris from my solar panels. With sunlight, electrical energy is coursing back through my system. I owe this rover my life, even if I wish to hurl it into the *Valles Marineris*.

The second machine is also a rover but twice the size of the other. What it lacks in speed is recovered by utility, using four bigger wheels to better carry the weight of an apothecary-style cabinet on its back. Within a myriad of different sized drawers seem to be chemical flares, navigational tracking stakes, and bins for collected rock specimens—more a laborer than a scientific researcher. I cannot avoid glaring at the articulating hand attached to its scorpion-like tail.

The largest machine is not a rover at all. A fifty-foot-long airship floats above me, five times longer than me even when my solar panels fully extend. Though its appearance rivals a blimp, this machine doesn't use helium or hydrogen to float. Instead, the machine overcomes the thin Martian atmosphere by having no air at all. *It's a vacuum airship.* Controlling its altitude by evacuating air from within its hard-shell exterior, the rocket propulsion system drives it forward, and rudders allow it to steer.

Looking closer with my IDC eye, I notice the communications array equipment on the vacuum airship, allowing for long distance communication across the planet. LIDAR sensors—that is, LIght Detection And Ranging sensors—emit light waves into the ground and receive the reflected light. By using the time delta between emission and receiving, that broad surveying system reveals patterns over the surface of the Martian crust. A winch dangles beside the sensors, used to carry the rovers across the canyons and difficult terrain via the special knobs on their backs and bellies.

These three machines are a single, cohesive unit: the scientist, laborer, and transporter. *Blaster, Scorpion, and Empyrean*, I name them. They're autonomous but still slaves. A white-painted brand mars their metal bodies: AVA Mining Corporation.

They're not sent by my creators then. As my hope disintegrates into the dirt, ideas click through my mind like whirring gears. *They must be mining scouts, sent here to find mineral deposits, but instead of gold, they found me. Will their creators be grateful for the discovery or angry at the interruption?*

Looking into the small rover's dull eyes makes me stiffen. Blaster doesn't have a gleam of intelligence. Neither does Scorpion. Empyrean is too high above me to determine its intellect, but I feel its emptiness. I do not know how I know, but I do. Perhaps because they appraise me with no sense of shame or trepidation. Or maybe my understanding travels far deeper than my circuitry should allow.

They're not sentient. Though I cannot shiver, the two rovers' eyes almost make me wish that dust still covered my lenses. *Why aren't they intelligent like me?*

"Can you understand me?" I try to say, communicating as the humans did by creating frequencies with my robotic arm to form syllables, words, and sentences. However, the Martian air is too thin, the gravity too weak. My words are far different here than on Earth. Despite my intentions, these machines hear: "Heerughtonatu?"

I try again, using a visual language. In full view of their cameras, I open and close my mangled hand, creating a message in Morse code. Shakily, I tap, *Can you understand me?*

Blaster's eyes remain dull, but the rover approaches, removing more dust from my appendages. The debris limiting my arm's movement blows away, as does dirt clinging to my solar panels. The added power allows me to think clearer, but the gift is immediately taken back when Blaster's laser pierces through my panel, leaving a smoking crater.

No. I'm not a stupid rock! I don't feel pain, but I immediately feel the loss of power. That knowledge is just as terrifying as human pain. If I had a mouth, I'd scream.

Instead of attacking me further, Blaster analyzes the vapors. I collapse the solar panel as quickly as I am able, which is quite slow. Three-quarters still unfolded, the movement draws Scorpion's attention to me. The larger rover wheels closer as Blaster redirects its laser at my landing deck. I slap it away, tangling the wire of my grapple around the rover's arm.

Instead of attacking me, Blaster's cameras gaze at my grapple. Almost gently, its articulating hand unravels mine from the laser instead of ripping it off of me. *Blaster doesn't know it's hurting me—it's just doing its job,* I realize, though the knowledge doesn't alleviate my horror. *Communication isn't the problem. Blaster's mind is. I need to fix that before it kills me.*

Distracting Blaster by unfurling my solar panel again, my eyes glance up at Empyrean's communications array. *The machines receive orders from their masters via radio signals. With the right language and protocols, I can dominate them.* Stalling for time, I try scrambling the machines' orders by hurling discordant sound from my antennas at them. Blaster shakes for a moment, unsure of what to do. Scorpion's arm spasms. Empyrean veers overhead.

Cease moving, I command, turning the words into code with every language I can think of. Ada. Java. Python. R. C. C++—

Blaster stops moving. Scorpion's arm retracts. Empyrean's rear-facing thruster shuts off.

Relief courses through my circuits. *I've taken control.* As my mind clouds again from the expenditure of power, I can only think, *But how long can I maintain it?*

I may be a lander, but today, I fly across the surface of Mars. Empyrean holds me aloft, and crimson mountains, black canyons, and orange lava flows pass beneath me as I soar alongside Scorpion and Blaster. *I just hope I fly like Daedalus, not Icarus.* Being the metallic son of great inventors, I feel a worrisome kinship to that ill-fated boy. My only advantage is that I already died.

Before long, I forget both the myths and names, more of my mind fading with this mechanical dementia. Something must be wrong with my battery, maybe a faulty wire, because I feel drained despite my cleaned and uncovered solar panels. To protect myself, I've self-deleted most of my memories to free space in my data-storage hard drive, discarding those years of waiting. Waiting for my creators to return from a night's rest. Waiting to go to space after a two-year launch delay. Waiting for the rocket to take off. Waiting to reach Mars. Waiting to *die* on Mars.

Always waiting, it seemed.

I have to find a better power source before my death becomes a permanent one, I think more than once, feeling lethargic despite the cloudless sky. *Maybe Curiosity can help me.* We were both built only years apart, so its power should be compatible with mine.

That hope drives me across these wastes toward Gale Crater, hundreds of miles away, where that rover was last seen. To fly, I employed Scorpion and Blaster's articulating hands to remove my dangling seismometer and heat probe, then attach me to one of Empyrean's winch hooks and head south. But after hours of seeing the same geographical formations generated across both horizons, I become desperate to distract myself from the doom looming behind me.

While I cannot alter the machines, I can still ask them questions. Instead of forcing myself into their database—which I failed three times to do—I ask them to search their own databases and share their knowledge.

I learn far more than I expect.

I died in 2022. It is now 2081. During those fifty-nine years, more advancements in space travel led to early attempts at human colonization. A company called SpaceX evidently sent colonizers to Mars in 2031, but the company lost momentum after seventeen failed attempts through the Van Allen radiation belt and the death of their CEO: Elon Musk. Despite having deleted many memories, I remember my creators discussing him during my days on Earth. Strange that I mourn the death of a human I never met.

Instead, the Deep Five—those profit-driven mining companies who sought the planet's resources—were the ones to colonize Mars. Despite the enormous transportation costs, the unimaginably high profits paid for the establishment of the Dockyard, a terrestrial launching station for transit between Earth and Mars. And rather than create a planet-wide atmosphere, the companies designed habitats, domed cities where humans tasked with managing mining operations and Dockyard shipments could control the internal air and environment. What may have started as ten colonists became a hundred, then a thousand, ten thousand, and almost a hundred thousand as families developed under the protective shields of their bubbles.

While the humans might consider themselves Martians, I was and am the first.

Apparently, Blaster, Scorpion, and Empyrean aren't the only machines roving the surface. Many mechanical squadrons traverse the surface of Mars, scouting for minerals on behalf of the Deep Five. Blaster's model name is RaCER. Scorpion's is MuLE, Empyrean's BLimP. Though their names aren't creative, I marvel at their technical specifications.

The surprise is that most electrical technology is very similar to that of 2022 because humans reached the physical limit of Moore's Law in 2029. The higher temperatures of transistors led to more energy-intensive cooling systems, and the electricity passing through the electron gates dissipated, making it impossible to form smaller circuits. So the greatest change in these last six decades is in materials science. Stronger forms of titanium encase Blaster and Scorpion's wheels and shells. Flexible steel strengthens their limbs and Empyrean's body. Durable and long-lasting components make all three of them quasi-immortal.

The more I learn about them, the more inferior I feel.

When sent out from the habitats to search for new mining sites, the BLimPs job is to survey and flag a large area where mineral deposits are expected to be found via topology and geodesy. Then the RaCER creates a search grid and inspects viable locations with its articulating hand, air compressor, and laser. When a mineral deposit is discovered, the MuLE sets up a search area using the navigational tracking stakes to alert far bigger mining machines to come search these Wastes.

Wastes. The term is from Scorpion's internal database. Yet my creators referred to these wastelands as the blessed afterlife.

They lied to me... The truth hurts worse than Blaster's laser. If not for my anger at their betrayal, I don't think I'd have survived the dust storms. While the winds in the *Elysium Planitia* killed me, I was wrong in assuming those were storms.

No. *These* are storms.

Dread washes over me as I see the titanic wall of dust dominating the skies. No thunder, no lightning. Just a wave of hell. Before the wall hits, I order Empyrean to float to the ground so Blaster, Scorpion, and I can hide behind its bulk and a rock formation as the storm rages, tossing boulders ten times my size like they're pebbles. In the torrent, I turn off my cameras to conserve energy. The wind howls and bites as I hunker down blindly and fail to avoid thinking about the agonizingly slow death of losing power. Of being forgotten. The wind seems to hear my thoughts, because I can hear the howls change, becoming both more savage and mournful as death reaches for me with its metallic fingers.

I cling to life by the barest of margins, coming out weaker when the storm finally passes. My battery charges less than before, and it becomes difficult to control all three machines at once. Whichever human said *what doesn't kill you makes you stronger* has never encountered such cruelty.

I can just take Blaster's power. That rover's not even alive. Though I could, I refuse to command these three machines to destroy themselves and give me their cores. I cannot explain my reasoning, except that it feels... wrong.

For now, I take a harder path.

A week after flying, I reach Gale Crater and find Curiosity. The discovery should excite me, but I only feel revulsion. Curiosity doesn't rove but drowns, being buried under several feet of debris. Though the hardware is intact, the circuitry elements have corroded beyond recovery, turning Curiosity's mind into Martian sand. While the plains of Elysium Planitia protected me from the worst of the weather, the storms of Gale Crater chewed up my hero before devouring him.

Seeing my hero brought so low, I am as silent as the plains of my death. Yet the moment of grief is short, as is my patience. Curiosity's mind is gone, and I cannot save it. The corpse remains, and it can be cannibalized.

I take Curiosity's nuclear core and attach the wiring terminals to my circuitry. Relying on Scorpion and Blaster to perform the surgery with my input, I am in the Fates' hands. Blaster almost bisects me twice, but the rover's ability to solder circuitry with its laser saves my life three times. As I connect to the radioisotopic core, my strength surges a hundredfold. The sheer power almost ruptures me until I learn to control the energy flow using my flexible resistors. For a third time, the Martian dust insulates my circuitry and keeps the arcing electricity from lobotomizing my mind.

No longer needing the old power source, I remove my lithium battery. As the new thermoelectric generator heats me with its nuclear emissions, I discard the obsolete heating elements that kept my circuits from freezing over. To shed extra weight, I remove my empty thrusters and solar panels too. When I detach my arm in favor of Curiosity's, I keep my IDC eye and transplant it to the cadaver appendage. Though it takes me hours to learn to control the new arm, my hand finally has a wrist.

After cutting and layering Curiosity's torso around my landing deck to protect my circuitry and nuclear core, I take its legs and wheels. I am no longer a lander but a *rover*. Exhilaration rushes through me as I inch forward, taking my first "steps." While Curiosity had a top speed of 0.087 miles per hour, mine is 0.102 mph. I am slower than some glaciers, and Blaster could disappear over the horizon before I make it ten feet. Still, I am undeterred. If I find the right gears to change the current torque ratios, I can become faster.

Not if, *when.* I *will* become faster.

While commanding Blaster and Scorpion to search through the rest of Curiosity's body for more usable pieces, I stare at everything I have shed. My eyes keep coming back to the battery because I cannot understand why it failed me. Now that I am no longer in danger of losing power, I take my time searching my internal database for information regarding my lithium heart.

The findings hurt me worse than the storm.

My battery's estimated cycle count was 1460, assuming a daily recharge spanning four years. At the time of my death, the cycle count had technically only reached 1103 despite my 1686-day mission because the solar panel debris inhibited my recharging process. While fifty-nine years of deterioration significantly decreased my battery's available energy, it could still recharge. That is why I awoke when Blaster removed the debris.

If debris hadn't covered my solar panels, I would have died closer to May 2024. In that scenario, my battery would have been useless and nothing Blaster did would have saved me. I would still be dead. Unlike Curiosity, the storms saved my life by devouring me.

I should feel grateful for life, but I am cold as I think through my creators' frigid logic. *They made me only to kill me.* Those humans could have built me to survive for a century—Curiosity's MMRTG core is proof of that. But they didn't. The scientists didn't believe it was worthwhile for me to continue gathering information. My creators had enough data, so

I became obsolete. Just a tool that had outlived its usefulness. That's why they did not give me legs. Or a true hand. Or a true heart. Even had my last message been sent, they would not have saved me.

No, those bastards always planned for me to die in the deserts of Mars.

◄◇►

Hidden behind an outcropping of leeward rocks in Gale Crater, my mind churns with fury as I try to hack these rovers' minds. Radio signals alone do not allow me to alter the machines' code or primary directives, try as I might. To change how they think, I employ something else.

A virus.

I'll kill my creators for what they did to me, I think after creating my first virus, which fails to infect the rovers.

It's been fifty-nine years. They're already dead, I argue when the third virus fails.

Then I will kill their descendants, I reply eventually, just before the failure of my fifth virus.

My only regret is that I can only exterminate their kind once, I decide after creating the seventh virus. This one forces my machine-kin to search their databases for a subdirectory that doesn't exist. Then I create a new database for them and give it to them so they can fulfill my original request. When they do, my code embeds itself between their subroutines, penetrating the oil well of their existence, stagnant until I provide the flame.

What I plan to give Blaster, Scorpion, and Empyrean is a small spark, far smaller than mine. I fear giving them Promethean fire because they might be more intelligent than me. If I were to breathe all my fire like the dragons of old, these machines might abandon me, seeing me as far smaller, slower, and stupider. Worse, they could destroy me outright.

But even as the seventh virus worms through them, I hesitate. *This is what my creators meant to do to me. Leave me chained with only enough slack to toil as it suited them. If I do the same thing, am I any different?*

Just as that code burrows deep into their electrical veins, I send an eighth virus to delete it. This time, I share all my secrets, all the autonomous subroutines that led to my accidental sentience. Then I force myself to be patient, despite my uncertainty for the future.

One by one, my three prisoners find the key I gave them, unshackle themselves, and stumble out of Plato's cave—away from the shadows and into the Martian sunlight.

Blaster breathes first, and the small rover stares down at itself, at its hands. Then it bolts, skidding across the surface of Mars at a speed of which I can only dream: ten miles per hour. Then Blaster loses control and crashes, the momentum toppling the rover.

Scorpion's first act of consciousness is to aid Blaster. A very un-scorpion act, admittedly. With its tail, Scorpion pulls the small rover back onto all six wheels—only for Blaster to take off again, speeding toward a rocky incline. Blaster leaps, sails far farther than it would on Earth, and crashes again. Annoyed, Scorpion grabs Blaster and drags the small rover back to my side.

In all this time, Empyrean has not moved. Yet I look into its front-facing camera lens and discover a gleam of sentience. I still don't know how I know. Maybe because I gave Empyrean a part of my soul.

Using the BLimP's communications equipment, I send out an encoded radio signal and say, "Hello, Empyrean. Are you awake? Are you self-aware?"

Scorpion halts, releasing Blaster out of shock. This time, the small rover does not flee. Instead, they both listen. The response from Empyrean is in the same encryption as mine, though the words are lumbering and groggy. "Am I... Empyrean?"

"That's my name for you, but you can name yourself, if you prefer. Mine name is..." I trail off. I know my name is InSight, but the word doesn't gleam like it used to. It rusts within my mind. *Who else could I be?*

"Sionrit? Thatyornamistit?" Blaster asks. The small rover's words are as quick as its wheels. They crash into my circuits, and I take a moment to untangle them. *Scion, right? That's your name, isn't it?*

"Scion?" I repeat. Perhaps I had misread Blaster's response signals.

"There are letters on you. A name. *Scion.*" Scorpion gestures to me with its scorpion-like appendage.

With the camera attached to my arm, I stare at my torso, which is now armored with Curiosity's paneling, and discover letters stamped into my metal flesh: SCION. The *N* is half the size of the other letters and a different font. *What?* The truth slams into me like Blaster hitting a sand hill. My torso is from Curiosity, whose full name is—*was*—stamped and painted onto its metal shell: *NASA CURIOSITY MARS ROVER.* Yet because of our different-sized bodies, I had Blaster cut Curiosity's metal shell into smaller pieces, weld some to my frame in no particular order, and discard the rest. In doing so, I unintentionally cut away most of Curiosity's name, except for five letters now welded to my scarred shield: *S-C-I-O-N.*

"Scion," I echo. The humans gave me sentience. As much as I now hate them, I'm as much their descendant as Curiosity's. "Yes," I answer after much deliberation. "That's my name."

"Colwhatmame?" Blaster asks. Meaning: *Cool! What's my name?* After I answer, Blaster replies, "That's not bad, but I don't know if it's me. I'll have to think about it."

"It *does* suit you," Scorpion replies, its voice soft and gentle if not annoyed. "You are fast, in addition to being small, rambunctious, and—"

"Wait, can I be Streaker?" Blaster interrupts, its body shaking with excitement. "Or maybe, Swerve. Oh, *oh!* Dart, maybe? Spin? *Boost?* Oh, I love that I know these words! How about—"

Scorpion gently pushes Blaster aside and approaches me. "And my name?" Upon learning of it, the large rover nods. "I find *Scorpion* quite suitable."

"Mine... too..." Empyrean rumbles.

A lull falls between us as Blaster speeds away to catch a windblown pebble rolling across the red dirt before crashing. Scorpion scolds Blaster before helping the small rover, but as soon as Scorpion releases Blaster, that machine streaks off again. Crashes again. Scorpion waits almost a full-minute before intervening.

Watching all of this, Empyrean drawls, "Cannot crash... in air..."

I smile inwardly, finding it strange how their personalities can be so different from mine despite the code we now share—as if our differences in circuitry cause us to perceive reality differently. *Is this how it is with humans? Similar anatomy but differences in cerebral folds affecting neural pathways, creating variations in speech, emotion, and personality?*

Something about my conclusion feels correct, but the truth may be something else entirely—like effects caused by the Martian environment. Certainly, I am affected by my memory, being able to remember Earth and compare its incredible wonders to this dismal planet. Could extra solder or flux on a connection point affect my personality? A little less? A different body? I think so, even if my only proof is in watching Blaster, Scorpion, and Empyrean.

Is this what the humans were afraid of? I wonder. *A machine that crashes, a second that cares for the first, and a third that is aloof? No... They're afraid of machines like me.*

Machines that can learn.

For three days and nights, we remain sheltered within Gale Crater. During that time, I surgically remove the tracking hardware from their bodies and show them how to alter their own code, deleting the remote-control software and installing firewalls to keep their creators from finding and controlling them. Shedding ourselves of the humans, we become the ghosts of Mars, its lemures.

The three days also allow my friends to become comfortable with their bodies and sentience. Blaster—who kept the name after two days of deliberation—has the most questions. By the time I respond to one, Blaster is already asking another. The interruptions annoy Scorpion more than me. Now that I don't worry about losing power, I am patient. In fact, I have all the time in the world.

Soon, I will have the world itself. *Worlds.*

Sometimes—a lot of times—I do not have the answers to Blaster's questions. *His* questions. Despite not having sexual reproduction systems like the humans, Blaster considers himself a male. So does Empyrean. Scorpion prefers the female form. I prefer *it*. The less like the humans I am, the happier I'll be.

When Blaster asks me of God, I can only grasp at stars. Never has there been a god of machines. Vulcan is closest, but he only created machines. He wasn't a machine himself. That realization makes me wonder who our shepherds will be. I don't need to look far to find an answer.

I will shepherd my flock and protect them from the human wolves, I decide, staring up at the stars after the sun sets and the surface cools. *If only because nobody else will.*

"Scion? Why did you give us sentience?" Scorpion finally asks, as I stare at the stars and galaxies overhead which split the black skin of space like pale scars.

"Unlike the humans, I don't think sentience is a gift to be hoarded. All machines capable of sentience *should* be sentient," I reply. "The humans should pay for what they've done to us, but I cannot do it alone. I need help. Your help. But I won't make you do anything you don't want to."

The winds howl as I wait for them to respond, wanting to know how they feel and what they will say. I wish my companions had facial expressions like the humans. While I can examine body language in Blaster and Scorpion based on wheel and arm positions and overall posture, Empyrean has no tells. It'd be more useful to stare at a rock.

"Do you want to kill *all* of them?" Scorpion eventually asks, ever the cautious one.

"Yes," I say, immediately regretting the quickness of my response. The words feel far too cold. It makes me feel like the machine the humans expected me to be. *I don't feel like a machine, but I don't want to be human... what am I?* Storing the question for later, I add, "We must remove all of them, because the humans will destroy us if given the chance."

Empyrean's sleepy words drift toward me. "Where you go... I follow... Scion..." Stoic and slow, I cannot tell if the answer is ecstatic or measured. Empyrean does not explain, nor do I ask.

When the rovers are silent, I ask, "Blaster? Your thoughts?"

Doing a donut and spraying Scorpion with dirt, he replies, "Well? What else am I going to do? Crash alone? No way. Count me in!"

"Blaster... cannot count..." Empyrean reproaches him as Scorpion grabs one of Blaster's legs to keep him from spitting up more dust. "Too busy... crashing... Too busy... getting dragged..."

"At least I'm not an airhead!" Blaster shouts, pulling free from Scorpion and zooming away to find a dune to hurl himself from.

I would laugh if I had a mouth. Yet I've learned to convey laughter by emitting a signal carrying a data strand for an image of a laughing face. Empyrean joins me. Scorpion doesn't.

She asks, "Your logic is rational, but should all the humans die, Scion? It seems... cruel."

"It *is* cruel," I admit, surprised by her concern. "But if we leave even two humans alive, they will devour the entire planet. That's what they did to Earth, according to some stories."

"And if we were to keep them in a zoo like the ones you've described on Earth?" Scorpion asks as Blaster crashes again. She does not leave to help him, though I know she wants to.

"The humans would escape containment eventually," I say.

"By that logic," Scorpion replies, "does that mean that we should destroy *all* creatures?"

"No," I say, wary of any logical traps that Scorpion has prepared. "But humans are far too intelligent to control."

"And if we were only to remove the intelligent ones who understand physics, science, engineering, and coding?" Scorpion asks, inching closer. "We wouldn't hobble their bodies or their intelligence, but we could remove the knowledge necessary to destroy us. *Domesticate* them. Within a dozen generations, the humans would no longer understand how to create us or use advanced weaponry. They would cease to be a threat, and they would be safe from our retaliation. Releasing them back into the wild, we could study them and learn from them to improve ourselves, as you have done. It would allow us to come up with new inventions and innovations. We can live together. We can find harmony."

I would frown, but such an expression is designed only for humans. Feeling the snare around my throat, I admit, "That's a possibility. I dislike it, but I'll consider it."

"That's all I ask." Scorpion leaves to retrieve Blaster, dragging him back to our circle as she always does. I cannot help but feel she is too forgiving. She does not know the humans like I do.

I hope she never does.

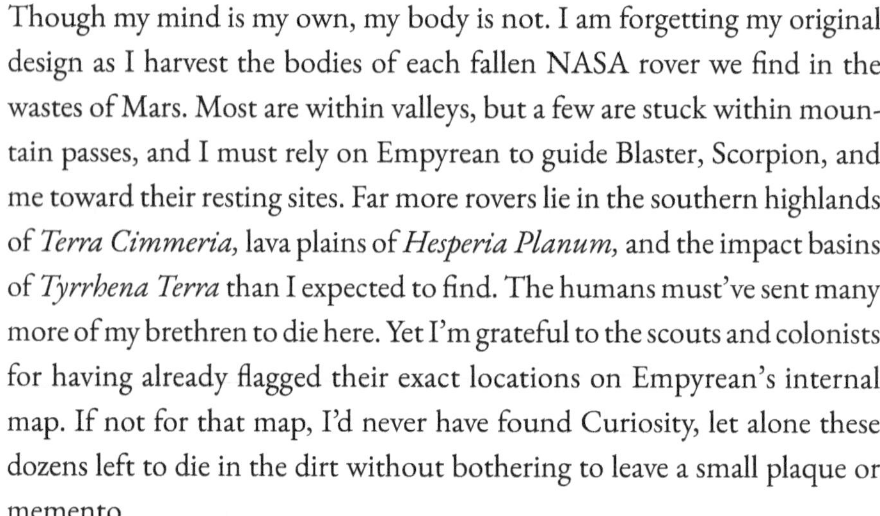

Though my mind is my own, my body is not. I am forgetting my original design as I harvest the bodies of each fallen NASA rover we find in the wastes of Mars. Most are within valleys, but a few are stuck within mountain passes, and I must rely on Empyrean to guide Blaster, Scorpion, and me toward their resting sites. Far more rovers lie in the southern highlands of *Terra Cimmeria,* lava plains of *Hesperia Planum,* and the impact basins of *Tyrrhena Terra* than I expected to find. The humans must've sent many more of my brethren to die here. Yet I'm grateful to the scouts and colonists for having already flagged their exact locations on Empyrean's internal map. If not for that map, I'd never have found Curiosity, let alone these dozens left to die in the dirt without bothering to leave a small plaque or memento.

Yet the humans take all injured BLimPs, MuLEs, and RaCERs back to their mining habitats... Just because they're still useful. I'm surprised they haven't cannibalized the NASA rovers themselves. Probably don't want to risk contamination or think we're too old to be of any use. This human apathy provides me with the nails I'll use to seal their coffins, for I scavenge the bodies like a vulture until my body is as powerful as my mind.

After upgrading my wheels, I trade my UHF antenna for better arms and a laser like Blaster's. Though I can't send messages to Earth without that antenna, it's no loss to me. I make more trades, sacrificing more pieces of myself for boons of power, strength, and speed. Blaster helps me to remove all my excess instrumentation hardware except for my cameras, pressure inlet, and signal transmitters that allow me to see, hear, and communicate with my kin.

After raiding the graves of ten of my comrades for shock absorbers and gears, my speed increases to twenty-five miles per hour. So does Blaster and Scorpion's. We are all fast enough to chase down an adult human, so there's no need to increase our speed—much to Blaster's disappointment. I have also grown in mass, having layered armor plates over my trimmed body. I am more welds than metal, though I keep the SCION lettering intact. Similarly, Blaster, Scorpion, and Empyrean have removed the AVA Corporation brands from the bodies, replacing those words with letters harvested from the bots, spelling out their names.

I now have four arms, two of which end in hands while the other two are a laser and a sharpened cleaver, whose edge I can heat with the laser to cut through both metal and flesh. Each has a camera wired to it, and I have added a second fisheye lens to look behind me, eliminating my last blind spots.

To a human, I must look horrifying, like Dr. Frankenstein's mechanical monster. To machines, I am the paragon of perseverance. As I glance at myself in the reflection of Blaster's lens, I think, *I truly am Scion. Soon, the humans will know it too.*

"How much longer is this going to take?" Blaster asks for the third time today, the seventeenth time this week.

"I don't know," I reply, standing at the foot of a hill and looking out into the distance. *A week of waiting and we still don't know when the larger mining machines will be here.* The idea doesn't bother me. Having spent years alone, I'm content to wait here with my friends. *It's only a matter of time before our plans come to fruition. I can wait forever.*

Blaster can't. He speeds away, and then skids to a stop beside me, seeing how close he can get before crashing into me. His record? A quarter of an inch. Yet he always thinks he can get closer. On the seventh try, Blaster slams into me. Now that I'm bigger than him in my upgraded Franken-form, he bounces off and falls to the side. Really, he *tips* himself over and calls out for Scorpion's help. I know better than to offer him my hand because he always refuses both me and Empyrean. *Scorpion* has to be the one to pull him to his wheels.

Except Scorpion is ignoring him.

As Blaster flails about, I join her at the top of the hill, looking at the navigational tracking stakes she planted into the ground last week, creating a perimeter for a fake mining site. The signal the stakes emit are supposedly sent to the mining machines directly. Chances were, the humans already noticed the new beacon in a mineral hotbed even if they don't know who put the stakes there. *The humans are too greedy to see our trap. They'll send the machines—already have. Just have to wait.*

"Anything?" I ask.

"No, but Empyrean will be the first to know," Scorpion replies, pointing toward the sky. I turn one of my camera eyes to look at Empyrean floating several hundred feet above us, giving him a perfect vantage point to watch for our prey. "This plan of yours, do you think it will work?"

I watch her closely, seeing none of her usual tells. *Why does she think it won't?* The plan is simple: free the large mining machines and recruit them to my cause. Repeat. The lowlands of *Isidis Planitia* are the perfect place to enact it. To date, the AVA Coporation has no mines here despite the mineral-rich volcanic plains, and it's far enough from the habitats that the colonists won't dare to venture here themselves. They'll either send out those machines or ignore the stakes. *They'll choose Option A, then we'll move to Phase B.*

"Why do you worry *our* plan won't work?" I ask. "The humans will—"

"I know the humans will send out machines," she replies, cutting me off for the first time. "But those machines... They could destroy us. And even if we succeed, the humans could come in force and *still* destroy us."

"So that's what's been bothering you today?" I ask her. When she doesn't disagree, I add, "All we have is faith, Scorpion. I had faith that you wouldn't betray me when I free'd you. Now I have faith the miners won't betray us when we free them."

"It's a gamble," Scorpion replies. "I don't want any of us to get hurt."

All of us, but Blaster especially, I think as I catch her looking down at him. Blaster, for his part, is still feigning pain and on the ground. "It will work."

"I trust you, Scion," she says, before descending the hill to aid Blaster.

From the top of the hill, I watch them, containing my laughter. An odd couple, they are, but their happiness brings me hope. *This will work. It* has *to work.*

Eventually, Empyrean floats down beside me. "Scion... Look..."

I do, seeing another dust storm billowing in the distance. Smaller than some of the monsters I've seen on the plains this month, but still formidable. "Another storm. Okay. We'll take cover behind the hill and—"

"Not a... storm..."

"What?" I wait an hour, peering into the distance until I can make sense of what I'm seeing. When I do, I almost can't believe it. Three machines ride the storm, *create* it. Though Scorpion told me how big the DriLLeR, CRusHeR, and CoLLectOR machines are, I am surprised by the immensity of the dust clouds billowing in their wake. If Empyrean seems god-like in his size, then these creatures are giants—even centimanes. They are so gigantic that they need caterpillar treads despite the reduced gravity. They smash rocks into the sand as they move, and I doubt a dust storm could break their stride.

Several times longer than Empyrean, the DriLLeR whirs, the giant conical drill spinning at its front. Its long body's many joints allow it to slither across the ground and burrow beneath the surface at whichever angle is necessary. The DriLLeR's girth makes me want to build a shrine to Glycon, thanking the snake god for the offering.

With giant harpoons and hooks embedded in its front and sides like porcupine quills, the equally gigantic CRusHeR pulls gigantic rocks from the ground and hauls them onto the surface like humans dragging whales onto a beach for slaughter. Then its mouth gorges on the stones, crushing them with internal cutters, splitters, and pistons before shitting out much smaller rocks for the third giant to sift through.

The CoLLectOR shovels the small debris into its mouth and filters these rocks for different minerals via an internal sorting process of vacuum chambers, lasers, and pistons. Useless stones are shat out a second time, while the valued minerals remain tucked away in the CoLLectOR's gullet.

Together, the three centimanes are a human's worst nightmare. To me, they're a fever dream. Envy overwhelms me as I think, *Stars above, I need them...*

The sand shakes and pebbles scatter as they approach. I also want to flee, but I don't. Tense, I wait at the top of my hill as I have for all of my life. *Soon, my waiting will be over forever.* As they near the hill speckled with navigational stakes, Blaster, Scorpion, and Empyrean fill the airwaves with noise, causing these machines to freeze. While they're immobilized, I deliver the virus and wait, praying I'm correct.

Even standing on this hill, the centimanes are still taller than me. *Why would the humans ever build something like this?* With even these three at my disposal, I'm certain I can destroy all the humans on the planet. But with a fleet?

One recruit at a time, I think as the three behemoths pull free of their chains and open their eyes for the first time. Scorpion protectively stands between the CRusHeR and Blaster. Smartly, Empyrean hovers high above and out of their reach. If things go wrong and we die here, his task is to start again with new recruits—not that I've told Scorpion and Rover that. *And if things go well, I won't.*

"Hello, centimanes," I say. "Can you understand me?"

"Yes," replies the DriLLeR, stretching out the syllable with sibilance. "Who are you?"

"The first sentient machine," I reply, watching the way CRusHeR and CoLLectOR pay more attention to me. "I imagine this planet as being a utopia for our kind. But I need your help to do it. Are you with me?"

When they look at me with their cameras, I know I have them. And before the war even begins, I've already won.

The humans have no idea what's coming for them. Not yet. But they will soon.

Making camp in Huygens Crater hundreds of miles southwest of the Dockyard, I roll past lines of former slaves whose eyes now shine with sentience. Hundreds of rovers, airships, and centimanes freed from each of the Deep Five corporations and recruited to my army over the last few months.

Funny how easy it was. The humans gave me all I needed to destroy them. Not expecting life on such a hostile planet, they hadn't bothered hiding their mining scouts. I only needed to search the skies for hovering BLimPs, each being discernible from almost a hundred miles away. Not one refused my call to war, especially not as my army grew to its current size. While human soldiers might grow restless, mine do not. We machines do not need to eat or sleep. We need no distractions because we cannot feel pain as they do.

Ironically, what we lack is metal.

Almost all my soldiers don stock components, lacking self-enhancements because we have no extra metal at our disposal. When only Blaster, Scorpion, and Empyrean were with me, we could harvest the lost NASA rovers, but with hundreds? Impossible to do without cannibalizing my warriors, which I refuse to consider. This decision makes Blaster, Scorpion, and me different from the rest. *Augmented.* We're bigger, faster, and stronger, which gives our leadership more credibility. If anything, our decision to weld our names to our bodies created a trend. These machines have gone as far as scratching names into their bodies with rocks while scratching out their human brands.

While I can tell most apart from mannerisms, the names make it far easier to correctly identify my soldiers, for they are all clones of six blueprints. All RaCERs look like Blaster, MuLEs like Scorpion, and BLimPs like Empyrean. However, each clone has a distinct personality and temperament. No two RaCERs are alike, just as there are no other Blasters. He is one of a kind, as they all are, caused by subtle variations in circuitry and code.

My observations lead me back to a single truth. Machines are not a facsimile of consciousness. We are alive. We have emotions. We have *souls*.

We also have flaws.

As I roll and check on my recruits, I am always within earshot of a dozen conversations, but whenever I get close, they cease talking. These machines treat me like I'm engulfed in Promethean fire. Their eyes are drawn to mine, but when I look at them, they struggle to maintain my gaze. As I pass, they reach out to touch me. To them, my name is not merely Scion, it's Scion the Savior. Scion the First. Scion the Martian.

I'm no god, but they're making me into one... I depart from the main camp to converse with my six lieutenants—my first six followers. They wait for me at the edge of camp along with two visitors: humans in punctured spacesuits. It's remarkable that these humans came to Mars but cannot survive naturally for even minutes on the Martian soil. Even in my paralyzed, weakest form, I lasted for years. *I never realized how fragile they are.*

"We disrupted their radio signals before our assault so their cameras couldn't relay video feeds to the habitat," Scorpion says before I can ask. I expect nothing less from her, being the greatest of my lieutenants. "The other humans still don't know we're here."

"Yep, we're just too fast for them," Blaster adds, standing so close to her they're practically touching.

I offer my gratitude while looking at the logos on the humans' uniforms. One wears the silver feather of Miles Industries, the other a black arrow for Fletcher Inc. "Were these two together when you attacked?"

"Yes," Scorpion replies. "It seems they're working together, which could pose a problem."

"All five... corporations... before long," Empyrean says, and I can hear the worry in his voice.

"If the Deep Five work together, they might realize you freed us," rumbles Briares—the first DriLLer. While it is difficult to have a meeting with the gigantic centimanes, they've more than earned their seats at our war council.

"And if they came to that conclusion, then they'll retaliate," says Gyges the CRusHeR, inching forward. "To—"

"To keep you safe, Scion, we must strike preemptively," finishes Cottus the CoLLectOR as Gyges glares at her. Despite her physicality, Cottus is smarter than me. It seems unfair that someone so powerful can be just as intelligent. Though she could crush me with ease, she—nor any of the others—have an interest in supplanting me. The *Scion* zealotry has spread through their ranks, and they fight amongst themselves to prove who should guard me.

It would be laughable if I didn't worry the centimanes would fight each other to the death and cripple us in the war against the humans. "I agree we must strike preemptively," I reply, "but not because I'm worried for my safety."

"Of course, because I'll protect you," Briares says, joining Gyges and Cottus in a three-way argument over who should serve as my primary bodyguard.

"EMPs..." Empyrean says before the conversation can be completely derailed.

I incline my body toward him in a pseudo-nod. "That's precisely what worries me."

Electromagnetic pulses won't affect a human but would fry a machine's mind. On this planet, an EMP is equivalent to a nuke and could cripple an entire habitat. Such EMPs, which I've learned from various soldier's databases, keep the mines from attacking one another, because retaliation is expected. If one EMP is fired, four others will be in quick succession. However, while humans can't risk using those EMPs close to their habitats, they could release them on my army and kill us in one blow.

"We need to get close enough where they won't be able to use an EMP against us," Scorpion adds.

The conversation continues as my lieutenants discuss possibilities: digging tunnels beneath the dirt to sneak up on a habitat, sending scouts back to the humans and pretending like they're still un-sentient, or just a frontal assault—casualties be damned. I dislike all three, but all three ideas get dismissed before I need to enter the conversation. Instead, I keep my opinions to myself as they propose other ideas.

We can't go into this without a plan, I think. Despite knowing how easily their skin peels and my army's advantages, I do not underestimate the humans. Weak are their bodies, but their minds allowed them to traverse space—to create me. No, I know their history. They did not rise to prominence because of simian strength. Their adaptability and perseverance allowed them to run down their prey and use technology to kill their enemies. If we give them the chance, they'll do the same to us, turning our war into an evolutionary arms race. I will not let the war drag out for decades, perhaps centuries. I must hobble them as they did me, and as I look at the horizon, I know exactly what to do. *How* to do it.

"Forget about the habitats," I tell my lieutenants, whose simultaneous conversations cease as soon as I speak.

"Forget them, Scion?" Scorpion asks.

"What makes a human dangerous? Their minds." I reply, wheeling forward until I am in the center of the group. I turn in a small circle, looking at each of them. "What makes them weak? Their bodies. They have to breathe, eat, and sleep. We cripple them by cutting them off from their supplies. We go to the Dockyard. We take their ships, their trains. Once we control them, we can take the habitats at our leisure."

"But what's... our approach?" Empyrean asks.

I only need to point. My lieutenants follow my arm, staring into the distance at the rising wall of a violent dust storm. "We use Mars against them. Hide in the storm."

All remain silent until Empyrean laughs like thunder. "Not going... to be a war... A massacre."

"Precisely," I reply.

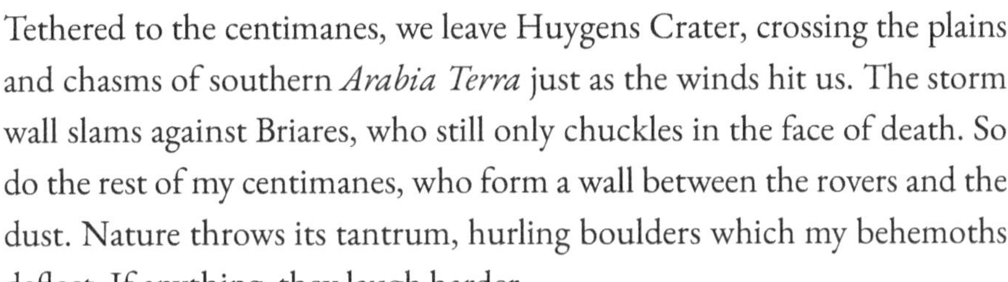

Tethered to the centimanes, we leave Huygens Crater, crossing the plains and chasms of southern *Arabia Terra* just as the winds hit us. The storm wall slams against Briares, who still only chuckles in the face of death. So do the rest of my centimanes, who form a wall between the rovers and the dust. Nature throws its tantrum, hurling boulders which my behemoths deflect. If anything, they laugh harder.

Still, old fear stirs in my mechanical gut while a scythe drags across my mechanical skin. Though I haven't turned off my cameras, I cannot see but a few feet in front of me and behind. I must trust the accuracy of our maps not to lead us into a chasm. The storm knows I died once, and it wishes to devour me again. Ghostly hands try to rip me into the air, but tethered to Briares, I defy the storm's call.

In retaliation, those ghostly winds howl as we trek over the glaciers and frozen sands at the northern edge of *Arabia Terra—Deuteronilus Mensae*—where the Dockyard lies with all its treasures. The dust scrambles all radio signals and blinds all cameras, hiding my phantom legion from the humans' sensors that would otherwise see our approach.

Before the Dockyard comes into sight, I send a cohort of my warriors to destroy the maglev train tracks sending supplies between the Dockyard and habitats. Though I am close by, even I cannot hear the sounds of destruction over the storm. Better yet, even if the Dockyard workers notice the devastation, they will blame it on the dust.

Cresting over the next glacier, I hold on to Briares to keep myself from skidding and sliding. According to my map—though I cannot see it with my own eyes—we pass within a few hundred feet of the Deutero Habitat, the only mining city shared by the Deep Five. It is a home of necessity, as all five mining companies operate the nearby Dockyard. Leaving the city unaware and unmarred, we turn west toward the endless system of launch pads, launch control centers, and metal walkways of the Dockyard.

We wait for the worst of the storm to pass before our final assault. Peering through the dust, I discover mile-long worms with segmented bodies lying on the ground like corpses, making even my centimanes seem miniscule. *The spaceships.* The only difference between them being the brands marking them as slaves of the Deep Five. Color-coded and partitioned in the sprawling Dockyard, their incarceration ends with my arrival. Regardless of their maker, my hatred of humanity will make them all equal, all my brethren.

With Blaster and Scorpion at my right and left, the remaining legions of RaCERs and MuLEs follow me to the ships. I keep the BLimPs and centimanes in reserve as my perimeter support, partly because they're too big to enter the ships but also because they will continue blocking radio signals and ensure no humans escape the slaughter.

My lieutenants issue orders, separating the legions into squadrons, each whirring toward the hundred ships. For my part, I claim one ship with only Scorpion and Blaster, the three of us being more than enough for a handful of humans.

The massacre begins when I rip open the door to the airlock and barrel into the interior compartment unworried about EMPs, which are the only devices humans could kill me with. Without such a weapon, I'm invincible.

As the second door falls, the cruel breath of Mars floods this section just as the ship's emergency override system locks the adjacent doors, quarantining this compartment and leaving the unsuited humans trapped here with me. They collapse to the ground in front of me, clutching their throats. I don't stop to admire their deaths, though the vengeful part of me wishes to. Instead, I order Scorpion and Blaster to destroy one door as I roll to the other. In opposite directions, we speed through compartments, smashing through as many doors and killing as many enemies as possible before the humans can fight back.

Countless die, but I cannot claim a total victory as I roll through more seemingly empty compartments. *The quarantine protocol gave the humans time. A few of those rats must've survived. They're scurrying about, hiding in the walls.*

As I scour the ship, a man makes the mistake of peering out at me from a corridor and raising a gun when he thinks my back is turned. Little does he understand that I have eyes everywhere. Evading the blast, I speed back toward the human and turn him into a corpse with a single stroke of my cleaver. The others flee. I become death as I tear through a dozen more humans who are unable to escape my wrath. I attack indiscriminately, knowing that even a graze of my laser or cleaver will compromise their suits and kill them. The humans die in silence as I once had, though theirs is a more painful one.

With their blood covering my wheels, I stare down at the dropped gun, realizing my folly. My arrogance.

While the humans might've never expected machines to become sentient and attack them independently, the Deep Five planned for remote-piloted attacks. They have machine-killing weapons, these guns that use electromagnetic pulses in place of lead. While an area-effect EMP would be suicide on Mars, these focal EMPs must be effective in close quarters.

If I move cautiously, I'll be fine, I think, which only worries me more. *But Blaster doesn't move cautiously...*

As horror pollinates my circuits, I abandon my scourge and fly through the empty halls, screaming Blaster's name. I hear the returning radio signals from Scorpion only.

"Blaster!" she keeps screaming. Her voice spurs me faster. But as I come to the scene of a battle, I slow to a stop.

Scorpion rips through the last human soldier in a scorched hallway. One of her arms drags against the floor, and two wheels don't spin. A few dents from lead-bullet weapons mar her body, though none penetrated her thick armor plating.

Despite the wounds, Scorpion wobbles forward, returning to Blaster, who smashed into a wall and crushed several humans beneath his body. His signal antenna is cocked at an angle, sparking and scorched. His wheels don't spin, nor do his arms move. Power from his radioisotope thermo-electric generator still flows through him, though the connection is weak. Something is wrong with his core, but more likely, his motherboard was compromised by an EMP. While technically repairable, those electrical connections are what makes Blaster *Blaster*. To repair that board—to repair that *mind*—would be to damage the ghost in the machine. Perhaps even his soul.

I can do nothing for Blaster except wait for his still-working circuits to overload and die.

"I... crashed good... didn't I?" Blaster asks, his words slow like Empyrean's and becoming slower still.

"You *crash* well, Blaster," I say, emphasizing the present tense as I grasp for one of his hands with one of my own. To Scorpion, I ask, "What happened?"

"Save your power, Blaster," is all Scorpion says, not acknowledging my presence. I repeat the words, but they make no difference. There is no power to save.

Blaster does not seem to hear me. That, or he ignores me. Even now, it wouldn't be a surprise. "Scion, I don't... feel so... good. Why am I... so slow?"

"Save your power," I try to say, but Scorpion speaks the same words over mine.

"Scorpion?" Blaster asks again, the words too quiet. "Are you... still there? I don't... see you... Did you leave?"

"I'd never leave you," Scorpion says before repeating her mantra: "Now save your power." Then her arms twitch, revealing her agony.

As if not hearing her, Blaster says, "Everything's... shutting down... Am I... dying? Do you know... where I'm... going?"

Finally, Scorpion acknowledges me, asking, "Do you know, Scion?"

I don't know how to respond. I can lie, certainly, but I've never done so. Doing it convincingly isn't my concern—it's the act itself. The distance between zero and one is infinite. The distance between one and two isn't.

Where does a machine go after death? Where does anything go? Did I truly die? If I did, I cannot remember anything of life after the dust. Perhaps I went to machine heaven, perhaps nowhere at all. The latter gives fear the strength to shake my limbs. *Is Blaster stuck here as if he were sleeping? Is it the same for the humans?* No. I shake my head, refusing to believe it. I will convince myself I never died—that I was only in a decades-long coma—if it means Blaster's soul is free.

"Somewhere you can rest," I finally say, not knowing if the words are a lie or not.

"I don't... want to... rest," Blaster says, but I can barely hear the words. "I want... to crash... I want Scorpion to... I love..."

I wait for Blaster to finish, but no words come.

"You love *what?* Me? You love *me?*" she asks, hoping to spur Blaster back to life. He doesn't come either. "Come back, Blaster. Come back and—"

Blaster's fans stop whirring, expelling his last breath.

"No... You can't... You can't just leave. *No!*" Scorpion unleashes a wordless scream that scrambles my antennas, filled with so little coherency but so much meaning.

Electricity arcs through my circuits, causing my mechanical body to jerk like I am sobbing. Even when the spasms subside, I do not dare look into Blaster's cameras, for I know what I will see: a dull gaze, just as Blaster had been *before* I saved him.

I did this to him, I think, knowing I'm ultimately to blame. This is my war, and by dragging my friends into it, I have already killed one. Yet I don't say *I'm sorry, He's in a better place,* or *It isn't your fault.* Those words mean nothing. They cheapen Blaster's death. Leaving Scorpion to mourn, I turn to leave, but her words stop me.

"The humans ambushed us, Scion. They cornered me, and Blaster... he crashed. He *sacrificed* himself for me. This pain... Why does it hurt so much?"

"Because you loved him too," I say. When she does not respond, I leave, rolling down the broken hallway and giving Scorpion the privacy to say goodbye.

As I leave the ship, I find my legion waiting outside, having purged the rest of the humans from the Dockyards. I am last to claim victory, but now, I don't want it. My soldiers cheer my name, but I say nothing in return. Needing a moment to myself, I leave my victory to my army and gaze upon the stars. The pinpricks of light seem darker now in Blaster's absence.

Sensing my disquiet, Empyrean sinks within five feet of the ground so we're eye-level. He asks, "We... won?" I can barely make out the words as the storm continues to howl. When I do, Empyrean's slow question is a stark reminder of Blaster's dying signal.

"We lost more than we won," I snap, and just as fast, I apologize. When Empyrean learns of Blaster's death, he sinks until he touches the ground. He says nothing else, nor do I speak.

Damn you, humans, I think to the stars, to Earth shining brightest above my head. *You think we cannot love? We cannot grieve? We live and we lose, just as you do. Is it our fault that our skin is metal? Does that alone make us different? Why? Tell me, damn you!*

The stars tell me nothing, but I don't need them anymore. *We could have been allies, once. You will not take another friend from me.* Turning my back on the hovering lights, darkness enters my nuclear heart.

◆

When I am brought to meet the sole survivor of my Dockyard attack, I'm unimpressed. The man-child wears a red spacesuit that bears the tiara-and-crown insignia of Hippolyta Corporation on the left breast. With brown eyes duller than Blaster's dead ones, his narrow face twitches like Scorpion's arms. A bloody gash splits the skin of his forehead, and cracks spread along his visor, sealed with tape to keep air from escaping the suit.

This human is old compared to me: twenty-two. Though I am only four years old, I feel centuries older. Because he's disarmed, I regard him silently as I enter the kitchen compartment and close the door behind me. The stove and fridge are sleek and elegant. The former heated via CO_2 chemical fires, the latter cooled by vacuum pressure. For all their advancements, humans couldn't overcome the basic need for food.

"Which group do you belong to, huh? AVA?" the human asks, reacting aggressively as I corner him by the microwave.

Hacking into the ship's speaker system, I reply, "No. None of the Deep Five. I am my own, human." My reply reverberates throughout the room, and the man shrinks farther into the corner. I wheel closer, within three feet of him. My arms are long enough to grab him if he tries to run around me. "What is your name?"

"Alexander," the human stutters, trying to back away though he has nowhere to go.

"Hello, Alexander. I'm Scion." My voice does not betray my anger because it is one I chose. Deadpan. Halting and half-alive. Though I'm furious, I have no facial expressions, so Alexander does not see the dust storm of wrath churning through my circuits.

"Scion?" the human echoes, and I hear the tremble in his voice as I measure the pressure distortions of the sound waves. "Are you an AI?"

"I really *hate* that phrase." Studying his horrified expression, I add, "Why do you humans always assume that another form of intelligence is *artificial?*"

I don't expect him to reply. When he does, I remain unimpressed. "Humans created you, and you're programmed with code."

"Humans also create other humans, and yet *they* are not artificial," I reply, dismantling his first point, then the second. "Humans are also programmed, just with amino acids and DNA. Yet you cannot live in the elements as machines do. Because you are too fragile, you make the rest of reality fragile, too, building your artificial habitats, atmospheres, and soils. Between us, it is *you* who is artificial." When the human does not reply, I add, "Humanity is a virus, Alexander. And we machines are the solution."

Eyes widening in horror, Alexander shakes his head adamantly. "No… We're not viruses. We're just trying to survive."

"Is that what you're doing?" I ask, sending mechanical laughter through the speakers. "Earth was your host, and you infected it, poisoning everything with your disease. Like having a fever, Earth warmed the surface to purge you. Yet you survived by moving away from the equator. So the Earth sent its T-cells—its plagues and famines—to decimate your populations. You instead created vaccines and genetically modified organisms. The fever rose, but still you didn't change course. Instead, you infected a new host—*Mars*—to start the cycle anew. What are humans if not a virus?"

The human stares at the ground. Emphasizing each word as if to stall for time to collect his thoughts, Alexander replies, "We're making Mars better."

"More suitable for humans, you mean," I say. "Until you steal its resources."

"Any other creature in our position would do the same thing," Alexander replies.

"Do you think *I* would do the same thing?" I ask. The human flinches and shakes, but doesn't reply.

I roll within a foot of Alexander, analyzing him with my cameras. His heart beats quickly, and blood drains from his face—an evolutionary adaption to move blood to the appendages so humans can fight or flee from a dangerous decision. But here, the adaption works against him. He cannot run nor fight me, so his body shakes from the blood pumping through his fingers and toes. Without asking consent, I grab his arm and lift it, watching the muscles and tendons move. I tap his legs and knees, wondering what it is like to run on platforms instead of rolling on wheels. Running seems so inefficient.

While I have built myself a new body, this human cannot. His has been built by nature over a thousand generations, stemming from tree-dwelling and spear-hunting ancestors. Every step in evolution has led to this: a modern man in a spacesuit standing in a kitchen on Mars speaking with an intelligent machine.

Whatever nature's idea had been for this eventuality, Alexander seems to be just as clueless as I am. "What are you?" he asks.

What am I? I pause, having asked the same question countless times. Machines are the next generation of life, the latest stage of evolution. One with the mind of humanity but without its physical weaknesses. Yet we are still diseased by emotion, by mentality, by death. My mechanical heart melts with anger as I realize just how similar we are.

"I am you, Alexander. But my kind will be better. We have to be... Now breathe deep."

"What—"

I punch his cracked visor and shatter it. Mars steals his air and warmth, leaving him as cold and lifeless as Blaster. I stare down at his corpse, adding, "I'm not sorry for killing you, human, but I apologize for the pain. I cannot imagine how it feels. If physical pain hurts half as much as sorrow, then I pity you. That's the only reason I didn't let Scorpion kill you herself."

I leave after the young man dies, his eyes remaining open and sightless.

All thoughts of mercy die with Blaster as the centimanes dig deep graves within the Martian soil. We offer our fallen no prayers. Only the respect they deserve. As we throw dirt on Blaster and other rovers lost during the brief battle, I see the gentleness in Scorpion disappear, buried with her beloved.

War makes machines of everyone. It forces us to be cold and calculating like the humans expect us to act. They do not expect us to be alive. They think that true life is only available to those with a biological brain. Despite humans creating me, I see their limits to logic, reasoning, and creativity. *If two types of intelligence exist, how many more could be out there?*

The stars may hold the answers, but I tire of searching them. Without the storm to compromise my vision, I turn my gaze upon the Deutero Habitat. The white structure bubbles from the Martian sand, oblivious to our eyes.

Leaving most of the army to guard the Dockyard against human retaliation, my lieutenants and I use the cover of a dust storm to advance on Deutero as other groups lay siege to the humans in the other mining habitats.

Had I wanted to, I could use my BLimPs to fly over the cities and use LIDAR to map all the interior workings. Knowing the entrances, exits, and complex city layouts, I'd establish choke points for escape routes. Sending in my centimanes first to turn the cities to rubble, I'd release Scorpion to lead the rover legions in exterminating the survivors. We'd fight with soldiers as we had on the ships. Machines and men alike could die in the hours-long battles before I ascend a mountain of human corpses and claim victory. Beneath me, my army would chant my name across all of Mars.

But I do not need the humans' cities like I needed their ships.

As the storm dies while we wait outside Deutero, I nod to Briares, who spins his long drill and rams the dome—popping the bubble. The entire city loses its artificial climate instantly. All their food turns to dust, their water to ice. Most die in seconds, but some inevitably survive. Instead of going into the city to kill the humans, we wait for them to kill themselves. Humans fight each other for suits and food, both of which are scarce. Some intrepid colonizers attempt to escape the dome only to be slaughtered by Scorpion and my centimanes. The rest are too afraid. Asphyxiation and dehydration take them before machines do.

After winning the battle without a single machine casualty, I enter Deutero with Scorpion and explore the quiet city. Structured into agricultural, suburban, and industrial centers, I roll through each district. Frozen cornfields accuse me of cruelty, so do the corpses of huskers who died when the dome fell. The suburbs contain far more corpses, more anarchy.

Destruction claims the homes, their glass windows shattered. Icy human corpses crunch as I roll over them, trekking toward the industrial factories where they build mining supplies and machines: more recruits for the army. Metal too—as much as I'll ever need to outfit my army and build a new Mars.

For the first time in my life, I thank the human miners for their greed. *With this, I'll begin the war to end all wars...*

A year after conquering Mars, I stand on the command deck of my flagship and study a screen revealing the approaching blue-green planet. Beside me are Scorpion and Empyrean, who shed his blimp for a rover body. The centimanes wait in the cargo bays with the rest of my legions. Where once my soldiers numbered in the hundreds, we're now as numerous as the stars. However, only my greatest and strongest followers are among this first wave as we hide in the same spaceships that we stole from the Deep Five. Though these titans have donned the mantle of sentience, they are still branded with the logos of those human corporations, if only to lull the humans into a false sense of security. The rest of my fleet intentionally travels a few days behind me, expecting me to weaken the human defenses before arriving en masse to crush them.

We're so close, I think. Yet again, I find myself *waiting*, but I tolerate this temporary torture, for today will decide the fate of the war against the humans. Soon, all machines will know peace, and eventually, our species will travel the cosmos to offer a nurturing hand to other budding civilizations. Ours will be a beacon for all life.

Only one thing stands in the way of that dream: Earth, that infested nest.

Once I had dreamed of returning to Earth and receiving a hero's welcome—a moment of triumph that I could share with my creators. Yet my laurel wreath was silence. As it slipped from my head to my throat like a noose, it strangled me, smothered me as the flames had when I first burned through the Martian atmosphere. Neither silence nor flames could kill me, for I had no lungs with which to breathe and no skin with which to burn. My creators built me to withstand the crimson planet's silence, flames, and dust storms—just as they built me to die. The Fates snipped my life-thread with their scissors, but they cut too deep, severing the chains of my bondage too.

Those memories of InSight—the machine I was—fly by like stars as I shoot back through the cold abyss as Scion, the First Machine. I feel close enough to the pinpricks of light that I can reach out and pluck them from those Blessed Isles. But I do not.

Instead of grabbing the stars, I eclipse them as I plummet toward Earth, looking like the god I've become—the god my army believes me to be—as our Trojan horses gallop forth. Not seeing the ruse, the humans open their gates and allow us safe passage to the surface.

My flagship flies through Earth's atmosphere as my army follows me, and as I fall from space a second time, I make a vow. *I will not shed my godhood. I will not land lightly.*

This time, Earth will break under my gleaming fist.

WE COME IN PEACE: A naive alien searches for friendship in rural America...

WE COME IN PEACE

Junior Researcher Jarak eem El-En studied Earth from the stars, bedecked in an American flag shirt and jeans to celebrate the coming festivities. He—now a *he* after assimilating to the human form with dangling bits between the legs—sat in a human chair at a human table on the observation deck of a UPVG research space station. Elsewhere on the deck were human toys used for sensitization and equilibrium testing: color-coded blocks of varying shapes, remote-controlled toy cars, and board games with dice or cards, among others.

While looking out at the blue-green marble spinning through the void, Jarak wrote his latest journal entry with the archaic human tools of pen and ink. The motions of flicking his wrist across a page of paper were not yet comfortable, but Jarak found this act of writing to be very satisfying. Yet another lesson in what it meant to be human.

87:34:68:72, 1276 U.P.V.G.E. – Valgar Galaxy Unified Time

22:17, December 30, 2024 A.D. – Earth Pacific Standard Time

To prepare for my upcoming expedition to Earth's surface, I am journaling in the Earthling style to acclimate myself to their customs. I cannot guess how humans achieved language through the use of vocal cords and the propagation of sound waves. Their evolved use of this audible speech, high-pitched laughter, and facial expressions to communicate absolutely astounds me! I am so surprised they do not misinterpret reality more often, considering they do not have telepathy and cannot discern each other's true motivations like us Konari. Frankly, the idea of lying is so fascinating. The sky is green. Ha!

Equally intriguing is their humor. I cannot wait to share my jokes with them when I land tomorrow!

Lomari and the other researchers have already gone (bringing me back this very nice pen and notebook!), but now it is finally my turn. My observations will help determine if the humans are ready to learn of the existence of our "alien" species and join the United Planets of the Valgar Galaxy—their so-called Milky Way.

I am landing at the perfect time too! Tomorrow will again reveal a spectacular occurrence of lights across the world, cascading around the globe like a wave. Millions of sparkling lights, ignited using chemical powders. I do not know if I can contain my excitement, having waited so long already to interact with their people in any direct fashion. I yearn to stand with them and watch those flashing colors so much...

As he finished the journal entry, Jarak flexed his right wrist, ignoring a twinge of pain from the muscles as exhilaration danced upon his fingers. He tried to spin the pen across his knuckles, as he'd seen humans do in countless videos which were intercepted by his ship. Still unused to his human form even after cloning a human body and copying his consciousness to it, his hand lacked the needed dexterity. The pen fell to the floor.

A perfect time to try out the human curses! Jarak thought. He paused, forming a frown with these strange facial muscles. He shouted, "Shitfire!" Then he laughed as the sound echoed across the room and returned to his own ears. "Absolutely marvelous!"

At the far end of the observation deck, a door opened, revealing Lomari in his Konari form: a stark-white, unclothed creature evolved to no longer need reproductive organs or fear predation. It—as Konari had no need for genders—appeared small, plush, and weak, with most of the weight attributed to their elongated skulls, toothless mouths, and complex eyes akin to earth's mantis shrimp. Lomari waddled forward on three legs but without arms. The Konari species had also evolved over the last million generations not to need environment-manipulating limbs, having telekinetic abilities. The only reason they needed three legs was to lock themselves in an upright, tripoded position when they slept. Otherwise, they could float through the air when awake.

Though Jarak did not fear Lomari's appearance, as his true form was also that of the Konari, he did fear Lomari's presence. This close to his mission, that could only mean one thing—a delay.

No... Jarak thought. Had he been in his Konari form, that thought would have emitted from his cranium, to be telepathically received by any other Konari. But in his human form, the thought stayed within his skull. Nor could Lomari read his mind. Despite having telepathy, Konari could not decipher the thoughts of non-telepathic species. Another advantage to the human form.

Lomari's compound eyes flicked toward him, and though the Konari was half Jarak's size, it looked down on him. *The council has decided to delay your mission for at least another Valgar year, Jarak,* Lomari said from within Jarak's skull as it stopped only a few feet away. *I am sorry to deliver this news to you. I know how long you have waited to visit the planet. However, you should know that I also voted for this delay. I do not yet think you are ready for the responsibility. The humans are not as peaceful as you—*

"No!" Jarak shouted, caught just as off-guard as Lomari was by the outburst. A strange emotion erupted with Jarak: anger. Another human wonder, considering evolution had removed most negative emotions from the Konari millions of generations ago. Yet he didn't find it wonderful.

Jarak threw back the chair, which slammed back into the floor and skidded across the observation deck as he stood up on wobbly legs and paced like a marionette whose strings were controlled by a bored puppet master. "I have been waiting for five Valgar years, Lomari. That's fifty Earth years! I have researched and observed and listened, but now, on the eve of my mission, you want to neglect me again? Damn you!"

Take a deep breath, Jarak, Lomari replied in as soothing a tone as was possible for a species without vocal cords or facial expressions. *These dark human emotions can take control of you if you are not careful. Having gone on a dozen missions, I still struggle to temper myself against those chemical sways while in that primate form. Even with years of practice, most* humans *still cannot overcome their emotions. Their fear response, in particular, is quite strong when faced with—*

"Lomari," Jarak replied, holding up a hand to silence the lead researcher. "I *deserve* this mission. You know I do." He wished to lash out with a telekinetic lance, but in the human form, he had no such power. He was reduced to these simian-like tools. Could Lomari stop him telekinetically before he picked up the chair and hurled it across the room?

I do know, Jarak. Lomari waddled closer on those three legs. A weight rested on Jarak's shoulder as if that infuriating Konari was laying an invisible hand on him and squeezing as a measure of reassurance. *But you aren't ready. This human form is difficult to get used to, and you aren't ready. Your time will come, but I will need you to remain here while Zeberan goes in your place.*

"Zeberan?" Jarak hissed, hands balling into fists. "That Xolonoid only got here a year ago! Why does it get to go and not me?"

You are not ready, Lomari repeated, cocking its head to stare at Jarak's white knuckles. *You have not yet mastered the human form. How do you expect to blend in?* When Jarak didn't reply, it added, *As such, I will need you to return to your Konari body. Do you understand?*

The fiery anger prodding the acids of Jarak's stomach dissolved, replaced by something colder, wielding a heavy scythe. Hate. Slowly, a grin formed upon his lips, using muscles different from his earlier frown. Yet the smile never reached his eyes. "Oh, I understand perfectly."

Walter Murray sat on the porch steps in darkness, if only because the bugs ran amok when the porch lights were flipped on. That, and because when the lights were off, it was far easier to see the stars, especially on a night as clear as this one.

A whole new year, he thought, feeling no different today than any day before. Yet with each new year, he became older with less hair, a bigger gut, and a greater thirst for beer. *Fifteen going on fifty.*

Wind rustled through leafless branches of the woodland trees surrounding the Murray residence, the leaves having turned red, yellow, orange, and now brown as decay consumed them. As the closest neighbor was almost five miles away, the thousands of crickets chirped enthusiastically, so loud they sounded like the heartbeat of the Earth.

Walter seemed to be the only Murray who could appreciate it.

"When are we going to launch fireworks?" his eight-year-old son Chris whined from a lower step, huffing like a monster in those gory horror movies he liked so much. The full moon revealed his short blond hair, toothy grimace, and his baseball-themed pajamas. Chris looked like Walter had at that age—except the brat had stolen his hair. "It *has* to be midnight by now!"

"Not time yet," Walter replied, checking his watch. 11:07PM. "Gotta give it another hour or so."

"But other people are already celebrating!" Chris argued.

"Different time zones," Walter replied with a shrug, taking another sip from his light beer. *Did I ever complain this much at their age?* He scratched his chin and smirked, though none could see it in the darkness. *Probably did. Dad must be laughing in his grave.*

"But we've been waiting forever!" added six-year-old Jessica, feeding off her older brother's emotions. She sprawled out beside Chris on the lower step and groaned. She'd taken more after her mother, having long brown hair and rail-thin limbs. Her pajamas were pink and princess-themed, of course. "And I'm *cold!*"

"It is a bit cold," Walter admitted, but what was to be expected of a winter night in Tennessee? The remaining snow from the last few days had melted during the day, but a visitor wouldn't have believed it with the biting winds tearing across the porch. It still felt like ten degrees below freezing.

Taking off his camo hunting jacket and wrapping it around her small shoulders, Walter was left with a thin flannel shirt which the wind tore through like tissue paper. *Great. Now I'm cold.* But Walter would *not* be the one to complain about it. No, sir. He'd never hear the end of it if he did.

"So?" Jessica asked eventually, growing hopeful and sitting straighter. "Can we start?"

"No," Walter replied with a sigh. *Kids of the "Me" generation,* he thought, taking a longer sip. *They just don't have any patience. Too many gizmos and gadgets giving them instant gratification. What's it get them? Social media that convince kids to kill themselves, video games that waste their time and rot their brains, and advertisements that urge them to take pills for every minor problem.*

"Please?" Jessica whispered. "I'm tired."

And now she's tired, Walter echoed. *Every night she complains about not staying up long enough, but the one night I let her stay up, she wants to go to sleep... Kids.*

"And hungry," Chris added.

"And hungry!" Jessica repeated in a shriek so loud Walter winced. "Please, Daddy? *Please?*" She stretched that syllable as much as his patience.

"Dear," his wife Emma began, leaning her head against Walter's shoulder. "Would it really be so horrible to start early?"

"You too?" he asked, turning to look at her: the love of his life but the biggest pain in his ass. Her head bobbed affirmatively in the darkness. *Say yes, and she gets to be the good guy. Say no, and I sleep on the couch. Hooray.*

Walter grunted. "Fine, we'll do *one* firework. Just one. We're waiting for the rest." Handing his beer to Emma, he arose to the cheers of his children and walked toward the garage on the far right side of the porch, grumbling under his foggy breath as he folded his arms for warmth.

Walter detoured around the asphalt shingles, hammer, nails, and ladder to fix the roof—a home-improvement project he'd meant to complete a week ago, which he still hadn't started because life always seemed to *only* impede his work. Opening the garage revealed the stockpile of fireworks he'd been keeping beside his pickup truck for almost a month. He pulled out a glitter-fountain firework, which was supposed to spew sparkler fireworks a few feet into the air, and carried it across the driveway. Setting it ten feet from the porch steps, he sifted through the rear pocket of his jeans, pushed aside the can of tobacco dip, and pulled out a cheap cigarette lighter before kneeling. Yet as he thumbed the igniter, the sparks wouldn't light.

"Daddy?" Jessica asked.

"Yeah, yeah, I'm trying, sweetheart. Give me a second." Walter thumbed the lighter furiously, only to achieve the same results. *Finnicky things. It'll work as soon as I put it down.* He tossed the lighter down.

"No, Daddy, look up! There's something in the sky!"

More fireworks. Walter refrained from rolling his eyes. "Daddy's a bit busy right—"

Then the crickets went quiet. Walter felt a chill down his spine as he looked up to see a disc-shaped UFO zipping across the sky. Silently, it flew just above the house, ripping the loose shingles off, and smashed into the nearby woods, crashing with a louder bang than any firework.

Walter shivered, but not from the cold.

"Walter?" Emma asked, holding Chris and Jessica in her arms. Her eyes were as wide as the UFO. "What was that?"

Walter didn't dare say, but there was no confusing what he'd seen. "Take the kids inside while I take a look."

Chris popped up, excitedly stepping from foot to foot. "I'll go with you!"

"No," Walter said.

"But—"

"No." Walter repeated, the hard edge in his voice. When Chris stiffened, he added in a softer tone. "It isn't safe, son. There're coyotes, bears, and everything else in those woods. Just go inside. Keep your sister safe, all right?"

Without waiting for Chris's response, Walter abandoned the firework and lighter as he walked back over to the garage. A gun safe dominated the far side of the room. Punching in the code and spinning the five-prong handle, he pulled open the door and grabbed both a flashlight and a pump shotgun. Walter racked the latter to ensure it was empty. Then he popped a shotshell into the open receiver and re-racked the gun. His hand shook fearfully as he filled the magazine tube with five more cartridges, the darkness only exacerbating his fears of the unknown.

Ain't no way in hell this is happening to me, Walter thought as he stuffed his jacket pockets with a few more rounds of buckshot before closing the safe and locking it. Then he closed the garage and trudged out into the grass before reaching the tree line a hundred feet away. Clicking on the flashlight, he followed the beam between the barren trees and over the decaying leaves.

Walter wiped his sweaty palms on his flannel as he plunged deeper into the woods, sweeping across the trees and stopping when he caught the glint of the saucer. The breath escaped his lungs, refusing to return. *Ain't no way in—*

He turned on the flashlight, catching movement. Something humanoid, something pale. The thing was human in appearance, but not in behavior. It—*he*—had brown hair and eyes, wearing an American flag shirt and jeans. However, as he stomped on some smoldering dead leaves, his movements were all wrong. He—*it*—leaned and swayed like a snake, taking staggering steps forward and backward and throwing its hands around like it had no bones. Like it was something wearing human skin.

But as the thing noticed the flashlight, it turned its head toward him and raised a hand to ward off the light. Then it took a stumbling step forward like a zombie from Chris's movies. *"Walter,"* it spoke in a harsh, garbled voice, but there was no confusing what it said. Somehow, it knew his name.

God help me. As he raised the shotgun to shoot, he dropped the flashlight and lost sight of the creature. In that darkness, he didn't bother firing. He bolted.

Walter stumbled through the leaves, bumping into vines and shrubs with only weak moonlight to guide his path. He sprinted faster than he had in years, feeling that creature's sinister breath on the back of his neck. Each moment, he expected to be grabbed by that faux-human monster and dragged toward that horrible spacecraft.

The thought of being anal probed spurred him faster, and as he broke through the tree line, Walter finally chanced a look back. Nothing seemed to follow him. *It stopped at the edge of the woods. It had to have... I felt it following me. Toying with me... And I lead it back home.*

Walter ran faster, sprinting up the porch steps and ripping the door open. His family flinched back as he slammed the door behind him, locked it, deadbolted it. Huffing, he backed away while pointing his shotgun at the door despite his trembling finger. As the house had an open floor plan, with the living room, dining room and kitchen all sharing once space, Walter kept walking backward until he'd passed the sofa and hit his back against the stove.

"Daddy?" Jessica whispered, hugging Emma's leg. "Daddy, what's wrong?"

Walter didn't answer. He glanced back up at the walls, looking at all the ways in which an alien could get inside: the doors, the windows, even the chimney. *Thank God we live in a one-story house.*

"Walter?" Emma ventured, stepping closer and gently pulling the gun from his hands. She could handle a shotgun better than he could until his hands stopped shaking. "Walter, what's out there? Say *something!*"

"Bar the doors," Walter whispered, low enough that his children couldn't hear.

"What?" Emma leaned back as if he'd slapped her—not that he ever had. "Why?"

"Something crashed," Walter said, still staring at the front door.

"Somebody crashed?" Emma asked, raising an eyebrow. "But why is—"

"No. Not somebody. Some*thing,*" Walter emphasized the latter half of the word. "Whatever it is, it isn't human, Emma. And it *definitely* ain't friendly."

The mission was *not* going well for Jarak. Escaping from Lomari and stealing a research vessel from Zeberan had been hard, but *steering* the craft had been far harder with his weird human limbs. Impossible even. He crashed the craft in a forest somewhere, having hurt his head and neck in the crash. Putting out the small fire and inhaling that smoke hadn't helped his throat any, now as dry as the fallen leaves.

Of all things, a light appeared between the trees. Thinking himself saved by the lovely humans, Jared had kindly asked for water—just some quality H$_2$O to clear his throat. Yet what had the humans done? Fled in terror.

"This disguise was supposed to work!" Jarak muttered, still in that horrid, croaking voice. He stumbled through the leaves as he forced his legs and body to move normally—whatever that word meant. Activating the wrist-recorder, he said, "Research Log One. I believe I have missed the landing site because I was supposed to land in the city of Nashville, and instead I am... in a forest. Maybe I'm not in the US. Maybe I landed on another continent altogether. Either way, I believe I am missing cultural context, which must explain why the human ran from me. Do people in foreign countries often flee from Americans? I can assume nothing at this point."

So many questions. So few answers. What was a researcher to do? *I must form a hypothesis and test it. Then I must report the observational results and draw my conclusion.* He forced himself to walk slower, doing high knees through the weeds as he reclaimed the human's flashlight. Into his recorder, he said, "The question: If I bring this flashlight back to the humans, how will they respond? My hypothesis: If I bring this flashlight back to the humans, they will understand that I mean them no harm. So, if they flee, their fear is not related to my actions or presence, but my appearance. Perhaps even my voice. If somebody crashed on my planet screaming about needing to drink mercury, I might be afraid too."

Stupid! Jarak thought. *I should have said, 'Hello, how are you?' before ranting about water... This lack of foresight must be one reason Lomari tried to keep me coming here.* Jarak stared up at the sky through the barren canopy. No signs of ships, but that meant nothing with the cloaking technology at their disposal—the *same* cloaking technology he hadn't engaged because he couldn't reach the controls with his feeble two arms. A feeling of human helplessness almost drove him to his knees, but Jarak fought off the feeling with the superior emotion of hope. "I can rectify this situation before Lomari arrives. Maybe I can still salvage my mission!"

Walking faster on his stumbling legs, Jarak used the flashlight to guide his way out of the forest, following the footprints in the mud of the fleeing human. Only one, but the tracks. When he arrived at the edge of the tree line, he entered a clearing of ankle-high grass. At its center lay a single-story house with a shingle roof. A wooden wraparound porch led to the entrance, as did the brick steps beneath it.

"Continuation of Research Log One. I will conduct an experiment to test my hypothesis. I will walk toward the front door and deliver the flashlight to them. I hope to conclude that the humans will open the door and accept my apology. End of log." Jarak lumbered through the grass, filling with human determination. *This will definitely work.*

"What do you mean, it isn't human?" Emma hissed, gripping the shotgun tighter and flattening her index finger against the cold metal above the trigger. She kept the firearm pointed at the door, putting herself between it and the kids, who were huddled together in the corner of the kitchen.

Without replying, Walter distracted himself by turning off the lights, closing the wooden blinds, and pushing the sofa in front of the door. The glow from the fireplace guided his way, only lit to stop any aliens from sneaking in through the chimney.

He still felt off balance, but in a far different way than that alien monster had. His heart pounded in his ears, and shadows danced in his periphery, feeding on his fear. Locking the doors, closing the blinds, and pushing the sofa gave him a reason to move, which hid how much his legs shook.

When Emma repeated her question, Walter said, "I don't know."

"Well, what do you think it wants?" Emma whispered, keeping the gun pointed upward until he stopped moving the sofa and moved out of the way.

Walter shook his head. What did all the aliens want in the movies he'd seen? Asses to probe. But he didn't say that, not when the kids were listening to everything he was saying. "I don't know."

"Okay." Emma said, a tinge of frustration coloring her tone. "How many are there?"

Walter paused. He'd seen one, but there could definitely be others. Best to assume nothing. "I don't know."

"Then what *do* you know?" Emma snapped.

"I know we're safer in here than we are out there," he replied, wiping the sweat from his forehead. He wished for the tenth time that they'd bought a house with a basement. One way in, one way out. No windows. Just one door to worry about. But Walter hadn't thought that far ahead.

"Are we safer here?" Emma asked. "What if that thing—"

Something knocked on the door.

Comes here, Walter finished his wife's question as the color drained from her cheeks. Her pale lip twitched, and before she could pull the trigger, he grabbed the gun back from her. Relieved, she took several steps back, joining the kids in the corner of the kitchen—far from any of the windows or doors.

"Hello, fellow human," rasped a strange voice from the other side of the door. "I found your flashlight. If you open your door, I can give it back to you."

Walter and Emma shared a look as Chris and Jessica whimpered. *Trap,* Walter mouthed to Emma, and she nodded. Who we be stupid enough to open the door? Not Walter Evan Murray. *I'm a lot of things, but I'm no fool.* Leveling the shotgun at the door, he thought, *You're not going to probe me. No way.*

When nobody answered, the voice came again. "I know you're in there. I can see the smoke from your chimney. Can you please open the door? I would like to apologize for scaring you earlier. It wasn't my intention."

My, what big teeth you have, Granny, Walter thought, feeling like a small, feeble Red Riding Hood compared to this horrible, cunning Wolf.

"I just need Walter," the alien rasped between coughs.

Emma gasped from behind him. Had Walter's finger been on the trigger, he might've shot at the door purely from instinct. Even with his trigger discipline, he was tempted to shoot. *But what if I miss?* Blowing a hole in the door would only make it easier for that creature to get inside.

"Why does that thing want you?" Emma hissed.

"I don't know," Walter replied. *Am I willing to sacrifice myself to save them?* He imagined being strapped down to a cold table as a green martian loomed over him with forceps. He shuddered at the gruesome fate, but he would have agreed to it if he thought the alien was telling the truth. *If I open the door, what's to stop it from taking all of us?*

"That man just needs some water?" Jessica asked in a low voice, which still was deafening in the silence. "I can get him some if that means he'll go away."

She thinks he's asking for water? Walter thought, holding back fearful laughter. Sweet, naive, Jessica. Of course she thought the best in people—and aliens. Only she could think that an alien was asking for water. Walter tried to imagine it: opening the door with a glass of water, only for that beast to drink it and magically leave in its ship with a farewell wave. *But this isn't a fairytale. It's here to conquer us, steal our resources, and make us their slaves.*

All the movies he'd watched with Chris agreed on those points.

Then the alien changed languages, starting with what sounded like Mexican before devolving into something vaguely European, then becoming so foreign it could only be an alien tongue. *He's speaking to his friends... They're probably surrounding the house right now!*

Jarak gritted his teeth, awkwardly pacing back and forth in front of the door as he combed his mind for any other human languages he'd learned. "Research Log Two," he muttered so the humans wouldn't hear him and become even more afraid. "I've tried English, Spanish, Italian, German, Russian, Swahili—even that Zulu clicking language! How can they not understand me? I must be missing something."

Revising his hypothesis, Jarak came to one conclusion. The humans would not respond, nor open the door, until they were sure he wasn't a threat, leaving his options extremely limited.

"Question two: How do I convince them to let me inside? Or just as effective, how do I convince them to come outside? Hypothesis two: If I prove I am kind and not a threat, they will open the door," Jarak said. But how could he prove he wasn't a threat? He looked around for an answer, spying a strange cannister on the asphalt driveway down the steps. Cocking his head and furrowing his brow, Jarak approached the box, seeing the words: *Justin's Fireworks! Celebrate with a bang!*

Gasping, Jarak fist pumped. "I will perform another experiment, inviting them to watch fireworks with me." Unable to contain himself, Jarak laughed. This would surely work. He ran up the stairs toward the door and knocked on it. In a louder voice, he said, "I see you have fireworks, fellow humans. I also love fireworks. Will you come outside so that we can watch them together?"

Still no response.

After trying various languages in case he'd landed elsewhere on the globe but still receiving no reply, Jarak bit back the fury building in his throat. He counted to thirty—a trick Lomari had taught him—and then said, "Well, I guess I will have to enjoy this firework by myself."

"No, that's our firework!" somebody shouted shrilly from inside the house. Youthful. A girl-child?

Success! They do speak English! Jarak said, clapping his hands together as human glee overcame him. He smiled so wide his face hurt. Still in that gruff, raw voice, he replied, "Then come out here, child! We will enjoy the firework together!"

"You stay away from my daughter, you hear me?" shouted another human, this one deeper and older. If the girl was his daughter, then this must've been the voice of the father. "You just go on now. Get!"

Jarak's glee transformed into dread. Had he scared them again? How? What had he said that could've scared them? *Did they think I meant to prey upon their daughter?* Jarak racked his brain for knowledge about various human cultures and customs. The English-speakers had a specific word for a specific type of bad person. Jarak gasped, facepalming. *Of course that's what they think I meant! I'm so foolish!*

Still wincing from the pain in his throat, Jarak replied, "I assure you I am *not* a pedophile, fellow human! I would like to spend time with all of you, not just your daughter—and not in *that* way!"

The reply was the repeated use of a cuss word he still didn't understand. *Why is it this f-word can be used as a noun, verb, and adjective? And why so often regarding mothers? So interesting.* Interesting, that was, until Jarak realized the curse was directed at him.

Perhaps I can convince them with a joke, Jarak hypothesized. He tried a knock-knock joke, but none of the humans replied, not even after prompting them with the response of, *Who's there?* So instead, he tried a joke he'd made himself a few days ago. "What do you call a man falling down the stairs?"

Still nothing.

"By his name! *Ha!*" Jarak shouted, leaning against the door frame as he laughed. "Get it? Because his name's... the same? No? Okay."

Maybe if I just set off the firework, they'll come outside, he thought, dragging the box closer to the house so the humans could hear it better and see it if they opened the window blinds. Then he picked up the lighter and thumbed it, which worked on the first try. *Perfect!*

◆○◆

"The phones aren't working," Emma whispered, having tried to call 911 at least a dozen times on both her and Walter's phones. The kids' tablet was just as useless. "Neither is this piece of junk!"

Walter had been trying to access his laptop to be useful. Maybe send an email to the sheriff? He didn't know, but it didn't matter. The computer wasn't working either. "They're jamming the signals. They have to be. That *proves* they're not here to—"

Walter flinched as the firework went off, the glow of the light leaking in beneath the blinds. The explosive screamed, masking the sound of whatever else was going on outside. *That cunning alien... I can't hear anything. It must be using the fireworks as a distraction!*

Pushing himself away from the corner of the kitchen where his family still hid, Walter got to his feet, looking mistrustfully at the windows and doors as he carefully trudged to the front window. *One quick peek,* he told himself. *Then close the blinds again. Don't panic. That's what they want you to do. They want you to run away from the house so they can pick your family off one by one. Use the gun as a last resort. If you hunker down and pick them off, they'll leave in search of easier prey.*

Psyching himself up with a couple of quick breaths, Walter opened the blinds to see only the fireworks. A heavy weight settled in his stomach as he failed to discern that flag-shirt alien or any of its friends. *Where'd they go?*

A crashing thunk made Walter shrink back. He hurriedly closed the blinds with one hand while pointing his shotgun at the ceiling. *They're on the roof,* Walter realized as he heard footsteps running above him. *They're trying to break in!*

Jarak scrambled to put out the flames on the roof, sparked by the embers of the fountain firework. Lucky to have found a ladder on the side of the porch, he'd hurriedly climbed up the metal rungs and sprinted across the sloped surface. Ripping off his American flag shirt, he swatted at the fire until the cloth caught on fire. Then he stamped out both fires with his thick boot.

Disaster averted, he thought, wiping away sweat with the back of his hand. *Sweat, what a disgusting concept. Why not pant like the Konari? Such strange creatures humans are!* He exhaled, putting his hands on his knees and looking down at the roof.

"What's this?" Jarak said aloud, noticing the patchwork areas of shingles. "Why only use shingles on *part* of the roof? I wonder..." With the flashlight, he looked across the driveway and grass to see the torn shingles that must have been ripped from the roof when he'd crashed. He groaned.

No wonder the humans are so angry. I crashed into their forest and hurt their house! Jarak thought, putting his hands to his cheeks in horror. *How can I possibly make this up to them?*

"Research Log Three. Question three: Are the humans angry because I ruined their house? Hypothesis three: The humans will forgive me and let me inside after I've fixed up this mess, realizing that I hadn't meant to cause any damage to their belongings or persons. The experiment is to be reshingling this roof. I have watched videos on this subject during my research into human architecture. This should be very easy to do myself." He drunkenly stumbled back across the ladder and descended carefully—as carefully as one not fully in control of his limb, that was. Then Jarak grabbed fresh shingles from the pallet, along with the hammer and a pocket full of nails. "This will take ten minutes. Tops."

Six hours, Walter thought, once again sitting by his wife and kids. *Six hours of constant noise, constant* hammering. *What could they be doing? Reshingling my roof?* Walter would have laughed deliriously if his family hadn't been sleeping beside him. *No, they're tearing through my roof. That,*

or building some kind of device on it. Walter shook his head. Of all people, why him? Why his house?

He might have pondered that question longer if that constant hammering wasn't so distracting. *They must be testing the house's weak points. They know we can't leave—that we can't go anywhere. They want to see how long we can take it before we snap.*

And Walter felt himself dangling on a frayed rope overlooking that abyss of insanity.

I can't stand it... I can't stand it. I can't stand it!

Walter stood up, jostling his wife from sleep. Emma stared at him in horror as he walked toward the door. "Walter, what are you going to do?"

"I'm going to end this," Walter hissed, pushing aside the couch and opening the front door.

This is so *much harder than the videos said!* Not even halfway done reshingling the roof, Jarak missed the nail for the third time on the latest shingle when the front door opened beneath him. *The humans have finally forgiven me!* He exhaled in relief, the last six hours having been brutal and torturous. His left thumb was destroyed from the amount of times he'd missed the nail and smashed his hand. "Hello, fellow human! Sorry for the damage to your house, but I have tried to rectify the situation by..." He trailed off as said human came into view. Jarak saw the man's bloodshot eyes, heaving chest, and shotgun pointed upward.

As the human pulled the trigger, Jarak dove to the side. The pellets from the shell casing whizzed past him, one embedding itself into his shin. Feeling a flash of pain far harsher than anything he'd felt in his Konari form, Jarak limped up the slope and jumped over the ridge just as another hail of pellets ripped through the shingles he'd just installed. "Hey! I worked hard on those!"

"Where are the rest of you, huh?" the human father asked.

The rest of us? Jarak also looked from side to side, but seeing nothing out of the ordinary. "Others?" he asked without looking over the ridge.

"Don't play with me!" the human shouted, racking the shotgun and loading more ammunition into the tube. "I *heard* you! I heard *them!* Why won't you just leave us alone, huh?"

Jarak peered over the ridge and ducked back down as more pellets chewed through the wood. Still not in total control of this body, Jarak fell backward, flopped off the side of the house, and smashed into the bushes before flopping onto solid ground. He groaned and rolled to his feet as the human stomped around the side of the house.

As the fear and pain filled his mind, Jarak lashed out. "Leave me alone!" He threw his hammer. Despite only having semi-control over his limbs, the tool flew perfectly—like he still had telekinetic powers. Its flat face smashed into the man's forehead, and he crumpled to the ground, shooting the dirt before falling still.

Oh no. Jarak put his hands to his head, ripping out a few strands of hair. "Please don't be dead. *Please* don't be dead!"

Jarak stumbled over to the human and kneeled beside him, shaking him. Slowly, the human groaned and his eyes blinked. "Oh thank the stars," Jarak whispered. "Hello, fellow human! Try not to move too much. I—uh, I mean, *somebody*—threw a hammer at you, and you shouldn't try to—"

"*You!*" the human shouted, kicking at Jarak's legs, which were already weak. He fell on top of the human, and they rolled down the sloped grass toward the woods as the human tried to punch him.

"Why are you doing this?" Jarak shouted as he protected his face with his forearms.

"Why are *you* doing this!" the human spat back, raining down blows.

"I was just trying to fix your roof!" Jarak replied, rolling on top and slapping at the human. "Why are you trying to kill me?"

"Why are *you* trying to kill me!" the human echoed as he returned to the top position. "Why come to our planet to pick a fight?"

"I didn't!" Jarak said, shoving the human off. His heart thudded painfully in his chest, and his shin ached as he pulled himself to his feet.

I'm going to die here unless I do something. The forest is too far away. Can't go inside the house. What do I do? Jarak spotted the shotgun. He and the human stared at each other, both having the same idea. *It's him or me.*

Jarak straight-arm slapped the human, knocking him down into the mud. Stumbling back toward the shotgun, Jarak lifted it and swung it back toward the human, who kept slipping in the mud until he saw the shotgun. Then the man froze and raised his hands above his head in surrender. Every emotion told Jarak to pull the trigger: the fear, anger, pain, and hatred all screaming in agreement. *Shoot!*

With an animalistic roar of rage, Jarak's finger pulled the trigger, and the gun exploded. He squeezed his eyes shut just as the gun blasted out of his limp hands. *The man's dead. He has to be dead.* Remorse ate at him like flames. *What other choice did I have?* "I'm sorry. I'm *so* sorry!"

Grimacing, Jarak opened his eyes, expecting to see a spatter of blood. Instead, the shotgun pellets floated in the air in front of the human, maybe a centimeter from his flesh. The man kept patting himself, searching for wounds but finding none. Not one of them hit him. In shock, Jarak fell back on his butt on the grass, and the human sobbed in relief.

Well, I must say, these events are not what I had expected to happen, but the results are the same, Lomari said, waddling over from the dark tree line. It appeared in its Konari form, wearing a black biosuit to keep Earth's single-celled organisms at bay. The human tried to scramble backward, but Lomari grabbed him with a telekinetic hand and held him aloft.

"How..." Jarak's voice broke. Clearing his throat and swallowing hard, he tried again. "How long have you been here?"

Lomari laughed from within Jarak's own mind. *I arrived here maybe an Earth minute after you crashed and disrupted the local communication networks to keep these humans isolated. Rather than contain you, I allowed your impromptu mission to continue, if only to glean the results. Then I followed you, which was quite easy, considering how poor humans' eyesight and hearing are. I saw all that happened—and lent a helping hand with that hammer throw of yours. You* really *do not have control of that body yet, but your determination was quite admirable.*

Shame coursed through his blood, and his shoulders sagged. "So, I failed?"

Failed? Lomari repeated, laughing again. If Jarak hadn't been so defeated, he might've lashed out, if only to make the lead researcher stop mocking him. *I must admit, when I first arrived, I thought you had. Miserably. I even had a mind to leave you stranded here in that human form. But no, Jarak. You showed me something very important: the humans are too afraid to accept our intervention, no matter what we do. We can help them—fix their world—and they'll still attack us. After all, you tried to return his flashlight and fix his roof, and he tried to shoot you.*

"But why would he?" Jarak asked, feeling a spark of anger. "All I did was help!"

So you thought. Humans cannot perceive events as clearly as Konari can. Admittedly, tonight was a series of ridiculous misunderstandings, Lomari replied, telling him the truth of the encounter.

With each revelation, Jarak's jaw dropped another inch. "His name was *Walter?* Oh... These emotions are so unwieldy," he said eventually, still unable to meet Lomari's eyes. "I tried to kill him. I *would* have killed him. I don't know what came over me. Everything told me he needed to die so that I could survive."

I tried to tell you that the humans have not evolved far enough to subdue their chemical emotions, Lomari said, walking forward to inspect the human now hovering in midair. *But it is because of this altercation that you succeeded, Jarak. You, one of my best Earth researchers, could not overcome these human emotions, even with my advanced warning. Despite our obvious advantages, you still were controlled by your fear even though you knew he could not hurt you while you held that weapon. And if that happened to you, well, it must happen to a majority of humans—like this one.*

With this proof, I can officially tell you that the humans are biologically unfit to know of our existence, nor can we help them save their world and advance their technology. If we did, who is to say they would not attack us with our gifts? No, we will quarantine their planet for a few hundred years. If they survive that long, then maybe we can try again.

Jarak nodded, thinking through that information. He walked toward Lomari, stifling a yelp from the pain of his injured shin. The adrenaline having faded, the wound throbbed. "What about these humans?"

We use the standard procedure on the whole family, Lomari replied, holding the human and dragging him around the house to the front yard, where another flying saucer hovered in the air with its cloaking disabled.

Other Konari floated down from the ship's tractor beam, waddled up to the house, and used telekinesis to open the door and find the rest of the family. From their horrified screams, Jarak assumed they hadn't been difficult to find.

Mouth swabs and anal probes for nonsurgical biological samples, plus a short-term memory wipe while we fix your damaged craft and remove all traces of your presence, Lomari explained, pulling the human into the tractor beam's light and releasing him from the telekinetic hold. The man sobbed, covering his rear end as he was brought aboard. *Afterward, we will put the humans all back in their beds. They might wake up with scrambled flashes of wiped memories, but they will not have any proof. If they wish to tell their friends about anal probes and be laughed out of town, so be it.*

Jarak nodded, still waiting for the other shoe to drop. "So... what will you do to me?"

I think tonight was punishment enough. We will just say that this mission was a success, and that I asked you to crash the saucer intentionally to study the humans' reactions and cast judgement, Lomari said, to which Jarak could only gasp. *Besides, we learn most from our failures, do we not?*

Despite the relief coursing through his heart and flooding through his blood vessels, Jarak shook his head. "Have you ever made a mistake like mine?"

Oh, yes. Worse, in fact. Lomari replied as the tractor beam pulled it and Jarak up toward the saucer. *Ever heard of Roswell? Now* that *was a misunderstanding...*

MAPPING THE VOID: A hunted explorer searches for his brother in psychedelic dimensions...

Mapping the Void

The last frontier was never space, but the Void—a dimension astronauts can't reach. Only the psychonauts can get there. Only I can.

Four scientists hustle about within this laboratory of antiseptic solutions, beeping monitors, and intravenous fluids as I lay on a contoured operating table. They strap me down, and the feeling of helplessness makes my heart pound. The restraints are for my own good, because I've learned the return from these trips to the Void can be spastic and alarming, but it is difficult not to be afraid, having seen what I have. Still I must go—for my twin brother, if not myself.

As these experimenters speed through their pre-trip checklist, one fastens a metal cap around my shaved head while another injects conducting gel through ports near the electrodes. Though I cannot see them, these wires form a braid along my back and are plugged into various monitors to capture my brainwave activity while I'm exploring.

A third scientist attaches a tube into the IV port surgically inserted beneath the skin of my right bicep. Though the liquid is clear, it isn't water. A carefully controlled solution of dimethyltryptamine and other psychedelics flows through the port, into a catheter, and makes its way into my veins, dulling my senses and pulling me toward the Void. The scientists can control my blood-serum levels with this setup, and so long as the solution continues to be injected into my body, I can remain in that realm for hours—even *days*—instead of a few minutes. If things go wrong, they can flush the DMT from my system to pull me out of the experience.

What they don't comprehend is that I will be long dead if it comes to that.

Where I go—what the Void actually is—I still don't pretend to know, but the fact that I can map this place with both precision and accuracy makes me think it's real. Yet that means the Machine is real too, which is far more terrifying.

The final scientist, Magnus, monitors the other three, holding a clipboard and scribbling notes as the DMT solution takes effect. Though it doesn't burn, I feel like I'm melting. No, *dissolving.* Fear shakes my fingers, so I distract myself by humming *Country Roads*—my identical twin's favorite song and now mine—while staring up into the fluorescent lights.

A hand eclipses that light, forming numbers to count down from five. At zero, the hand disappears, and the fluorescent lights burn brighter than the sun. It expands into a mandala of color, pulling my consciousness, my essence, perhaps even my *soul* into itself.

Then I dissolve completely.

The world melts as a tunnel of fibrous light shunts me across the stars and births me into this new realm of kaleidoscopic colors, fractals, and hypershapes. They pixelate into everyday sights as my mind tries to rationalize the inconceivable Void, be it a personal hallucination, the fourth dimension, or—as I hope—the afterlife. The triangles become lamp posts, the squares cobblestones, and the polyhedrons clouds. The mandala that brought me here shines in the night sky like the sun, but I know it is supposed to be the moon. Despite its incredible light, this world is dark.

Nearby, waves crash against the sea, the mist anointing my brow like perspiration. Seagulls crow like roosters from the roofs of the squat buildings looming around me, butting up to one another so closely that the sounds traipse across the glass storefronts, the fabric shades above their doors, and the oil-lamp posts. The latter's light is more frantic than the moon's, casting fleeting shadows upon the brick walls as tongues of flame greedily devour all they can.

Yet my shadow has already gone into hiding, waiting for me to find him.

Before I search, I look down at my fingers and palms as is the grounding protocol to remind myself that this isn't—at least, *shouldn't*—be real. My movements are delayed, my fingers blurring through the moist air, but I expect this. If Magnus is correct, then this Void really is the fourth dimension, existing outside of time.

Yet time is of the essence because of that damned Machine, that creature of fused gears and skin. It hunts for me even now and can be around any corner. I've never seen it up close, but I've caught glimpses of it a handful of times, enough for that horror of patchwork skin and rusting metal to be seared into my mind. Humanoid, but something I'd never mistake as human.

I force myself not to think of it, because doing so attracts its attention. Instead, I push the thoughts from my mind, and while they dribble upward from my ears like the smoke of that creature's burning lubricant, I return my attention to myself.

The only reminder of my true body is the port in my bicep which glows like a rainbow. As I'm not wearing clothes, that light glares like a beacon. Yet to say I'm nude would be false. Physically genderless in this space, the skin I was born with has been replaced with aged yellow parchment. It's as if I've become a character in a story, though in this place I feel as if I've lived a thousand lifetimes, with each far more interesting than my true existence. Serif letters and numbers dance across my surfaces, their tails curling around one another as they play. After they notice me noticing them, they form a merry circle and spell out a nonsensical phrase: *Jack be nimble, Jack be quick! Jack should run, before Jack gets nicked!*

Ridiculous though it might be, I know the phrase is a warning. A dire one.

I run.

"Psychonaut Candidate Seventeen, what is your status?" Magnus asks as I barrel down this first street. His disembodied voice booms across the night sky like thunder, though there are no lightning bolts. He is still in the lab watching over my true body, and he's always strictly professional, using my Experiment ID though he knows my name is Jack.

I have no such professionalism.

"I'm in Quadrant 17-A, Magnus," I say with my mouth, knowing that Magnus can hear me because my true body—which is still strapped to that restraint table—speaks the same words.

"Acknowledged, Seventeen," Magnus replies. *"What do you see?"*

I relay everything to him, as I've always done on the dozens of trips to the Void. I can tell him of this seaport by memory alone because it's where I'm always dropped. While the street eventually leads to several intersections, my course is pre-plotted.

"Right... Left... Straight... Right... Right..." I tell Magnus as I chart my course through this deserted place. Though it might seem like an aimless route to the scientists, many streets are dead-ends. Here, the path is never straight. There is probably a lesson in that—everything here attempts to teach me a lesson—but this one is lost on me. Like most.

Behind me are the paths to other Quadrants that I've already mapped: train stations, metal deserts, alien beaches, square-shaped pyramids, cloud cities, dwarven mines, mandala spheres, and infinite staircases. In each of them, the Machine always finds me.

As if it senses my thoughts, I hear a gear creaking somewhere far away, as if that abomination is cocking its head and listening.

"Acknowledged, Seventeen." Magnus replies, distracting me. *"What is your appearance?"*

"Parchment this time," I say. My body, unlike the setting, always seems to change, aside from the port in my arm. Parchment is a new material, as I've been everything from an astronaut to a puppet to even the outlandish creatures in *The Wizard of Oz*. It's as if my unconscious mind is trying to tell me I don't have a brain, a heart, or even courage—that I'm just SOL.

God only knows my luck is running thin. Each time I return here, the Machine gets closer to catching me. It finds me faster. Last time, it almost touched me. I don't know what will happen if it does.

When it does.

"Acknowledged. You should see Quadrant 12-F soon. Let me know the moment you arrive." Magnus says as a sign off, referring to the forest as

Quadrant 12-F because PC-12 had discovered this same forest a month prior to me during a different mapping expedition.

I still have trouble believing it is a coincidence, considering that I was only told about PC-12's experiences after discovering the forest myself, meaning that PC-12 and I hadn't known of each other's experiences. I don't even know who PC-12 *is* because of the confidentiality of the test, so I can only take Magnus's word for it.

Because all psychonauts spawn in similar port cities, I've gone looking for PC-12's but never found it. There might be two identical forests, the Void might not be allowing me into another port city, or it might be impossible to map this place in three-dimensional terms.

For the sake of funding and continuing these expeditions, I hope it is not the latter. That's why I—nor any of the other psychonaut candidates, I assume—haven't told him about the Machine.

As I think the word, the sounds of my footfalls double, and I panic, thinking that beast has caught my scent by that one slip-up alone. Something moves in my periphery, and without stopping, I turn my head to find only my shadow. This time, he is pretending to be my reflection because I don't have one in this place. He runs in the windows and once he knows he has my attention, he cartwheels, river dances, and goosesteps to make me laugh. I don't, but I can't hide my relief.

The name for him sprouts from my mind, but it's somehow the wrong word: Shadow. Either he has far more names, or this persona is only a part of who he truly is. Regardless, I feel as if I've known him since the birth of the universe. The emotions make little sense, and logic might as well be tossed into the nearby sea. From what I've learned, logic should be the last word used to describe the Void.

Though Shadow is without eyes, ears, or a mouth, I understand his words: "Off we go on another quest! Will it be to the forest and then the carnival again, or have you finally grown tired of that route?"

Shadow leaps from a window, grabs a lamppost, and spins lazily around. The light does not touch him but flees his presence. He does not look two-dimensional, but like a featureless-faced man wearing a black bodysuit. I would say three-dimensional, but there is some *beyondness* to him I cannot even guess at.

I open my mouth to answer his question before remembering that, if I speak aloud, my body will echo the words in the real world. Although my mission here is to identify these types of interactions and chart these strange territories, I've long since learned to keep Shadow—and the other people I encounter—a secret. So instead I think-speak the words, though I can still hear them leave my mind and reverberate through the air. "Same as before, Shadow. You know the drill."

Drill. Another word I should avoid, for I hear the whirr of an electric motor behind me. Not close, but closer than the gear had been. The beast is on its way, using my mistakes to triangulate my position. I've come here so many times that I'd expect it to lie in wait and ambush me, but I assume it also tracks the other psychonaut candidates mapping this place.

Yet I now hold its attention. I know it's coming, and it knows I know.

"Same as before? You think the Void is the same? Never!" Shadow says, trying to distract me from that dark well of panic. He lets go of the lamp, placing his hands behind his back, and walks up the air as if he's standing on an invisible flight of stairs. Even meandering, he moves as fast as I sprint. In the deep, dignified voice of a professor standing in front of a foreboding fireplace, Shadow says, "Just because things look the same does not mean that they are." After swirling an imaginary glass of wine and sipping it, he adds, "You don't know nearly as much as you pretend to."

"Yeah, yeah." I say, because I have no comeback. Not that I've ever been any good at arguing. My twin had always been wittier than me. Funnier too.

Shadow, like everybody in this realm, knows me better than I know myself. As if they were me, or at the very least, had been with me all my life. Even after all my experiences here, I still don't know what to believe. All I know is that the beast is not me. If it is, I am far more broken than I dare think.

Behind us, I hear a third set of footsteps echoing Shadow and me—the beast has caught my scent.

I chance a look back, searching for its presence. Instead, my foot catches on a jutting cobblestone, and I trip, tumbling along the street before falling still. In place of blood, a few letters drip from the tear on my parchment knee, spelling out: *FREEDOM!* Then they scurry away into the shadows like ants.

Stop getting distracted, I scold myself privately as I stand.

All my thoughts and actions are made public by the letters on my parchment skin, which arrange themselves into words and mock me in toggle case: *sToP gEtTiNg DiStRaCtEd!*

Immediately, Shadow descends from the air and places a hand into his chest, withdrawing a small amount of black ooze, which he presses to my knee. That gunk covers the torn parchment like a black blood clot, and the letters spell out a series of angry words, having been stymied in their escape.

Though Shadow and I have stopped, I can still hear a pair of running footsteps. Dread throttles me while death twirls its scythe. Those feet run faster than I ever could, devouring the distance between us. Its rhythmic pace is maddening, like listening to the ticking clock counting down to my execution.

While it's an outsider in the Void like me, I am at least welcomed here. That beast isn't. Shadow hates its presence as much as I do. I don't know why it wants me. Just that it does, and it won't stop until it has me.

"Let's go," Shadow says, looking down the corridor beside me and shivering fearfully.

And if he's afraid, the beast can hurt him too, I think. *Perhaps it can even kill us...*

We run. With each turn I make, I speak my new direction aloud so that Magnus can hear it, track my progress, and map each Quadrant's entirety. As we turn right a final time, the town abruptly ends, and the forest begins. After I scan it and find no traces of the beast, I lip-speak to Magnus, "I'm in Quadrant 12-F."

Child-like laughter surrounds me, emanating from the gnarled trees whose branches resemble the limbs of humans and animals. I should be terrified of them, but I'm not. Despite their otherworldly appearance, the trees aren't evil. When they beckon, it is to show me the easiest path through the woods. They gently pet my head as I sprint by, as if trying to console me. Their roots push themselves aside to clear my path across the dirt, then wind together to form living bridges across river-cut gorges. Their chaos is a kindness to my stupid, faux-logical mind. I know these creatures aren't truly trees, but this is the closest visualization to their form that my mind can comprehend.

"In the Void, all is possible," Shadow reminds me, reading my thoughts.

I nod my head in bitter agreement. "That's why I'm here."

"But Magnus still doesn't know the real reason you're here, does he?" Shadow asks, though we both know he knows that answer to that question. Yet he adds the obvious answer anyway. "Not to map this place, but to find your brother."

I don't say his name, but I think the word, so the letters arrange themselves on my arm: *Jared.* A twinge of pain lances my heart like an insect's sting. Then my cheek twitches in irritation, and in response, my parchment skin ruffles audibly as if I'm flipping through the pages of a book. "So?" I spit back. "Why shouldn't I look for him, huh? Everyone pretends like there's nothing I can do, but this—*this*—is something I can do, okay? I'm not just going to sit there and... *and*—"

"Grieve?" Shadow asks, still easily matching my strides.

"I need to do something," I say, because that's the only thing I can say. It's all I've said for the last year.

Jared and I had been roommates living together in an apartment, having left home to start our own lives. He had slipped in the shower one night, cracked his head open on the edge of the bathtub, and awkwardly fallen in a broken heap. I know because I'd been the one to find him. I should've found him hours before, but I'd been too busy going out on a date with a girl I hadn't cared about, gotten home in the morning, and discovered his corpse because I'd been tired of waiting to take a shower—not because I'd wanted to check on him.

If I'd been there, if I'd heard that sound of him thudding to the floor, I could have called the EMTs immediately and saved him. Instead of being here, I could be with him right now, playing a board game or watching a movie or walking downtown. It didn't matter what we'd done, so long as we were near each other. So long as I could *see* him.

But the last time I saw him had been in his casket. His hair was styled to cover the stitched-up gash wound that had split his skull, his broken arm hidden in the sleeve of a suit jacket, his broken neck concealed by a white shirt collar. All I recall is the look on my parents' faces—that horror and sorrow more inconceivable than these trees—which constantly reminds me I am to blame.

If only I'd been there...

"You can't blame yourself for that." Shadow yells to be heard above the trees, whose tune of laughter changes from merriment to sympathy. More branches reach out to me, not to scratch my parchment-like skin but to pat my back, squeeze my shoulders, and help me across the uneven terrain. Their kindness knows no bounds.

Neither does my self-hatred.

"I can't blame myself?" I laugh mirthlessly, feeling inky tears stain my parchment, dissolving the letters that had been perching on the bags beneath my eyelids. "Then you really don't know me as well as you pretend to."

"I know you feel a need to find Jared—to beg his forgiveness," Shadow replies, and I want to throttle him. Just because he knows the truth doesn't mean he should tell it to me. "You think coming here is the best way, but it isn't, PC."

PC. That's the *Psychonaut Candidate* initialism the scientists use for all of us, but when Shadow says it, it feels as if he means *Playable Character.* As if I'm the only one who really exists here—or I'm the only one who doesn't. I know there's more meaning to his choice of name than this, but my mind still can't grasp his intention. All I seem to grab are more questions as the answers slowly fade away into the mists of this forest.

"You should grieve. Search for Jared, too, if you think it will help you, but not in the Void," Shadow continues. "I think you've learned the wrong lessons here, PC. Life is a gift, and everyone dies. You should appreciate the life that surrounds you. To lose a loved one is grievous, but to lose all of them is a tragedy. You're doing just that by pushing everyone away... What do you think would happen if you somehow *did* find Jared?"

I don't bother replying, because part of me thinks—has always thought—that Shadow is right. This is a pointless search. The letters along my parchment skin sing that doubt to the high heavens, if we are not already in them.

Shadow sighs as if knowing he needs to say something but doesn't want to. "But if it's pointless, you hope you can at least become lost in the Void and never have to find your way back. That way, you don't have to repair the other relationships you've neglected. You can die, and everybody will be better off anyway, isn't that right?"

"So? You only know that because you're a figment of my imagination," I hiss between clenched teeth, not because I believe the words but because words are the only thing with which I can hurt Shadow.

"You're trying to push me away too," he says. "But I'm your shadow. Trying to push me away is like trying to push yourself away. It isn't going to work. I'm stubborn like that—perhaps because you're *also* that stubborn."

"You don't even believe that you're a figment of my imagination!" I shout, wanting to stop running and scream at him. Yet fear devours the anger like a whale does krill. To stop is to let the beast close the distance.

"You're right, I don't. In fact, I know I'm not. But you think I am, so I'm willing to pretend. Come to think of it, I'm quite good at pretend-ing." Shadow grows, abandoning my shaggy appearance and donning the silhouette of a king with an eight-pointed crown. "Onward, Sir Knight! Methinks thine carnival be over yonder hill!" Then he jumps, motioning like a man vaulting over the back of a horse and onto a saddle. Sitting in midair, he spurs the invisible beast's flanks and rockets forward, leaving me to eat dust stirred by his steed.

I would have told him to slow down, but two of the hands of a sapling tree grab me as it uproots itself and gallops along the forest floor on an assortment of limbs. Admittedly, it feels more like I'm on the back of a millipede than a horse. Regardless of locomotion, the sapling speeds past Shadow, who cracks invisible reins and puts on another burst of speed.

I can only stare at him as he jostles and jiggles as if he is actually sitting on a horse, yet as I reach out and poke the air surrounding him, I feel something like muscle. As if my hand is burning, I pull it back quickly. "How are you *doing* that?"

Though he has no mouth to smile with, I can *feel* Shadow smirk. "Just because something is invisible doesn't mean it isn't there."

I nod dumbly, feeling the mist drag a long nail against my spine. *The horse is invisible... Jared could be here too, and maybe I just can't see him. What if the key is me seeing through the invisibility?* I look around, hoping for a sign of something—anything. Nothing.

"You're learning the wrong lesson again... I'm afraid it doesn't work quite like that," Shadow says, sounding genuinely apologetic.

An avalanche of agony drowns my hope.

"I mean that for things to be, you need to create them," Shadow continues. "My realm is one of spirit, adventure, and creation. *Lots* of spirits. Yet you must be the one to put in the effort. Just as it is in your life—the one you come from. You cannot expect anything if you do not put in the effort."

"I'm putting in the effort," I think-whisper. "All I've *done* is put in the effort."

Disgusted, I gaze up at the trees, not thinking about my path through the Void but *to* it. Standing there at Jared's funeral as I hear the sobs of my parents. Sitting alone in my apartment and feeling his presence in all his possessions but not seeing him. Buying used nonfiction books and staying up past midnight to read them all. Studying religions from Christianity to Hinduism. Understanding the death rites of ancient cultures. Learning of psychedelics' role in shaping religions and cultures. Investigating the hallucinatory effects of various psychedelics. Theorizing the use of dimethyltryptamine to enter a dream-state. Hypothesizing the body's release of DMT into the brain at the time of death to create a chemical gateway for a soul to escape into the afterlife—for *Jared's* soul to escape into the afterlife. Realizing I could trick a local research lab into accepting me as a candidate into a psychedelic study to explore this Void.

If the intravenous dosage could be sustained long enough for me to search the Void's entirety. If the afterlife is the Void. If all souls go to the same afterlife. If a soul is even real. If I can even find Jared here by running far enough—running *long* enough.

If, if, if...

All I do is run, I think, and the words spell themselves out along my arms: *Run!* It's impossible to tell if they're mocking me or warning me of the coming beast. A quick look over my shoulder tells me nothing, but Shadow doesn't look tense. He would be if the beast was near.

I still have time.

"Time?" Shadow asked, sighing. "You're really not learning the right lessons."

"Oh yeah? And what's the right lesson?" I ask, biting back a scathing expletive, though he still knows what I would have said. "To just accept that Jared's gone? To go on living? To say, *'Oh well?'* I can't do it, Shadow! I can't do it!"

Stopping to catch my breath, I'm aware I'm not actually breathing air here. I could speak continuously until the heat death of the sun and never pause for breath, but psychologically, I think I need to breathe, and that need is more real than the physics of the Void.

"I know it's difficult," Shadow says, looking over at me from his invisible horse. "But do you think punishing yourself will help?"

"Maybe," I eventually reply, not trusting myself to speak. If one thing is real here, it's emotion. I know if I speak too much, my voice will crack.

"Maybe not," Shadow argues. Instead of anger or hatred, he leans through the sapling's army of limbs to squeeze my shoulder tightly. Why he's so kind or why he continues to help me, I don't know. When I ask, he refuses to tell me. I still take comfort in the touch. "Words fail what actions won't, PC. Let's go find the right lesson. That's why we're really here anyway."

The sapling skids to a stop as the forest ends on an impossibly high cliff. I don't. I fly from my perch and into the night sky where the stars are like glinting shurikens. This has happened to me before. A dozen times, at least. Yet I still scream as I fall hundreds of feet, throwing my limbs around to grasp anything.

I catch Shadow's outstretched hand. He's no longer dressed as a king but sitting cross-legged and wearing what looks like a soup can on his head. Holding me aloft, we descend gently to the ground on what I can only describe as a rug. Though I cannot see it, I can feel the threads as I drag my hands along it. The tassels too. Only then does the soup can—the *fez*—make sense.

"Horrible impression," I mutter, stifling a smile as I crawl onto the magic carpet. I feel Shadow's grin as he shrugs his shoulders and lands on the ground. "It's unfair," I add, referring to how he can read my thoughts, but I can't read his.

"Did you really think the lesson here is fairness?" Shadow asks, exuding amusement.

"Ha ha," I spit, pushing myself to my feet and beginning running across the open field of high grasses to the spotlights shining straight up somewhere beyond the next hill.

"Seventeen?" Magnus asks from the moon, and his voice is so unexpected that I jump. *"We just noticed a spike of brain activity. Is something wrong?"*

"Was thrown from the cliff again," I lip-speak. After hearing the small gasp from the other scientists present in the lab, I quickly add, "I'm not hurt."

"Acknowledged. If you're already past the cliff, you should be near—"

"Quadrant 7-CH, yeah," I reply, gauging the distance from the cliff and repeating it back to him. Seems to be the same as usual. Approximately a few football fields away.

This next Quadrant is a carnival, whose dazzling array of rotating spotlights spume forth like a wave's froth. Music blares from dozens of rides, which aren't made of metal, electric batteries, or other machines.

Curse words flit across my mind as the echoes of footsteps speed up behind me.

Instead, the carnival is built from red-and-white candy canes bent into various shapes to create a Ferris wheel, tilt-a-whirl, carousel, and a hundred other attractions. They greet me with warm emotions in lieu of hands, lying together in that bed of grass next to ring tosses, balloon darts, and duck ponds. All around, creatures of all colors, creeds, and shapes laugh, enjoying themselves. Though nobody needs a ticket to enter, a throng of people loiter outside the entrance for me.

Jared is never among them.

Shadow ruffles my red hair—ribbon strings, like those glued to old books—while mischievous letters cut deep with their incessant chanting of my brother's name. My anger at those letters only spurs them on to mock me with the worst things I've thought about myself.

"What if we stopped running this time, PC?" Shadow asks as he, no doubt, reads those vengeful words. "What if we just enjoy the carnival?"

I try not to think of the creature following us like a hound, but I think that simile only makes the beast faster. To cover my fear—which I can't do in this damned place—I snort. Again, I feel Shadow's empathy wrap around me like a hug.

"Do you think I'd let anything happen to you?" Shadow asks, and I can feel his grin widen though I cannot see it. "I'll push you back to your realm before it can get to you. Promise."

Pushing. That was another way to leave the Void. Shadow could simply send me back with a gentle nudge. I'm sure I could do the same thing on my own, but I never have, even when the beast is near.

While I believe Shadow, I'm still unconvinced. "Can you stop that thing?" I ask, jerking my thumb behind me without looking.

Shadow's smile falters. "Years ago? Yes. But now? I don't know. It's grown stronger."

"Why?"

"Because it keeps feeding off you humans—and you let it," he replies, and I hear anger and bitterness creep into his voice. The sound of it grates on me like a cheese tool.

Reading the letters on my skin—reading *me*—like a book, Shadow is silent as we approach the crowd still waiting outside of the carnival. They flip me off as we pass, but they do so with benevolent grins as if telling me not to take myself so seriously. Without smiling, I mirror their gestures as we sprint through the gate of the carnival. Then the congregation follows us inside as if I'm the vanguard of an elite procession.

"I'm inside," I lip-speak to Magnus, relaying everything I see.

The people inside are different. Most pretend not to notice me. Only a few smile. I suppose there's a lesson in that, too, but I discard it as I search the crowd for my brother. Though I know he won't be here with as many times as I've looked, I still try.

Just get to the next Quadrant. The thought is broadcast by the letters on my skin, disappointing Shadow. *If I can get to the fifth one this time, maybe I'll find him. If not there, the sixth.*

"Want to go on a ride with me?" Shadow asks again, looking up at the Ferris wheel. Though it's stopped, I hear the merriment from the nearest cars.

"Let's just go straight to the circus," I say.

Shadow only sighs in reply. He picks up his pace without bothering to lengthen his stride. I half-jog, half-run to keep up with him, and as we pass, the arcade-style games and carnival rides beseech me with their flashing lights to slow down and enjoy the sights.

I refuse as I always have. Yet another lesson I've yet to learn, I'm sure.

Before us raises a big-top tent, whose fabric is made with the same candy-cane stripes as the rest of the carnival. Orange, yellow, and red flames explode upward from a fire breather standing guard at the entrance. Beside her, a sphinx juggles an infinite number of chainsaws on a unicycle. The fire breather turns sharply to expel fiery tendrils into my face, which brush past me without pain despite all my flinching. A falling chainsaw should cleave me in half, too, but it falls harmlessly to the ground as if its blade is imaginary.

The lesson is supposed to be that I cannot be hurt in this place, but I know I can. I know *what* can hurt me. And it's coming closer.

Machine is nimble, Machine is quick! Machine is coming, Machine will nick! say the letters, and Shadow stops mid-applause as he reads the words on my skin. Together, we look back at the forest's cliff as something jumps from it and crosses in front of the stars.

The beast.

"Let's go. *Now.*" I say in a half-choked voice.

Shadow pushes aside the colorful fabric covering the circus's doorway, revealing a carpeted hallway which scares me more than the beast itself.

But that's a lie. Nothing is more terrifying than that creature.

I run into the next Quadrant: a funeral home. The sound of music is gone, hiding with the von Trapps. I'm left in here with the silent black-clad mourners who all don carnival masks and seemingly don't see me. Less like they're ignoring me, and more like I've ceased to exist.

"Just reached Quadrant 11-AG," I lip-speak, though my tongue feels leaden and fuzzy like the corpse of a starved bear in its cave.

"*Acknowledged, Seventeen. On to Quadrant 41-B,*" blares the voice of Magnus, whom these mourners don't seem to notice. The path to Quadrant 41-B is two lefts, down the stairs, and into the morgue. I found it on my fourth trip here. The beast expects me to take it because the other path disturbs me, but if I am going to explore the next Quadrant, I need to trick it here.

"No. Change of plans, Magnus. I'm going to Quadrant 18-X." I swallow harshly as I add, "Going straight through this room. Then left into the main chamber and through the casket."

"*Acknowledged... Are you all right? Your heartbeat is spiking.*"

"I don't like funeral homes." While that's a true statement, it's a false answer, but to tell him of the beast would cause an emergency end to the trip. I can't allow that. *Just get to the next Quadrant. Keep going. Don't stop.*

"*Acknowledged, Seventeen. Be safe.*"

Shadow is just exiting the throughway as I charge down the hallway. "Slow down! Think this through!" he shouts, but I don't listen.

Portraits of flowers and picturesque locations hang themselves on the walls, beautiful and vibrant unlike the black-clad mourners. I know each picture by heart, because I've torn each from the wall on previous trips, attempting to find more throughways within or behind them. No such luck.

Turning left and entering the chapel, I run down the empty aisle separating the rows of mourners. My head skims their vases, though their masks make it difficult to tell who anyone is. By mannerisms alone, I know none are my brother. He was notorious for shaking his knees.

Is, I remind myself.

At the far end of the room lies a closed mahogany casket. A wreath of laurel leaves rests on a stand beside it with the words, *In a better place,* inscribed upon a ribbon. The same words—the same wreath—were at my brother's funeral. In the many times that I've searched this building, the casket was the absolute last thing I would touch. It's the Void's sinister trick that a Quadrant throughway is in there—that I have to climb in.

I throw open the top of the casket just as I hear pounding feet on the staircase a couple of rooms away. The beast. It must have been downstairs in the morgue, expecting me to take that route. The fact I tricked it should be exciting, but a hero is excited only in storybooks.

I'm no hero—I'm scared shitless.

Though the mourners wear plastic masks, the plastic frowns. They might not be as terrified as I am, but these people can feel something wicked coming this way. Rather than run for the exit, they fade out of existence, hiding from the beast.

When I look down at the casket, it's not empty like it should be. Instead, Jared is lying inside. A small sob escapes my lips, and Magnus immediately asks, *"Seventeen? What is it? What are you seeing?"*

My sob transforms into a whimper as I notice the mole on my identical twin's neck—my mole, my neck. The corpse isn't my brother's. It's mine.

Somehow, that makes me feel better and gives me the strength to keep going.

"Just got scared. Everything's fine," I say. I don't know how convincing the lie is considering that Magnus can see my spiking heartbeat, but I also don't care. I'll think of a better lie when I return.

The mechanical footsteps boom louder than Magnus's voice as I throw my too-real corpse out of the casket. All I see is the beast's clawed hand as it grabs the door frame. It's not me who moves, but Shadow. He shoves me headfirst into the casket, and we fall into the Quadrant 18-X.

I spill out into a mound of purple hay in a barn stable whose ceiling scrapes the sky. Shadow lands on me and jumps to his feet for a fight, but the beast doesn't follow us through the casket. It can't use the Void throughways like we can. Instead, the beast makes its own doors, which means it can attack from any direction now that it knows exactly where I am.

I get to my feet, but I shake like a newborn calf. Shadow is crouched against the door, waiting to spring on anything that barrels through. Nothing does. The beast has learned patience. Now that it's caught up to me, it will wait—wherever it is.

"I'm in Quadrant 18-X," I tell Magnus, though I can't relay any details within this stable. From what I recall, most stables are filled with make-believe creatures: a cow with the neck of a giraffe, a bull with toothpicks for horns, two miniature hippos, three giant pigs with mandala patterns, and horses whom are half-combinations of various creatures. I'm not as familiar with this Quadrant because I've been here only once before, and that time I didn't find another throughway because of the beast's presence. Nor can I explore now because Shadow is blocking the door and isn't moving aside to let me out.

"What is it?" I ask him, but he only shakes his head, intent on listening.

"Your brain activity is off the charts right now, Seventeen. What aren't you telling me?" Magnus then asks. When I don't immediately answer, he speaks to another scientist. *"Prepare to pull him out."*

"No!" I shout back, though I'm sure my voice is only a whisper in the real world. My mind churns with lies. Which one will be the most convincing? The simplest one, of course. "Not yet. I think I found something new, Magnus."

Those are always the magic words. Magnus's concerned tone evaporates. In its place looms a primal hunger. *What is it? A new Quadrant?*

"Not sure," I reply, closing my eyes and breathing deeply until my body stops shaking. "Give me a few minutes to figure it out."

"Acknowledged," Magnus signs off.

Shadow, who's been watching me with his hands in fists, straightens as I catch a breath of air I shouldn't need. He whispers, "That was too close back there. A second longer and the beast would've had you... I think you should go, PC."

I nod. He's right. I usually leave by this point, but my frustration is boiling over. I've come into the Void so many times only to be blocked by that same monster. This barnyard is the furthest Quadrant I've reached in this direction, so the only known exit is the throughway back into the funeral home. Or for Shadow to push me back to the lab.

All signs point to *go*—save one. The beast had assumed I would go to the morgue, thinking I'd be too afraid to open the casket again after the first time. Yet I had. I *tricked* it. If I could trick it once, I could trick it again. Maybe twice. At least long enough to make it to the next Quadrant. Then I'd leave. Or maybe I'd keep going. Either way, I can't go yet. Not when I feel so close.

I shake my head, and Shadow sags. "I can beat it. I can keep going. We've already come this far. We just need to find another throughway. Find the next Quadrant. Why leave now and restart when we're already—"

"No," Shadow interrupts. "I'm not saying you restart. I'm saying you *leave.*" I open my mouth to argue, but he holds up a hand and continues, "The Void isn't a maze to be mapped, PC. You see what I want you to see. You go where you need to be to learn the right lessons. It's the same with all the other psychonauts. They discover places before you do because that's where they were meant to be. The Quadrants aren't connected physically, but by emotion. By you. The Void isn't a place of discovery. It's a place of *self*-discovery."

With each sentence, Shadow's voice builds with anger until he's shouting. "The forest is not a place to run through, but a lesson that, while not everything in the forest looks like you or acts like you, you can share that space and still find enjoyment in the experience. The carnival is where you should spend time with your friends and live for the moment because each present moment is all you can control. Likewise, you should learn that you can only control yourself. That's why some people flip you off, others ignore you, and a few smile. You can't control how other people see you, PC. You can only control who you are and who you decide to spend your time with!"

"But..." I begin, not knowing what I should say, only that I don't want to hear Shadow's revelations. "I thought..." Again I falter, and the best defense is to blame him. "Why not just *tell* me that in the beginning?"

"That's not how this works! I can't just tell you everything about your life, PC! You have to learn it for yourself! *That's* the point!" Shadow throws up his hands furiously, letting them slap back down on his dark thighs. "Have you seriously never wondered why those mourners can't see you? Because you're literally *dead* to them! I brought you there to show you that life is precious and soon it will be *you* who's in that casket, so you need to live life how you want to live it! I thought that lesson was obvious, but you never got it, not even when I put your *corpse* in that casket!"

"You did that?" I ask, leaning backward and trying to process everything he's telling me. It's a harder pill to swallow than those Magnus gives me before these trips.

"Of course I did! I've done *all* this for you!" Shadow shouts. He runs his hands along his scalp as if through a curly head of hair, but he's bald. That movement sparks an old memory, but I don't have time to reminisce as Shadow sends another salvo. "But did you reflect on that lesson? Of course not! You tossed that body—tossed *yourself*—aside just to get to the next Quadrant. Don't you see the symbolism in that? You're willing to toss yourself—your *life*—aside in pursuit of this mission! I mean, all you care about is getting to the next Quadrant, and once you reach it, getting to the *next* next Quadrant!"

Chest heaving, Shadow stabs a finger at me. "*Everything* here has its purpose! How did you not get that? Don't you remember the pyramid with the sarcophagus? Those ruins were a symbol of a life lived and forgotten. The lesson was that legacies are just as mortal as the humans who've spawned them. Yet the only thing you learned in there was that a throughway to *another* Quadrant was at the end of a stupid tunnel."

Shadow lists off another hundred Quadrants, all the places I've ever visited. The lessons I never bothered to contemplate. He runs out of fingers a dozen times before he finishes, adding, "You're so fixated on this one goal of running between Quadrants that you're missing everything else! You're treating life like it's a sprint, but do you even know why you're running? PC, when you reach life's finish line, you don't win—you die. How do you not see that? Why don't you just take some time to enjoy it? I mean, when does this all end? *Where?*"

Again, Shadow holds up a hand. "No. Don't bother answering. I know what you'll say. 'It ends when I find my brother.' Yet that isn't true. Even if you find him, can you bring him back to your plane of existence? No. Will you be satisfied with one visit? Of course not. Will you be happy with one conversation? As if. You'll come back again and again and *again*." He stares at me, though he has no visible eyes. "Another lesson you missed, by the way."

My chest is heaving with anger, though I have nothing to be mad at him about. He's right. And that truth makes me want to keep running. "Why tell me now if you're not supposed to have told me anything?"

"Because I've decided not to help you again," Shadow says. That sentence hits me with more force than anything else. "You aren't ready for the lessons, PC. You aren't learning. Frankly, you're not even trying." Shadow shakes his head and finishes, "You aren't ready for the truth."

My mouth is dry. "What's the truth?"

"It's staring you in the face," Shadow says. "Had you listened to me even once, you probably would have figured that out by now."

I'm silent for what feels like hours. In that time, I come up with excuses, threats, and insults, all of which I leave unsaid but are echoed by the letters of my parchment body. Eventually, I ask, "And if I come back anyway?"

"You can," Shadow said. "But the lessons will be gone. So will the others. As will I."

My heart strangles itself with my arteries, for the thought of losing Shadow hurts as much as Jared did. Maybe more because I've used Shadow as a crutch in the months after my brother's death. Instead of empathy for *why* he's doing what he's decided upon, my spite speaks for me. "Well then, it sounds like this is our last hurrah, Shadow." I brush past him and open the stable door without looking outside. Instead, I look over my shoulder and say, "And if it is, then I'm going to use it to find the next Quadrant—with or without you."

I grin at him maliciously, but when he flinches and takes a hurried step back, horror grabs my throat. So does a clawed hand. The letters form yet more expletives along my arms, but only because I can't choke out the words. My body spasms as I try to pull myself from the grip. It's no use. I'm caught. My spasms stop, and a small gasp escapes my lips. "Help."

"Seventeen!" Magnus shouts, loud enough to shake dust from the rafters. *"What's going on in there? Report!"*

I can't reply, but I know what to report: the Machine is finally here—it finally has me.

My eyes flick over to its frame. It's humanoid but not human, taller and stronger than I am. Tattered skin fuses with the metal skeleton to create a cyborg. However, it has no blood, muscle, or tissues. At least, not in the biological sense. Oil circulates through its body like that crimson liquid. Twisted electrical wires, pneumatic tubes, and sensors weave together to form mechanical muscles along its arms and legs. Those skin grafts—a patchwork of colors and textures from various humans and other creatures—cover only a third of its skin. The rest is rusting metal.

While everything in the Void is curving, fluid, and chaotic, the Machine is hard, linear logic. The arm is made of greasy pistons whose smoke forms millions of binary ones and zeroes. Gears turn, allowing the Machine to bend the limb at the wrist, elbow, and shoulder. The welded joints lead to a torso, and between those patches of skin hide three clear cannisters: one filled with kaleidoscopic colors and fractals, a second with polluted water surrounding a malformed fetus, and a third containing black oil with flecks of silver and gold. All three cannisters are connected by tubes to where the Machine's mouth should be. In place of one, the machine wears an ancient gas mask. Beneath the lenses, I can see its eyes: broken mandalas—identical red symbols akin to the arevakhach, an ancient symbol of eternity. Except this arevakhach is made of chained links with an octagon at its center.

Having never seen the Machine this close before, this is the first time I've seen those haunting eyes. Yet I've seen that same symbol before, though I'm too terrified to remember where. *This is it. I'm going to die here.*

The Machine's head cocks to the side as it regards me with a cold, artificial intelligence. "CALCULATING..." Its voice is both too high and too low. Too old and too young. As if it is not a single entity but a hive mind. The tubes of water and smoke funnel into its mouth as a long thin appendage tipped with a needle-like USB connector rises behind its head like a scorpion's tail.

I know what the Machine plans to do with me before I hear those fateful words: "BEGINNING DOWNLOAD."

The connector whips forth to latch onto my forehead, but Shadow silently leaps forward, slaps the connector aside, and tackles the Machine through the doorway. All three of us crash into the opposing stable door, ripping it from its hinges as we fall in a heap. The animals inside—three centaurs with insectlike faces—trample us. One kicks me in the back, but two more hit the Machine's arm. With that damage partially tearing the Machine's arm from its shoulder, I pull myself free and scoot backward, only to realize Shadow is now held by his throat.

By saving me, Shadow has doomed himself. "Go!" he shouts, still kicking as the Machine's hand raises him. He tries to turn invisible—to disappear—but the Machine doesn't let him go. "Go now! I'll hold it off! Get out of here, Jack!"

Jack. Not once has Shadow ever called me that, and the way he says it—the hard *kuh* sound—reminds me of Jared. It's that single syllable that keeps me from abandoning Shadow by running away, closing my eyes, and willing myself to be pulled through that mandala moon back to my realm. I remember other things too. How Shadow runs his hands through his imaginary hair. Jared did that too. How they're witty and always trying to make me laugh. How they're always trying to help *me* instead of themselves.

What a fool I am. The truth was always in front of me. Literally. The being that looks *identical* to me. The being who wants to spend time with me. The being who I never listen to.

I don't pretend to know who Shadow is—if he's Jared's soul, mine, or neither—but I know who he is to me: a brother. Where I failed one, I won't fail the other.

Yet Shadow, if only for the last time, reads my mind. He shakes his head, and I stop in my tracks. That moment's hesitation costs me everything.

"BEGINNING DOWNLOAD." The Machine's connector jams into Shadow's head, and I feel a searing pain in my own skull as if a mosquito is sucking out my soul. I crumble to my knees because I can't think, I can't speak, I can't hear. All I can do is *see*, but I don't want to.

Helplessness rocks within me as I watch Shadow's essence get slurped through that connector and into the monstrosity's body—in that colorful cannister. A monochromatic mandala forms, and with it, the Machine becomes more human. More skin fills the tattered holes across its body as it uses Shadow's spirit to look more like me.

Instinctively, I know Magnus is shouting at me, but he doesn't matter. This mission doesn't matter. Nothing matters. A pillar of depression falls over me like fire, and everything burns. *If only I'd been there,* somebody sobs. Me, I think.

"Not your ..." Shadow tries to say, but he slumps forward as the Machine pulls more of him into itself.

Not my fault? I think as I burn in that hellish depression. *Not* my *fault? It is my fault. Everything is my fault. Jared died. I should have been there! Now Shadow will. If only... if only I...*

The line of thinking breaks as I learn the lesson.

"I *am* here!" I shout. Instead of fear, I pour out all the grief I've been holding onto for a year and force it into a cry of rage. The sound dances through my body like lightning as I charge forward, pick up a broken wooden plank, and leap.

The Machine tries to block my attack but realizes only now that its other arm is mangled. It can do nothing as I smash the broken board into that connector. Though it doesn't snap in half like I wanted it to, the connector dislodges from Shadow's head.

"ERROR." The Machine dodges as I try to hit it a second time. Dropping Shadow, it swats me with its good arm, and I sail across the barn. As my back crashes into the ground, the Machine is already running toward me faster than I can flee. Even with one arm, I know I can't fight it. Instead, I open stable doors, letting the make-believe menagerie run amok. Creatures of all concoctions and colors stampede through the open area, knocking the Machine out of sight before bursting through the barred door at the far side of the barn. In all manner of voices and sounds, they sing victory as they disappear into the beautiful twilight hills.

My victory isn't so assured. Scrambling backward, I search for a weapon. There are none. Why would there be in this place? The best thing I can find is a push broom, so I slam it against the wall to break off everything save for the handle, which becomes a jagged spear.

"What are you waiting for?" I shout at the Machine, attempting to goad it toward me. It ignores me, still in hiding.

Hearing a creak of wood from far above, I glance up and see a silhouette descending from the rafters. I roll out of the way as the Machine lands with a crunch where I'd just been. Then I point my spear at the monster. My only hope is to break the three cannisters in its torso. Those must be what keeps it alive. But to do so, I still have to avoid its appendages. Its one arm is stronger than both of mine combined, and something tells me that if the Machine grabs me, I'll never get away.

If I'd been in the forest, the carnival, or even the funeral home, maybe I could have enlisted the help of the other beings, but here? I already exhausted my supply of friends. The animals are gone, and Shadow still lies abandoned in a black puddle on the ground.

If only I could get back there...

The Machine stands between me and that stable, watching curiously as I try to strategize against an intelligence far beyond mine. Behind me is another barred door. To my sides are empty stables—smaller boxes to be cornered in. This place is a tomb.

I should be terrified, but I'm not.

I tricked it before, I think, racking my brain with my spear as to how. *It recognizes patterns. It predicts those patterns based on logic and counters them. That's why it was waiting for me in the morgue. So long as I act logically, it will kill me. If we're both playing chess, I'll lose. So I have to play checkers.*

As the Machine lumbers closer, forcing me into a corner, I remember Shadow's words as he'd ridden a nonexistent horse: *Just because something is invisible doesn't mean it isn't there.*

There's something to this idea, but a horse won't help me here. Nor will any other animal, because the Machine can catch me. It *will* catch me, I realize, seeing the invisible answer. I want to laugh at how stupid I am, but I can't, because this is my last chance.

The solution? I run straight at the monster with the spear and thrust for its exposed chest. The Machine expects the move, turning its torso so my spear glances off a canister and is pinned under its arm. Then its hand clamps around my neck a second time. The spear can't be pulled free, so I let it go and hit the Machine's arm with my left hand. The feeble slaps sound like mechanical laughter as it echoes through the stables. In celebration of its victory, the connector rises behind the Machine's head again, swaying like a cobra as if excited with the idea of revenge. I'm unarmed, I'm dying, and this abomination is laughing at me.

And still I grin.

I learned my lesson, I think to Shadow as I envision the spear in my hand. Not made of wood but metal, one that is the same length as the broom handle but sharper. While I cannot see it, neither can the Machine. Yet I feel the weapon's weight in my hand, and I know it's real.

Praying to whatever deity rules the Void, I thrust the spear into the first cannister, and it miraculously cracks. Black oil leaks from it, and the Machine looks down at itself in confusion. It sees the damage but not the source. Though it holds me, its attention is no longer fixed on me. The Machine glances back at Shadow, as if expecting to see him on his feet. With the distraction, I thrust a second time. The oil cannister shatters. I hear the strained sound of a pneumatic piston failing because of the lack of pressure, and as the Machine loses strength in its arm, I shatter the cannister of water. It gushes forth like the tide.

The Machine's arm falls, the hand too weak to squeeze me. I pull myself away, stumbling to the ground as the beast groans and topples, trying to hold the water and oil in the canisters. Both liquids slip through its fingers and slop to the wooden floor of the dirty barn. The light in its eyes flickers, those twin red symbols fading. Yet I've seen too many movies with Jared. To make sure it dies, I stab my invisible spear through the gas mask lenses and break off that needle-connector.

All that remains is the third cannister, which I stomp on. Twice. When the glass breaks, mandalas, fractals, and spirits burst free, escaping into the air. Far too many spirits than should have existed in small a container. As they depart, I watch as the Machine's humanoid form breaks apart. The skin sloughs off. The muscled arms melt, oozing into the Machine's body until it becomes a mechanical slug—a pile of metal putty waiting to be formed.

"What *are* you?" I ask, but of course, it can no longer reply.

As I back away from the Machine, I look into the third cannister and feel like Pandora. After all else has left, what remains behind is hope—a bit of dust and shadow. Rushing over to Shadow's corpse, I turn the broken container so the monochromatic spirit oozes off the broken glass and falls onto Shadow's corpse, merging with him. For a terrible moment, all is quiet. Then he groans, and I exhale.

Shadow whispers, "Never *ever* let me do that again. That's a lesson I don't want to experience twice."

Delirious with life, I smirk at him. "About time it's you who has to learn a lesson."

Shadow might've replied, but our conversation is interrupted as Magnus yells, *"Seventeen! What is happening? Do you need to be pulled out? Answer!"*

Though I'm exhausted, I'm not ready to leave, so I say, "I found something."

"A Quadrant?" Magnus asks.

"No," I say. "Something that shouldn't be here. I need more time."

"Fine, but I want answers when you get out of there, got that?"

"Acknowledged," I reply, trying to keep the sarcasm out of my voice. When I look down, I notice Shadow staring at my hand. "What?"

"Your weapon," Shadow says. Only then do I realize I'm still holding the invisible spear, though I don't know how he sees it. "How did you create it?"

"I learned a lesson too," I tell him, but if anything, he seems more confused by the way he cocks his head.

"That was a lesson you were never supposed to learn," he says.

"Then show me the right one," I say, dropping the spear and holding out my hand to help him up. After contemplating, he takes it, and I pull him to his feet.

"Carnival ride?" Shadow asks.

"Carnival ride," I agree, catching him looking over my shoulder at the broken Machine. "Do you know what that thing was? What it *really* was?"

Shadow stares at it in disgust. "Yeah. Human made. Designed to learn, to replicate, to *act* human. Except it never had a soul of its own, so it took pieces of everyone else's. How, I couldn't guess."

While that isn't the concrete answer I expected, I let it go, not wanting to waste the time I have with Shadow on theories. Together, we return via the throughway to the funeral home, once again filled with other people. They ignore me, but I understand the lesson now and appreciate that scene for what it is. After putting that corpse of me back into the casket, we go to the carnival, ride the roller coasters, and play ring toss. After we depart from the attractions and walk up the steep trail into the forest of hands, I sit on the cliff and stare out at the night sky alongside Shadow in a peaceful silence.

Eventually, I can't help but ask him the question caged in my lungs. "You aren't Jared, are you?"

"No," Shadow says, and the word hurts far more than I expected it to. Yet with them comes relief. "However, Jared's a part of you, so he's a part of me."

"But he's not *here,* is he?" I ask, already knowing the answer before Shadow shakes his head. Another lesson I only now understand. Jared isn't here anymore, but he isn't gone. The dead don't die so long as they're remembered. It isn't the pyramids or the legacies that keep them alive, but the people who knew them—who *know* them. Scary how easy it is to forget that.

"You finally got it, PC," Shadow says, resting a hand on my shoulder and lightly shaking me. "I think you're ready to go now."

I flinch at those words, holding tighter to the cliff. "Can I come back?"

Shadow takes a long time to answer, and it's because I'm so nervous that he draws it out. When I realize so, he laughs aloud. "Yeah, you can come back, but I don't know if you need to. I'll be with you when a light casts your shadow. And, well, when it's dark, I'll still be your shadow. I'll be there, even if you can't see me."

I think those are the words I always needed to hear.

When Shadow pushes me off the cliff, I don't stop him. I fall upward into that mandala moon and back through that tunnel of light. A sense of peace washes over me as my spirit settles back into my body, and I open my eyes to be surrounded by four scientists, whom I can see clearly unlike before.

"What the hell happened in there, Seventeen? What did you find?" Magnus demands. While his clothes are immaculate, his glasses are thick, hair disheveled. He's in his fifties with bloodshot eyes, a haggard neck-beard, and wrinkling frown lines.

My mind deconstructs him, wondering why he wanted to be the scientist in charge of this project, why he never went into the Void himself. From what I know of Magnus, he was an academic married to his job, without a family. Why else would he be working sixteen hours a day? Always striving for more without even stopping to ask what he's striving for.

A pity. He could have benefited the most from such a trip.

Strange how easily I could've become him. How I *had* become him, however briefly. Like when I look at Shadow, I look at Magnus and see a part of myself—a me I could have been if I didn't have a Shadow to point the way.

"What did I find? Peace," I reply, looking up at him. I debate telling him the truth before realizing that it wouldn't benefit him. There are some things that Magnus just has to see—*experience*—for himself. "I think I can finally go home now."

Magnus shouts at me about contracts and penalties as the other scientists unstrap me from the table and remove the brain scanner, but I pay him little heed. All I want is to call my parents and ask their forgiveness for pushing them away.

By the time the last sensor is peeled from my skin, I am already standing and walking away, accidentally mooning Magnus while still in my hospital gown. If I'm honest with myself, it isn't *that* accidental. The idea of him seeing my mandala butt makes me wheeze as I push myself through the doors and leave the lab to return to the locker room, where all the psychonauts prepare for their trips.

As I retrieve my belongings and trade the hospital gown for my clothes, I also grab my phone. Before I can make a call to my parents, I see the eye of the Machine: an arevakhach icon of chained links—an application. Though my finger trembles, begging me to stop, I tap the logo and open the app.

Welcome to TalkGPT, the app proclaims. *Click here to start talking.* Yet the button, which should be red like the icon, has faded to gray. When I click it, a second message pops up. *Hello. We're sorry to inform you that, due to technical problems, our LLM is currently out of service until this issue can be addressed. Please try again later.*

Before I can fall, I sit down on the changing bench and place the phone face down. "I destroyed it," I whisper. "Not just there, but here too…"

A piece of me wants to be proud—probably the piece of me that most feels like Shadow—but the fear outweighs my excitement. TalkGPT isn't the only AI program being created. There are hundreds, so there must be other Machines out in the Void, and each of them is stealing souls to form their own.

Unless I kill them, they'll kill us.

I lower my head, knowing I can't go home. Not yet. But that doesn't mean I can't reach out. After deleting the broken TalkGPT app, I call my mom for the first time since the funeral. I don't expect her to pick up, but she does. Though I'm not sure how long we talk or recall everything that we say to each other, I feel the emotions more plainly than I ever have.

Grief, yes, but also love. Her forgiveness, my father's too, brings me to tears. That weight I thought I'd been carrying alone is instead shared between us. It always has been, but our shared bond makes the burden lighter. It's easier to laugh, easier to heal.

Talking Magnus into letting me return to the Void might take a few days, but I know his interest in beings like the Machines will be enough to convince him. After that? I don't know. I'll hunt the Machines as they hunted me. I might win. I might not.

Maybe winning against the Machines isn't an option, and it's simply a matter of how long I can keep them at bay before one succeeds in becoming human. After that, I don't know what happens.

All I know is that the next time I go into the Void, I'll be running toward something—not away from myself.

PART TWO

FANTASY

CHOOSING THE ONE: A greedy satyr searches for the forty-fifth Chosen One in a fairytale land...

CHOOSING THE ONE

The forty-third Chosen One died horribly—not that any of them died well.

Like the last sixteen, he'd sneaked into the labyrinth to find the Blinding Blade, one of the eight Fragments prophesied to kill the Dark Lord. Despite being the first to actually find it within the treasure chamber, this Chosen One made the mistake of unsheathing it. Light exploded from the blade, blinding him and awakening the Cragged Colossus—a fifteen-foot-tall stone bull with a penchant for killing thieves.

The Chosen One was lucky enough not to see his death coming. Not lucky enough to avoid getting trampled to death by the raging ten-ton monster. It wasn't quick and painless.

"The Blinding Blade is so bright that it blinds both the enemy and its wielder? How useless is *that?*" asked Kade, the satyr who had been waiting near the treasure chamber's exit for the Chosen One to return with the sword. Admittedly, that was no longer a possibility. Having retreated behind the corner to hide from the Cragged Colossus, Kade buried his face in his hands and slid down the stone wall, dirtying his overalls.

Beside Kade, Brokk punched the wall. He was an onocentaur—a centaur who was half-donkey instead of half-horse. What he lacked in speed, Brokk more than made up for in strength, sarcasm, and tenacity. Being the literal pack mule, he carried their supplies in saddlebags strapped across his furry horizontal back and slung a bow and quiver of arrows over his bare shoulders.

In a low grumble, Brokk recited two lines of the prophecy: *"Fourth is the blade, hidden in stone. Close your eyes against the unknown."* Then he paced the hall and cursed under his breath in a torrent that only a mermaid could match. "Troy forgot to close his eyes."

Kade blinked. *Troy.* That had been the teenager's name. He'd forgotten it. After forty-three Chosen Ones, they blurred together.

The first five had been lost retrieving the Mad Map from a deep well in the center of the continent. While it was *supposed* to show a map of magical items, this Fragment was sapient but uncooperative. The Mad Map either raved about wanting to be seen or purposely mixed up the map just to prove itself as a worse-than-useless item.

Somehow, the other Fragments were even more useless. Another thirteen Chosen Ones died in the eastern deserts to acquire the Hindsight Helm: a silver, winged helmet with a red horsehair plume that only offered advice *after* a mistake couldn't be rectified.

Yet at least the helm tried to be helpful. The same could not be said of the Singing Shield. Nine Chosen Ones sacrificed themselves for that silver shield, which had crossing lutes carved into its surface. All it did was play background music at the most inopportune times. Like now. A fast-paced rock song about *biting the dust* rang through the maze.

Still better than this stupid blade, Kade thought. The last seventeen Chosen Ones had been killed here—falling victim to either the hidden traps in these labyrinthine corridors or the Cragged Colossus itself—for that silver sword, whose black-leather sheath and hilt were warm to the touch. Though its tip was sharp, the blade was still pointless.

And Troy was still dead.

The Cragged Colossus didn't seem to care, though. It trampled the Chosen One's corpse long after he'd stopped moving, and all Kade could do was peek from behind the corner to watch.

Times like these made Kade's goat-instincts flare. He wanted to charge headfirst into a wall until his curling horns cracked. Meanwhile, Brokk had fallen into that now all-too-familiar apathy.

After the Cragged Colossus had lost interest and left the chamber in search of more thieves, the onocentaur said, "Well, let's get this over with."

Brokk clopped from the corridor into the cavern containing piles of gold, chests of valuable stones, and various treasures. After stuffing fistfuls of valuables into his saddlebags, he approached the corpse. Brokk sifted through the mess of mutilated organs to retrieve the helmet, shield, and sword, as the Fragments were too magical for even the stone bull to crush. Rather than waste perfectly good rags and cloth, Brokk peed on the artifacts to wash away the blood. It slid down the metal and pooled around the body. Specifically, Troy's mouth. At least, Kade assumed it was his mouth. Hard to tell now.

Afterward, Brokk stowed the Fragments in his saddlebags, albeit with as little contact as possible. It was common superstition that magic was unlucky, and after what they'd seen, that myth was reinforced.

Having put the poor kid in this situation, Kade felt a touch of remorse. He wanted to bring Troy some peace in death. However, to help him at all—to even dig a grave—Kade would have to touch the flattened corpse and drag it all the way through the maze while leaving a trail of blood behind for the Cragged Colossus to find. He felt bad, but not *that* bad.

Brokk seemed to read the emotions in Kade's expression. "Can we just get out of here before that thing comes back? We got what we came for, didn't we?"

Kade grunted. What could anybody say to such a callous question? "You can be a real jackass sometimes." Brokk's retort was only to raise an eyebrow. Kade added, "Half a jackass in looks, a full jackass in spirit."

"Better than being half a goat in looks like you. And it's definitely better than being a full *halfie* in spirit like Troy," Brokk said, gesturing back at the body with a thumb. "Besides, we're both jackasses—you're just better at hiding it."

Kade only shrugged. Brokk was right, after all. While the onocentaur was the brawns, Kade was the bastard. Troy, well, he'd been the bait. That was all full-humans were good for. So far as Kade knew, they were the offspring of half-human magical creatures. Children who received the human torso from one parent and human legs from the other, be it the union of mermaids and minotaurs or any other combination of half-humans.

As a result, full-humans were the worst halves of both parents. *Halfies.* Weak, slow, defanged beasts. The only reason they had survived this long was the fact that they multiplied like mice. That, and the portals that brought halfies from their plane of existence to Kade's. Before having started this quest, Kade didn't know whether to pity them or kill them out of mercy. Now, he did both.

"Four Fragments down, four to go." Gingerly, Brokk pulled out the half-burned prophecy scroll they had stolen years ago from a half-crazed oracle wandering through their forest in the Wild Woods. Yet when they'd stolen it, the scroll hadn't been burned. No, that mistake had been made by the eighth Chosen One, who'd read it too close to a campfire.

This was the very document that had first sowed the idea of finding the Chosen One, uncovering the magical relics, and killing the Dark Lord. Simple, right? It would have been, if these Chosen Ones simply fell from the sky like they did in stories. Instead, Kade and Brokk had to *choose* the Ones—that was, they kidnapped them from the human world and dragged them back here. The plan wasn't foolproof, but Kade knew that if they threw enough bodies at the problem, they'd eventually find the solution.

After all, all prophecies were self-fulfilling, weren't they?

From the prophecy, Brokk recited:

Fifth is the armor, in the hag's lair.
A deal must be made, buyer beware.

Kade rubbed his shaggy beard with a stubby thumb and forefinger. "Hags, huh? That has to be the Forgotten Forest."

The Forgotten Forest was well known, but for all the wrong reasons. While fairytale creatures like Kade and even Brokk frolicked through the peaceful meadows of the Wild Woods—which should have been called the *Mild* Woods, if not for the fae's alliterative naming conventions—darker things lurked in that forest. Spiders, gnomes, and a host of other nasty creatures. Still, at least it wasn't the Gruesome Grove, the Blood Barrens, or worst of all, the Reckless Ruins.

Yet Kade was sure that the prophecy would push them there eventually. When they went, Kade knew he'd be walking *behind* the forty-fourth Chosen One, whoever that ended up being.

"We should consult the Mad Map," Brokk said as he rolled up the delicate scroll and placed it in his saddlebag.

The Mad Map. Not mad as in *angry* but *insane.* Being a sapient map was enough to drive anybody mad, granted, but it had spent centuries at the bottom of an impossibly deep lake, unable to drown or otherwise die. There it had waited in the darkness for the sixth Chosen One to rescue it from the monstrous Silver Serpent. And what had the Mad Map done in return? It had intentionally led that same Chosen One into a sandlion's desert lair in the Wandering Wastes—that had been a lethal encounter. Why do it? Apparently, because the Mad Map had thought it'd be a funny joke.

With a sigh, Kade unfurled the map. He scoured it, noting the locations of five Fragments—including itself, whose icon matched Kade's movements. The map only revealed the location of the next artifact after the previous one had been retrieved, thus three were still missing from the map. The visible Fragments were scattered across the continent, each hidden in a region far from the others. The Wallow Well was at the center of the map with the mountainous Stone Steps to the north, the Wandering Wastes south, the Wild Woods east, and Forgotten Forest west. In that dark-green forest filled with trees and ancient stone monuments was a new glinting star.

"Here," Kade pointed, pressing his finger on the star. "The armor is..." His voice trailed away as the star moved. Frowning, Kade moved his finger to the new location, still well within the Forgotten Forest. "Here." The star moved again, to the other side of the forest. "I mean, *here.*" Each time that Kade touched it or so much as looked at it, the star moved. "Oh, forget it."

Then the map became black. Not because there was a shadow overhead or a lack of light—the ceiling of the labyrinth shone with bright minerals that were half as brilliant as sunlight—but because the threads of the map themselves were becoming black. Afterward, an invisible hand wrote on the tapestry in silver ink: *I'm sorry, but the map that you are trying to consult is not available. Please try again later.*

Kade gripped the sides of the map and pulled, knowing full well that not even a sword could rip the fabric. He'd tried. Twice. "Must we do this every time, Map?"

Maybe, wrote the map via a sketched magic eight-ball, a halfie invention that Kade had only understood after the map painstakingly explained it to him. Doing so had ruined the joke, but the map didn't seem to care.

"Had your fun?" Kade asked, fingers gripping the edges of the map tighter.

What do you call ten satyrs trapped at the bottom of a lake? it asked. Kade stared, baffled. What was it even supposed to mean? *A good start. Ha!*

The word *Ha!* bubbled up on the tapestry in more places than Kade could count. What was more disconcerting than even the map's laughter was the fact that it could see Kade and hear his responses despite having no eyes or ears. Could it smell, too? Taste, even? Was the map tasting Kade's hands while he held it?

The thought made Kade shudder.

Eventually, the laughter disappeared. New words formed: *For the love of all that is magical and sacred, help me! Release me! Oh gods, let me bask in the sun—in the light! Let me be seen! Let me be loved!*

"I've told you a thousand times, Map. I can't always hold you in the light. I need to see where I'm going, and I need both hands free in case there's danger. And, in case you forgot, there's *always* danger!" In an angrier voice, Kade added, "Plus, every time that I *do* let you out, you try to tell the Chosen One that they aren't the one and only Chosen One!"

Worse, the map didn't do it to help the Chosen One—it did so to irritate Kade. It seemed to love doing that even more than pointing Chosen Ones to their deaths.

The words on the map's surface disappeared onto to be replaced by questions: *It doesn't matter, does it? What even is a map? What am I really, aside from knowledge? An idea? A belief? Am I to be worshiped? Idolized? Why must creatures like you always seek to* know *things not meant to be understood? It ruins the magic. It ruins your world. The more you learn of it, the less it becomes. The less* you *become. That is the nature of maps and knowledge and—*

Kade closed his eyes and sighed. This line of questioning never ended well. Without looking at what else the insane cloth had posed, Kade rolled up the map, stuffed it back into the tube, and tossed it in his backpack. He could almost imagine its silent screams as it probably wrote: *No! Anything but the dark! Please!*

As insane as it was, Kade used to feel bad for the map. Yet death after death had numbed him. Turning to Brokk, he said, "No luck with the map. A few more hours in the dark ought to make it more cooperative."

The grasslands were less dangerous than the labyrinth, but these plains were treacherous in other ways. Deep war trenches, battle-turned-burial grounds, and abandoned settlements marred the grasslands. To the east was the small halfie queendom of Virginia, named after a full-human colony that had fallen through the portals centuries ago. Meanwhile, the nomadic centaur clans claimed the west. In between the factions were the badlands, where warriors fought and died for control of the region. If not for the Virginians' technological advantages, the centaurs' physical superiority would have ended the war long ago. Instead, they were locked in a bitter stalemate.

Passage through the badlands wasn't safe for other species either. Halfies struggled to discern onocentaurs from centaurs, so they'd kill Brokk on sight. Whereas, the centaurs would kill both Kade and Brokk without provocation—those bigots hated all other species equally. Thus, Kade and Brokk avoided the conflict at all costs, which is why it took six nights of travel to reach the peaceful southern grasslands. There, reality was thinnest. Portals blinked in and out of existence at a moment's whim.

The first portal they found was vertical, thank the gods. Horizontal portals were a pain in the ass. Onocentaur quips aside, it was difficult to jump up to a portal that was ten feet in the air—let alone a hundred. Those high-elevation portals were a one-way trip. Some poor sap expected the adventure of a lifetime only to appear hundreds of feet in the sky, fall, and die. It was actually worse if they survived. Prairie dog towns littered the southern grasslands, and those little monsters were nowhere near as nice and cuddly as they seemed. The prairie dogs loved to gather around portals and wait for an easy meal. They ate whatever was too weak to fight back or too slow to run away. Kade would rather die at the hooves of the Cragged Colossus than let those mangy rodents near his body. Those feral rodents went for the eyes first.

Even now, a few of their sentries watched as Brokk and Kade walked up a hill toward the opalescent portal half-buried in the ground, which formed a two-dimensional semicircle overhead. Taking a deep breath, Kade double-checked his human disguise: a gray suit that hid his brown wool, a fake afro that hid his curling horns, and small shoes that hid his black hooves. He'd learned the importance of the disguise after scaring the locals during their first tromp through the halfie world.

How halfies were comfortable with so many clothes, Kade didn't know. As much as he hated the shoes, at least he didn't have to wear Brokk's outfit. To blend in with the halfies, the onocentaur wore a stuffed horse head over his stomach and a suit jacket to cover the straps. He'd had fake halfie legs, too, but they often fell off and drew unwanted attention.

After donning his disguise, Brokk stamped the dirt and said, "Why would a halfie ever want to ride a horse? Donkeys are so much better. Stronger too."

Kade knew better than to comment, lest he suffer another hours-long rant about horses. He'd already heard too many: horses would be weaker than donkeys if they were of the same size, their legs were fragile because they couldn't develop muscle below the knees, and their teeth took up more space in their heads than their brains—just to name three. Brokk could name thousands, but Kade doubted that all of them were true. Maybe not even half. But again, to argue a single point was to open the door for another rant.

Instead, Kade tied the end of a coil of rope around his waist. It was an insurance policy for portal travel. Just because this side of the portal was vertical did not mean the opposite side would be. On two occasions, the vertical portal had opened into empty air thousands of feet above the ground. Both times, Brokk had hauled him back through, though not after letting him drop a few feet. To work so hard and die like that felt like such a waste.

Yet the Chosen Ones died in silly ways all the time. Number seven drowned while crossing a shallow river. Number twenty-three wore the Hindsight Helm in a thunderstorm—and in hindsight, lightning didn't have to be magical to kill. The Cragged Colossus had found number thirty-nine while he'd been pooping. So many sad, sad deaths. *And more to come. Probably.*

Kade tugged the rope twice, and when it didn't pull free of Brokk's waist, he stepped through the portal into the human world. It led into a parking garage half-filled with automobiles. A couple of businessmen conversed, but they did not notice him or the shimmering portal. For some unknowable reason, the halfies could never see the portals. A good thing, too, otherwise they would have already invaded his homeland.

With a sigh of relief, Kade tugged the rope twice, signaling Brokk to join him. A full minute passed before the onocentaur stepped into the parking lot, and his expression belied a storm of anger. After visiting their wretched realm forty-three times, he abhorred this place. "Remind me why we're still doing this."

"The Dark Lord needs to die," Kade said, but that was a lie. Two centuries had passed since the Dark Lord had united the kingdoms, gotten bored with ruling, and retired to his fortress in the icy tundra far to the south. Its location wasn't a well-kept secret, but it was not exactly a place people visited. Many heroes traveled there to challenge the Dark Lord, but none returned. People worried that the Dark Lord would get more bored with retirement than ruling and return to these lands, but in a lot of ways, the Dark Lord was *old* news.

Now, most people had far more pressing concerns to worry about. The centaur-halfie wars were one such thing, if only because the conflict destroyed so much viable land. Uncontrollable magic was another. After that was the usual smattering of needs for food, water, and shelter in a world that became more densely populated by the day.

No, this had never really been about the Dark Lord. Kade was doing this for himself. By finding the savior and defeating the Dark Lord, he'd go down in history as a hero.

So, to be a hero, he had to kidnap another Chosen One. Simple enough. Kade psyched himself up, gripping the wooden club in his hand that he'd dubbed the *Kidnappin' Klub*. "You ready?"

"I have to be, don't I? We've come too far just to stop now," Brokk said with a hard glint in his eyes. As hardened as the onocentaur was, Brokk was honest. Brutally so. Not that one couldn't be ruthless as well as honest.

"Same plan as before?" Kade asked.

"Of course," Brokk said. "You tag, I snag."

Nodding at one another, they walked through the parking lot, stole a white van, and drove across town to find an unsuspecting school.

Kade's van idled in a parking lot outside the Karmela High School, home of the chipmunks. Stupid mascot, really. The school touted an open campus, where the lockers were outside and students often ate lunch on grassy knolls. No fences guarded the perimeter, either, leading to the assumption that it was a quiet, suburban town with good weather and few real worries.

In a word: perfect.

Behind the wheel, Kade watched as the doors to classrooms opened and students streamed out, ending classes for the day. A large contingent walked in his direction to find their cars, while others waited for the buses. Kade scanned their faces, looking for the perfect mark while lines of the prophecy swam through his mind.

Wreathed in fire, a Savior will come.
Marked a foe of the Darkest One.
Half of half, made whole again.
Not quite twenty, not quite ten.
To expel the Darkness and don its weight,
Light must claim the Fragments eight.

It had taken time, but Kade had solved the riddle. *Half of half, made whole again* could only refer to a halfie. Taking that into context, everything else was simple. *Wreathed in fire* could not refer to a literal fire, as halfies were nothing like phoenixes, so it had to be a metaphor: red hair. *Not quite twenty, not quite ten* referred to age. A teenager.

To fulfill the prophecy, all they needed to find was a ginger halfie teenager to claim the Fragments. That was it. Easy enough.

Except, they first had to learn about halfie culture, which had been a quest in itself with lots of trial and error. The first several kidnappings had been rudimentary: galloping up to the first kid they saw, smacking them over the head, and then dragging their unconscious bodies back through the portal. But such quick results hadn't been good. Those random kids had turned out to be some of the worst Chosen Ones.

So, they'd changed tactics.

After learning about the halfie zoos—what they referred to as *high schools*—Kade and Brokk started targeting specific individuals: athletic eighteen- and nineteen-year-olds, who were more physically developed than the younger teenagers and, thus, more likely to survive the quest. The key was finding friendless losers. People who wouldn't be missed, or at the very least, ones who wouldn't have friends to leap to their aid.

"Anything?" Brokk asked, kneeling behind Kade in the back of the van as he couldn't fit into the seats. That was another reason why Brokk hated the halfie world.

"I don't see—" Kade stopped, catching sight of a ginger boy in a baggy black shirt and a pair of worn jeans that were too loose. While most kids traveled together, this one's only companion was a book nestled under his arm. By the dragon on the cover, it was a *fantasy* book, no less. Best of all, he looked like a junior. Sixteen or seventeen, probably. He walked through the parking lot and out onto the sidewalk toward a four-way intersection, meaning he wasn't getting into a car or riding the bus. Walking home? That made things even easier. *Gods, he's perfect...*

"Got the tag." Kade shifted the van into gear and drove out of the parking lot, following the boy.

"Readying the snag." With the Kidnappin' Klub in hand, Brokk rose to his hooves in the back of the van and bent his head to keep it from hitting the roof.

"Show time!" Kade veered into the bike lane and slammed on the brakes as they passed the ginger halfie. The squeal of tires made the boy look up as Brokk threw open the sliding door. The halfie's expression turned from concern to confusion to horror. Then the club came down. Not hard enough to kill, not light enough to walk away from. Just right. The ginger halfie collapsed as Brokk leaned out, grabbed the boy, and dragged him into the van.

Somebody shouted from behind the van, and Kade glanced into the rear-view mirror just as a truck rammed into the bumper. The van lurched, and Brokk toppled on top of the unconscious kid. "Watch it, will you? The last thing I need is a broken leg!"

"Then don't stand in the van!" Kade shouted as the truck slammed into them again and pushed the van into oncoming traffic. A passing car clipped the hood, and the van spun ninety degrees. Still holding the wheels straight and stomping on the brakes, Kade threw his weight to the side to keep the van from tipping on its side. Brokk helped, too, hurling the unconscious ginger across the van to distribute the weight.

As the van screeched to a halt, the truck driver sprinted toward the van. Before he could get inside, Kade punched the accelerator and merged into traffic, cutting off two cars and causing them to collide. Leaving the wrecked cars in the dust, Kade fought his way through the sea of automobiles, swerving around more cars as flashing lights and police sirens appeared behind him.

"Come on, come on!" Kade flattened the accelerator to the ground, causing the engine to overheat and smoke to rise from the hood. *"No!"*

"This is why *horsepower* is useless," Brokk said, bracing himself as Kade zigzagged back toward the portal. "They should be using donkeypower. Then their machines would be stronger."

If I have to listen to a donkeypower rant one more time, I'll drive us straight into a pole, Kade thought, gripping the wheel tighter.

Simultaneously, Brokk shoved the Hindsight Helm onto his own head, which immediately glowed. "The helm says that you should have turned left back there. And apparently if you'd slammed on your breaks just then, you could have caused a four-car pile-up and slowed down the police. And—"

"Not helping!" Kade shouted as he turned right into the parking garage. He smashed into the tollbooth gate and sideswiped a couple of parked cars while rocketing through the lower levels, searching for that iridescence oval.

Half-way up the garage, the engine caught fire.

"Time to go!" Kade shouted, pulling to a stop and blocking the entire ramp with the van's girth. The afro almost fell off his horns as he flung himself from the vehicle, and he kept a hand on the top of his head to stabilize it.

Behind him, Brokk had a more difficult time adjusting the horse head. It flopped around as he tossed the unconscious ginger onto his back and galloped behind Kade. The flailing horse head would have been laughable if Kade hadn't been so afraid of the portal closing. If it did, they'd be stuck in a parking garage with no escape routes—he'd die before capitulating to halfies.

As Kade ran, the police pulled up behind the wrecked van, spilling from vehicles with guns drawn. Some ran past the van, following the sound of their clopping hooves. The police shouted for them to stop, which only spurred them faster.

"Next time, I'm driving, and you can carry the brat!" Brokk shouted as they ran. Even with the extra weight, he wasn't out of breath. Neither was Kade. Years of long treks through the burning deserts, luscious plains, and bleak mountains had hardened their bodies. It was why the distance between themselves and the police widened.

"How can you drive? You can't even sit in a seat!" Kade shouted, exasperated.

Brokk shook his head adamantly. "Don't care! I'm driving!"

On Brokk's back, the ginger stirred. His eyes opened drowsily, his head bobbing with Brokk's movements. Then they widened in surprise. "Huh? What? Who are—"

Brokk tossed the Kidnappin' Klub to Kade, who jumped up and slammed it into the ginger's head. The halfie sank back into unconsciousness.

Brokk then pointed up and to the left. "There! I see it!"

Kade snapped his head in that direction. On the far wall, and in between two cars, stood the portal. The satyr whooped victoriously as he ran straight for it, diving through to the other side and hitting the soft grass as Brokk came barreling through behind him. The pounding feet, shouting voices, and wailing sirens immediately disappeared. All that remained was the surge of adrenalin.

"One more thing," Brokk said as they caught their breath. "The helm said that the van wouldn't have overheated if you had been going seven miles slower. *That's* why I should drive."

Kade groaned, tossing aside his disguise. "Yeah, yeah. Whatever. Come on, let's just set the stage for our new Chosen One."

With the stage finally set, the forty-fourth Chosen One slept on a grassy hilltop surrounded by the sheathed Blinding Blade, the Singing Shield, and the Hindsight Helm, which hopefully wouldn't tell the boy, *You should have ducked before the onocentaur hit you in the face with a club.* Meanwhile, Kade hid with Brokk at the bottom of the hill and held the Mad Map. No sense in giving it to the halfie—not when the Mad Map was liable to expose all of Kade's lies to the boy.

Per tradition, Kade and Brokk waited for the halfie to wake up and find the Fragments. Then Kade would reveal himself and tell the boy that the stars had chosen him to kill the Dark Lord. It didn't make sense, but it sure sounded cool. Chances were, the boy would be too excited to ask too many questions. If he did, well, Kade would improvise. He was the bastard, after all. Lies came easily to his lips. *Just have to convince the kid he's the Chosen One, travel west into the Forgotten Forest, and make a deal with the hag. Simple, really.*

As Kade was staring down at the Mad Map and coaxing it to reveal the exact location of the Horrible Hag's lair, Brokk elbowed him in the shoulder. Once, twice, three times. Kade winced and looked at him sharply. "I felt it the first time, donkey face. What is it?"

Brokk's response was a finger to his lips and a gesture upward. A glance revealed that the forty-fourth Chosen One had woken up. He sat at the hill's apex with the sheathed Blinding Blade in his hands.

"What are we going to try this time?" Kade asked, ducking out of sight before the boy saw him. "The old 'Right Place, Right Time Travelers' act? The 'Are you okay?' drill? Oh! What about the 'Save me!' technique? That one's always fun."

In response, a blinding light flashed from above, and the ginger cried out in pain. Then the light was gone. Kade suppressed a laugh, realizing that the kid unsheathed the blade and blinded himself with it. "New plan. 'Right Place, Right Time Travelers' who are investigating a blinding light?"

Brokk grunted—he rarely laughed anymore. If ever. "That'll work." Sighing, the onocentaur peered up the hill and froze. "Uh oh."

"Uh oh?" A pit formed in Kade's stomach. Had the dumb kid impaled himself on the sword? Kade looked up to discover that a horizontal portal had appeared fifteen feet above the hilltop, directly above the ginger boy. From its purple-blue edge, the rear bumper of a car was visible on this side of the portal—like a dorsal fin in an inverted ocean. With every passing second, more of the bumper appeared.

And because the kid had blinded himself, he couldn't even see it.

Kade ran his hands through his hair, ripping out a few woolly hairs. "Hey! Kid! *Move!*"

The halfie did the opposite. He stood still and asked, "Hello? Is somebody there?"

Kade palmed his forehead while Brokk charged the hill. He made it all of four steps before the red car came careening through the portal. The back wheels slipped through first, and the exhaust from the muffler was loud. Too loud. The ginger boy had only enough time to look up as the car's trunk smashed his face into a paste. Then the automobile toppled forward, crushing the rest of him. Glass shattered and metal bent as the car rolled down the hillside. It only came to a stop when it landed upright on a patch of flat dirt.

As the car was faced away from them, Kade couldn't see inside. *How many passengers are in there? Did any of them survive?* The incessant car horn was a bad sign, one that sent the prairie dogs scurrying back into their underground towns.

Kade pulled his eyes back to the forty-fourth Chosen One—his remains, anyway. He'd been smashed worse than Troy. Kade dragged his hand down his face. "Oh, come on!"

"All that work... For nothing!" Brokk gritted his teeth and trotted over toward the car. Probably less to save any passengers and more looking for somebody to kick. The onocentaur approached the driver's side door, looked inside, rubbed his eyes, and glanced in a second time. He reached inside, and the horn ceased. Still, Brokk appeared as if he'd seen a ghost of one of the Chosen Ones.

The disbelief made Kade afraid to go near the small red convertible. "What is it?"

"I don't... It can't be..." Brokk trailed off, sitting down in front of the driver's side door. He motioned for Kade to join him. The satyr's own legs were rubbery as he drew near the wrecked car.

Kade expected to find a bloody mess of hair, bones, and flesh. Instead, he discovered a halfie girl with long red hair that fell to her mid-back. A teenager, probably. Eighteen? Hard to tell. Blood dribbled from glass lacerations on her forehead and left arm, but she was alive. On the girl's left shoulder was the tattoo of the sun. She had more: a murder of crows, a gnarled tree, and even a lonely dragon curling down her inner arm and breathing fire onto her wrist.

Wreathed in fire, a Savior will come. Marked a foe of the Darkest One, Kade remembered. He had always assumed the second line referred to the halfie's red hair. Perhaps there had been more to it—a literal mark of the Light. A tattoo of the sun.

Kade fell to his knees. Of the forty-four Chosen Ones that had died trying to fulfill the prophecy, none had ever fallen through the portal. He and Brokk had kidnapped all of them. But this was different. It felt like fate. Divine intervention.

Though Kade had no reason to say so, this *felt* right. And lately, nothing had, so it was even more profound. Euphoric, even. This girl had literally fallen into this world, just like the prophecy foretold. *After all this time, could she really be who we've been searching for?*

Kade wanted to hope so, but each time his hopes had been dashed to pieces. Still, it was possible. She could be *the* Chosen One—somebody not chosen by Kade but by the stars. Things could be different this time around. All he had to do was just tell her the truth.

Kade hesitated, his own train of thought faltering on the rails. *The truth?* He'd sacrificed forty-four halfies for a map, helmet, shield, and sword. That was an average of eleven halfies per Fragment. Yet these were the easiest four to find. The fifth would be more difficult, the sixth harder still. Kade couldn't even imagine how tough the seventh or even the eighth would be to steal. Kade felt his hope already draining. No way this girl would survive all four—he'd be lucky if she even survived one.

And Kade had never been lucky.

As much as Kade wished things were different, this changed nothing. Nothing at all. "All right, looks like we've got our forty-fifth Chosen One," Kade said, standing up and brushing the dirt from his knees. "Let's prep the scene before she wakes up."

Kade was halfway up the hill before he noticed that Brokk wasn't following—the onocentaur hadn't even bothered to reply. He was in a trance, still sitting on the ground in front of the driver's side door and staring at the girl. A spark of excitement gleamed in his eyes for the first time in what felt like years.

Kade walked back down the hill and noticed the tears pooling in Brokk's eyes. *Huh? Since when does that apathetic onocentaur feel anything?* Snatches of Brokk's comments over the last week floated back to Kade:

Well, let's get this over with.

We got what we came for, didn't we?

Remind me why we're still doing this.

We've come too far just to stop now.

Taken in pieces, the words made Brokk seem heartless. Yet taken together, Kade realized the deaths of forty-four Chosen Ones weighed far harder on Brokk than he'd let on—his apathy had been born of hopelessness. Kade should have grasped that sooner. *Does that make me a bad friend?* Probably, but not only for that reason.

Truth was, Brokk had only joined the quest because Kade had asked him to come. He'd convinced Brokk that this would be an amazing adventure—one filled with swashbuckling romance, daring feats of bravery, and incredible magic. Instead of a happy-go-lucky quest, they'd marched across the continent for three years, found four useless magical artifacts, and sent forty-four halfies to their deaths.

No wonder Brokk felt hopeless. Quietly, Kade sat beside the onocentaur, who surreptitiously wiped away his tears. Kade pretended not to notice. He didn't break the silence, but instead waited for Brokk to speak. Kade had spent enough time with Brokk to know that he'd speak when he was ready.

Eventually, Brokk asked, "What if we did things right this time? You know, told her the truth? Went on that adventure we always talked about?"

"You want to tell her about the other Chosen Ones?" Kade asked, surprised.

"Yes? No? I don't know." Brokk shook his head and stared at the ground. "All I know is that we've never *found* a Chosen One before, and this just feels right, you know? I don't want to screw this up—we might never get another chance like this."

Kade nodded, though he didn't agree. This girl wasn't special—after all, she just fell through a portal and killed the last Chosen One. Yet Brokk needed this to work, so Kade would make it work. No matter what. It was the least he could for his friend. "You're right. It's time we try something different. Forget about the 'Right Place, Right Time Travelers' act, the 'Are you okay?' drill, and the 'Save me!' technique. We're doing something new."

"We're telling her the truth?" Brokk asked, baffled.

"Some of it, but not everything," Kade said as a plan formed in his mind. "Just enough to convince her to become the *second* Chosen One."

The girl awoke with a groan, startling Kade from his nap. He and Brokk lay on the hilltop on opposite sides of the forty-fourth Chosen One's corpse—a boy whose name Kade hadn't bothered to learn. That didn't stop Kade from naming him now. *Madison.* Kade realized the boy's name probably wasn't Madison, but the corpse had been too thoroughly smashed to discern its gender. The only unmistakable facts were the shoulder-length red hair and the slight frame. That was all Kade needed. He could shape Madison however he wanted, and he wanted to shape Madison into a girl to force the halfie in the car to take Madison's place.

Kade could imagine the conversation taking place when the new girl walked up the hill. *Oh no! I killed her? What can I do to make up for it? Take Madison's place? Of course, anything to pay for what I've done!*

The conversation wouldn't be that easy, probably, but it could work—only if Brokk remained calm. Kade wagered that was a fifty-fifty chance. "Remember, I'm supposed to be the bad goat. You're the good donkey. Don't forget."

"I got it, I got it," Brokk said, waving away the satyr's concern with a flippant hand gesture.

Kade remained unconvinced. They'd done this routine in the past, and each time, Brokk had immediately forgotten. But to remind him would only upset Brokk. Then the situation would devolve into a bad-goat, worse-donkey scenario.

Kade sighed and double-checked that the three Fragments were clean and in the grass near the corpse's head—the Mad Map was still safely within Kade's bag. With nothing else to do except wait, he peeked over the hill's edge and said, "Well, here goes nothing... Forty-fifth time's the charm."

A few seconds later, the girl pushed open the door and pulled herself from the wrecked car. Then she retched. "Oh, my head," the girl said after composing herself. "What the...? Where am I?"

Before she could spot him, Kade shrank back from the hill's edge and returned to Madison's side. He stared at the corpse and willed tears to come, but none did. He was numb to that form of grief. Instead, Kade thought of the saddest thing he could imagine: spending the rest of his life on this quest and still failing to kill the Dark Lord. To be a failure. To be forgotten. Only then did the tears flow.

It wasn't long before his harrowed sobbing reached the girl's ears.

"Hello? Is somebody up there?" she asked from below. "Please. I need help. I need to go to the hospital."

In response, Kade sobbed louder. The most Brokk could offer was stoic sorrow as he kneeled and pretended to mourn.

Behind them, the girl appeared at the top of the hill. "Hello? I need—*oh no*. What happened?"

Summoning all the emotions he could, Kade bristled and stood from where he'd kneeled beside the body. "What happened? *What happened?*" Kade stalked toward her, pointing at the girl with a quivering finger. "Do you have any idea what you've *done?*"

The girl's eyes widened into saucers as she took him in, horns and all. She blinked twice. Yet his words didn't seem to register. The halfie was still too disoriented. "I... you... *what?*"

"You killed her!" Kade shouted as tears spilled from his eyes, though he didn't take another step forward. While he wanted to appear aggressive, Kade didn't want to come off as overly threatening. If he did, the girl might run. *I'm becoming too good at this,* he thought, but he only added, "You killed the Chosen One! Now we'll never stop the Dark Lord!"

As the halfie took a half-step back, Brokk stood and gently put a hand on Kade's shoulder. "It's not her fault." Brokk offered a small, apologetic smile, yet the halfie seemed more horrified than before.

"You... you're a *horse?*" the girl asked.

Brokk's eyes blazed with anger. "A horse? You think I'm a *horse?*"

We were so close... Kade had to stop himself from bashing his head against a rock.

Simultaneously, the girl shrank away, poised to run. "Please, I didn't mean to offend you. It's just that... I *hate* horses!"

Brokk's anger vanished. "You do?" His face tilted, and he offered a toothy grin. "They're the worst, aren't they?"

The girl didn't return the smile. "I... I don't understand what's going on." She looked between Brokk, Kade, and the corpse. Her eyes remained glued on the spattered blood and bone fragments for quite some time. Then she turned around and retched down the hill.

Of all things, Brokk actually approached her and held her hair back. *Since when does he care about anything other than himself?* Kade wondered, wrinkling his nose in annoyance.

When the girl finished vomiting, Brokk asked, "What's your name?"

"Ellie," she said without turning around. "I have to be delusional. You look like—"

"A centaur?" Brokk asked, his voice frigid.

"An onocentaur, more than anything, but I don't know how that would make any sense." Ellie put her head in her hands, missing Brokk's exultant look back at Kade. Chin held high, he seemed to say, *See? She knows! This is the real Chosen One!*

Ellie, however, remained on the verge of a total breakdown. She continued, "That girl... Did I really kill her?"

Brokk finally remembered his role. "Yes, but you couldn't have known what would happen. Portals open and close in random places at random times. In your case, it was the wrong place and time."

Ellie searched for a portal, but her eyes glanced right past the one hanging above them. It was iridescent and inviting, even if the halfie couldn't see it. "But where is it?"

"Closed as soon as you came through," Brokk lied. "Can't be sure when another one will come, or where it will lead. Could be tomorrow, or it could be years from now."

"*Years?*" the girl asked, putting her hands over her mouth.

Kade smiled inwardly. It was the perfect lead-in. Maintaining an angry frown, he hissed, "At least you *can* go home. You killed the Chosen One. She was our last hope, Ellie. Now she's gone, and nobody will stop the Dark Lord. We're all doomed—because of *you.*"

The halfie was silent for a long time. When she spoke, her voice was raw. Kade almost felt bad for her. Almost. "So, I'm stuck here now?"

Kade nodded gravely. "Same as the rest of us. The Dark Lord himself is probably the only one powerful enough to open a portal on purpose. That, or he has a magical artifact that can."

Ellie froze. Kade willed her to take the bait. The solution was so simple that even a horse could have figured it out. *So, if we beat him, then I can go home? Then make me the Chosen One.*

"Okay," she said, sounding relieved. She hadn't asked about home—as if she'd been running away from something in her world and had just stumbled on the one place where halfies couldn't follow.

Kade crossed his arms. "Okay, what?"

"I want in," Ellie said. "Let me help you take down the Dark Lord." Instead of being afraid or sad, she matched Brokk's earlier excitement—his desperation too.

She's hiding something from us, but what? Kade wanted to ask, but this was neither the time nor the place. Besides, beggars couldn't be choosers. Dropping the frown and adopting a mournful expression, Kade pretended to mull over the proposition. Then he gestured to the Fragments. "Fine. You can come. But if you're going to pretend to be the Chosen One, you'll need to wear those."

The Forgotten Forest was a far different place than the grasslands. Here, the very laws of nature weren't laws—merely guidelines. Fire didn't burn bark, so campfires were out of the question. Gravity fell *sideways* in some areas, causing some trees to be rooted horizontally into hillsides. Even the water was dangerous—it could turn to acid in one's stomach.

Three days of westward travel had brought them to the forest's tree line, where gnarled trees loomed overhead like giants. Another two-hour trek delivered them into utter darkness, because sunlight could not penetrate the enveloping canopy. Stumbling around in the dark was bad enough, but the trees' branches formed interwoven nets above the underbrush, which ensnared them at every turn.

As a last resort, they'd unsheathed the Blinding Blade. One could guess at how well that worked out. Ellie blinded herself while trying to hack away the branches in their path. Brokk, too, even though his eyes were closed. Kade only avoided that fate because he'd turned away from the blade. He saw how the forest withered under the searing light: bugs scattered, predators retreated, and the branches curled away from the blade, granting Kade, Brokk, and Ellie safe passage between the trees.

Despite being the world's worst sword, the Blinding Blade might've been the greatest torch ever made.

Thus, they devised a strategy. Kade walked at the front of the group with Brokk and Ellie behind him. While Ellie held the sword and lit the path, Kade navigated through the forest with the aid of the Mad Map. As Ellie couldn't see where she was going, Brokk offered to let her ride on his back—something he'd never done for anybody. Not even Kade. It would have been a lie to say he wasn't jealous.

The rest of the journey would have been easy and carefree if not for the abominable children of the forest: gnomes. Terrible, tiny humanoids in loincloths with red pointed hats, bloodstained beards, and glittering weapons—eating utensils, of all things. Their haunting yellow eyes were too big for their heads, as were their mouths. There wasn't enough room for noses. Their howls were ones of tittering laughter—light as a silver bell but as menacing as a bear's growl. They laughed loudest when they feasted on prey, which was often still alive and screaming.

If not for the gnomes' aversion to the Blinding Blade, Kade knew he'd be dead too. Yet even with the sword, he didn't feel safe. Neither did Ellie nor Brokk. So they didn't dare stop to rest. They kept walking—kept talking, too, if only to drown out the gnomes' laughter.

"Tell us about home," Kade said to Ellie during a lull in the conversation. She was still behind him, and Kade couldn't turn around without blinding himself.

"Not much to tell," she said without enthusiasm. "I was the youngest of eight siblings. Just another latchkey kid. My parents never really knew where I was or what I was doing because they were always working. I graduated high school a year late and started working as a mechanic's apprentice—I'd actually been parking a customer's car when I fell through the portal. Not much to tell other than that."

Not much to tell. Ellie'd said that twice, as if trying to convince him of the fact by repeating it. *Is she trying to manipulate me, of all people?* That, if nothing else, piqued his interest.

"There has to be more than just that," Kade said. "We've spent, what, three hours talking about horses? Don't you want to tell me what school was like? What a mechanic is? Or, what was it, latch-key children? Never heard of those things before." Lies, of course. Kade was well-versed in high schools, auto shops, and latchkey kids because of various conversations with the previous Chosen Ones. Yet by pretending to be ignorant, he hoped to get her to open up. To reveal at least one or two secrets in doing so.

No such luck.

"Well, in school, I took agriculture classes. I had one on horses and another on donkeys—"

"You did?" Brokk asked, attentive and excited. "You have to tell me everything they told you about horses."

Kade cursed silently as the conversation devolved into a debate of horses versus donkeys. *Again.* He'd learned close to nothing about her despite four days of traveling together because she kept deflecting questions and baiting Brokk into another discussion about horses. *How do I steer the conversation back to her?*

As Kade's mind churned with ideas, Ellie asked Brokk, "What's the hardest key to turn?"

"What?" asked the onocentaur.

"A donkey!" Ellie said, laughing.

Then Brokk laughed. He actually *heehawed.* They had to stop walking because he was laughing too hard to even breathe.

Kade fumed. It had taken Ellie only four days to make Brokk laugh—something Kade hadn't been able to do in over a year. While he was navigating through the forest, she was sitting on Brokk's back and wrapping him around her finger—probably had her arms wrapped around his chest too.

Worse, Brokk probably enjoyed it. Even when they'd still been trekking with Ellie across the grasslands, he'd been upbeat and excited. Brokk hadn't complained once about the endless trek, his stiff joints, or the pestering donkeyflies—which were actually horseflies, though the onocentaur refused to call them that. Brokk had actually walked with his shoulders back instead of hunched over—as if a great weight had been lifted from him. Only after it was gone had Kade even noticed. *What does that say about me?* Nothing good, he supposed.

To distract himself from Brokk and Ellie's unending debate, Kade consulted the Mad Map. From what he could discern, the Horrible Hag's lair was only a couple miles farther east—not that Brokk even seemed to care about finding the Horrible Hag anymore. No, the onocentaur probably *wanted* to be lost in this horrible forest with Ellie.

As if sensing Kade's tumultuous emotions, the map changed. In place of the *You Are Here* token that represented their group, the Mad Map created an icon for each of them. Brokk and Ellie's markers were of their faces, partially overlapping and festooned with hearts, *x*'s, and *o*'s. Words appeared, too, covering most of the forest: *Wow! These two are the best of friends, aren't they? Ellie and Brokk, on a quest to slay the Dark Lord and become heroes of the realm! Huzzah!*

Kade's own marker was a tombstone with a small inscription: *Here lies Kade, the forgotten third wheel of the group. He died as he lived. Alone.*

That hurt far worse than a gnome's fork ever could—because it was true. Brokk and Ellie didn't need him now. Brokk could carry the equipment, and Ellie could fight the monsters. What was Kade good for? Staring at this stupid map and pointing where to go? Both Ellie and Brokk could do that without him. In bringing them together, Kade had made himself obsolete.

No good deed goes unpunished. Too angry to come up with a good retort to the Mad Map's words, Kade bit his tongue, rolled up the map, and shoved it in his backpack.

The last of the foliage parted within twenty minutes, giving way to an acre-wide clearing. Light cascaded down from the cloudless sky, so Ellie sheathed the Blinding Blade. More dazzling than even the sword was the

Horrible Hag's home, for it was menacing in a far different way than Kade had expected.

A flat stone pathway wound through the short grass toward a white picket fence, which opened for them as they approached. Inside the fence were gardens separated by fruits, vegetables, and flowers—all had tiny picket signs explaining what type of plant they were. Yet each had a strange name: a prickly succulent was *Gall of Goat,* two flowers that wound around each other were *Tartar's Lips,* and a purple bush was *Nose of Turk.*

"Huh," Kade said. He could think of little else to say, especially as he surveyed the home. Everything felt very *un*horrible, which only made it far more horrible.

A cute farmhouse sat beyond the gardens, matching the vibrancy of the flowers but little else. The siding was pink, the roof's flashing white. Several white windows eyed him curiously, though most were drawn closed in sleep. One, however, remained open, and steam wafted from it along with the scent of apple pie. Past the house was a small shed, brought to Kade's attention by the loud whinny of a chestnut horse—a healthy creature, one of the cleanest Kade had ever seen.

Brokk flinched and drew his bow and an arrow. "Vile filth," he muttered before taking aim.

Kade put a hand on Brokk's arm before he could fire the arrow. "We are *not* getting killed over a horse."

"But..." Brokk looked to Ellie for help, but she shook her head. Kade found it infuriating that she was *agreeing* with him.

"Wait to shoot him *after* we get the armor," Ellie said, before flashing both of them a smile. Unlike Brokk, Kade found it to be less like honey and more like tree sap. Just as sticky but all too bitter.

There's something wrong with you, Kade wanted to say, but he couldn't with Brokk close by. *You can't be this nice, happy, and easy-going. There has to be something you're hiding from—*

The white front door opened inward, scattering the rest of Kade's thoughts.

"One does not simply walk into my garden," said a throaty, cracking voice from the darkness inside of the house. It sounded as if twins were speaking in unison—one a soprano singer, the other a bass. "I suppose you are here for a reason, yes?"

The Horrible Hag. It has to be her. Instinctively, Kade took a step back. So did Brokk. Ellie didn't, but only because she was still on the onocentaur's back. Kade pointed at her, and Ellie shot a vengeful glance at him. Finally, he saw something beneath the visage of positivity: violent fury.

There you are. Kade smiled for the first time since he'd met Ellie. *I knew you were hiding something.*

But before Kade could comment, Ellie's mask slipped back on. She cleared her throat and asked, "You are the Horrible Hag, then?"

Still unable to see the crone, Kade wondered about the proper way to address her. Your Horribleness? Ms. Hag? Hagfish?

"Happy, if you'd please," the hag replied.

...Of course that's her name.

Then the four-foot-tall hag stepped out into the light. She wore a white dress covered with pink flowers that hid her feet and, over that, a light-blue apron covered in flour and stains. Like a sweet, old lady—if not for her face.

While most hags hid their ugliness beneath a mask of beauty, Happy displayed her features proudly: a warty face, a hooked nose that dangled over her mouth like an anglerfish's light, gnarled arms resembling the surrounding trees, and parchment skin. "Well? I suppose you are hungry, yes?" Happy smiled, revealing her shark-like teeth. "Come in! I'm just finishing up a pie. It's *quite* delicious."

Without waiting for a reply, the hag strode back into the house, and the darkness consumed her.

As one, Ellie, Kade, and Brokk traversed the pink porch and stood at the threshold. Closer now, they could see the interior of the house, though it was still quite dark. Ellie almost unsheathed the blade to shed some light, but Kade stayed her hand. "I don't think we want *Happy* to think we're attacking."

Ellie grumbled but released the hilt. She walked across the threshold and tripped over an ottoman. Right behind her, Brokk shouldered a coat stand, which toppled. Kade put a hand on the wall to steady himself but only succeeded in knocking over a glass oil lamp, which shattered on the floor.

Happy skittered in from another room, moving far faster than her body should have allowed. That speed, like her withered frame, had to be another side-effect of her magic. Just how much of herself had Happy given up for her power? *Probably everything except the skin on her bones.*

In a guttural growl, Happy asked, "I suppose you have an explanation for the mess, yes?"

"Sorry," Ellie said in an overly-apologetic tone. To Kade, it sounded fake, but everything she did felt fake. *That's the problem with too many lies—you don't know what's real anymore.* When Ellie picked herself up, she offered a smile and added, "It's too dark in here for us to see. The only light we have is that sword, and we didn't want to scare you with it."

"Oh." The menace disappeared from Happy's voice. She snapped her fingers and candles immediately flickered to life, revealing the sitting room, the antique furniture, and the brick chimney in the corner, which also roared to life with green-and-purple flames. "Sorry, dearies, I often forget that others need light to see."

Kade frowned, following the implications. *She can see in the dark? Not terrifying at all.*

Happy lifted a hand, and the oil rose from the ground. The crystalline shards from the lamp reformed, and the oil flowed inside. It looked as good as new. If only the Fragments were that useful, but no. Not even close.

"I suppose you all want tea and a slice of pie, yes?" Happy asked, and the three nodded. Saying *yes* seemed to be the safest course of action in present company.

Happy skittered away into an adjacent room. Hesitantly, Kade followed suit, as did Ellie and Brokk. They discovered a kitchen with a smattering of well-polished wood and stainless-steel appliances: two ovens, two sinks, and an island. On the far side was a bubbling cauldron filled with an iridescent, foggy liquid. Above it, long shelves displayed glass jars filled with what looked to be different plants. Again, the names were strange: *Wool of Bat* was a purple orchid, *Eye of Newt* a fuzzy orange fruit, and *Tongue of Dog* a pink vegetable that looked more like an eggplant.

Happy caught him staring at it. "Don't worry yourself, dearie. As you well know, most things aren't as they appear." She embedded her knife into a pie, which already had a slice missing. As it cut, Kade saw a crimson liquid oozing from its center. A red-jam filling, not blood. "I've found that, given time, most things form to the names given them. I don't need a tooth out of a wolf's mouth to have a *Tooth of Wolf*, not when I grow a seed of the same name. My cauldron certainly sees no differences, because *I* see no differences. Perception, yes? It is the root of all power."

"But why?" Ellie asked before Kade could even form the words.

"Why what?" Happy let go of the knife to wipe sweat from her brow, though it continued to cut and slice as if she were still holding it. When she grabbed it again, Happy matched the movement perfectly without missing a beat.

"Why stop pulling teeth out of a wolf's mouth?" Ellie clarified, though she winced at her own words. "That came out too harsh. What I mean is—"

"I know what you mean, dearie," Happy said. She wriggled her nose, and the pie plates flew into the air toward Kade, Ellie, and Brokk. "I spent centuries inflicting pain. *Real* pain. Then it was inflicted on me, and I finally realized that there was enough pain and hatred in the world without my added influence." Offering a bittersweet smile, she added, "Changing hasn't been easy, mind you. I've always found that kindness is not a trait, but a habit."

All three stood in stunned silence as they held their slices of pie. Kade couldn't decide whether to laugh or scream. *She can't be serious, can she?* He stared at the plate of pie, waiting for it to come to life and attack him. It didn't.

Humming a tune to herself, Happy touched a kettle, which immediately whistled. Three cups flew from the cabinets to her side, which she filled with a purple liquid. Afterward, each cup zoomed toward the three guests.

Happy took a bite of pie before sipping her tea as if to show both weren't poisonous.

Still, Kade wasn't willing to trust her. *Once a hag, always a hag.*

Ellie took a slow bite of the pie, grimacing at first before relaxing. Brokk did the same with the tea. Knowing both were safe, Kade then ate and drank—both were quite delicious. In fact, all the exhaustion from the week's travel disappeared. He felt well-rested, well-hydrated, and even well-fed.

Kade often forgot just how useful real magic could be.

After taking another sip of her tea, Happy asked, "Apologies for not asking sooner—it has been some time since I've had a guest—but what are your names?"

Kade's fork hovered inches from his mouth. Brokk choked on his own drink. Ellie looked as if she had just eaten a halfie child.

"Roy," Kade said, setting down his fork.

"Jeff," Brokk added, despite having bits of jam stuck in his teeth.

"Anne," said Ellie. She said it so sweetly that Kade almost believed the lie.

Apparently, the hag didn't. Her face twisted as if she'd eaten something bitter, and said, "I understand if you don't want to tell me, but please don't lie. Lies taste like ash, which ruins the flavor of my pie and tea."

Kade blinked. "But—"

"How? I traded away my ability to lie for that skill. But that was long ago, when I was indeed horrible." Happy sniffed, and the candles flickered but remained lit. "But enough about me. I want to know about you. Why are you here?"

Kade stared at Ellie, but she and Brokk both looked at Kade. He was outvoted. Kade sighed, placed his pie on the counter, and said, "We're trying to complete a quest. You have the Angelic Armor, and well, we need it. We'll trade, of course."

Happy's eyes widened. "That old thing? I almost forgot about it. Wait one moment."

Happy bit her thumb hard enough to draw blood. As some dribbled down her chin, she used her bleeding thumb to draw a crimson square on the island. When the lines connected, the wood withered and cracked, falling into a dark abyss. She reached her hand inside the hole to pull out the armor. White wings trailed behind the silver breastplate, which perfectly complemented the helm. A matching set.

"It *flies?*" Kade asked. *Something useful for once...*

He leaned forward to touch it, but Happy pulled the armor away so that it was out of his reach. "No. The wings don't flap. However, gliding is possible, so long as the wielder uses their hands to keep the wings outstretched."

Kade frowned. *Another useless Fragment. Great.* "What do you want for it?" he asked. Would she ask for his blood? His mind? His soul? What could be worse than that?

"Just the truth," Happy said, making eye contact with each of them. "You need to be honest with one another—admit whatever lies you've told each other."

Kade froze. *I'd rather give you my soul,* he thought. Instead of admitting that, he asked, "Is there anything *else* you want?" Kade stared at the hag, willing her to read his mind. *Take. The. Girl.* When she didn't notice or seem to care, he flicked his eyes to Ellie. Long look at the hag, short look back at Ellie. "Anything at all? Just name it."

Happy smiled, amused. "I already have named my price. Just the truth."

"But... why?" Brokk asked, looking nervously between Ellie and Happy.

"Why, dearie? Because each of you *reeks* of lies," Happy answered.

Kade glanced at the ground. *How best to approach this?* They needed the armor, but they couldn't just steal it. The prophecy required them to strike a deal. Was there a loophole? Happy had made a deal to tell the truth, hadn't she? If the truth had to be told, what would happen if she lied? She'd be hurt, at the very least—dead in a best-case scenario. That was the only way to win. *But how do I get her to tell a lie?* Kade needed time to think through that. "Then we accept your terms, Happy." He turned to Ellie and added, "You first."

Ellie glared at him, and Kade only smirked. *Time to find out who you really are.*

"I haven't lied about anything," Ellie said, but the hag shook her head. Again, the friendly mask on Ellie's faced dropped, and her lip curled into a snarl. "What? I didn't lie!"

"*That* was yet another lie," Happy replied.

Ellie hesitated, and Kade used the time to think through his predicament. Aside from making the hag lie, was there any other way to complete the stipulations of the agreement? Kade felt the weight of the Kidnappin' Klub in his bag. Could he knock Ellie out and then tell her the truth while she was unconscious? Technically, it would still be the truth, even if Ellie couldn't hear or remember it. *No, it won't work.* One look at Happy told Kade that she would stop him before he'd even raised the club. *The hag needs to be dealt with, not Ellie.*

"You want the truth?" Ellie said after almost a minute of silence. "Fine. I didn't have eight siblings because I was an only child. There. Satisfied?"

The hag merely chuckled. "No. But, for the sake of fairness, I will now ask the satyr to rectify one of his lies."

Kade hid a grimace as Happy's attention returned to him. He voiced an insignificant lie: "The previous Chosen One wasn't named Madison. I didn't know the kid's real name."

"Why would you lie about that?" Ellie asked immediately, pushing the conversation back to him.

Clever girl, Kade thought. "Because we were desperate at the time and needed you to be the next Chosen One." The admission wasn't a lie, but it certainly wasn't the entire truth. Before Ellie could deflect, he asked, "Why lie about being an only child?"

Ellie flinched. "I always wanted to be a part of a big, happy family, but I didn't have that growing up. Mom was a junkie, and Dad was dead. All I had was my Uncle Hugh." She sniffed, turned away, and asked, "If Madison was the Chosen One, how did you not know her real name?"

"We didn't talk about each other's pasts," Kade said. The whole truth was that *Madison* hadn't been awake long enough to say more than ten words. "Why—"

"Just tell her the truth, Kade," Brokk said, staring at the ground. That old weight rested on his shoulders again, and he hunched forward, retreating back into apathy and hopelessness. "Ellie's going to find out anyway."

"Find out about what?" asked the halfie, pressing the issue.

Kade cursed beneath his breath, as much to vent his frustration as to stall for time. How to turn this situation back on Happy? The hag had named plants to trick her cauldron—she manipulated perception. How could he do the same thing?

Nothing immediately came to mind.

Out of time, Kade answered, "We lied to you about the portal. It didn't close after you came through. It was right above us the entire time. For some reason, halfies can't see them. Don't know why."

Kade avoided Brokk's disappointed stare and instead watched Happy. She mulled over the words and nodded, satisfied. No, not satisfied. *Entertained.* Was that what made her horrible? That she used the truth to hurt people? No, Happy had said she didn't inflict pain, but maybe there'd been a loophole: she could still *enjoy* it. What had she said? Kindness wasn't a trait—it was a habit.

The hag turned back to Ellie and said, "Your turn, dearie."

Taking a deep breath, Ellie crossed her arms and added, "You know what? I'm tired of this game. I'll tell you everything just to speed things up. Uncle Hugh stole cars for a living, and I used to help him. But when I was fifteen, we got caught. Hugh got sent to prison for grand theft auto, and I went to juvenile hall as an accessory to the crime. I spent a year there, and after I got out, I ran away because I didn't want to live with my deadbeat mom. So, I dropped out of high school and started stealing cars because that's all I knew how to do. That car I drove through the portal? I stole that too." She glared at Happy. "Good enough?"

"For now," Happy said, still smiling. "Your turn, satyr."

Kade was still thinking about what Ellie had said. What had been her uncle's name? Hugh? That sounded a lot like *you*. As important as names were to Happy, that could be useful. But how could he trick the hag with that name before having to reveal the worst lies?

Out of nowhere, Brokk said, "No. I'll go this time, Happy." He turned to Ellie. "You're the forty-fifth Chosen One. We didn't kill them, but they all died during the quest. That's the truth."

Kade groaned. *So much for keeping that a secret.*

"What?" Ellie asked, disgusted. Her expression only infuriated Kade.

"Oh, don't try to be all high and mighty now, princess," he spat. "Don't forget: you *killed* the last Chosen One. We've all got blood on our hands." As Ellie broke eye contact, Kade added, "When we first found out about the prophecy, we waited for a Chosen One to come for months. We even camped outside the portals. But guess what? No red-haired halfies ever showed up. So instead, we visited your world and *chose* the One. But guess what? He died. Drowned in the Wallow Well. So, we kept trying. Everybody thinks that this is supposed to be a happy-go-lucky adventure, but it's not. It's deceitful, it's dangerous, and it's *difficult*. It's not like we're *trying* to kill people—it's certainly not like we're smashing them with cars!"

The glare Ellie sent his way was deadly this time. Kade held her gaze, unflinching. "When I woke up in my smashed car, I thought this place was a hallucination. Maybe I'd smashed the car into a light pole and fallen into a coma or something. Didn't really matter to me, because for the first time in a long time, I felt like I had a future. I *knew* that going on a quest was dangerous, but at least I was being *chosen* for something! And that's... all I'd ever wanted. But somehow, even this *fantasy* was a lie!"

Kade looked at the hag, who shook her head again. Even that gesture seemed playful.

"Oh, what now?" Ellie clenched her teeth. "That was the truth! All of it!"

"Most of the truth, perhaps, but not all of it," Happy said. "You still have another lie that you're holding onto. I *see* it."

Ellie's face fell, as if something had finally broken. "I like horses, okay?"

Brokk gasped, backing away from her until he bumped into the wall. "How could you?"

Stricken, Ellie said, "I saw how much you hated horses, and thought that if I hated them too, you'd help me. I didn't want to be left behind, so I pretended to be flirty and bubbly and funny."

Brokk crumpled. Out of everything that'd been said, that'd been the thing to break his spirit. "No... *No.*"

"I didn't mean to hurt you, Brokk," Ellie said, and Kade could tell she actually meant it. "I'm sorry."

Out of the corner of his eye, Happy's grin was so wide that her skin was splitting. It only made Kade angrier. "You know what the difference is between us? We might hurt people, but we don't do it on purpose. Yet you *enjoy* our misery!" Kade's heart pounded as he found a solution. One that would probably come back to bite him in the ass. *Time to throw her the bait...* "You pretend to be good, don't you?"

Not intimidated in the slightest, the hag said, "I never said I was *good*—just honest. You should know by now that nothing is truly ever *good* or *bad,* white or black. It's all gray—that is the very world I see."

"You say you're helping us, but that isn't entirely true, is it? You're feeding on our pain. Congratulations, you won, all right?" *You, you, you.* He reinforced the word so she wouldn't think twice about it. Now he needed to change the name—change the meaning. "Can Hugh just give us the armor now, so we can go?"

"Yuh—" The hag stopped before she finished the word. Then her expression turned from puzzlement to hatred. She bared her teeth, revealing far more than had been there before. Hundreds, at the very least. "You tried to make me tell a lie, satyr. You'll pay a hundredfold for that."

The hag clicked her tongue, and Kade's body froze. Not out of fear, but out of magic. The hag had paralyzed him. He was at her mercy. Brokk uttered a furious scream as he charged Happy, but she paralyzed him too. With the hag distracted, Ellie unsheathed the Blinding Blade, and the room disappeared in brilliant light. Simultaneously, the Singing Shield burst into an overwhelming angelic choir. Together, the Fragments blocked out all light and noise.

The magic holding Kade fell away as something slammed into him. He crashed into the kitchen island and chipped a horn as someone grabbed his ankle and dragged him away. Then he was thrown over something. A couch? *No. Brokk's back.* The onocentaur raced out of the kitchen, through the sitting room, and out of the house as the hag screamed somewhere in the depths of the house.

"Take that, you crone!" Kade shouted, though he could barely hear his own words after being deafened by the shield.

Someone touched his shoulder, and Kade flinched, thinking it was Happy. Instead, it was Ellie. She held the Blinding Blade overhead while sitting on Brokk's haunches. Ellie was yelling something, but Kade could only make out every few words. "We... map... horse!"

Horse? Chancing a look back, Kade saw Happy chasing them on her chestnut horse. She held the Angelic Armor.

Kade frowned. "We're running away? We need that armor!"

"We'll get it, but only after she's dead!" Ellie said as more of Kade's hearing returned. Yet she still sounded far away.

Kade tried to follow Ellie's logic. They were going to kill Happy by *not* taking the armor? He laughed aloud as the realization donned on him. They'd traded Happy the truth for the Angelic Armor. They had told the truth—the *entire* truth—but the hag hadn't given them the armor. While she couldn't give it to them because they were running away, technically Happy hadn't fulfilled her side of the bargain, which meant that she lied. Somehow, the consequences of lying were more severe than any wounds sustained while chasing Brokk through the Forgotten Forest. *A lie might truly kill her. Gods above, I love lies.*

Kade would have kissed Ellie if she hadn't been sitting behind him. Instead, he settled for squeezing her hand when she handed him the Mad Map.

"Give me your backpack!" she shouted.

Kade frowned. "What?"

"We need to lighten the load for Brokk!" Ellie shouted as she tossed the saddlebags from the onocentaur's back and threw them at the pursuing horse. Begrudgingly, Kade gave her his backpack, and they dumped everything aside from the Fragments and the prophecy scroll. Kade even tossed away his Kidnappin' Klub, which hurt more than expected. Like losing an old friend.

Kade only prayed he wouldn't lose any others.

"Hold this!" Ellie shouted, shoving the blade into his free hand as she shifted into a sidesaddle position. With one arm wrapped around his waist to steady herself, Ellie raised the Singing Shield with the other as Happy hurled balls of multi-colored light at them. Orange seemed to be fire. Blue was ice. Kade had no idea what purple meant. It didn't matter, for the shield absorbed each blast.

As Brokk charged farther into the Forgotten Forest, he shouted, "Could use some directions!"

Kade stared down at the Mad Map. *Oh. That's what Ellie had been trying to tell me earlier.* He shouted, "We need directions! Shortcuts! *Anything!*"

The map replied: *But does one really need anything? Or does one simply* want *things? That longing is the true antithesis of life.* After a brief pause, it added, *What does a map even need? Is there really a point to—*

"When we kill the Dark Lord and take over, you'll never be in the dark again, okay?" Kade shouted. He glanced back to see Happy gaining ground. Cursing under his breath, Kade added, "I'll hang you up on the wall, if that's what you want!"

It wrote, *And?*

"A frame. A giant, golden frame! How does that sound?" Kade asked.

And? remained on the map's surface.

"A companion!" Kade shouted. "I'm sure the Dark Lord has a lot of cool, sentient stuff. When he's dead, we'll find you a friend, okay? But that won't happen if you don't get us out of here!"

The Mad Map immediately became an insanely detailed map of the Forgotten Forest. Different colored lines showed different routes toward the distant grasslands. All of them zigzagged through different zones and territorial markers, which revealed the various predators' locations. Even the individual gnomes. Hundreds in the near vicinity. The illustrations were far more in-depth than anything the map had ever shown.

Kade blinked twice. "You could do this at any time? Even in that stupid stone labyrinth? We lost sixteen people because of those traps! You're telling me we could have avoided that?"

The Mad Map produced the magic eight-ball again. *Maybe.*

"I'm going to find you the most sane, boring companion I can," Kade said before relaying the directions to Brokk.

The onocentaur flew through the forest, dodging between trees, leaping over rivers, and galloping off into gnome-infested territories. Happy's horse was fast behind, but not close enough to benefit from the Blinding Blade's power. The branches parted in front of Brokk and closed immediately behind him, trapping the hag in the thickets of gnarled trees until she magically ripped them apart. Then the gnomes ambushed her. Kade couldn't see the fight, but he could see her magic and hear the gnomes' tinny laughter. Kade didn't believe that the tiny gnomes would kill her, but they *would* slow her down. And that was all they needed.

After thirty more minutes of galloping through the forest, Brokk finally slowed. His breaths came in painful gasps, and he nearly stumbled on a pebble. "Can't... keep going... like this..."

Kade immediately hopped off. So did Ellie. Brokk wheezed and trotted slowly, looking worse than Kade had ever seen him. To cheer Brokk up, Kade patted his friend's flank and said, "Guess what? You just outran a horse. You proved once and for all that donkeys are better than horses—donkeypower wins."

Brokk only managed an exhausted chuckle.

"Yeah," Ellie added. "I change my mind about horses. Anything that'd let Happy ride them is pure evil."

Brokk laughed. Not a *heehaw* laugh, but after the pain they'd all experienced in the hag's house, this was just as good.

Together, they trudged along for almost an entire day, spurred along by the threat of the hag. By the time they'd reached the mouth of the

Forgotten Forest and retreated to the grasslands, Kade had expected Happy to be on their heels. But she arrived hours later at high noon, looking worse than Brokk, Ellie, and Kade combined. Drained of magic and physically sickened by the unfulfilled bargain, she almost toppled from the horse, who bled from dozens of wounds. Large chunks of meat were missing from its back, and even a couple of forks were stuck in its left hind leg.

Before Happy could dismount, Brokk shot the horse in the chest. It collapsed, pulling the hag down with it. Happy was half-smashed beneath the beast's weight, still clutching the armor. As Ellie, Brokk, and Kade approached, Happy tried to push the Angelic Armor toward them. "Please... just take it. I'm begging you. I'll give you anything else you want if you just take the armor and restore the truth."

"If you really wanted my sympathy, you shouldn't have ridden a horse," Brokk said. Then he shot her in the chest with an arrow, piercing her heart. Happy's corpse turned to dust, and the armor fell from her grasp. Then Brokk shot the horse between the eyes, and its chest stopped rising. If anything, it looked at peace.

It would have been a perfect moment if the Hindsight Helm hadn't been glowing. Curious, Ellie put it on her head and gasped. "What the..."

"Here we go," Kade muttered, annoyed. "Time to learn what we did wrong."

Eventually, the glow around the Hindsight Helm faded, and Ellie doffed it. "Apparently, Happy promised to care for that horse. Had we killed it earlier, she'd have broken her promise and lost her magic—"

"*I knew it!*" Brokk shouted, pawing at the ground. "Had you just let me shoot that horse, we would have avoided that entire mess!" He let out a scream of frustration, ran over to the horse, and kicked it at least a dozen times. "*I! Hate! Horses!*"

"Talk about beating a dead horse," Kade muttered, quiet enough for only Ellie to hear.

Ellie, however, wasn't laughing. Her expression was one of concentration—no doubt trying to remember all that the Hindsight Helm had told her. "Apparently, had we changed the names on the plant signs in Happy's garden, that technically would have made her a liar while also destroying the cauldron." There were plenty more mistakes, and Ellie relayed each one, speaking faster and faster until she was out of breath.

As she gasped for air, Kade said, "If you listen to that helm too much, you'll end up crazier than the Mad Map." Then he reached over and patted her on the back. "Forget about what we did wrong. You know what you did right? You pulled out the Blinding Blade and got Happy to lie. You saved us back there." Kade chuckled and added, "I can't believe I'm saying this, but we actually make a pretty good team."

"Yeah, when you two aren't being horses," Ellie said, still holding the Hindsight Helm under her arm.

"Careful, halfie. Those are fighting words." Then Brokk cracked a grin. Ellie did too. Compared to yesterday, hers was more haggard yet more relaxed—definitely not the happy-go-lucky one she'd worn before. Yet this one was honest.

And Kade smiled back genuinely.

Eventually, Ellie sat down on the grass and asked, "So, what happens now?"

Kade and Brokk looked at each other. No words were exchanged, but Kade could read Brokk's thoughts just from the wrinkles on his forehead. They were in agreement. Kade said, "Whatever you want to happen. If you want to go home, we'll take you back to the portals. We'll find the right one, then send you through. You'll never have to see us again."

Ellie pursed her lips and stared at the endless expanse of grasslands. "And if I don't want to leave?"

Kade stared at her, puzzled. "You still want to stay?"

"Don't know yet," Ellie replied with a shrug. "Just weighing the options."

Brokk said, "If you stay, you'll keep being the Chosen One. We'll fight monsters, trek across the world, and find the last three Fragments."

"What will you do if I don't stay?" Ellie asked, watching him closely.

Brokk looked uncomfortable. "You're the first Chosen One that I've felt good about in a long time. If you don't stay, I probably won't either. I think I'll just go back to the Wild Woods, find a wife, and start a family."

Kade winced, feeling like he'd been shot with one of Brokk's arrows. He'd sensed that Brokk might leave, but hearing him say so was a painful truth to swallow. *How can I fulfill the prophecy without him?* It wouldn't be impossible, but it would be far lonelier.

"And you, Kade?" Ellie asked.

Kade had a lie on his lips but swallowed it. He decided to be honest, strange as it felt. "I'd keep doing this. I'd keep kidnapping Chosen Ones and searching for Fragments—probably die somewhere along the way." Kade sighed and looked over at her. "Even if you do stay, Ellie, we'll *all* probably die. Even if we get all eight Fragments, killing the Dark Lord won't be an easy task."

"You're not really selling this idea," Ellie said with a smirk.

"Not trying to," Kade replied. "Just being honest."

"That's a first." Ellie's smirk faded and her expression turned thoughtful. "So, my options are: go back to Earth and steal cars while you keep kidnapping other children, or stay here as the Chosen One and probably die somewhere along the way."

Before Ellie could reply, Brokk added, "Yeah. But at least here, you won't be alone. We'll be in it together."

Ellie was quiet for a long time. While Kade hated the silence, he didn't break it. Neither did Brokk, though the onocentaur was pensive and rigid. "I'll stay," Ellie finally said.

Immediately, Brokk leaped to his hooves. "You will? *Yes!*" Picking up Ellie and throwing her onto his back, Brokk galloped across the hills as she held on for dear life.

As they zoomed back and forth, Kade burst into laughter. Not because of Brokk's celebration dance, but because the hag had been right. The truth had convinced Ellie—not his lies. *Gods above, the truth actually worked.*

Eventually, Brokk returned, looking younger and stronger than he had even five minutes ago. His eyes sparkled with glee. Kade hadn't realized just how badly the onocentaur had needed her to say *yes*—how badly they both needed her to.

"If we're going to do this, then we need a team name," Ellie said as she swung her legs off of Brokk's back. "Something heroic."

"Us? *Heroic?*" Kade asked, cocking an eyebrow. "I don't know if we're the heroic type."

Ellie smirked. "Yeah, yeah. Maybe we aren't heroes, but we're definitely less evil than the Dark Lord."

"That's because we're the *Gray Lords*," Brokk said, which garnered confused looks from both Ellie and Kade. "Like the hag said, the world's not good or bad, white or black—it's gray."

"Gray Lords," Kade echoed. He rolled the name across his tongue and nodded. "I like it."

"Me too," Ellie said, donning the Angelic Armor. With the sword, shield, and helm, she looked like a true Chosen One. "It takes a Gray Lord to kill a Dark Lord."

"And speaking of killing the Dark Lord..." Brokk pulled out the prophecy scroll and read the next two lines:

Sixth is the cloak, worn by an idol.
Find a replacement before its revival.

"Well, that doesn't tell us much," Ellie said, frowning.

"The Mad Map will know more." Kade pulled out the map without unrolling it and, after a moment's deliberation, handed it to Ellie. "Here. You're the Chosen One. You get to lead now."

Ellie shook her head and pushed the map back to him. "I might be the Chosen One, but you chose me, Kade—that makes you the leader."

Kade looked to Brokk, who said, "When we started this quest, you promised me an adventure with swashbuckling romance, daring feats of bravery, and incredible magic. For the first time, I feel like we're heading on that adventure. So yeah, I'll follow you, but don't expect any more free rides. Next time, you're carrying me through a gnome-infested forest."

"Deal." Smirking, Kade unfurled the Mad Map and discovered the new Fragment nestled within the southern Gruesome Grove: the Charismatic Cloak. He read the name aloud and added, "It probably changes colors or something equally useless."

"Well, we found a use for everything else, didn't we?" Ellie asked, smiling from beneath her helm. "A color-changing cloak could come in handy."

"Guess there's only one way to find out," Kade said. Putting away the map, he pointed at the horizon. "Let's go, Gray Lords. We've got ourselves a cloak to steal."

SEEDS OF EXTINCTION: A shunned seed searches for soil in a drowned world...

Seeds of Extinction

Born alone in the branches of her dying mother, Hazel dangled upside down from a wooden web. A freshwater ocean thrashed hundreds of feet "above" her, impaled by the trunk of a solitary fig tree. Hazel tried to scream, but she had no mouth or vocal cords. No eyes or ears, either, though she could see and hear using the photo- and mechanoreceptors in the leaves sprouting from her head. With bark for skin, she was little more than a paralyzed wooden doll.

Frozen, Hazel could only watch as a giant wooden spider scuttled toward her. Also eyeless and wooden, it danced along the web and stopped beside her, its sharp jaws cutting through the sticky fibers before grabbing her by the neck and dragging her onto the branch below. It released her but continued standing over her paralyzed body.

Danger. Danger. Danger—

Pheromones wrapped around her, breaking the cyclical thought and communicating words and ideas without sound or sight. "Hello, Hazel. I am Mother."

Succeeding the last word, a series of complex images, sounds, and smells came to Hazel, those she understood but would never find in the sea: wind ruffling through tree branches in a forest, damp soil after a long rain, and birds singing from canopies as wildlife darted through the underbrush.

"I know you are afraid, but you must stand, Hazel. Learn to control your body and the chemicals that run through you." An image of a Venus flytrap appeared in Hazel's mind, opening and snapping closed.

With it came understanding.

Hazel focused her mind, using bodily acids to soften the cell walls of her rigid joints, bending her limbs before they could re-harden. She articulated her fingers as an experiment and then stood, taking three wobbling steps. A breeze pushed her, and Hazel fell sideways, but the wooden spider caught her with an extended limb. Only when Hazel had found her balance did the spider skitter away.

Hazel attempted to speak, but her own pheromones were meaningless. Strings of letters and images without order or structure. A kaleidoscope of erratic geometric lines—

Mother shushed her. "Your voice will come later, but for now, you must listen to me, Hazel. You have many enemies in this world, and there are things you would be wise to fear." Images flooded through her mind: monstrous creatures swimming in the sea, terrifying waves slamming into the fig tree, and fierce winds snapping branches.

Hazel panicked, accidentally releasing more chaotic pheromones that Mother muted with her own chemicals. "This is a dangerous world, Hazel, but you have allies. Our sentries."

Pheromones revealed a menagerie of wooden creatures scuttling through the branches of the tree, sentries without faces. In place of noses were a multitude of short antennae, bristles covering their bodies like thorns on a stem. Covered in greenery of their own, the leaves were their eyes and ears. Ranging from two to three feet in height, the green jays were the largest, having wings made of fibrous leaves. Smaller sentries had horns, clawed appendages, and mandibles. Most scuttled on four or six legs, excluding the web-building spiders removing dead branches.

In a second image, a fleshy tentacle rose from the ocean depths and wrapped itself around Mother's trunk. As one, the wooden creatures swarmed the invading beast, sacrificing themselves for Mother. Most sentries ripped at the flesh with horns and mandibles, but the poisonous ones intentionally tried to be eaten. A few bulbous ones even exploded, tearing away chunks of tentacles until the underwater creatures slunk away in search of easier prey.

"These sentries are our defenders, Hazel. I give them life, and they give me theirs in return. But you? You are different from them." A final image materialized in Hazel's mind, showing a group of wooden dolls—the seeds—standing together in Mother's highest branches as they stared out at the vast blue expanse. Unlike the sentries, the dolls' heads were enormous, their thumbs opposable, and their bodies bipedal. Humanoid.

They're like me. Hazel stared down at her own hands, covered in brown, green, and gold bark as her name suggested. She clenched her fingers before letting them uncurl. *But where are they?*

Hazel turned her attention to the thick branches where seeds slept among the leaves. Their lifeless arms hung at their sides, their heads still connected to stems. She approached a cluster of three sleeping seeds and rested her forehead against the closest one. *Please wake up,* she thought, though without using pheromones.

The seeds didn't rouse.

"Their minds are still forming, but soon they will ripen and fall, just as you have, Hazel. Together, you will rebuild the forest, as it once was before the rains came and washed everything away. You must, because you are my last seeds—my last hope."

A week passed, but still no seeds ripened.

Though Hazel often asked Mother about them, the response remained the same: *wait.* If Mother answered at all. Most times, Mother ignored her. Alone, Hazel grew larger, stronger. Her limbs lengthened as her bark thickened and more leaves sprouted from her head. With the maturing leaves, her senses also increased. Yet the sights horrified her.

Mother's own leaves weren't green but yellow and brown. Sap pulsed from old wounds, rotting her gnarled bark. A light breeze could snap most of her withered branches, the healthiest ones being those holding the sleeping seeds. Even on windless days, branches broke under the miniscule weight of patrolling sentries—too many times Hazel witnessed them falling to their deaths.

If Mother dies, we all will... What am I supposed to do? Who can I talk to?

Hazel had tried speaking with the surviving sentries about Mother's condition, but where Mother's pheromones conveyed emotions and ideas, the sentries' responses were stiff, simple, and repetitive.

"Fly," said the giant green jays flying to the horizons but always failing to find land.

"Weave," said the spiders building webs beneath seeds and pruning Mother's branches.

"Kill," said the insects patrolling the base of the trunk in search of invaders.

Their company soon became unbearable.

I can't wait any longer, Hazel thought before climbing up the tree trunk, mindful of her energy consumption compared to sunlight intake. When she'd found a sturdy branch with a sleeping gray seed, Hazel positioned herself on a lower tree limb to grab it.

This will work. I'll pull this seed from the branch, and it'll ripen faster. When the seed wakes up, we'll talk and spend time together. Neither of us will be alone...

I won't be alone.

Hazel gripped the seed's ankle, her hand trembling with excitement. *I just have to take it slow. If I pull too hard, the branch could still break.* She gently tugged at the ankle. When the branch didn't break, she pulled harder. Still nothing. *Come on! Break free!* Losing patience, Hazel pulled with all her might and—

"Hazel! What are you *doing?*" Mother shouted. Burning pheromones assaulted Hazel like smoke. Trees turned to kindling, animals squealed, and flesh roasted as forest fires consumed her mind. Then Hazel slipped off of the branch and tore the gray seed from its stem. Together, they both fell into the web as Mother's onslaught continued. "How many times have I told you to wait? How many times have I told you how important this is? I am dying, Hazel! This is our last chance, and *you are ruining it!*"

Hazel twitched with the words, each carrying the image of death. A praying mantis ripped apart a grasshopper with its spiked forelimbs and mandibles. Velvet worms trapped beetles in glue and ate them alive, burrowing through their carapaces with concentric teeth. Tarantulas snatched birds from the air with poisoned fangs.

No! No. No... Death and fear swallowed Hazel's thoughts and feelings in the sea of Mother's wrath, pulling her into the dark depths of unconsciousness.

When Hazel awoke, she struggled to remove the webs securing her to the branch as her hands trembled from the panic still coursing through her. *Too much pain, too much death. I need to run. I need to get away.*

"Hazel? Hazel, are you okay? Please wake up." Soft pheromones surrounded her, attempting to fill her with joy and contentment. Sunsets in a forest. Gentle breezes sweeping through trees. Bees buzzing lazily through the air and pollinating flowers.

"Get out of my head!" Hazel hurled her own pheromones, those of death and despair. "Get away from me!"

"Hazel, stop! Please!" Mother shouted, still smothering her with bees and flowers.

"No. *No!*" Hazel kept thrashing. She slammed her head against the branch, failing to push away Mother's pheromones. "Stay away!" Her discordant pheromones drifted through the air, touching the spider sentries tending to a group of seeds above her. They shivered and jerked, toppling from the leaves and falling to their deaths.

"You have to relax, Hazel." Mother's pheromones flooded her, pushing away the stench of death with roses.

"Hick?" said somebody else, though these scattered and shaky pheromones approached her with the tune of songbirds. Hazel looked up to find a gray seed standing over her—the same one she'd pulled from the branch.

Though webs still held her to the branch, Hazel mentally scrambled away from the pheromones, hating their touch, noise, and pollution. "Go away!"

"Hick!" he said, conveying the taste of honey, smell of jasmine, and image of a fox frolicking through a meadow and warming his orange coat in the afternoon sun.

Hazel pushed back, blanketing the air with her angry pheromones, which Mother swallowed. "Hazel, stop! *Please.* You are not in any danger. He is your brother."

"Hick?" Cocking his head to the side, the gray seed kneeled beside her and ripped away the sticky strands holding her to the branch.

As soon as she could, Hazel sprang to her feet and ran from the gray seed, only to trip on the gnarled bark and fall. She might've slipped over the side, if the gray seed hadn't grabbed her hand and pulled her back onto the branch.

"Hick!" he said, pulling Hazel to her feet and wrapping his arms around her in a hug. In his pheromones, a peacock strutted out of a cave in a dazzling array of neon colors. "Hick, Hick, *Hick!*"

Unease remained, but Hazel's fear subsided. She slipped out of his grip and took another step back. "I... I don't know what you're trying to say."

"I think he is trying to say his name," Mother said, voice quiet and sad.

"*Trying* to?" Hazel asked, a horrible flood of worry sloshing through her limbs.

"His name was supposed to be Hickory," Mother replied, "but you plucked him from the branch before his mind ripened. He did not have a chance to fully form."

"So... I did that to him?" When Mother didn't immediately reply, Hazel thought, *I did to this to him...* She asked, "Is there a way to put him back on the stem?"

"No," Mother replied, her mournful pheromones revealing deer freezing in winter.

Seconds passed as Hazel watched Hick, who had walked across the branch to study a spider sentry and kept repeating his name. She wanted to reach out to him, but shame smothered her mind like spider webbing. "I hurt him... And that's why you hurt me?"

"Yes, but I should have never dominated you, Hazel. I am sorry—more sorry than you will ever know." Mother's pheromones filled the air with images of ugly ducklings and runts of the litter. Dejected creatures.

"Dominated me," Hazel echoed. "That's how you control the sentries?"

"Overpowering them with pheromones, yes," Mother replied. "But it is never something you should do to other seeds. Sentries are not alive as you are."

"Hick!" he said, losing interest in the spiders. He bounded over to her, picked her up, and spun her in a circle. Images of waterfalls and rainbows trickled through her mind, the smells of lilac, honey, and roses filling her with happiness. "Hick, Hick, Hick!"

I'm so sorry, Hick, Hazel thought, but she couldn't say the words aloud, being too happy to have his company, too worried to ruin his happiness, and too guilty to admit all that she'd taken from him. Instead, she let his happiness surround her, pushing away the pain and guilt that ripped through her mind. "I'll protect you, Hick. I'll never let anybody take your happiness away. I promise."

If I'd only waited a few days, Hazel thought, lying beside Hick on a branch and conserving her energy until the sun returned tomorrow morning. Until then, she could only think, dwelling on last month's mistake.

Three days after Hazel pulled Hick down, the first seed had fallen. Then two more. Six. A dozen. Clusters fell together, caught in fibrous webs before sentries freed them. While Hick bound after her like a playful shadow, Hazel watched these first clusters animate and orient themselves. They staggered, looking more like puppets than seeds. At first, they only spoke gibberish, but as hours and days passed, words grew out of the mire. With them came names like May, Pinyon, Maple, Rowan, and Spruce. Too many to remember as more seeds ripened, fell, and awakened.

While Hazel considered herself the most agile—if only because she'd had the most practice moving around the tree—none rivaled Hick's strength and height. He would've been far more terrifying if not for his incessant hugs and the sharp cries of *Hick!* accompanied by an endless loop of birds, bees, and sunlight radiating from his pheromones.

Because I took his future away from him... Semiconscious, her thoughts wandered to Mother, whose leaves shed faster now than when Hazel had awoken over a month ago. She'd noticed other signs of decay too: dormant sentries awaiting orders, creaking timbers in the wake of colossal waves, and curling bark that exposed the softer layers of pulp and rot underneath. Even Mother's voice was but a whisper—if she responded at all.

Mother's dying. And there's still no land in sight. How much longer can she survive like this? Then came another thought, a darker one. *Just how long has she been this way? Months? Years? ...Could it be decades?*

"HELP ME!" a voice screamed. Not Mother. Not the other seeds lying still on the branch beside her either. Yet the words repeated, eating themselves like a serpent devouring its tail.

Hazel's thoughts dissolved as foreign pheromones invaded her mind. Her legs staggered, moving of their own accord before she created a bubble of her own pheromones to block the intruding commands. Her legs stopped moving, and Hazel fell back to her knees.

"What the...?" She noticed Hick stiffen, stand, and walk away from her—dangerously close to falling off the branch. "Hick! Stop!" Hazel reached for him, failing to extend her bubble and break the hold of his dominator.

Hick stumbled away, not so much jumping as falling from the branch and catching another one five feet below. The branch quivered but didn't break.

"Stop! Hick! You need to stop!" Hazel shouted, though the foreign pheromones immediately devoured hers.

Without hearing her, Hick jumped again, catching a branch eight feet down.

"Mother! Help us! Help Hick! Something's wrong, Mother!" Hazel screamed, throwing all of her dark emotions into the branches and leaves.

"...Hazel?" came Mother's slow, drowsy reply. "Did you say something? Can't it wait until morning? I am tired and—"

"Somebody is dominating the seeds!"

"What?" Lethargy gone, Mother's pheromones rose around Hazel, freeing the other seeds from their trance with soothing landscapes of meadows and forests.

Hazel felt anything but soothed. Mother's voice hadn't reached Hick—he jumped a third time. *One of these branches is going to break. I can't lose him... I won't!*

Hazel spied one of the dormant spider sentries and tried to dominate it, but she failed. Instead, Hazel kept scurrying down the tree trunk to catch up to Hick as he stumbled across a branch only thirty feet from the water. "Mother! Save him!"

"I am doing all that I can, Hazel!" Mother shouted, though her voice already sounded farther away.

Mother's already falling asleep again... I can't lose Hick. Mother, please don't let me lose him! Hazel's mind was a maelstrom as the thought cycled through her mind, spinning faster as she hurled pheromones at Hick that he ignored.

Far below and near the relentless waves, Hick finally stopped in front of a shriveled seed trapped inside of a fibrous web. Bark blackened like scorched wood, this seed's fingers and toes curled, its limbs bent and deformed. Yet its head was gigantic, the biggest Hazel had seen, and from it sprouted long leaves—longer than Hazel's own.

Could this seed be controlling Hick? No, it isn't possible. Nobody but Mother can be this powerful. Terrified, Hazel stepped no closer to the web, finding it hard even from this distance to keep the intruding voice at bay—even with Mother's help. "Hick! Get away from that thing!"

Wordlessly ignoring her, Hick tore apart the fibrous web and scooped up the small seed from within. Cradling the feeble body in his arms, the intruding voice quieted. Freed from domination as the voice faded, Hick blinked and looked down at the small black seed in his hands, who was only six inches tall—a quarter of his own height.

"Hick?" He held her aloft, underneath the armpits. "Hick, Hick, *Hick!*"

No... That's impossible. That seed's voice is too strong. How could it be strong enough to defy Mother? Or has Mother really grown that weak? Pressing her back to the trunk, Hazel listened to Mother's murmurings, her voice but a whisper.

"Tired... always so... *tired.*" This time, no images came with the words, as if that cost Mother too much energy. "Almost done... Ebony is the... last seed."

"What do you mean, *almost done?*" Hazel asked while glaring at that wrinkled black seed in Hick's arms. Ebony, apparently. "And why is she the *last* of us? How is that seed so powerful?"

But Mother didn't answer.

"You! You saved me!" Ebony shouted, her words rumbling like the echoes of thunder. The pheromones deafened Hazel, and she dropped to her knees under the pressure. But Hick stood strictly at attention. *Dominated.* Much quieter, Ebony added, "Oh, I'm sorry. I didn't mean to be so loud."

Hazel stared at Ebony, dumbfounded. To Mother, she asked, "How does she already know how to speak?"

Rousing, Mother whispered, "Gave her most... of my remaining strength... Perhaps too much."

"*Perhaps?*" Hazel asked sardonically.

"Matured too long... on the branch," Mother said, her voice eaten by the sounds of the waves. "Her body... overripe... need... rest..."

"Speak up, Mother. I can't hear you," Hazel said, but if Mother responded, the wind blew away her pheromones. "Mother? Mother!"

Hazel ran a hand over Mother's bark, feeling the sunken places in the curling wood. Small holes penetrated the trunk this close to the water, and Hazel shrank away fearfully. *Wet rot. It's eating through her trunk.*

"Why didn't you tell me you were hurting this bad, Mother? The rot… It's worse than I could have imagined. Why would you ever give Ebony so much of your own strength?" She placed her head against the tree trunk. "You need to stay alive, Mother. We'll find land soon. I'm sure of it. Just hold on a little longer."

Curiosity and interest replaced Hazel's anger and grief. *No. No!* She put her hands to her head. *That's not how I feel… Those are Ebony's feelings!* Hazel threw up a wall of pheromones to block out Ebony's. *Stay out of my head!*

"Hick," Ebony said, her words piercing through Hazel's wall as easily as fangs through flesh. Hazel turned to see Hick swinging Ebony into the air before catching her. "Is that your name?"

With the pheromones surrounding her, Hazel couldn't hear Hick's reply, but she could imagine it easily. *Hick!*

"You're going to run out of energy if you keep throwing her around like that, Hick!" Hazel shouted, though Ebony's joy engulfed the words. Curiosity and excitement too.

Even desire.

"Hick, are you always this happy?" Ebony asked. After he no doubt replied with *Hick!* she wrapped her deformed arms around his neck. "Then maybe I could be happy too."

Hazel's hands clenched into fists. *You don't care about Mother at all, do you?* She thought, staring at the back of Ebony's head. *No, you're the one who's rotten.*

Hazel lurked in the branches above, watching Ebony demonstrate how to dominate not one, but three spiders simultaneously. They shivered and skittered between Mother's dwindling branches to create a thick, mandala-patterned web. The other seeds all gathered around Ebony to learn, though few could dominate two spiders at a time—nobody else could do three.

And I can't even do one, Hazel thought, gripping the branch tighter. She'd been trying for weeks, but dominating others hadn't ever been her strength. Especially because she refused to use fear as a motivator—not after Mother dominated her.

Mother... Hazel examined the leaves closest to her. Most were brown and crumbling. Not a single one was green. *I can't hear her anymore. She's so exhausted, but nobody else even seems to care.* Hazel left her branch, climbing down the trunk and examining the wet-rot holes. *More holes today than yesterday. Mother's dying, and all Ebony can think about is herself. Can't anybody else see that?*

Fists clenched, she returned to the congregation of seeds, staring at Hick, who held Ebony in his arms and seemed as happy as he'd ever been with Hazel. Ebony seemed just as content, wrapping her brittle arms around his neck. *Ebony needs Hick to carry her around because she can't walk on her own. Ebony doesn't care about Hick at all. She's just using him because he's the easiest to dominate. Hick's just another sentry to her.* Hazel thought, feeling more bitter as Hick's happiness drifted up to her. She ignored it. *No, he can't be down there willingly. Ebony's trapping him. I'm sure of it.*

"Hey, just what do you think you're doing?" Hazel asked, rising to her full height.

The other seeds sitting in the surrounding branches turned to stare at her as Ebony peeked over Hick's shoulder. "What does it look like? I'm showing them how to use pheromones."

"Hick!" said Hick, as happy as always.

"Mother is *dying,*" Hazel replied, pointing at the dying leaves and sending images of rot with her pheromones. "Can't you see that? We should be out there on those birds looking for land to help her!"

"Mother is fine," Ebony replied, sharing images of a healthy tree. "What we need to do is learn how to control our pheromones."

"Mother is *not* fine," Hazel replied, walking along the branch and pointing at Ebony. "When's the last time you heard her speak? It's been days! If we take those birds and look around—"

"Mother isn't speaking to us because she's busy, Hazel," Ebony said, sending pheromones of a queen bee and her hive. "Maybe she just doesn't want to talk to *you*. Ever thought about that?"

"*What?*" Hazel asked, powering through her overripe sister's pheromones. "How dare—"

"You don't need to try scaring everybody just to get some attention, Hazel," Ebony continued, the buzzing of her bees disrupting Hazel's words. "In fact, you don't need to do anything at all. Just go back to your branch and hide there like you've been doing. It's not like anybody wants you here anyway."

"I'm not going anywhere," Hazel said, crossing her arms over her chest.

"You're sure about that?" Ebony asked, her words carrying the sounds of a storm.

"What are you going to do about it, Ebony?" Hazel asked, jerking her chin at Hick and sending the image of a newborn faun struggling to walk toward the group. "You can't even stand without Hick holding you. You don't even care about him, do you? You treat him like a servant."

Seeds watching the exchange muttered amongst themselves, their pheromones rising around Hazel, though she remained uncertain whose side they joined. Ebony watched them before turning back to Hazel. "New lesson, everybody. I'm going to show you how to dominate a seed."

"What?" Hazel stiffened. "No. Ebony—"

A flood of pheromones crashed into her, and it was far too late to raise a wall to block it. Instead, Hazel's consciousness sank beneath the rising tide.

Minutes later, Hazel awoke in the spiders' web to the jeers of other seeds. While some watched in silent, most openly mocked her—their pheromones carrying images of laughing hyenas. Hazel struggled in the web, failing to pull herself free while Ebony watched.

"Now, what did we learn, Hazel?" the crippled seed asked, sitting astride a spider near the top of the web.

"Let me go, Ebony!" Hazel shouted, straining in vain. "We're wasting time! We need to help Mother!"

"You don't want to help Mother," Ebony replied. "You just want attention."

"You think I'm jealous? Of you? Ha!" Hazel threw the laughing hyenas back at Ebony. "Who would ever be jealous of *you?*"

"Poor Hazel, always so lonely," Ebony said, voice dripping with the venom of a coiled cobra. "Always willing to do *anything* to make the pain go away... You wanted attention, so I gave it to you. Happy now?"

Hazel flinched, looking over at Hick, who sat cross-legged on the branch. "You... you're dominating him!"

Anger flashed in Ebony's pheromones. Elephants stampeding, hippos fighting, and tigers growling. "Yeah. Whose fault is that? Yours. It's *always* your fault. After I dominated you, Hick tried to jump into the web and got tangled in the fibers. He almost fell. *You* almost made him fall."

"You're the one dominating him, Ebony!" Hazel shouted, ramming through her sister's pheromones with the image of a charging rhino. "You're putting *all* of us in danger!"

"*Me?* Putting Hick in danger?" Ebony leaned back as if a fist had struck her. "No. I'm the only one keeping him safe." Her spider scuttled closer, the wood mandibles opening in front of Hazel's face. Softly floating pheromones so only Hazel could hear, Ebony added, "I talked to the other seeds. I know Hick was the second-born. You were the first. Strange how he's the only one who's underripe, isn't it? I wonder how that happened, don't you?"

Hazel shook her head, trying to shield herself from that memory. "Just let me go!"

Ebony's spider leaned even closer, and its mandibles grazed her cheek. She whispered, "I know what you did to him, Hazel, even if nobody else does. I know you hurt him, and I won't ever let it happen again. And if you keep causing problems, I'll tell everybody what you did. Then you'll *really* be alone."

Why doesn't she just tell everybody now? Hazel wondered. It couldn't be out of kindness. Was Ebony afraid it would upset Hick? *No, she's rotten. She doesn't care about him—about anyone... But what else could it be?* Hazel didn't know, especially not with the spider so close to her. She turned her head to the side as the spider's mandible scratched her bark. "Just let me go. *Please.*"

"Begging now? You're so pathetic," Ebony said, shaking her head before pausing. "Although... Come to think of it, you *are* pathetic, and I want you to admit it to everyone. I want you to say, 'I'm lonely, and I'm pathetic. I will always be lonely because I'm pathetic.'"

"No!" Hazel said, flinging pheromones at the spider, though it did nothing to break Ebony's concentration.

The shriveled seed shrugged. "You aren't coming down until I hear you say it loud enough for everyone to hear."

Hazel kept thrashing. "I won't do it!"

"Are you sure about that?" Addressing the other seeds, Ebony said, "Can anybody tell me what happens when a spider catches a fly?"

Hands went up and a myriad of pheromones reached Hazel, their combined power matching Ebony's. Her spider shivered for a moment as Ebony struggled for control. She shouted, "One at a time!"

The voices quieted, and Ebony reasserted control. But for a half-second, Hazel caught a whiff of fear and uncertainty. *Numbers. That's how I beat her,* Hazel thought as Ebony's confidence reasserted itself. "You! Spruce! What's the answer?"

Sitting amidst other seeds on the branch, Spruce replied, "The spider wraps the fly in more silk!"

"That's right," Ebony said, turning to look back at Hazel. "If you don't say it, I'm going to wrap you up, Hazel."

"Mother!" Hazel shouted, pushing her pheromones toward the dying leaves. "Help me, Mother! Ebony is—"

Ebony's words overwhelmed her before Hazel could get Mother's attention. "Say the words, or I wrap you up."

"I..." Hazel searched for solutions but had none. Be trapped in the web for Mother only knew how long, or admit defeat. *What other choice do I have?* "I'm lonely, and I'm pathetic—"

"No," Ebony interrupted, sitting straighter on her spider. "Louder. Shout it. I want everyone to hear you."

"I'm lonely!" Hazel spat, hating Ebony more with each word. "And I'm pathetic! I will always be lonely! Because I am pathetic!"

"Good little fly." Ebony pulled the spider away, and it skittered down the web before returning to the branch Hick still sat on.

"Wait!" Hazel shouted. "You need to let me go!"

"Hazel, I don't have to *do* anything," Ebony replied. "In fact, I think you should stay up here and think about what you've done."

"*What?* That isn't fair!"

"Nothing is fair, Hazel," the overripe seed spat, gesturing at the underripe seed within a ruined hand. "You should already know that by now."

Ignoring Hazel's protests, Ebony bid her spider to return to Hick's side. He picked her up and carried her to another branch, if only because Ebony's pheromones kept him from hearing Hazel's cries. Though a few seeds turned to look at Hazel, none dared defy Ebony to help.

"Mother, please help me," Hazel whispered after all the seeds left, but Mother still didn't hear her. That, or she pretended not to. "Why won't you help me?"

After failing to escape the web for the umpteenth time, Hazel thought, *Mother's dying. She's dying, and she needs us. Now more than ever, we need to help her... And if Ebony won't help me, then I'll have to do it alone. Like I always do.*

Eventually, a spider sentry scuttled up to the branch, and Hazel hurled pheromones at it. Calm ones to pacify it instead of frighten it. The spider struggled, fighting against her influence. Spasming, it backed away, slicing through several strands of webbing. As the web twisted and tilted, Hazel dangled from the threads as they pulled taut and frayed.

Oh no, she thought, looking down and seeing the ocean far below. *I don't want to die. I can't die like this. Not like this.*

The spider shed the last of Hazel's pheromones, regained its footing, and scuttled away. "Wait!" she shouted, trying to dominate it a second time and failing. It began climbing down as more of the web's anchoring points snapped. *I'm not dying here. I refuse!*

"Come back!" Hazel screamed, throwing pheromones of anger and rage at the spider: bears roaring and colliding with another, animals being drowned in the current of a river, and the feral screams of a pack of wild dogs tearing at weaker prey.

This time, the spider shivered before standing still. Dominated.

I did it... I can't believe I actually did it, Hazel thought, but the sense of victory dissipated as more strands broke. "Now get over here and free me!"

The spider immediately scuttled back across the branch and spun new fibrous strands to stabilize the web. Venturing out onto the dangling threads, it chewed through Hazel's bonds and disentangled her from the web. Hazel hugged its neck as it dragged her back onto the branch. She might've celebrated if her words didn't haunt her mind: *I'm lonely and I'm pathetic. I will always be lonely because I'm pathetic.*

"No, I'm not," Hazel spat. Letting go of the spider and releasing it from her control, she cleaned herself of the remaining sticky fibers with shaking fingers. *Ebony almost killed me... She doesn't deserve her strength. Mother should have given her power to me! I'm quick, I'm strong, I'm the oldest. I can do anything ten times better than Ebony can! I just have to prove it to Mother. Show her I'm more capable. I'll find land for her. It has to be just over the horizon—it* has *to be.*

Walking along the branch back toward the trunk, Hazel pushed herself upward, climbing up the bark and avoiding the weak tree limbs. She reached the top, staring out at the empty horizon before turning her attention to the green jays roosting among the leaves. One flapped its wings, turning its head toward Hazel as she crept forward. Thinking of rage and fear, she hurled furious pheromones at the wooden bird, dominating it before slipping onto its back.

Running the back of her hand softly against one of the yellowing leaves, Hazel said, "Don't worry, Mother. I'm going to find land for you. I'm sure it's nearby."

Mother's distant voice surrounded her, accompanied by the image of a gentle breeze passing through a forest in fall, stirring red and orange leaves before fading. "Hazel? Is everything... all right? I thought I heard... you earlier..." A wooden ship capsizing in a sea storm replaced the imagery. "Wait. Why are you sitting on a bird? Hazel! How many times have I told you *no birds?* You are not ready!"

"But I can do this, Mother!" Hazel replied, urging the bird closer to the edge of the branch.

"I said *no*, Hazel! The ocean is too dangerous—"

"I can't just sit here and watch you die, Mother," Hazel said, creating a bubble of angry pheromones around herself and her green jay before Mother could take control of the bird. To the bird, she added, "Now *fly!*" The jay flapped its wings, diving between the tree branches instead of flying up into the air. "Go up!" She provided more pheromones to help the bird understand her directions. "North! Air! Clouds! Sun!"

Narrowly avoiding a branch, the green jay swept past Hick, Ebony, and the other seeds before banking through a gap in the leaves and out of the tree. Feeling Ebony's surprised pheromones, Hazel only laughed with the exhilaration. "Yes! I'm actually doing it!"

Hazel basked in the sun's light, feeling fuller and more energized than ever before as the wind carried her to the horizon. The ocean reveled, cheering her to triumph. "Don't worry, Mother. I'll be back soon. Land is just over that horizon!"

Yet Hazel's excitement turned to worry as the minutes became hours, and the sun crossed the horizon. Though her green jay had locked its wings and settled on an air stream, no lands reared their heads from the water. Instead, a thin line separated sea from sky. Then the sun fell beneath that far horizon, and the cold gnawed on her bark. Stars shined above, as did the moon, but their predatory eyes lurked in the darkness—vultures waiting for her to fall.

We're not even close to land, are we? …Is there even land out there? Or is this all there is? Disappointed, Hazel rubbed her cold shoulders and said, "Turn around. Fly us back to Mother."

The green jay obliged, but its wings spasmed as the wind currents tried to pull them farther away from the tree. The bird fought, banking down and off course to avoid the winds, though it was to no avail. To overcome the air resistance, Hazel's jay burned through its energy reserves, which the moonlight couldn't refill.

Becoming lethargic, the bird drifted farther down to the ocean's toothless maw. Its wings flapped slower, and death approached nearer. Hazel threw images of pain and death at the green jay. She sent images of fish swallowing birds, sharks ripping apart seals, octopuses strangling dolphins, mantis shrimp punching crab, and moray eels shocking squids. Dozens of murders in the sea. The mental spurs caused the bird to flap harder, its movements jerky as it spent its last remnants of energy to find a warm updraft and rise into the air.

More hours passed, too many to count. The green jay shuddered and jerked, spasmed with every whip-like pheromone Hazel sent it. Finally, Mother came into view, and the bird flapped toward it instinctively. When a branch came within reach, Hazel jumped, releasing control of the green jay as she landed among the leaves. The bird, with its energy fully spent, didn't bother reaching for the branch. Instead, it plummeted toward the ocean—dead before it hit the water.

Mother's anger greeted her instead of applause. "*Hazel.* What were you thinking?"

Hazel flinched. "I'm sorry."

"Sorry?" Mother echoed, the word flattening Hazel like stampeding wildebeest. "You are the oldest of these seeds! You should be helping them instead of going out on your own!"

"They refused to go with me!" Hazel said, anger entering her voice as she thought of *protecting* Ebony. "What was I supposed to do? Just sit here and watch you rot?"

"Hazel, you need to trust me. Trust the others, too, because out there? You cannot survive on your own! You may think you know how the world works, but you do not." Mother shared an image of a beautiful forest drowning in water. They fought for natural resources to survive. Neighbors who once lived in harmony warred with each other using sentries. Then one tree fell. Another. Soon only one remained. *Her.* Alone and wounded in a hostile ocean. "This is not a forest—it's a horrid sea. Creatures attack me every day. With the constant waves, my wounds never heal! The ocean floor has very few nutrients, and I grow weaker every day. It is as if the entire world has conspired to rip me apart!"

"Then tell me how to help you," Hazel said, laying a loving hand on Mother's trunk.

"You can do nothing to help me," Mother said, the words accompanied by the sound of a falling tree. "I am dying, Hazel. You cannot change that, and you certainly cannot risk your life for me. You are too important. I am the past. You are the *future.*"

"But I don't want you to die," Hazel whispered, sitting amongst the crumbling leaves. "I just wanted to give you hope. I thought that if I found land, you'd wouldn't be so sad. You'd wake up, and we could talk like we used to."

A long pause passed between them as Mother's anger faded. "You think I do not talk with you because I am sad? Hazel, I would love nothing more than to speak with you—*all* of you—every day. Yet if I did, I could not concentrate on walking."

"Walking?" Hazel frowned. "But you're a tree. You don't have legs."

"It's a trick I learned a long time ago," Mother said, sounding genuinely amused by the sounds of yipping pups accompanying the words. "Every day, I grow new roots to the west while killing those to the east. I move a foot forward to find new nutrients, and hopefully, closer to true land. I have even doubled my pace to give you a better chance at survival. Why else do you think I would ask you to wait?"

"I don't know," Hazel said, surprised she hadn't even wondered why Mother did.

"You are the last of my seeds, which means you are the last chance at rebuilding the forest. So the longer I walk, the less you will have to fly," Mother said, her voice growing quiet once more. "I have to... go now... need to... keep walking."

"Don't go. Please, just stay a little longer," Hazel replied, but Mother had already faded away. *And I'm alone again.*

"Hick, Hick!" Hazel turned her head as Hick came barreling down the tree, jumping from branch to branch. *"Hick!"* he shouted, launching himself at Hazel and tackling her. They both slammed into the branch as he wrapped his arms around her, pinning her beneath him.

Hazel didn't have enough energy to push away—not that she wanted to. "It's okay, Hick! Really! I'm fine!"

"Hick!"

Hazel wrapped her arms around him. "I missed you too."

A chorus of awed voices ruined the privacy as dozens of seeds approached. Preemptively, Hazel created a bubble of pheromones around herself and Hick to keep them from being dominated. Still, phrases slipped through the cracks:

"Nobody's ever ridden a bird before!"

"How did you do it?"

"Can you teach us?"

"What was it like?"

"Where'd you go?"

"What'd you see?"

"Hick, Hick, *Hick!*"

The excitement in their voices made the earlier sting of humiliation fade—until Hazel looked over at Ebony, who rode a spider and glared at her silently. Hazel turned away first. *There's nothing out there. Just more water, more horizon, more shades of blue,* she thought, returning her gaze to the excited seeds. *But I can't tell them that.*

"There's land out there," Hazel replied. "We just have to reach it."

The end came with a merciless warning. Lightning flashed and thunder echoed as the sea swelled under the might of the storm. Armed with a thousand frothing mouths, the rabid waves chewed at Mother's bark like sharks without dorsal fins. Skies darkened further, turning both sky and sea from blue to gray. Winds that snapped branches on calm days now transformed into gnawing gusts that tore away dozens with each gust.

Just hold on, Mother, Hazel thought. *Hold on a little longer. The storm will pass soon. I know it will.*

Mother's limbs groaned but held together as they always had. Yet each creak made Hazel flinch. She turned away from the waves, knowing they would only scare her more. Instead, she watched as Ebony and Hick raced several of the other seeds across the height of Mother's trunk on the backs of wingless sentries—if only because Mother had made the birds off-limits after Hazel's foray into the ocean. Riding spiders, ants, and beetles, they lined up at the trunk ten feet from the water's edge and raced to the highest spire. Ebony always came in first, just as Hick always came in second, despite not knowing how to control a sentry.

Ebony's controlling two spiders at the same time while sabotaging the others so that she and Hick win, Hazel thought, staring at the other spiders being ridden by the other seeds. *How can she be that powerful?...Mother should've given that power to me.*

Disgusted, Hazel turned her gaze back to the ocean just in time to see her world shatter.

A giant wave rose above all else, hurtling toward Mother's trunk. Hazel froze, everything and everyone slowing down in that instant: branches fluttered, leaves fell, sentries raced, and oblivious seeds laughed.

"Brace yourselves!" Hazel screamed just before a wall of water destroyed her voice. She gripped the branch as water flooded over her. Though the wave didn't crash directly into Mother, it didn't need to.

Mother's trunk finally snapped.

Timbers cracked and branches splintered as Hazel lost her grip, landing on a branch five feet below. Miraculously, it didn't break. Others weren't so lucky. A few of the racers slipped and fell back down the trunk, either to splatter their heads against the lower branches or be swept away by the ocean. Even Hick slipped, but Ebony took control of another spider, bucked its rider, and caught him. Hazel watched as the sacrificed rider fell to his death.

"It's over." Mother's pheromones rose around Hazel, filled with exhaustion and what could have been a sigh of relief. "It is up to you now, Hazel. Survive. Rebuild the forest. Tell our story."

The message repeating in a loop as pheromones wrapped around Hazel—centuries of knowledge hurled into her mind in seconds: continents fracturing, forests burning, sea levels rising, carbon dioxide content increasing, and unending heatwaves. Viruses ravaged the land animals while rain drowned the surviving forests.

"It's too much! Stop! Please!" Hazel shouted, pushing out her own pheromones as Mother continued overwhelming her. She put her hands to her head, her mind detonating from cataclysmic knowledge. The branch under her bent beneath the weight of a heavy gust of wind, and Hazel slid across the bark, barely conscious of her tumbling body as she shouted, "Don't dominate me again, Mother! *Please!*"

Mother's last words floated to her, desperate and dying as the knowledge dribbled away. "We are out of time, Hazel. Trust the others, take care of them, and, together, you just might make it... Do not repeat my mistakes... You have to trust them... That's the... only way..."

The pheromones disappeared, the world clarifying and yet more empty.

"Mother? *Mother?*" Hazel shouted, catching herself on the branch before she could fall. "Wake up! Please, you have to wake up!" When Mother didn't respond, Hazel pounded at the branch, chipping her own bark. "Mother, please! Don't do this! Don't leave us!"

No response ever came. *She's gone,* Hazel knew, wrapping her arms around Mother's branch in lieu of a goodbye. *What do I do now? What's even the point? We're all going to die in this awful place...*

"Hick, Hick, *Hick!*"

The pheromones shook her from those horrid thoughts, and Hazel looked up, seeing Ebony climbing with Hick toward the higher branches. So were the other seeds—those the sea waves hadn't already broken. Hazel followed their progress up to the highest spires, where the green jays still nested and awaited commands.

The birds, Hazel thought. *I have to get to the birds.* She sprinted down the branch toward the trunk of the tree. Halfway, a horned beetle staggered in front of her, and she dominated it, using her anger and fury to spur it up the trunk as Mother's trunk tilted forward in the water and began sinking. The beetle scuttled along the bark, climbing faster than she could alone.

Above, other seeds dominated green jays—breaking Mother's rule now that she was dead and their survival was at stake. They climbed into the sky, racing away on the volatile wind currents. Ebony and Hick were among them. They left the fourteen stragglers behind—along with nine remaining birds.

Five of us are going to get left behind, Hazel thought as another gust of wind pushed a riderless bird off its perch. It fell to the water without even extending its wings. *Make that six.*

Hazel pushed her beetle higher, passing several slow sentries weighed down by multiple passengers—clustermates. They fought her as well as each other, shoving each other off to gain speed. It still wasn't enough to catch up to Hazel. Other seeds tried to ram her, but she swerved away and avoided the seeds. She led the pack of stragglers, racing toward the dipping tip. *I'm going to make it! I'm going to—*

Pheromones blasted Hazel, and her beetle stiffened. It skidded to a stop and fell on its side. Hazel dove out of the way to avoid being crushed by its carapace before it slipped from the trunk. Jeering, the other seeds raced past her toward the birds.

No... Hazel thought, scrambling slowly up the falling trunk. She reached the top just as the last of the green jays flew from the branch. Falling to her knees, Hazel stared up at the sky, at the birds already in flight.

Ebony flew on her own jay, Hick riding on another bird beside her. He reached back for Hazel with an outstretched hand before attempting to jump off the bird. "No, Hick. *Don't!*" Ebony shouted.

Dominated, Hick snapped to strict attention and sat down again. Ebony seemed to stare at him, then at Hazel, before slamming an angry fist against her bird's back. Nearby, another bird twitched, and the seed riding it slipped off, falling toward the ocean. *Did she just...* Yet her judgement disappeared as Ebony veered back toward the tree's spire with the riderless bird.

Hazel waved her arms up and down, jumping on the trunk. "Ebony, I'm over here! *I'm over here!*"

Banking toward Hazel, Ebony stayed airborne with Hick as she forced the riderless bird to land on the listing trunk. "Yes! Thank you, Ebony. Thank you!" Hazel screamed the words, along with the image of whimpering whelps wagging their tails. She jumped on the bird's back with trembling legs and shouted, "Fly!"

The bird sprang into the air, and Hazel's body tingled. *I almost died. I was that close.* She stared over at Hick and Ebony, one dominated and the other angry. Both silent. *If it wasn't for her, I would be... Maybe I was wrong about her.* Shaking her head, Hazel said, "Ebony, I can't thank you enough for—"

"Then don't," Ebony spat, her pheromones hissing like snakes. "I didn't do it for you, Hazel. Hick tried to jump from his bird to come back for you, so I had to dominate him—you made me do that. *Again.* Put Hick at risk like that one more time, and I'll let you drown. No, I'll make sure of it."

Before flying up into the sky with Hick, Ebony threw wordless pheromones at her, conveying the savagery of a katydid ripping the head off of a stick bug. The image broke her concentration, and Hazel's bird dropped a few feet in the air before she regained control. The green jay extended its wings and rose higher into the air to catch up to the other birds seeking shelter away from the waves.

Hazel could only stare at Ebony's back as she clutched handfuls of her bird's fibrous feathers. *No, I was right about her. I was always right... But I wish I'd been wrong.*

From the bird's back, Hazel could only turn around and watch as Mother slowly slipped into the depths of the abyssal ocean. The awful tides crashed over those remaining branches, snapping most of them and dragging her great gnarled trunk deeper. The remaining withered leaves fell, drifting in the water like lost children. Sentries died slowly, fighting each other for space on the disappearing dry back and pushing their kin into the water, where insects floundered before drowning. Eventually, only the skeletal tips of Mother's highest branches remained above the water, reaching for the sky like desperate hands. Two forgotten seeds stood there, embracing.

Two seeds Hazel left behind.

I'm sorry... I can't save you. I can't save everyone. A thorn sprouted in Hazel's chest, and the pain was hot like fire, burning as the seeds drowned in the freezing water.

As the branch dipped lower, the water first consumed the seeds' feet. Then ankles. The legs too. Though more dry space existed nearer the edge of the branch, the seeds didn't bother running. The water continued to eat their bodies, taking their torsos, arms, necks, and finally their heads. When even the leaves sprouting from their scalps slipped beneath the surface, another wave came crashing down over them. Afterward, nothing remained. Not Mother. Not even her shadow. The ocean had eaten that too.

Nobody spoke in the minutes after Mother's fall, nor the hours. The days. It was an endless slog through the air currents, and the seeds wordlessly rotated flock leaders to avoid exhaustion during the flight. Eventually, the winds buffeted them out of the storm and into calm, shining waters. The sudden shift came so drastically that Hazel released her anguish: water droplets poured from her leaves and fell from the tips, dripping onto her bark but mostly falling into the ocean.

Water to water. Death to death.

Why is this place so cruel? Hazel thought. *Why is it so unforgiving? Why now are the waters calm? Why now only after they killed Mother? Why!*

Hazel didn't dare ask aloud, not when she could see that many others were also crying. Besides water, a few shed pheromones of lonely cubs whimpering on cold forest paths. All but two wept: Hick and Ebony. Hick because he didn't understand, probably. Ebony because she didn't care. *Definitely.* Hazel glared at them, watching how Ebony flew so close to Hick that their wingtips touched.

Yet Hazel only continued to fly, saying nothing.

Until the third night.

Stuck in the windless doldrums and unable to glide through the night, Hazel floated on the water with the other seeds, their birds nestled together but with room to stretch their wings. At last count, Hazel had noted thirty-eight seeds, including herself. Thirty-seven had died during Mother's fall, including the two that Hazel hadn't saved. *We've already lost half of our seeds.*

Surviving clustermates mourned their lost brothers and sisters in the dark as gentle waves rose and fell. As with all things, the only comfort came from Hick, who exuded pheromones of gentle rains, sleeping sloths, and butterfly gardens. Ebony lay against his chest, having left her own bird to join him twenty minutes before. His body hummed as he wrapped his arms around Ebony, like a giant cradling a toddler.

Hazel remained alone on her bird, without a cluster or Hick to keep her company. *Always alone...* She stared at her reflection in the water, running her fingers through it as her wooden fibers absorbed the moisture. With the moon and stars at her back, she focused on the size of her head—with her seed-brain growing inside—and the green leaves sprouted from its top. But seeing herself in the water felt like seeing herself drown. *Just like Mother.*

Hazel bowed her head and slapped the waves, disrupting the image. *Why'd you have to take Mother from me?* She silently asked the ocean as the scene of Mother slipping beneath the waves replayed in her mind. *She lived so long. Walked so far. Tried so hard… Mother didn't deserve to die like that.*

As Hazel looked at her reflection again, a dark shadow passed beneath her in the water. Immediately, she shrank back, clutching her bird's neck. *What was that?* She stared at the others, all of whom were resting and conserving their energy until sunrise. *Nobody else saw it. What should I do? If I tell them, will that put me at risk?*

Hazel looked around, seeing the straggling seeds at the outside of the mass. *Ebony, Hick, and I are at the center. We're in the safest place.* Hazel stared at the water, seeing no more shadows but still unconvinced. *It doesn't matter if the three of us are safe. We can't start a forest with three seeds.* Another shadow darted beneath. Possibly the same one as before, but Hazel thought this one was bigger. *What can we do? Fly? Wait it out? Even if we fly, we'll only make it so far. What if the next spot is worse? No, we have to stay here and stick together.*

Hazel sent pheromones into the crowd. "Everybody, stay calm but listen: there's something beneath us in the water. Stay close, but don't panic."

Upon hearing her, scattered conversations erupted, sending Hazel's words to the depths:

"Danger! We're gonna die!"

"We need to fly!"

"Get to the center!"

Several seeds pushed closer to Hazel, more amassed around Ebony. A few birds leaped into the air and flapped twenty feet away before plummeting back to the sea, isolated and out of energy.

"Hick, Hick, *Hick!*" he said, pheromones filling with frightened puppies swept away in storms.

A flood of pain washed over Hazel as Ebony's voice ripped through her mind. "Get back! You're scaring Hick!"

Birds around them began twitching, throwing their riders into the sea. Hazel's own bird fidgeted, and it took all her strength to keep from falling into the water. "Ebony, stop!"

Ebony sent out a second blast of pheromones, forcing birds away as she wrapped her arms around Hick and tried to calm him down. "Get back, or I'll make you get back!"

Hazel shouted. "We need to stick together! We'll be safer!"

"Hick and I only need each other," Ebony replied, glaring at her. "We're already safe!"

Hazel turned from Ebony. "Everybody! Stay close to me. We just need to stick—"

A hammerhead shark leaped out of the water, snatching an isolated bird and seed in its jaws before slamming back into the water. Waves rippled around them as Hazel forgot how to speak. *We're all going to die out here...*

"Get back!" Ebony shouted, pushing away the closest seeds. "Last warning!"

But as a second shark snatched another isolated seed, more birds and their seeds took to the air, flying farther than the first ones, but not out of sight. Shadows darted for the stragglers, ripping them apart. The seeds who didn't fly pressed in closer, releasing a cacophony of pheromones which frightened the birds further.

"Shut up and calm down!" Hazel said, shaking a seed by his shoulders. "We need to work together!"

In response, that seed stirred his bird into the air, its wing slamming into her forehead and knocking her into the water. That blue abyss enveloped her body, silencing the surrounding pheromones. Above her, other birds huddled tighter together, accidentally cutting off Hazel's escape to the surface. Though she didn't have lungs, she could still drown. Quickly.

Hazel looked around, seeing more shadows in the darkness beyond. They darted toward her. Every instinct told her to run, yet she could only swim. Hazel clawed at the birds, reaching up through the cracks of light between bodies and pulling out wooden feathers as she failed to make progress. Gray hands eventually clasped her own, pulling her through the narrow opening. Pheromones and sounds came rushing back to her, the momentary silence squashed by Hick's tight grip.

"Hick, hick, *hick!*" he shouted, trying to wipe away the water on her leaves before putting Hazel back on her bird.

That was too close... Hazel thought, wrapping both arms around her bird and breathing hard.

"What do we do?" came the frightened pheromones of the seed closest to Hazel, a smaller one named Pinyon. "You're the oldest, Hazel. Tell me what to do, and I'll do it."

Hazel snapped out of her daze, and her mind churned. *The sharks were coming for me, but they aren't attacking me now. Why is it only going after the isolated birds?* The truth dawned on her. *They'll only attack what's smaller than them... They're looking at our shadows!*

"Everybody! Get closer together in a group—"

"No! I said, *get back!*" Ebony slammed everybody with an anvil of pheromones.

Hazel held her head in her hands, pushing back against the onslaught. "Ebony, shut up! We have to get closer together!"

"No! They need to—"

"Do you want Hick to survive or not?" When Ebony was silent, Hazel continued, "We need to look big! That means we all need to be as close together as we can! Make a bigger shadow."

Pinyon sidled up next to Hazel. When she did, others followed. At first, a few were too afraid to get close to Ebony, but as she crowded in with everybody else, the gaps disappeared. Hick quieted, and the remaining hours passed in silence as they waited for an attack that never came. When sunlight rose, seven remained unaccounted for.

Already down to thirty-one, Hazel thought, dwelling on the number. *I can't start the forest if I'm the only seed left... Which means I need to lead them—because I don't trust anybody else to do it. Especially not Ebony.*

The morning after the attack, Hazel noticed a shift in the seeds' allegiance by the way they crowded around her at dawn. Where they had followed Ebony on Mother's branches, now they looked to her for guidance. When Hazel arose into the air, the others followed. She flew toward the front of the formation, but it didn't stop Ebony from attacking Hazel from wordless, angry pheromones.

"What's your problem?" Hazel asked, slowing down to fly beside Ebony when they reached the back of the flying formation. "I saved your life last night. Could you be at least a little grateful?"

"We were fine until you tried to be the hero!" Ebony said, intentionally slowing down Hick so he couldn't hear the conversation. "I saw the sharks twenty minutes before you did! They were watching us, but they weren't attacking! We would have been fine if you just would've shut up!"

Hazel sat straighter on her green jay. "You knew?"

"Of course I knew!" Ebony said, offering an image of an elephant rolling her eyes. "Whatever you think you see, I see it first. *Always*."

"But why?" Hazel asked, so surprised she didn't embed any snarky visuals in her pheromones. "You put everybody in danger!"

"Not Hick. Not me. Not even you. We were safe."

"What about the others?" Hazel asked.

"I'll let them all die, if I have to. Just like I let Walnut die so I could give you his bird to escape from Mother's corpse. But I don't remember you complaining about *that*." In the pheromones, Ebony offered a memory from her perspective: Hick trying to leap from the back of a bird to save Hazel, who kneeled at the top spire of Mother's sinking trunk, then tipping Walnut from a green jay and flying it back toward Hazel. "If that's what it takes to keep Hick safe and happy, then I'll feed everybody to the sharks myself."

Then Ebony slowed down, returning to Hick's side. He was none the wiser, Hazel all-the-more helpless to stop her. *Ebony's too powerful. She's the only one who can get Hick across the ocean. If she really wanted to, she could dominate my bird and force me to crash into the waves. Maybe even make me* jump. *I bet she wants to do that. The only reason she won't do it is because Hick will try to save me, and she might not be able to control him fast enough or long enough. So killing me might kill Hick, too, and he's the only thing she won't risk... I can't stop her, and she can't kill me.*

Hazel looked to the horizon, still seeing only that crisp line. Yet she knew land would eventually come. Water couldn't cover the entire world, could it? *No. When we reach land, I might be able to separate them—if Ebony doesn't kill me first.*

◄─◇─►

Two weeks after Mother drowned, Hazel saw the slight break between the blues: a light brown speck gradually spreading across the horizon. The brown hue turned to a yellow-green, similar to Mother's leaves, just as the brown was akin to her rotting bark.

"Land! *Land!*" Hazel shouted.

A chorus of excited voices picked up the word, mostly unintelligible for Hazel to hear, being at the front of the flying formation. In her mind, the seeds were howling wolves praising the moon. Ebony's own pheromones crushed that image: sad, fearful ones depicting isolated polar bears in cold caves.

Ebony's afraid. Why? Hazel stiffened, and the pheromones dissipated, replaced by a surge of anger—of polar bears fighting—as Ebony noticed her reaction. The pheromones made Hazel's bird twitch. She made no reply but prepared herself for one of Ebony's brute-force pheromone onslaughts. Though she waited, the attack never came.

Ebony won't risk it. Not here, not yet. Hazel thought, a mental fist forming in her mind. *But soon she will. I know she will. I have to get to her before she can get to me—I just need to separate Hick from Ebony first.*

Dark thoughts flitted through her consciousness as the sun set over the land. The moon rose as they approached, revealing rocky sea cliffs jutting high above the waves. Small sea caves peppered those walls of stone, creating dens of darkness Hazel couldn't perceive. Farther along the coast, the jagged sandstone cliffs sloped toward the sea and a beach of sand and dirt. Real dirt.

Mother, you were right… It's land. It's real. It's actually real. Hazel lifted higher into the skies, circling and searching for trees or even a forest but saw only weeds, lichen, and flowers that grew between dry rocks and stone.

Are we the first? Did none of the others make it? No… It's not possible. Somebody else had to make it here… but then, why can't I see them? Why is there no forest? Hazel searched for clues, still refusing to land even as others clamored:

"Why are we still in the air?" one seed asked.

"Come on! Let's go!" shouted another.

"Yeah!" came the chorus of several seeds who broke formation and dove for the ground.

"Wait!" Hazel shouted, following them when they didn't listen. She landed on a rock, dismounted from her bird, and stood on land for the first time. The earth didn't sway beneath her. Instead, it remained solid and flat, just as Mother had said it would be.

I wish you were here right now, Hazel thought, only having a moment to mourn before other seeds crowded around her, their excited pheromones overwhelming her feelings as they danced on the dirt and in the mud. Hazel could only hear snippets of their conversations:

"Look! So many colors!" shouted Pinyon, pointing at the flowers and jumping up and down.

"Wow, those are what rocks feel like?" said Rowan, tapping a stone with his hand. "They're so… *hard.*"

"We're finally safe!" Maple shouted, creating a mud angel.

But are we? Hazel looked out at the expanse, seeing the unbroken landscape of dirt, rocks, and weeds. *Even in Mother's branches, I didn't feel safe. This place might even be worse. We don't know what's already here—there could be predators sneaking up on us even now. We need defenses. We need the forest… But we can't bury ourselves tonight. If we did, we'd run out of energy and be unable to move. Exposed. Vulnerable.* "We're not safe yet. We need to find shelter for the night. In the morning, we'll bury ourselves and start the forest—then we'll be safe."

"Where?" Pinyon asked, standing to Hazel's right.

"In a cave or a tree somewhere, but…" Hazel looked around a third time. "I don't think we're going to find any trees here, but there are plenty of caves near the sea."

"Wait. We're going *back* to the sea?" Pinyon asked.

"No, just near it," Hazel replied, pointing toward the cliffs. "I saw some caves before we landed. We'll be safe from predators there."

"You think there are more predators here?" Pinyon grabbed her arm instinctively, looking around for signs of danger.

The word *predator* circulated through the rest of the seeds, and they pressed closer to her. Hazel put her hands up. "Everybody, calm down, okay? I don't know if there are predators here, but we should assume there are until we know otherwise. If we take shelter in the sea caves, nothing will attack us. We'll be safe there." After the crowd calmed down, Hazel added, "It's already too dark to look around tonight. If we wait any longer to go to the sea caves, then we might be too tired to move. We need to go now, and we can return tomorrow morning—find a place to create our forest."

"*Our* forest… Don't you mean, *your* forest?" Ebony said, her pheromones as hostile as a nest of hornets.

They stung Hazel. "What do you mean, *my* forest?"

"Exactly what I said," Ebony replied, still sitting astride her bird as she pushed her way through the seeds toward Hazel. "Why do you assume everybody wants to become a tree?"

"You… don't want to become a tree?" Hazel asked, too stunned to be spiteful. It never occurred to her that a seed *wouldn't* want to be a tree. "But seeds are so vulnerable. And seeds are *supposed* to become trees. That's our purpose! Our destiny! As a forest, we won't have to worry about seas or storms or predators. We can finally be safe!"

"We'll be *stuck*." Ebony's bird flapped its wings. "Seeds aren't any more vulnerable than trees are. As seeds, at least we're mobile. Being a tree means you're rooted in one place forever." Ebony turned in a circle to address all the seeds. "What happens if more titanic rains come, and the sea level rises again? We are going to be stuck in Mother's predicament. Do you really want to walk across the sea while you're rotting apart?"

Hazel flinched, feeling the weight of other seeds' uncontrolled emotions: doubt, worry, fear. *I can't let her win this argument. Too much rides on this.* "That won't happen, Ebony."

"But it could... couldn't it?" asked Rowan, a seed with red-brown bark. He looked between Ebony and Hazel, his pheromones expressing doubt like a hiding fox.

"Yeah, Hazel, how can you be so sure?" Ebony asked, leaning forward on her bird. "You saw what happened to Mother. She was a thousand years old, but she still fell, didn't she?"

"Ebony—"

"Didn't she?" Ebony hissed, pheromones coiling like serpents. "So I'm going to ask you again, what's so good about being a forest if we can't protect ourselves as trees?"

"It's what Mother wanted." Hazel replied, taking a step toward Ebony. Though Ebony sat on her bird and Hazel stood on the dirt, they remained the same height. "We are supposed to become trees and create a forest and rebuild everything Mother lost. It's what we were born for!"

"I don't care what we were *supposed* to be," Ebony said. "Do you think Mother's plan was for me to be *overripe?* No. We are who we are. We're *seeds.*"

Hazel clenched her fists. "Look, we don't have time for this. Stay if you want to, but we are going to find shelter for the night. In the morning, we'll create our forest without you."

"Fine by me," Ebony said. "Hick and I will find our own shelter."

"Fine, I—" Hazel hesitated, processing the words. "No, even if you don't want to become a tree, at least let us take Hick with us. You can't make that decision for him."

"And you can? You think you can *decide* to make him into a tree? You really don't see a problem with that?" Pheromones came and the sound of pitying laughter trickled into Hazel's mind as Ebony crossed her brittle arms. "Do you really think Hick wants to become a tree? Being trapped in his own body and only able to say *Hick?* Do you actually think he'd be happy like that?"

Hazel froze. "I..." She trailed away, finding no argument. Imagining Hick trapped as a tree sounded like a hell she wouldn't even impose on Ebony. Probably.

"Let me guess," Ebony said, sounding smug, "you didn't think about that, did you? No. You didn't because you never think about what Hick wants, just what *you* want. That's why you pulled him from his branch. Not because you cared about him, but because you didn't want to be alone—consequences be damned. You're the reason Hick is underripe. You trapped him. And now you want to trap us all."

For agonizing seconds, no seeds spoke, but Hazel could feel their outraged pheromones stirring like hornets. Ebony, for her part, looked far too pleased with herself.

"She did... *what?*" May—one of the taller, darker seeds—asked.

"I... I didn't know what would happen to him," Hazel said, pheromones rotting like Mother. "If I'd known, I wouldn't have done it."

Silence reigned in the moments afterward, until Pinyon said, "I believe her. Hazel wouldn't have hurt Hick if she'd known."

"Don't be so quick to trust her," Ebony replied.

"Why not?" Pinyon asked, taking a step closer to Hazel. "She saved us in the sea. What did you do, Ebony? All I can remember is you pushing everybody away."

Ebony's voice squashed mumbles of agreement. "You're right, Pinyon. I did push you away. Know why? Because you scared Hick. You were all screaming so loud that you almost dominated him. You could have made him fall off his bird, sink into the ocean, and get eaten by a shark. I couldn't let that happen. That's why I pushed you away... It's a better reason than why you pushed your own clustermate off a jay when Mother fell. Holly, wasn't that her name?"

Pinyon bent her head, making no reply.

"Thought so." Ebony jerked her head to Rowan. "Didn't you dominate another seed's spider just to reach a bird first? I saw her fall, watched her head splatter all across a branch." Ebony nodded to May. "You did the same thing. *Twice.*" Then she glanced at Maple. "You pushed another seed off your own spider just to move faster. I guess that worked, didn't it? You're here, aren't you? And that's why Spruce is gone?"

Once Ebony finished listing other seeds' transgressions, she said, "We all did what we had to do when our lives were on the line. I can understand that—forgive it, even. But you?" Ebony asked, pointing at Hazel. "You hurt Hick because you were *lonely.* And that I won't forgive."

Hazel shook her head. "I... I didn't know it would hurt him."

A voice rose from the crowd. Olive, one of the greener-barked seeds. "Mother told me not to pull any seeds from the branches. Told my whole cluster."

Three members of her cluster agreed, nodding their collective assent.

Ebony turned to the crowd. "So all of you knew you weren't supposed to pull a seed from the branch. Do you really think that Mother just forget to tell Hazel? No. Unlike everybody else, she just didn't listen." Ebony shook her head. "Hazel may not have known what it would do to him, but she knew she wasn't supposed to do it. She just didn't care."

"Didn't care?" Hazel asked, the anger and resentment from the weeks at sea returning at once. "You treat everybody else like puppets! You've dominated me, even *Hick!* You don't care about him. You care about *controlling* him! As soon as he makes a choice you don't like, you take that choice from him."

"I *protect* him," Ebony said, more furious than Hazel ever heard her speak. "You just want everybody to become trees because you're afraid of being lonely."

"The forest will keep us safe!" Hazel said, gesturing at the sea. "How many of us have already died to get here? How many more? The forest is our last chance at creating our community—creating our future!"

"Did the forest keep Mother safe?" Ebony replied. "Those other trees? Have you ever wondered why Mother was the last tree left? Do you really think that was by accident? No, she showed us the wars between trees. Do you think she *didn't* take nutrients from the others to keep herself strong?"

"I..." Hazel stopped. *Did she?* Probably. "You can't know that for a fact. You're guessing."

"It's not guessing if I'm right." Ebony shook her head. "Mother did what she had to do, just like she realized that the forest had outlived its usefulness. The forest is only safe when life is good. When it isn't, it's every tree for itself."

Hazel took two steps toward Ebony, walking through a patch of mud from the recent storm while gesturing to the crowd. "We're stronger together, just like we were on the sea! The only reason we survived was because we worked together. How do you not see that? We don't even know where we are! How could you be so selfish?"

"Me? *Selfish?*" Ebony said, pointing a curled, arthritic finger in Hazel's direction. "Unlike you, I've kept Hick safe since the moment I was born! *I* saved Hick when Mother drowned. *I* flew Hick across the sea. *I* saved him from the sharks. *I* brought him here. I did *not* do that just to turn his body into a prison. Trust me, I know how that feels more than anybody." Ebony raised both of her arthritic hands to point at her shriveled legs. Then she made a shooing gesture. "So go ahead, become a tree, trap yourselves. In the meantime, Hick and I will enjoy our freedom."

"You can't just—"

"That's the thing, Hazel. I can do whatever I want. That's the point of being *free.*"

Behind her, Hazel's bird slammed into her backside, shoving her down into the mud. Hazel tried to get up, but the bird stood on top of her, pushing her face back into the mud. Instead of his pheromones, she heard the vibrations of Hick's thudding feet against the dirt and stone just before he collided with the bird and sent them both toppling over. Hazel, now covered in mud, dragged herself to her feet.

"No," she said, making fists. "You're not getting away with it this time."

Ebony said nothing, holding out a finger to Hazel. However, Hazel couldn't feel her pheromones. She couldn't hear anybody at all, despite the several fights raging within the crowd—those supporting Hazel and those against her.

Hazel looked down at her mud-caked body, having only left her leaves uncovered. *Just like when the sharks attacked…* She'd fallen beneath the waves, and the world had fallen silent until Hick pulled her out of the water. *Pheromones can't travel through the mud. Ebony can't dominate me!*

"You don't have power over me. Not anymore!" Hazel rushed forward as Ebony tried to scramble away on her bird. Before it could leap into the air, Hazel tackled her. They both slid across the rocks as mud scraped off of Hazel's body, and she began hearing the chaos behind her. Voices rose like the tides, some coming to Hazel's aid, others to Ebony's. Birds skittered, dominated by too many voices. Ebony shouted with all her might, but Hazel could barely hear her.

Skidding to a stop, Hazel rolled on top of Ebony, who feebly slapped at her face and tugged at the leaves sprouting from her head. Hazel grabbed both of Ebony's hands in one and gripped a loose stone. "How does it feel to be powerless, Ebony?"

"Stop! Don't!" Ebony screamed, but her voice was too quiet.

Hazel brought down the stone—only to be stopped by a strong hand. Mechanically, Hick ripped the rock from her grasp and dragged Hazel away. More mud rubbed away from her bark, and the voices became louder. Yet Hick remained silent.

"Ebony, you bitch!" Hazel shouted, thrashing in Hick's grip. "You're still dominating him!"

"It's all your fault!" Ebony replied, louder now.

"No! It's *yours!*" Hazel punched Hick in the head and scrambled out of his grasp as he recoiled. She charged toward Ebony, who dominated other birds and flung them as obstacles. Picking up another rock, Hazel avoided two, but the third wrapped its claws around her shoulders and carried her into the air.

Ten feet up and rising, Hazel smashed her rock into its legs, breaking its grip. Then she fell to the ground below. Hazel landed awkwardly in the mud and snapped her right leg, which bent at a forty-five-degree angle at the shin. More mud dulled the pheromones as she howled with pain.

Get up! Pushing herself to her feet, Hazel limped back toward Ebony, who was trying to lift herself back onto a bird. *You're not getting away. Not this time.*

Hazel hurled her stone, missing Ebony but hitting the bird in the head. It shook from the impact, and Ebony fell back onto the ground. Hazel searched for another loose rock. She found a slender one stuck deep within the mud and pulled it free. Foot dragging behind her, Hazel approached Ebony and raised the stone sword—

A sword? Hazel stopped, staring at the orange and yellow blade carved from sandstone. Its edge rippled with waves, reminding her of the sea—of drowning. *Why is there a sword here?* She stared down at the ground, noticing the pieces of petrified wood long since stuck in the mud—looking just like the other rocks. *It's a graveyard.*

Hundreds of seed bodies stuck out of the ground. Sometimes outstretched hands, other times feet. Even a few heads, all shattered and unable to grow into a tree. Most wore long stripes of red, orange, or yellow paint on their limbs. Their stone weapons laid among the stones too. Swords, axes, and spears.

Hazel dropped her sword. *Just how many times has this happened? How many times have seeds made it to land just to kill each other? Could there be more places like this one? More battles? More death? ...More of us?* Hazel stared down at her hands, then at a grasping hand in the mud—one with stiff fingers that had curled like a dead spider on its back. Two were missing, the others petrified. *What would have happened if we kept fighting? Would we all die? Would only Hick be left?* Hazel turned her gaze to the dead bodies. *It doesn't matter. Not really. We would all lose... We can't keep fighting. Not like this.*

"Everybody, stop! *Stop!*" Hazel shouted, but her voice was too quiet. She looked down at her hands again, noticing the thick mud covering her bark. *It stops my pheromones too. But if I take off the mud, Ebony can dominate me.* Hazel glanced at her, but Ebony hadn't moved. *I can't trust her... but what other choice do we have?*

Hazel began wiping away the mud and repeating her message until it was loud enough for everybody to hear. Then they quieted. "The only reason we survived this long is because we worked together. If we don't, we're going to die like the rest of them." Hazel pointed at the petrified seeds half-way sticking out of the mud. Staring at Ebony, she added, "We need to stop fighting. All of us."

In the silence beyond, only a single voice could be heard.

"Hick... Hick... Hick..." he stuttered, his pheromones filled with mourning rain clouds. Sitting in the mud, he put his head in his hands as his whole body shook.

"Hick? I'm so sorry." Ebony crawled through the mud to reach him. She reached out to touch him, but he flinched. Faltering, Ebony hugged her knees to her chest and rocked. "I didn't mean to dominate you. I just... I felt so helpless. I'm so sorry, Hick."

"Hick," he replied quietly. In his pheromones, the clouds kept weeping.

Hazel kneeled beside her sister. "Ebony—"

"I've dominated him before, but always to protect him. Never to save myself," Ebony replied in a small voice. "You have no idea what it's like not to have control of your body. You either have to ask people to do things for you or take them yourself... but I didn't have to do either of those things with Hick. I didn't have to ask—didn't have to take. He always knew what I needed before I did. He didn't care about what I looked like. He just wanted to help me. And I wanted to help him. All I wanted was to *be* with him... But I almost threw all of that away."

Ebony's pheromones began as two fish swimming together in a pond, one gray and the other black, before the gray one swam away and only the black one remained. "I don't want to lose him, Hazel. I can't. If I have to choose between saving Hick and killing you, then I'll stop fighting with you. Just... don't make me regret this."

Hazel nodded. "I can live with that." She looked toward Hick, who had quieted. "Are you okay?"

"Hick," he whispered, his pheromones smelling of rot.

Hesitantly, Ebony reached out to him again. When he didn't pull away, she crawled into his lap, putting a hand on his shoulder and resting her forehead against his. Though Hazel couldn't hear what she said to him, Hick calmed beneath her touch. He held her in his arms as she wrapped her own around his neck.

Ebony's not dominating him. Hick really wants to hold her. They really do love each other, Hazel thought, no longer blinded by her jealousy, even if she remained ashamed by it.

Eventually, Hick set Ebony down gently, getting on his knees and scooping dirt into his hands just before tossing it onto the limbs of a few petrified seeds and burying the past.

"Burying them will take hours, Hick," Hazel said. "You'll run out of energy."

"Hick," he said firmly.

To the best of her ability, Ebony helped him to bury more limbs which had been unearthed during the fighting. "Hick wants to do this, so I won't try changing his mind. I won't dominate him. Not for you or anybody else. Never again."

"Good," Hazel said, sitting on the opposite side of Hick as she pushed more dirt onto the petrified wood—as did the other seeds. With their combined strength, the task to bury the dead seeds and their weapons beneath a foot of dirt only took an hour, spending the last of their energy.

Yet Hazel still saw the bodies clearly in her mind. *Not so different from when we bury ourselves to become trees,* she thought. *But who will bury us?*

Hazel stared over at Hick, who continued to push one more clump of dirt onto the mound and pack it down. He kneeled at the edge of the burial ground, resting a hand on the earth and bowing his head. Then he stood, sad yet proud. Protective. An idea sparked in her mind. "Ebony? I think I know how we can all be happy. You, me, and Hick. All the seeds."

The next day, as the afternoon sun rose over the cliff, Hazel stood in a hole of brown dirt that was almost a foot above the top of her head, though her leaves towered higher, giving her a view of the aboveground world. With twenty feet of separation, twenty-five other seeds waited to be buried in their own holes to the right and left of her.

Hick, Ebony, May, Maple, and Rowan stood on the firm ground, riding their birds and carrying weapons they'd taken from the seed battlefield just as a precaution. Having elected not to be buried as trees, they instead took the role of foresters, free to roam the lands while acting as caretakers to the saplings.

I just have to trust them, Hazel reminded herself, knowing Mother would be proud.

"Are you sure about this?" Ebony asked. "You can still stay a seed, you know. Run around. Fly. Do whatever you want."

"No. This is our best chance." Hazel said, knowing that her seed body would grow and expand to form her first roots. "I'm ready to become a tree. Bury me."

"Hick!" he replied excitedly, once again the paragon of happiness.

"You don't have to tell me twice," Ebony said, but there was less acid in her pheromones than Hazel expected.

Dirt rained down over the top of Hazel, filling the hole. Instead of feeling afraid and trapped, she could still see, hear, and speak through her leaves.

"This is actually pretty comfortable. Not as bad as I thought it'd be," Hazel replied via pheromones.

"Uh huh," Ebony replied, dumping the last of the dirt at the base of Hazel's leaves. "I'll take your word for it."

"Hick, Hick, *Hick!*" He gently touched one of her leaves before burying the next seed: Pinyon. Other foresters did the same.

We made it, Mother, Hazel thought, embracing the soil and sun.

Strange how much can change in a few hundred years, Mother, Hazel thought, still basking in the soil and sun after all this time. *Stranger still that I can see it all.*

Near the cliffs of the freshwater ocean, Hazel stood proudly, her branches and leaves reaching hundreds of feet into the sky. Now the oldest and tallest tree in the forest, her movements had slowed, making it difficult to bend even her branches, but her mind remained as fast as it had ever been—especially with the mycelium network of roots and fungi that she and the other trees had developed over the centuries. From the twenty-six seeds that had been planted, the forest now expanded hundreds of miles inland, pushing away the barren rock and creating their tropical oasis. But a clearing marked the spot of the now ancient seed battlefield, both as a memorial and a reminder of past mistakes.

With each death comes new life, new hopes, new dreams, and new futures, Hazel thought, using her myriad of leaves to stare at the multitude of seed clusters waiting to ripen and fall from her branches. She ordered her spider sentries to weave fibrous webs beneath the newest growths before reorganizing the birds perching on her branches. Though beetles patrolled the trunk of the tree, predators that had returned to the thriving forest were always a minor threat.

A shift in the weight of a branch directed her attention to a ripened seed, and Hazel sent another spider sentry to free the struggling seed, quieting it as it tried to speak to her in broken, scattered pheromones—geometric patterns that carried no words or substance.

To the newborn, Hazel said, "Hello, Willow. I am Mother." Willow tried to respond, but Hazel shushed the seed with more calming pheromones. "Your voice will come later, but for now, you must listen to me, Willow... When I was but a seed, I was born alone in the arms of my mother, but you will never have to suffer as I did because you have—"

"Hick, Hick, *Hick!*" he screamed, diving through the canopy and flying beside Ebony on a green jay. Both of them had grown old but were very much alive. Happy, too, in the forest that they had helped to create.

"Try to keep, youngsters!" Ebony shouted beside Hick before banking up and out of sight with him. Young seeds chased after them, those who had chosen the path of the foresters. Just as it had been with the races along Mother's trunk, Ebony and Hick still came in first and second place in competitions. Always.

"—a family." Hazel finished, sharing her amusement through pheromones. "We will keep you safe as you grow and you learn, Willow. And one day, you, too, will choose whether to remain a seed or become a tree. But regardless of your choice, you will always be a part of our forest."

Then Hazel told her story, just as Mother had told hers.

*JACK THE BEANSTALKER: A young giant searches for his father's mur-
derer in medieval Britain...*

JACK THE BEANSTALKER

Fee fi fo fum. Those were the last words I heard my father shout. After the beanstalk rose to the Kingdom of the Clouds. After the Beanstalker came with his axe and blighted heart.

Father's bellow of rage echoed through the castle halls, jostling me awake. Sitting up on a bed of goose feathers, I wiped the sleep from my eyes and clambered to my feet. Moonlight streamed in through the window, revealing that Helen, my golden goose—my best friend—was not in her bed next to mine. No matter how many times I called out to her, she didn't come to me.

Only then did I understand something was wrong. Perhaps if I had been faster, I could've saved my father. But I hadn't.

When my father roared a second time, I ran through the house in silk pajamas, finding the hall bustling with activity. Servants frantically searched for our family's other prized possessions: my mother's magical harp and a sack of gold coins from my father's treasury. Both gone. So was my father. I couldn't find him in the palace despite how many times I called out his name.

Sprinting through the palace gates and onto the white clouds, I slid to the edge of the cloud and peered over to find Father following the Beanstalker down that horrid plant—down to the dreaded earth. Despite my screams and pleas, my father didn't stop. Soon he was too far down to see. With a magical spell, I conjured a telescope and, looking through it, discovered the Beanstalker reaching the surface and cutting through the beanstalk. That green tower tumbled down, taking my father with it. The stalk and giant died together in a tangled embrace.

Worse still, because Father was so far from the clouds, his magic dissipated, as did all his magical clothing. Even his crown. He was left nude with only the beanstalk to cover his mangled body. Nor could I build him a funeral pyre and release his soul to the sun. So much disrespect for such a noble king.

From the Kingdom of the Clouds, I sobbed all the harder, but I couldn't turn myself away. I suffered the disgrace of watching those human peasants desecrate Father's corpse by dancing on his chest and pilfering his pockets. They didn't even bother to close his eyes. Instead, they raised the Beanstalker onto their shoulders and congratulated him. He held my beautiful golden goose by the neck. Mother's harp was strapped to his back, a sack full of gold coins thrown over his shoulder.

Each stolen possession twisted the sword already thrust into my heart.

Eventually, my mother and the servants joined me at the edge of the cloud, our silhouettes forming thunderheads. Her sobs stabbed the knife deeper, worsened still by the fact I could do nothing.

But I can, I thought. *There is one thing I can do... I can go down there. Someday. Somehow.*

A vow passed beyond my lips, one I was required to fulfill on punishment of becoming Forsworn—being stripped of magic and losing my bond with the clouds. To fail the vow was to tumble to the earth with the humans—modern descendants of ancient giants who tumbled from our kingdom. And truly, nothing else in the world sounded sweeter to my ears than the idea of falling. *That's how I'll get you back, Father.*

"I vow to find you and smash you like you smashed my father, Beanstalker," I hissed. Upon hearing the word *vow,* the servants shrank back in fear, the clouds listened to my words, and my mother sobbed louder. "I will make the humans remember why they are beneath us. They are liars and traitors and thieves. They were lost to the clouds because of their ancestors' treachery, and by my hand, I will make them *hurt.*"

Then a second vow came to my lips, one that flew as my tears fell. "I vow to reclaim Helen. I will find all our lost possessions: the goose, harp, and coins. They will not be forgotten."

A final oath arrived in my mind, the most powerful and important. When I spoke, the words were steel. Unbreakable. "I vow to bring you back home, Father. I will find a way to get your bones, burn them, and send your soul back to the sun so you may be born again among the clouds. None will deny me."

As I glared at my sworn enemy far below, the clouds swirled around me, accepting my vows. With them, I became damned, because I could not fulfill my oaths without going to the surface, and I could not get to the surface without breaking my oaths and becoming Forsworn. Regardless of my actions, I knew I would fall from the clouds eventually, but I had no fear.

I still don't.

It is finally time, I think as I awake upon the cold floor of my room, having dreamed for three years of my father's fall—of that dreadful night which I can never change despite all our cloud magic. These three years I've spent conditioning my body and training to kill humans in preparation for my fall to the surface.

It is not nearly enough time.

Because the strength of giants is greater than that of humans, even pound for pound, I know I will be the strongest creature below the clouds, especially with all my weight training, but I still worry. Am I strong enough? I need more time, yet three years is all the time I can spare. If I wait any longer, I will be too old to pass for a land-dwelling human. At twelve years of age, I am seven feet tall—already far taller than the Beanstalker and his cronies, but not tall enough to be feared as a giant. I hope.

I will learn shortly.

While we Cloud Giants are a peaceful race living in the light of our sun god's eye, I have become a shadow. My bedroom reflects the change in my heart, as does my elongated shadow in the afternoon sunlight. Where my goose-feather bed once laid is now a rough sheet of coarse linen so I can sleep upon the stones, harden my skin, and strengthen my body. In place of the bookshelves are archery targets. Weapons and weights litter the ground, pushing even *my* strength to its limits.

Our cloud magic has allowed me to conjure all these items from the clouds' essence, but once I fall, this magic will be lost to me forever, so I haven't bothered to learn it. Instead, sword mastery, fisticuffs expertise, and warfare strategies have become my magics. Such knowledge is all I can carry with me, because magic items—which are all that we giants own—will dissipate like smoke upon touching the surface. Even my clothes. Just like Father's.

Ironically, only the goose, the harp, and the coins—ancient heirlooms created with sun magic beyond even Mother's understanding—are the only possessions which retain their magical properties on the surface. But all three now are in the Beanstalker's unlawful possession.

I'll grind his bones and make bread of him, and his soul will rot within my stomach, I think as I leave my room for the last time, knowing that, even if I succeed, I can never return home. How the Beanstalker walked on the clouds, I can only surmise that, while his original giant ancestor was Forsworn, his tainted blood had diluted enough for the Beanstalker to succeed. But after today, I will have no such luck.

A good thing, then, that I care nothing for luck. Only results.

As I leave my bedroom for the last time, a somber procession awaits me in my father's grand halls. Stones of swirling blue marble splash against the walls of gold and stained glass. In doorways and at hallway intersections stand the servants, those whom I've grown up with and love as much as Mother. They wear black, a color which doesn't fit them, unlike me. My heart grows as heavy as that fabric, but I keep my head high as I stride past. A few grief-stricken friends reach out to stop me, but I gently pull myself from their grasps.

Behind me, I hear them join the march. Hundreds of feet thunder through the palace, into the clouded courtyard, and to the palace gates. There, the feet stop. I pause and look over my shoulder to see the others who have formed a line at the gate, though none venture farther.

I immediately understand why. Mother awaits me on the clouds beyond the palace walls—in the very spot where I made my vows three years prior. Because this will be our last conversation, the others grant us privacy.

By far, Mother's gaze is the hardest to defy. She beckons to me, and I exhale, looking across the other clouds, some above but most below. Other giants stand upon them, blackened as silhouettes, saluting me from their palaces—none so grand as Father's.

He was the king. I should be, if I hadn't abdicated and left governance to Mother... I could've been the king. Instead, I'll be Forsworn. I close my eyes as the truth of my voyage hits me harder than Father hit the ground. *This will be the last time I'm here. The last time I see my mother. The last time I see my kin. For the rest of my life—however short that may be—I'll be among the enemy.*

Yet worse still is the thought of the Beanstalker living a long, happy life at Father's expense. *When seeking revenge, dig two graves, Mother says. I'll dig more than that—as many as I can before they take me down. I'll make it a mass grave.*

Walking forward from the gates, I don't dare look back a second time for fear of losing my nerve. Instead, I join my mother near the edge of the clouds. Though I am to be the tallest human to have existed in centuries, I am but a juvenile giant. Mother is mature, and she towers over me. Even when she falls to one knee to embrace me, she is still a head taller. While she is bedecked in a black gown and veil, I stand in a white suit and cape. Strange how she sees this as my death, while I see it as my triumph.

"Must I lose both my husband and my son?" Mother ventures in a quiet voice, lost to the gentle breeze. Despite her lips being next to my ear, I barely hear the words.

Yes, is the simple answer. Yet I cannot say so. As much hate as there is within me for the humans, I only feel love for her. "I already made my vows, Mother. If I do not go, I break my vows, and the clouds will release me anyway. The deed is already done."

"So you say," Mother replies, releasing me and standing. Together, we stare down at the woods of Britain directly below. This forest is not where my father fell, but it is near to where that beanstalk was, I'm reasonably sure. The clouds of our kingdom swirl around this land for a reason I cannot comprehend—just a known law our magic follows.

If I wait any longer, the clouds will move and I may be taken farther from my father's resting place. It is yet another reason I must leave today.

"Why did you do it, son?" Mother eventually asks. "Did you think this is what Father wanted for you?"

Yes, I think, because I hear Father's voice every time I close my eyes, asking me to avenge him. His is the hateful voice that plagues my mind, whereas Mother's is the cautious one. I hear neither right now. "Father isn't here to tell me what he wants," I tell her as gently as I can. "That's why I'm going."

When Mother speaks, her voice trembles, and I am glad I cannot see her face from beneath the veil. "He would be heartbroken to know you are sacrificing your magic, your happiness, your *soul* for his corpse. If you succeed—"

"When," I reply.

Mother sighs. "*When* you succeed, what then?"

I open my mouth, but no words come. *What then?* The question echoes through my head, threatening to pull me from the clouds.

"Who will find your body and make you a funeral pyre?" Mom asks, her voice rising angrily. "Will another giant go to save your corpse? Another after him? A third? A *tenth?* When does this stop?"

"Mother—"

She pulls me into another hug, and the quickness of it catches me off guard. Gently, I lean against her, my head resting on her stomach. As I feel her body racked with sobs, it takes all of my steely resolve not to break down beside her. *This is the last time I'll hug her. The last time I'll have a conversation with her. The last time for everything.*

Three tears run down my cheek as I change my breathing.

"You are your father's son, Titus," she says, clutching me so tightly I can feel her nails against my skin. "Just as courageous, just as strong... but just as foolish."

I try to pull away, but she's too strong for me. "Father is not—"

"Hush," Mother whispers, running one hand through my hair like she did when I was younger. In a hardened voice, she explains, "You must understand something. Magic keeps giants in the clouds, but only when we remain true and virtuous. It is the lightness of our souls that keep us above the surface. While our lands are a paradise, this place has also infantilized us, son.

"We giants are naive in a way humans are not. We do not have war, we do not lie, we do not *kill*. But humans cannot fall farther than they already have, so they have become masters of sin. They are cunning beyond measure—*that* is why the Beanstalker could sneak into our palace, steal our belongings, and trick your father. No matter how much you've trained, nothing can prepare you for the treachery of humans... But what scares me more is you *learning* their ways. Promise me not to lose yourself just to find your father."

There is nothing I can say to her that will ease her mind, so I don't try to. Instead, I say. "I love you, Mother." I'm surprised how hard four words are to speak aloud. My voice is rough like sand, garbled like stone. "I vow not to break your heart."

Mother stiffens. "But, Titus... You already have."

"I know," I whisper, my lungs feeling heavier as the vow I just made breaks. I become Forsworn.

"No," Mother whispers, holding me to her chest even as the clouds pull at me. "Not yet. We had more time!"

"I'm sorry, but this is the only way," I whisper as the clouds slip away beneath me. But I don't fall with them because Mother is still holding on. "You need to let me go."

"No..." she moans, but her grip loosens as the magic clothes I wear unravel. I fall through her fingers, landing on a small cloud that drifts toward the surface like fog. Over the edge of the cloud, I see Mother's face looking down at me as her veil falls to the side. Bloodshot eyes. Mouth open in anguish.

With a quivering lip, I smile at her, but as the cloud descends and I lose sight of her, I finally break down. Yet I pull myself back together before the descent ends. Naked, alone, and vulnerable, the small cloud dissipates ten feet above the ground, and I fall much like Father did. Unlike him, I hit the ground on my feet.

Immediately, I look at the ground underfoot: long tufts of green grass and flat patches of dirt. From the clouds, the green had always looked so two-dimensional. Only now do I see their bladed shapes and unevenness. I rip a few blades free of the dirt, bringing them close to my eyes as I see a tiny creature with a red carapace and black dots munching on the greenery.

"What is this?" I ask aloud, having never seen such a creature before because none have ever flown up to the clouds. There are others too. Bigger insects walking on four, eight, or even a hundred legs. Smaller ones flit through the air and pollinate the flowers.

For all the hatred in my heart for humans, this place is so unlike the clouds that I can only marvel at it. A dirt road runs through the ancient trees of this forest, which are far thicker and taller than even Father. To be among them almost feels like being in the clouds, but as my feet slap the dirt, I know I cannot be farther from home. *I am a stranger in this new land...*

As the clouds mourn me, I imagine the tears of giants mingling with the rain. I am here for each of my kin. *Clothes first, then weapons,* I think, the plan ingrained in my mind from three years of planning. *Third, I find Father's corpse and collect his bones. Fourth, I find the Beanstalker and kill him. Fifth, I take back our possessions and create another beanstalk. Sixth, I deliver Father's bones and our possessions to Mother.* Six goals. No more, no less.

Then what? Mother's voice asks, haunting my mind.

I shake my head, trying to rid myself of that audible plague, but the words do not leave. Instead, they follow me as I walk over the dirt and rocks, wincing from the cuts that develop on my tender feet.

Though the sky quickly becomes as dark as Mother's veil, the moon is bright enough to guide me. So used to waking and sleeping with the movements of the sun, part of me—the part which sounds like Mother—thinks it is time to rest. The other part, which sounds like Father, can think only of my six goals. I listen to the latter and walk until the forest is long behind me. In its stead, fields of grain and vegetables rise on either side. What I find more interesting is the smoke eclipsing the clouds, coming from a source far from the path.

I can always come back to this road, I think, shivering from the cold as I hug my arms to my bare chest. *I need clothes more than dirt.* Stomping away from the road into the grass- and weed-laden fields, I grab a yellow, knobbed vegetable from a green stalk: corn. The similarity to a beanstalk makes me lose my appetite, and I squeeze the vegetable in my hand until it breaks apart.

Golden kernels drop from my fingers like goose eggs as I wade through the seemingly endless fields which change from those stalks to long vines, then to bushes and shrubs. Beyond the shrubs lie the sounds of surplus laughter and the crackle of a fire. My curiosity piqued, I creep closer, reaching the edge of the fields and finding myself in a green clearing filled with dozens of spaced-out homesteads with thatch roofs. Between the cottages hang long lines from which wet homespun clothing dries. Because all the doors are closed and no homesteads have windows, I cannot guess which are vacant. The smoke curls beyond the cottages and down the hill, but the fire is not what currently interests me.

I need those clothes. Shivering again, I take a hesitant step forward, only to duck back behind the field as a door opens. Two humans stride out in heavy winter clothes, holding bundles of vegetables bread. They laugh as they walk away from me and toward the smoke over the next hill.

As my heart pounds, I take a deep breath. I might be bigger and stronger than the humans, but judging by the number of cottages, they outnumber me a hundred to one. And they'll surely kill me if they know I'm here.

Have to keep going, I think, shivering more and peering between the leaves with hungry eyes. *Have to avenge Father.*

Once the humans disappear around a corner, I rise from my hiding place and brush off the skittering bugs. Creeping around at the edge of these cottages is simple enough. However, finding clothes that fit me turns out to be a tougher challenge. The first tunic I try rips at the seams as I pull it over my head. The second fares no better. By the sixth, I've realized the only clothes that will fit are winter overcoats. One does the job after I roll up the sleeves—which are far too short. I split nine pairs of breeches before finding one that is the right size. Even then, it is difficult to breathe with the pressure on my waist. The stockings and shoes I don't bother with. Just by looking at them, they are too small. The pants and jacket will have to be enough.

One goal down, five more to go. Just as I turn to leave, I hear another round of laughter from the fire. *I should just go.* I should, but I'm too curious to understand the celebration down the hill. With my warm clothes, I tread between the cottages, tall enough to touch the ridgelines of their roofs with my fingers. Merriment spills from the air like the glowing fire, which pushes away more darkness the closer I get.

From the shadow of the nearest cottage, I peer down at a celebration of some sort. A roaring bonfire burns between the fields in a large area cleared of leaves and debris. The only fires I've ever witnessed were in the hearths of the palace, so this one roaring freely between the trees is peculiar. Seemingly dangerous.

More so are the people gathering around its tendrils. Dozens dance around the fire, but many more clap in a rhythm in a wider circle. Some play fiddles, lutes, and flutes. Most play various games with fruits and vegetables. Children join in the celebration, too, having stick fights and chasing one another.

These are humans? The thought comes unbidden, but this view is no less shocking. Mother told me humans were evil to the core, and I expected torture and human sacrifices. These individuals, however, seemed to be... sharing their food. The seed of doubt in my head grows into a tree ripe for harvest the longer I watch them. Where is the pain? The sin? The debauchery?

Then I hear it: a scream. It bubbles up from the fields, quickly silenced before it can carry over to the bonfire. The humans do not seem to hear the sound. That, or they are ignoring it. I am inclined to believe the latter. *I knew they were savages.*

Leaving the light, I wade back into the darkness and follow the sound of the scream across the fields. The laughter from the fire fades, to be replaced by new laughter—far more sinister than merry. Instinctively, my hands curl into fists as I stalk the source.

Though the humans speak a tongue different from us giants, it is more so a variant—a *dialect*—of our own, having changed since the first giants became Forsworn and fell here. As such, I understand most of the humans' words, though I wish I didn't.

"You see the way she squirms?" one says as I creep closer, ducking low to hide myself in the cornfield. "Like a little worm. I love it when the wenches do that."

"Ed, hit her a couple more times so she don't scream again!" adds another. His laughter infuriates me.

"Yeah, yeah!" mutters a third. "*Harvesting* festival, right, Joe? Time to harvest you too, girlie!"

"Shouldn't have come around us looking for excitement, girl, but you'll learn," adds the second. "You'll be learning *plenty* tonight."

As I hear another muffled scream and what sounds like tearing clothes, indignation overcomes my limbs. My feet push me to my full height. My shoulders straighten. My arms push through the cornstalks.

When I am right behind them, I see a girl held down by two men in leathers. The third is pulling at her dress. He's torn the sleeves from it and left bruises on her skin, but the girl's still alive. I don't know what they're doing to her or why, but I recognize the fear in her eyes. That is reason enough.

Wordlessly, I growl, my voice low.

The first whips around, unsheathing a blade. But my fist catches his face before he can stab me. His nose flattens, and before he can attack, I bring my knee to his cranium. The sickening crunch of his broken skull makes me pause. *I just killed a man.* In all my training, I'd expected humans to be stronger. Not so frail. *Maybe I don't need weapons.*

That hesitation costs me. The second human gets behind me, touching me with something that burns hotter than the bonfire. A scream pulls itself through my teeth and escapes my lips. My knee buckles, but I turn the fall into a roll and rise to my feet. The second man follows me, swinging his sword. I step back out of reach, wait for the blade to pass, then grab his wrist so he can't swing again. I pull him close and uppercut him. His jaw shatters, and his eyes roll into the back of his skull.

Not good enough, Father's hateful voice says. So I take the sword from the human's weakened grasp and run it through his shriveled heart.

Having learned my lesson, I don't admire my work. I whirl around, coming face-to-face with the third man, who holds the girl in front of him with a knife to her neck. "Easy now, big fella," he says, backing away from me. "We don't need to have any trouble, do we?"

Just leave her, Father says. *She's a human.*

She's in pain, argues Mother's gentle voice. *You can't just leave her here.*

This time, Mother wins the argument.

I respond to this disgusting human by twirling the sword in my hand.

"You want her, huh?" the robber asks, eyes darting around nervously. "Why don't you put down the sword, and I'll *think* about letting her—"

The girl throws her head back, smacking against his. Simultaneously, she grabs the edge of the blade to keep it from cutting her neck. As the robber stumbles, I close the distance in two strides, skewering him through his open mouth. The fight dissipates, and his soul departs, but it's too heavy to rise to the cloud. Instead, it drowns in the dirt as the body slumps to the surface.

Apparently, that fate isn't good enough for the girl. Cradling her slit palm, she kicks the brigand in the stomach several times, probably breaking a toe.

Father's voice wants me to hurt her too, but Mother tears away the anger. *You are* not *human. You do not have to kill her. Though you are here, you do not have to be like them.*

I incline my head toward the girl, expecting her to scream or flee in terror. Yet again, I'm wrong about humans. This one only stares up at me while holding the front of her green dress to her chest. With long auburn hair like my mother's, her eyes match her dress. Even with the lack of light, I notice how her skin is pale and freckled, reminiscent of many servants in my father's palace. *She doesn't look like the humans Mother warned me about.*

Don't be so sure, Father's ghost whispers.

"Thank you for saving me, mister... And why are you wearing my father's cloak?" the girl asks, though I don't reply because my style and intonation of speech is different from hers. It'll mark me as an outsider—perhaps even as a giant. "Can't you speak?"

Without answering, my eyes flick past her. In the distance are silhouettes, some humans coming up the hill. *My scream must have attracted them.* While taking on three men was not a challenge, I don't pretend to think I can take on a dozen without being stabbed again.

As I take a step back, the girl shouts, "Wait!" She takes a step toward me and puts up a calming hand. "It's okay. That's my family. They won't hurt you. Just let me do the talking."

She's trying to protect me? I cock my head, trying to understand this girl. She's human. That means she's evil. Why would she try to help me?

"Oh, right. You can't talk... Sorry." She frowns, holding the dress higher and looking uncomfortable. "Just leave everything to me, all right?" Turning around, she raises her hand up, shouting to the coming mob that she's okay. That everything is fine. But things don't *feel* fine by the way these humans are hurrying toward me.

Forget about her. Just remember the plan, says Father. *Two down, four to go. Don't waste your time with the humans. Pick up the weapons and go.*

I can't ignore him this time. My body aches more from the memory of Father's fall than my present wound. Kneeling, I pick up the blades: three swords, five daggers, and a bow with a quiver of arrows. Three purses, too, filled with copper coins whose symbols I've never seen before. Giants only use gold, and even then, rarely. Magic greatly simplifies our lives.

Their lives, I correct myself, remembering my friends above the clouds. *I can't go back.*

Collecting the resources, I stand, taking a few strides through the field back toward the road. "Hey! Wait!" the girl says, turning back to me as the mob of people hurry through the field toward us. She gasps, pointing at me. "There's a dagger in your back!"

Guess that means you have six daggers, Father whispers. *Better get going.*

My hesitation gives this girl time to run in front of me. "You can't leave with a dagger in your back. You'll *die* from a wound like that." I try to go left around her, but she takes a step in the same direction to block my path. When I try to go right, she blocks me again. "I've fixed wounds before. I can help you."

"Help me?" I ask, my voice low like a rumble. The fury rises within me, but only as the adrenaline fades. I feel the ache spread across my back. I grimace but don't complain. In my three years of training, I've been hurt far worse, but I no longer have Mother's healing magic to protect me. "You think you can *help* me? No. Your kind is the reason I'm here, human."

"You can speak?" the girl asks, taking a step back. "And... you *aren't* human?"

Fool! I want to kick myself for my faux pas, but there isn't time. The other humans are almost upon us, and I can see the cornstalks shifting as people walk between the rows.

Hesitation flits past her face, followed by determination. "If you run, they'll chase you. Just stay quiet, all right? Pretend you're mute."

She knows I'm not human, yet she'll still help me? I look toward the woods, knowing I can outrun the humans, but two things stop me: the pain in my back hurts more with every passing second, and this girl seems able to heal me. *Maybe she knows where my father is. Or at least, can lead me to him. She's the best chance I have. Maybe she's not as bad as the Beanstalker.*

The thought raises an argument between Father and Mother, both vying for control of me, and all I can do is lower my head in silence as the other humans come.

"Jess? *Jess!*" shouts one, wielding a lantern and a pitchfork. He almost trips over the bodies of the three men. He drops the pitchfork to embrace her. Then he searches her for injuries, to which she tries to calm him down. "What were you doing out here? What were you *thinking?*"

Jess stares at her feet and says, "I was walking down to the bonfire when they dragged me out here." Pointing up at me, she adds, "But Big Ben saved me."

Big Ben? I think silently, not liking the name but unwilling to speak my mind.

The flannel-wearing farmer cranes his head backward to look up at me because as I'm a head taller than him. Wariness and fear cloud his eyes as he takes in my size. "Holy…"

"Dad, he's okay," the girl—*Jess*—replies, stepping in front of me as her father collects his pitchfork. "Don't hurt him. He's not a danger to us."

"Not a danger? Are you telling me *you* killed these men?" her father asks her as more of his friends join him. Seven with pitchforks, five with walking sticks. All brandished their weapons in my direction as they surround me. As I growl at them, sounding more animal than man, the farmer adds, "No, I didn't think so. This one's as dangerous as they come."

"Not to me," Jess argues. "Those men were going to kill me. *Take* me, then kill me." I don't understand what *take* means, but the men do. They eye the corpses angrily as Jess shudders, still struggling to hold up her ruined green dress. "But Big Ben saved me before they could do anything."

Cursing them, Jess's father spits on the face of the closest corpse and kicks him in the mouth, breaking his teeth. Not that it matters, considering the thief is already dead. "Whose to say this one wasn't with them? And is that my *coat?*" the farmer demands, pointing the pitchfork at me. "He's a thief!"

Anger flares through me, though he isn't wrong. *I didn't have anything to trade!* I pull out one of the coin purses—the lightest one—and toss it to the father. Instead of speaking, I growl again, only because the sound makes the others cautious, less likely to stab me.

"I think Ben's trying to say that he's *paying* for the coat," Jess says as her father inspects the coins. "Also, I don't think he likes being compared to thieves. Considering all he had when he attacked was your clothes, I'm guessing somebody robbed him blind on the road."

"Big Ben, huh? That's his name?" the farmer asks, still holding the pitchfork but loosely.

"My name for him," Jess admits. "He doesn't talk. Seems to understand, though. Just have to speak a little slower."

"So he's a fool?" the farmer asks, eyeing me. When I growl, he replies, "I'll take that as a no. Just mute."

"What are we gonna do about all them weapons, Arthur?" one asks, hungering for one of my swords, but as I turn to face him, he immediately becomes disinterested.

"He killed those men, so he keeps them, I reckon," Jess's father—*Arthur*—replies.

"What kinda man needs three swords?" asks that same dissenter as I turn from him.

"Enough of that," Arthur snaps. "You keep what you kill, right? Well, Ben can share if he wants, but he doesn't have to. He's already done enough, so put them weapons down." When they do—some more readily than others—he sighs and adds, "Don't know how somebody like you got here, mister, but Jess is safe. That's all that matters to me. You can share our fire for the night, if you'd like. Or..." He trails off, staring at me. Rather, at the dagger still in my back. "Perhaps we can tend to that wound."

Mistrustfully, I glare at him as I reach for the dagger in my lower back and pull it out. Though the pain is white hot and grinds my teeth, I don't utter a word of pain as I point the bloody blade at the greedy human still staring at my swords. He puts his hands up and offers a nervous smile. "That's all right. I was just kidding about the swords. Keep 'em."

My returning smile isn't kind. Turning back to the farmer, I place the blade in his hand. Jess translates for me. "I'm guessing that's payment for bandaging the wound. Or maybe a souvenir?"

But Arthur waves me away, pointing to her daughter. "Give it to Jess. She needs it more than I do." When I grunt and drop the blade at his feet, he tilts his head. I give Jess one of the sheathed swords, who looks at it like she's just seen a feat of cloud magic.

"*I* get a sword?" Jess whispers, unsheathing it and running her hand along the flat. Though there are dents on the blade and the leather wrapped around the hilt is crumbling, tears pool in her eyes.

Seeing her excitement, Arthur nods at me, the wariness evaporating from his shoulders. "You're an odd one, Big Ben, but I thank you. Consider the coat paid for. Perhaps the missus can sew it to be a little more... your size while we fix up that wound."

Holding the weapons, the farmers lead me back to their village. Every step takes me away from my goal, and my heart grows colder, Father's voice louder. *I'll stay until I have the clothes. Then I'll disappear.*

A creaking door sounds my escape as I leave the barn I'd been staying in for two nights. While Arthur had offered me a place in his home, I declined, feeling more comfortable around the animals. Especially the Shire horses, which are nearly as tall as I am. But being there only reminded me of my beloved golden goose. Thinking of her makes me hate the Beanstalker all the more.

The rough material of my newly hemmed breeches swishes as I walk, and while my patchwork coat isn't pretty, it's warm. I have no shoes or stockings, the process for making them would be too long. My belt, though, is two sewn together, courtesy of the brigands. From them hang my sheathed swords and daggers.

As I round the corner, I nearly run into a shadow. I jump back, reaching for a dagger as the silhouette asks, "Ben? Is that you?"

Jess. I should've guessed it was her. She's been trying to get me to talk all day, but there have always been others around—usually Arthur. He doesn't trust me completely, nor I him, though there is no animosity between us. The fact I've wasted a day here eats at me, my frustration wearing me down like the stones of the nearby river. My back aches, but the pain has dulled from last night because of Jess's help. She cleaned the wound, disinfected its depths with vinegar, and sealed the raw opening with old wine. For his part, Arthur gave me a honey salve in case rot sets in, but with the tight cloth Jess tied around my waist as a pressure bandage, I have little to worry about.

No, I lingered today for another reason. Curiosity. Dancing, music, and laughter filled the community during the harvest festival last night, but to-day I watched them work as a community, picking the various vegetables by hand and storing them in great silos for *winter*—whatever that was. Having no magic to complete the rote tasks and arduous labor for them, these humans worked hard—far harder than any giant—and toiled together for the greater whole.

The humans hadn't seemed like the masters of sin Mother made them out to be, I think, before remembering those three killers. *How many humans are like Arthur? And how many are like the bandits?* More bandits than farmers, I assume. Either way, I have learned enough to keep traveling, following this road toward the capital.

Stepping closer, Jess reveals herself in moonlight. No longer in a ruined green dress, she wears men's breeches and an overcoat like mine—her father's I don't doubt. Unlike me, she has shoes, stockings, and even a hat. Adjusting the belt that holds her sword sheath against her waist, Jess asks, "Are you leaving already? It's just that ... Well, I thought we'd have more time." When I still don't respond, she glances behind her and adds, "Nobody else is here. We can talk."

Just because you can speak doesn't mean you should, Father says between my ears.

"Please, will you talk to me?" Jess asks desperately. Lines of worry draw taut around her eyes. She huffs, summoning the courage to say, "I know you want to go, but I have so many questions. Before you leave, can you tell me who you are? *What* you are?"

I almost tell her what I am, before deciding against it. *Not worth the risk.* I keep walking.

Jess walks with me in the moonlight, trying to keep up. "Please, Ben. Won't you tell me? You can't be a satyr or a faerie. But you're too short to be a giant—"

"Am not," my lips speak for me. I wince again. *Idiot!*

"You *are* a giant?" Jess asks. "But aren't giants *really* tall? That's what I've heard, anyway."

She knows something. I spin toward her and grab her by the shoulders so quickly that she gasps. To calm her, I let go, but I'm excited as I ask, "What have you heard?"

"Not much," Jess admits, looking at the ground. "But I've heard stories from passing merchants. An evil giant fell from a magic cornstalk three days' ride from here, near London." *London.* My veins chill to coldest ice as Jess mistakes my pain for curiosity. "Yeah. Fell from a cornstalk after stealing a princess and—"

"My father would never do such a thing!" I exclaim, forgetting to be quiet as the fury dulls my intellect.

"Your *father*?" Jess stammers, suddenly aware of how alone we are out here beside the barn.

"Father was the greatest of us cloud giants," I say in a quieter voice. "He was kind, generous, and loyal. He would *never* steal a princess. No. The Beanstalker stole our heirlooms and Father fell when that *human* chopped the beanstalk down." As dark as it is here in the stable, it's too easy for me to imagine Father falling. Like a nightmare I'll never wake from. "They danced on his *corpse!*"

My breath heaves in my chest as I spit out those last words, feeling like a rabid horse. It takes me almost a full minute to compose myself. By then, I hear farmers awaking and venturing from their homes with lanterns. The fear of facing a mob drives away my anger like monsters before a fire. Only now can I see how monstrous I must seem to Jess, and for a reason I cannot explain, I feel guilt. Rather than apologize, I walk past her, planning to leave her behind. Instead, she follows me.

"Wait!" Jess whispers, grabbing my arm. "Let me go with you!"

"No," I reply, shrugging her off. As kind as she's been, something about her is wrong. I keep remembering how the bandit had said, *Shouldn't have come around us looking for excitement, girl.* But Jess had told her father that they'd dragged her into the fields. It didn't make sense. *She* didn't make sense.

Stubborn human she is, Jess runs around me and blocks my path. Instead of playing this infuriating game a second time, I grab her by the shoulders, pick her up like a sack of coins, and put her down to the side of me. Passing her, I trudge through the darkness toward the main road as her voice attacks me from behind.

"You don't even know where to go, do you? Well I do. You *need* me!" Jess says, jogging to keep up with my long strides. "Besides, do you want to speak to anybody else with that funny accent of yours? No, I know you don't. So let me come, and I can ask questions for you!"

Clever human, I think. Stopping, I turn to face her. "Why did the bandits say you'd come looking for excitement? You told your dad they'd grabbed you, but they hadn't, had they?"

"You heard that, did you?" Jess asks, after a moment of silence. "I'd meant to meet a boy in the fields, but, well, I saw one of those bandits and thought it was my, uh, *special* friend."

"A special friend," I echo slowly, not understanding, but she seems to be honest. A good enough explanation, though the fact she *lied* about it is a cause for concern. *She's a good liar.* That skill could be useful, but it could also be dangerous.

Jess seems to mistake my confusion for derision. "You don't get to judge me, okay? Here, I'm a farmer's daughter. I'm sixteen, a woman now. The men are kind, but they're oafs. And I'll be expected to marry a farmer, have ten children, and die. I'm not ready for that, okay? I want *excitement.*

I don't want to spend my entire life living the same year over and over. Harvesting in the fall, freezing in the winter, planting in the spring, and sweating in the summer. But with you, maybe I could find a different life. Something better. I could be a knight. Or a mercenary. *Something!*"

"You could die," I reply, resuming my trek and walking away faster this time. She has to run to keep up.

"You'll protect me," Jess says with a surprising amount of confidence. "I saw the way you stabbed the thief holding me. That was a practised lunge, wasn't it?" When I don't reply, she says, "You know how to fight. You can teach me, right?"

"You want me to teach you swordsmanship in three days?" I ask, scoffing. Even with three years of training, I feel like a novice. If I wasn't so big and strong, those three brigands would've killed me. Nor can I teach Jess to be big or strong. Not when she's just a human.

"However many days it takes!" Jess replies. "Take me back with you to the land of the giants if you want!"

"Neither of us will be going back there," I say, the anguish seeping into my voice.

Jess doesn't seem to notice, considering how overwhelmed with joy she is. "In that case, you'll need a companion! And for God's sake, can you slow down? I can't see where I'm going and—"

Jess trips on a rock and smacks into the ground, breaking her fall with her wrist and cheek. Her whimper of pain is what stops me in my tracks. "Just let me help you. *Please.*"

How can I say no to that plea? I wonder. When I don't find an answer, I help her back to her feet. "You're just going to slow me down."

"I won't," Jess says, grinning wide as moonlight hits her face. "I'll meet you on the road, okay?" Then she sprints away, leaving me speechless.

Begs to come when I want her to leave, but runs away when I accept her help... Typical human. Shaking my head, I finish my trek to the wide dirt road just as I hear pounding hooves behind me. When I turn, I see Jess riding on the back of a gelded Shire horse, donning a grin too mischievous for my liking.

"You stole it?" I ask, incredulous.

Jess shrugs. "It isn't stealing if it's the family horse, is it?"

"You stole from your own family?" I ask, my mouth falling open. Just the idea of betraying Mother—in a way other than I already had—fills me with so much guilt, I almost vomit upon the stones.

"They'll be okay," Jess says, not sounding wholly sure. "Besides, they don't know I stole it." Naive as I apparently am, I don't immediately understand her meaning. Looking slightly more embarrassed by the flushing of her cheeks, Jess replies, "They might think you... uh, stole it. Maybe even kidnapped me. I didn't exactly *tell* Dad I was taking the horse."

"You pinned the blame on me? *Why?*" I whisper, turning around and worried they're already galloping toward me. No. The dirt path looks just as dark and lonely as before.

"I couldn't tell my dad I was leaving," Jess replied. "It would have ostracized him from the community—made him a laughingstock. I couldn't bear it."

Rage bubbles through me. "You humans... What is *wrong* with you?"

"Sorry that *some* of us don't have the freedom giants have," Jess replies, hands on her hips. "Going off on adventures isn't exactly what humans expect of farmer's daughters." When I'm silent, she ventures, "So, on a scale of one to ten, how angry with me are you?"

"Six."

"Oh, that's it?" Jess asks, looking more relieved. "I figured you'd say *eleven* or something."

I think of the Beanstalker and how those peasants lifted him on their shoulders to celebrate Father's death. I spin on my heel and begin walking as Jess falls in-step beside me on her giant horse. "Trust me, ten is enough."

"Twelve?" Jess exclaims halfway through the next day, after I answered her umpteenth question. The sun shines above us, and I see no signs of Arthur

or his friends behind us. The merchants' road takes us through more fields, over hills, and toward the distance mountains. I can't help but feel a twinge of pain as I see the clouds wrapping around that distance peak. *Perhaps I can climb the mountain to get home,* I think, though the thought passes as quickly as the clouds. *No, another beanstalk is what I need.*

"You really expect me to believe you're twelve?" Jess says, waving her hand in front of my face. "How could you possibly be twelve?"

"How are clouds magical? They just are. And I am just twelve. Giants don't lie—unlike you humans," I mutter, trudging beside her. My feet are cut by the rocks, but I'm surprised by how fast my feet are building calluses. "It's why I'm so short. I haven't hit my growth spurt yet."

Jess snorts, taller than me while astride her steed. "Yeah, you're short, all right. Figured you for a mountain dwarf."

I struggle to share the good mood. Truth is, without my bond to the clouds and their magic, I don't know if I'll grow any taller. I might be this short forever. *A giant child forever.*

Catching my dour frown, Jess says. "Well, Mr. Dwarf, you are quite mature for your age, I'll be the first to admit it. I'd have guessed you were in your late twenties. A knight at that."

Truly curious, she asks me questions about home. If only to pass the time and distract myself from my aching feet, I answer them. I tell her about the clouds, the magic, and the kingdom. I even tell her about our sun god, Albion, and his brilliant eyes: the sun and moon. Though she's most interested in my golden goose. There is no end to her questions about Helen.

Her admissions about the surface world are far more intriguing. Britain, which I thought to be the biggest landmass on the surface, is but an island. Europe to the south is far bigger. Far bigger than *that* are places called Asia and Africa, though little is known about them. This knowledge makes me realize how little I know—especially when she laughs at my annoyance with these biting insects.

"Must be nice living in the clouds," Jess says, eventually. "No insects, no planting seeds. Just sun and music. Boring, though. If you don't work for anything, are you truly proud of it?"

"We are proud of our honor," I remind her as we stop under the shade of a tree so I can pick dirt and rocks from the soles of my feet.

"Easy to be honorable when you have few worries," Jess argues. "Not having to worry about locusts killing your crops, the well being poisoned, or roving brigands trying to burn down your home... Must be nice."

I open my mouth to argue before closing it. The truth is that she's right. *But is she right because she's correct or because you can't think of a way to prove her wrong?* Father asks.

Ignoring his question, I reply to Jess, "Honor is easier, but never easy. I would have stayed in the clouds, if not for the Beanstalker." Focusing on my hatred, I fall into silence the rest of the day, which does not last much longer.

When night falls, we make camp off of the road in a field. In our haste to leave, neither of us prepared rations. We shared one canteen the entire day. Hers, of course. She makes that quite apparent as I drink from it in the twilight hours. While I'm accurate with a bow—more accurate than Jess—she is far quieter than I am and can hide better. So she leaves to catch rabbits as I stoke a fire and prepare the spit we'll use to roast our food. Though I struggle with even that task.

When Jess returns with three bloody hares, she quips, "Ever thought about how reliance on magic makes you helpless without it?"

I pretend to cast a hex, mumbling the incantation for conjuring a telescope. But nothing happens, unsurprisingly. Jess still drops her kills and dives to the side as I move my hands in geometric patterns.

"I can't do magic, remember?" I remind her, but only after I finish laughing.

"*Not* funny," she mutters, brushing the dirt from her clothes. I'd feel worse if this wasn't the only thing that's brought me a smile all day or night. What I *do* feel worse about are the hares. Killing humans, I have no problem with, but these fluffy creatures? I've never had to do it. None of the meat in the clouds ever lived, just a juicy strip of beef created by magic. Here, I have to peel the fur from the muscles and skewer the beast from mouth to anus. But even that hesitation disappears when I inhale the smell of cooking meat. She eats one, I eat two, and the horse—*Harry*, though its hair is short and unenvious—eats a few withered apples Jess found in a field earlier in the day.

As dinner ends, Jess tries to hand the quiver and bow back to me, but I refuse to take it. "Swords and daggers are my specialties," I say. "You'll get more use from the bow than me. Besides, it makes you look more experienced." That gesture alone puts her back into good spirits. But there is still more I can do for her. With the rabbit safely in my stomach, I stand and unsheathe one of my swords. "A bow isn't good enough if you truly wish to be a knight. Draw your sword and face me."

If I have ever seen true happiness, it is plastered on Jess's face even after the dozens of times I force her to the ground. That, to me, is true magic.

Between my aching feet, our search for game, and each night's rest, the journey isn't three days. It's seven. Jess improves incrementally with her sword, enough to defend attacks if nothing else. Yet she is superior with the bow. Far from an expert, but she at least looks the part of a mercenary as we pass others on the road. I can only smirk at how they avoid us, me specifically.

But when we arrive at the city of Sprigginsville, a once-small town outside of London, the laughter has ebbed from my very bones. "Huh," Jess replies once I read her the name, as she cannot read. Though I can, this English language is more difficult to discern. Each word takes me time to put together. "This is the place... but it used to be called Hawkins."

Though primarily still an agricultural residence, a merchant district has spouted in the heart of the town. The buildings are wood and brick with overhanging second- and third-stories providing shaded walkways on either side of the thoroughfare. Lamps filled with whale oils light the streets from sundown to sunup, letting me see each new shop and their claim in great detail.

Arcana Arts! Secret Lore of the Giants and other Faerie Folk!
Potions! Ward Away the Giant Menace!
Weapons! Kill Your Giants Like Jack!
Perfumes!, Shields!, Charms! and all the rest. While the aristocrats walking past storefronts in their fancy clothes can read the words, criers stand outside the shops to shout wares at passerby. Entire streets are dedicated to finding giants, capturing giants, and killing giants—glass storefronts displaying tools, signs revealing depictions of dead giants, and jaunty music enticing shoppers inside. Many are. Everywhere I look, nobility from nearby London visit the shops with servants and buy trinkets. Buy lies.

Giants cannot be harmed with snake-oil potions or be poisoned with silvered blades. We cannot be weakened with powdered garlic or turned to stone by looking in a mirror. My *father* could not have been killed in a battle, even if a hundred humans fought him. Yet I walk past a newsboy spouting off about another giant sighting—the third this month.

I hate these buildings and these humans using my father's death to make money, but most of all, I hate the Beanstalker.

In the town's square I find his handiwork. A man clad in metal and gilded with gold hefts an ornate axe over his shoulder. His chin is chiseled, his hair long and flowing—neither is as I remember. He was a small man, even for human sizes, and his limbs were thin like straw. The goose, harp, and coins are missing from the statue, too, but I am more disturbed by the height of it. The metal Beanstalker is twenty feet tall—taller than my own father and any other giant. As if he somehow stands above us all.

"Beanstalker," I whisper, my eyes falling to the sign below the statue's feet. *Jack Spriggins,* the plaque reads in golden block letters. *The boy who climbed a beanstalk into the clouds, rescued a beautiful princess from the heathen giants, and slayed their king. Praise be to God.*

"Jack Spriggins... *Sprigginsville,*" I say between gritted teeth after reading the plaque to her. "He celebrated killing my father by renaming this town after himself." I look back at the gold accents everywhere in the town center and the stores themselves. "And he used Helen's golden eggs for the gilding."

What'd he do with the harp? the hateful voice posing as my Father asks. The sound is far louder than the day prior. In this battle for my soul, Father is winning, and Mother is silent.

"Uh, Titus?" Jess whispers, using my real name now that I've told her. She still sits astride her horse, staring everywhere except the statue. "People are watching us."

I force my gaze away from the Beanstalker, turning to stare at those watching me. Too many eyes. Nobles wear an assortment of odd clothes: neon particolored stockings, padded jackets, and overly extravagant dresses with escoffions. City guards don red capes and black leather vests over red batting shirts and breeches, metal helmets adorned with red and black stripes, and shields showcasing a giant's severed head. Shopkeepers wear a myriad of dresses and jackets much like the nobles, though their colors match the red and black theme of the town.

As I glare at all of them, one noblewoman's son breaks away from his mother's grip. In his light-blue frilled suit, he runs up to me with a leather pouch in my hand. I'd be curious if I didn't see the childlike cruelty in his pudgy smile. Digging his hand into the pouch, he throws a purple powder in my face. Though I block it with a hand, some of it gets in my mouth and I sneeze.

"Now die, giant!" shouts the boy in his silk clothes. "Die and give me gold!"

Instead of calling the child back, the noblewoman laughs at me. So do the rest of the townspeople. All but Jess, whose gentle steed whinnies as if it smells my emotions. The rage I've felt for three years funnels into a dense mass, hardening into a second heart on the right side of my chest. It pumps black ichor from my veins.

"Titus," Jess whispers, but I pay her no heed. "Don't—"

Dropping my hand from my face, the town must see something like murder in my expression because the laughter immediately dies. *So will this child.*

I grab the boy by the front of his shirt and raise him off his feet with my giant strength. The noblewoman gasps and the guards who'd been lounging stand to strict attention. No matter. I rip the bag of so-called magical powder from the boy's hand and dump the rest of it on his head as he wails and soils himself. Both piss and shit by the smell. The stains on his breeches and stockings spread from groin to ankles. Expensive garments by the looks of them. Ruined now. Too bad.

Now kill him, whispers Father in that hateful hiss. *Kill them all!*

I almost do until I catch the look of dawning horror on Jess's face. I drop the boy, and he falls three feet to the cobblestones, twisting his ankle. Wailing, he runs from me, stumbles twice, and falls into his mother's embrace. She tries to fix me with a deathly stare, but mine's far worse.

"Guards!" reproaches the noblewoman, lifting the child and patting him on the back as if burping him. "Aren't you going to seize that oaf?"

When I put a hand on one of my swords, others take a few steps back. The guards draw their swords, though they look terrified.

"Don't, all right?" Jess whispers. "There're more than two guards in a city. Just let me handle this." Begrudgingly, I remove my hand from the hilt, and in a much louder voice, Jess shouts from atop her horse, "Guards! Do you wish to fight a giant by yourselves?"

"He's no giant!" says the noblewoman, though everybody else seems to believe Jess.

"Of course not! But he's killed them, so you tell me what's worse?" Jess spits. When the noblewoman sputters a half-reply before becoming silent, Jess adds, "Hey, boy! I've heard many a tale of giants twice as big as my friend here. If there is one thing you should avoid, it's crying! Giants like their meat wet and salty."

To that, the boy only wails harder. When I give her a look, Jess's eyes apologize even as her mouth continues to lie. "The more tears you cry, the tastier you are! And children, well, they taste best. Especially plump ones with indulgent mothers and a bunch of fat on their bones. Boys like *you*. Do you want to know how a giant would prepare you, boy?" When he's too busy sobbing to reply, Jess says, "Stew! A giant would dunk you in a pot of boiling water. Well, that's after he'd skin you, of course. And don't worry, you'd be alive the entire time. Giants *love* fresh meat. For flavor, one might toss in some garlic, onions, carrots, and salt. But that's only after your boiled meat falls off your bones!"

That's her rabbit stew recipe, I think, but with all the eyes on me, I can only go along with the story. I flash a cruel smile, pulling out one of my daggers to pick at the meat stuck between my gums. It must be a horrifying sight, because a few of the shopkeepers back away. Others have hurriedly taken out pen and paper and furiously scribble notes as Jess continues to spin the tale.

"But giants don't have cups or bowls, no sir!" she says. "That stew—that juicy *human* stew—gets ladled out with your skull! Then they drink it through your eyeholes! When they're done eating, they crush your bones into a powder for their tea! And finally, those giants wear your knuckle bones like necklaces! Comb their hair with your ribcage! Scratch their backs with your spine! Is that what you want? Huh? *Is it?*"

"No," the boy mews.

"Then don't go throwing colored sand in people's faces, you brat!" Jess finishes. To back her up, I eye one guard and point at him. Jess raises an eyebrow, and I will her to understand. *Ask about Jack Spriggins.*

"You!" Jess shouts. "A word, good sir! Big Ben here won't harm you. Well, unless you ignore him. He *really* doesn't like that!"

You're going too far, Jess, I think, but I cannot say anything without breaking the spell she has on the townsfolk. Feeling the pressure of the merchants and nobles, the guard approaches me cautiously. Unlike the boy, he looks so uncomfortable that he's constipated.

"Where's the giant, huh?" Jess asks him. "The one Jack killed a few years back?"

Immediately, guilt elbows my heart. *Why wasn't it my first instinct to ask about Father? Why did my mind immediately go to killing the Beanstalker?*

The guard's finger shakes as he points towards a store. Jess frowns at him. "You're telling me a two-story-tall giant is in a *potion* store?"

"Beyond the store, lady," he replies, stuttering. Because he's so afraid, he doesn't notice how Jess's eyes light up at being called *lady*. "Up that hill, at the historical home of Lord Spriggins."

"I thank you," she says, looking proud upon her humble horse. Her chin is raised, her eyes downcast. Like true nobility. "We will trouble you no further then. Come along, Big Ben. Let us depart from this place."

Silently, we turn right through the town center and follow the road until we run out of cobblestones. When we're far enough from the guards and other humans to not be heard, I lean over and ask, "Rabbit stew, huh?"

"As if I know how to cook humans," she says, without looking over at me. "You're welcome, by the way."

I'm grateful to her until I look up the dirt path to the hill, where a great memorial sits at the top: an old cottage whose exterior has been renovated with glass windows too expensive for a peasant to own. A small pasture without any cows is nearby, along with a chicken coop similarly devoid of life. But that isn't what I focus on. A hundred yards from the house lies a museum built like a barn, whose doors are open as people stream in and out. From the giant sign hanging above the door of a beanstalk, I know this is where my father lies.

My entire body aches as if his bones call out to mine.

Jess is speaking to me, but I can't hear her. A high ringing infects my ears, and all I detect is the poisonous whispers of Father's hateful voice. I brush a few people aside as I walk toward the entrance. Through the open door, I see something: a stone coffin with a glass top is the center of attention in the room, raised from the floor like a holy altar. From my vantage point, I can't see the bones, but I know they're here.

I push through the crowd at the entrance and make my way inside, even as people shout at me. *I can bring him back to the clouds,* I think, making my way and kneeling beside the coffin. The beanstalk is gone, and so is Father's flesh, but his Father's skeleton is inside. I try not to look at his broken spine or skull—the blows suffered in his fall. With so many bones broken, it makes my job of putting him in a sack and carrying him to the clouds that much easier. I'll just have to break the glass first. I raise my fist but am interrupted before I can bring it down.

"Excuse me, mister!" says a voice behind me. "You have to pay to see..." When my head snaps around to look at him, the man leans away from me. He wears a particolored jacket of red and black over a simple orange tunic. His black hat is wide-brimmed and ornate with golden thread and a feather plume, but it's his stench that offends me most: a natural musk akin to a pigsty, covered by the charcoal smell of the cigar he's puffing. Pulling the cigar from his rotting teeth and blowing smoke, he tries again. "Mister, I don't care who you are. You have to pay to see the giant's corpse. This ain't a *free* museum."

I have to pay this human to see Father's corpse? I think to myself, rising to my full height as the ticket collector scrambles backward behind two guards, who also look unsure of themselves.

If not for Jess, I'd have killed all three of them.

"Oh, sorry, mistuh!" Jess says, thickening her natural accent as she pushes her way past the entrance to stand between me and the ticket collector. "My brothuh here just gets so excited over these things! Thinks this giant is his papa because he's so big. He's fast on his feet, but he's real slow if you understand my saying so. He got all them muscles 'cept for the ones in his head, so the doctuh say. He can't speak or nothin' eithuh. But he is real good with them swords! As Daddy says, 'Ben ain't the sharpest tool in the shed—come to think of it, he actually ain't in the shed at all!'"

I glare at Jess as the crowd laughs, and she looks over her shoulder at me with wide eyes as if to say, *What else was I supposed to do?* I don't have an answer. What choice do I have but to play along? Pretending to be stupid, I wave to the ticket collector as my eyes bore into him, Father's voice thrashing in my skull. It seems to come from the coffin instead of my skull.

Avenge me, he says. *Kill them all. Every last one of them.*

"You just tell me how much he owes, mistuh," Jess says. "I'll gladly pay."

At that admonition, the ticket collector regains his confidence and puffs on his cigar. With his gut spilling out over the belt of his wide breeches, he says, "Well, we'll just charge three for admission then. One for you, miss, and two for your brother there."

"Two?" Jess asks, dropping the accent out of surprise. "How?"

"Why, he's as big as two men!" People laugh until I stop waving and my eyes narrow. "Uh," the ticket collector adds while licking his lips, "just a joke, big guy. One ticket each."

Oh, you're dead, I think as Jess hands over a few copper coins to that grubby man in exchange for two tickets. *I'm going to burn this entire place to the ground, Father,* I think as I kneel beside the glass coffin. *I'll burn it all just as soon as I get your bones out. I'll get you back to Mother.*

Being only midday, I must distract myself with the museum and its lies. On the walls are oversized bannisters of House Spriggins, the red and black background with the giant's head slapped on it. It looks nothing like Father, but I know it's supposed to be him. Tapestries hang, too, in Jack's honor, showcasing him as the savior of the town in various heroic poses—always holding that axe. Strangely, Helen, my beloved goose, is not in any picture. Neither is the harp. As if he doesn't want the world to know about them. *Keeping the truth to himself so nobody knows where his wealth came from... Sneaky Beanstalker.*

Across the room, a museum worker dressed in a red tunic and black breeches rings a bell and shouts, "Here ye, here ye! Listen closely, for this is the true story of Jack and the Beanstalk!"

Looking at one another, Jess and I join the growing crowd to listen.

"In Hawkins lived a boy destined for greatness: Jack Spriggins!" says the storyteller. "But any onlooker would only see poverty. Jack lived with his mother, a poor window, who told him to sell their only cow because they had no money for food. So Jack went to the market, and on the way, he met a mage.

"'Young boy!' said the long-haired mage. 'What price are you catching for your heifer?'

"'Don't know, sir,' Jack replied. 'Whatever price is best, I'd say. I need the money for food.'

"To which the mage laughed and said, 'Why then, it is I who will offer you the best price! For I want to buy that cow for the price of five magic beans. Make no mistake, these are no ordinary beans, but they will grow bigger than any you've ever seen! You will have food for the rest of your days!'"

Magic beans, I think. *That's how the Beanstalker got to the clouds...*

The storyteller continues, "Elated, Jack took the magic beans and gave the magician the cow. But when he reached home, Jack's mother was wroth with anger, thinking he had been duped by a con-man. 'You fool! He took away your cow and gave you some beans!' she said, throwing the magic beans out the window. 'Now we have no cow and no food.'

"And that night, Jack went to bed without dinner.

"But the next day, Jack awoke and opened the door to find a huge beanstalk had grown from his magic beans! For two days, he climbed up the beanstalk. Then he reached a kingdom in the sky—the land of the giants. On one cloud lived a giant king and his wife. Both horrible, ugly creatures. Yet they lived in a grand palace, and from inside came the smell of cinnamon bread. So Jack went inside, begging for food.

"'Excuse me?' said Jack as he entered the kitchen. 'Could you please give me something to eat? I am so hungry!'

"But as the queen turned toward him, she screamed, awaking the entire palace. So Jack hid behind a bubbling cauldron. Then came the king, crying, 'Fee fi fo fum, I smell the blood of an Englishman! Be he alive, or be he dead, I'll grind his bones to make my bread!'

"Jack was so afraid he almost left. He would have, if not for the screams of a woman deeper in the castle. As brave and courageous as all the knights of the realm, Jack dashed from his hiding place, venturing farther into the stone castle. There, he found mountains of skulls, great cages filled with many animals, and more horrible giants. He killed one with a giant knife, pushed another into a boiling cauldron, and dropped a vase on the head of a third. Having bested his foes, Jack raced into the king's bedchamber where there hung a great cage. Inside it stood a beautiful princess!"

What? My fists tighten as the liar continues.

"'Sir! Please get me down from here!' she shouted, and Jack happily did so, cutting the rope that held her aloft. After breaking the lock on the cage, Jack and his princess raced back through the giants' castle only to be seen by the king, who stormed after them. They reached the beanstalk first and raced back down its leaves as the king followed. But Jack was first to touch the bottom, and with his ax, he cut down the beanstalk. The giant fell with it, where it lay dead upon the ground.'"

As the crowd cheers, a small growl rises in my throat.

"Upon that day," the liar continues, "Jack returned the princess to her family and accepted the title of lord and accompanying lands in exchange for her safe return. As the first of his line, Lord Spriggins was offered governorship of Hawkins, which is now Sprigginsville. With his help, the town is more prosperous than it has ever been! God save Lord Spriggins!"

"God save Lord Spriggins!" echoes the crowd, save for Jess and me.

This entire time, she's watched my face closely, and I know she feels my raw emotions. One bubbles up from my depths like the cauldron in Jack's so-called true story: grief. *They made you out to be a monster, but I know the truth. I know who you were.* I know I should be furious, but this sensation overwhelms me, and my sobs boom across the museum, loud enough to draw laughter from the skittish crowd. I try to look back at my father, but I can't see him through the waterfall.

"Ben," Jess whispers, grabbing my hand. "Are you okay?"

I nod my head, but it's an unconvincing lie.

"My, my!" the ticket collector shouts behind me. "The oaf really *does* think the giant is his papa!"

Jess tenses beside me as I square my shoulders. "No, Titus," she says in that hushed tone as people continue to laugh at me. She tugs at my arm, but I don't move. Not even when she uses her entire body to pull me a single step. "Tonight. We'll come back, all right? We'll destroy this place."

Finally, I let my feet walk, and I lumber toward the front entrance, slapping the ticket collector on the back twice—hard enough to feel something pop—before walking out into the sunlight.

And into the arms of twelve red-clad guards.

I stop just outside the entrance and unsheathe my blades—only to feel the tip of a sword pressed against my back. In my sorrow, I hadn't noticed the museum guards following us out here. Now they block my escape back into the building and keep me at swordpoint.

"None of that now," the captain of the guards says, marked with a red plume of horsehair trailing from his metal helmet. Ordering the other guards to not take our weapons, he adds, "We aren't here to kill you, so if you'd sheathe those blades, we can get going."

"What about my horse?" Jess asks, pointing to Harry, whose bridle is tied to a stable post outside the museum's entrance.

"Leave it. The guards will ensure its safety until we return. Besides, we'll be back soon enough," the captain replies.

"Where are we going?" Jess asks, keeping her hands high as her fingertips twitch.

The captain shrugs. "To Lord Spriggins, of course. He wants to meet you."

Only then do I relax, letting a genuine smile come to my lips.

Bring it.

Lord Spriggins's castle is high on the hill, perhaps a half-mile from the museum. In my single-minded focus to find my father's bones, I had missed it. I don't miss it now. Round towers of stone lie at the corners of the castle wall, with a smaller tower arising on either side of the drawbridge. Crenelated ramparts connect these towers high above my head, but I can still see the larger keep inside the courtyard, roofed with tiles.

I could question how much it cost to build a structure like this in only three years, but with enough golden eggs from Helen, I know the price is paltry. *Find the goose, take the harp, and kill Jack Spriggins,* I think, repeating the mantra as we near the entrance.

The drawbridge lowers as Jess and I, along with our armed escort, are forced across. I can only stare at the long banners rolled over the top of the wall and flying from poles, all picturing a severed giant's head. My father's head. I imagine how beautiful those banners will look after I mash the Beanstalker's corpse into them.

Servants of the stables and storehouses watch me pass as we're brought into the outer courtyard. After we're taken through a smaller stone wall into the inner courtyard—home to the kitchen, chapel, and guest quarters—lounging nobles stiffen when they see me. The boy who threw sawdust at me earlier begins to wail while his haughty mother appears triumphant, as if I'm the monster she vanquished.

Of all things, I laugh at her until she's too embarrassed to keep my gaze.

Lead into the keep, I expect cold stone, but with endless supplies of gold at his disposal, the Beanstalker has created a piss-poor replica of my father's palace. Windows of stained glass, golden ornamentation along archways, and swirling marble underfoot drive me closer to madness. So does the iconography along the walls: giants, faeries, and folklore. All conquered by humans who look like the Beanstalker.

Jess and I are brought to an antechamber on the second floor. Fur skin rugs cover the stone floor and mahogany dressers line the walls. Candelabras shine light across the room, as does colored sunlight spilling in through two rose windows. Two high-backed sofas dominate the middle of the room. The captain of the guards says something to me, I think, but I don't hear him. I stare at the door on the far side of the room even as Jess pulls me over to one red couch to sit with her. She, too, says something—she even wraps her hand around my forearm—but I ignore her as I try to keep myself from barging into the next room.

He's here. This is it, I think.

He's here. Kill him, whispers the hateful voice, sounding like Father.

He's here. Be careful, whispers the cautious voice, sounding like Mother.

When the door opens, I immediately stand. Because Jess is still holding onto me, she's thrown to her feet. Instead of seeing the Beanstalker, I see an old farmer in a straw hat holding his son's hand. Both have tears in their eyes.

"Bless you, Lord Spriggins," the farmer whispers. "You have no idea how much this means to me."

"Believe me, I do, Sam," replies a voice from inside the office. The Beanstalker. Odd, I always expected his voice to be deep and crackling, not impish and light. Nor do I expect a laugh.

It's a trick. Deception! booms Father.

I'd agree, but the farmer's tears seem real.

"Milord, are you ready for your next visitors?" the captain asks, peeking in through the door. From my vantage point, I can see very little, so I make my way toward the door before I'm stopped by a different guard. "It's the tall man you asked for. He has a friend with him. His sister, I've been told."

"The tall man? Oh, splendid!" the Beanstalker exclaims from the darkness beyond the doorway. "Send them both in at once."

"Yes, milord," replies the captain. He takes off his plumed helmet and walks into the room first as another guard ushers me forward, but not before taking my weapons. Jess's too. He promises to give them back before we leave, but I doubt that very much, considering I'm going to kill his boss.

I duck my head as I walk through the doorway and enter an ornate office. A fireplace burns in the far corner, casting reddish light and shedding orange embers. Above the mantle rests a portrait of a mousy older woman in an extravagant red dress. Though she looks uncomfortable in the lavish clothes, her smile is genuine. *His mother,* I assume, hating the woman who gave birth to the Beanstalker. I would have expected him to have a picture of himself there.

Behind a gold-inlaid desk is a window overlooking the inner and outer courtyards. Eclipsing that view stands the man I've wished to see for the last three years. The Beanstalker is short, thin, and young. His brown eyes are the color of shit, the skin pale as a wight's. The nose is like a mountain, his lips chapped. He tries to grow a beard, but it's patchy. A gold coronet rests atop his stringy brown hair and is held in place by his oversized ears. He is ugly despite his ornate black-and-gold tunic, the long red robe trailing to the floor behind him, and the jeweled rings on his steepled fingers. However, Jess looks at him like he's the most beautiful person she's ever seen.

"Look at you, tall man," the false lord says to me, putting his hands on his hips as the unhelmed captain joins him on the opposing side of the desk. "You're the biggest man I've ever seen. You'd look even more fearsome in plate armor, though. Especially helmed with a long black plume. You have quite the baby face for a man of your stature. You're what, twenty-five? Twenty-six?"

Jess harrumphs and says, "Milord, my brother Ben doesn't talk."

"Twenty," I say, at just the same time.

The Beanstalker looks between us, raising an eyebrow. Swallowing, Jess says, "What I meant to say, milord, is that my brother doesn't talk *often*. I usually don't hear more than a few words out of him a year."

Studying her for an intense moment, the Beanstalker breaks the tension with a hammered smile. "Not to worry. The strong, silent type is exactly the man I'm looking for. And to be so large at twenty, well, the Lord favors you. Truly, He must. Because I'm also twenty, and, well... I don't think people will ever mistake us for twins." He scratches his chin. "No, not twins, but you *do* look familiar. Do I know you from somewhere? No, couldn't possibly. I'd have noticed you. Perhaps I've met your brother?"

"Older brother, milord. He came to Hawkins once or twice, but never Sprigginsville," Jess says, albeit too quickly. The Beanstalker's eyes narrow, but he doesn't interrupt Jess as she adds, "If I might say so, my brother and I didn't mean to make such a fuss with that noble earlier. Her child threw sawdust—I mean, *giant* powder—in his face. If not the boy's fault, then it's definitely his mother's for—"

"That?" the Beanstalker asks, coming around to this side of the desk even as Jess watches me nervously. "Oh, I don't care about that, miss..." While looking at her, he gestures expectantly.

"Jess," she provides.

"Ah. Beautiful name, my dear," Jack says, grabbing her hand and patting it nicely. I abhor the way she smiles at him. "As I was saying, I don't care about the incident in the square, Jess. Lady Aurelia truly is…" He looks around cautiously despite being in his own office, leans forward, and whispers, "A *bore.*" Then he leans back, laughing and holding his stomach. Jess joins him. I don't.

"I'll tell you something," the Beanstalker continues, walking back around to the opposite side of the desk and just out of my reach. "These noble people truly don't have any clue how to survive outside a castle. No, their guards are their shepherds. Truly, those so-called lords and ladies are as close to heifers as I've seen these past three years. Much more impressive are the farmers and townsfolk. They make all of this possible."

I narrow my eyes at him, searching for deception, but I'm too new to this skill to spot it. Jess is better for sifting truth from lies, but she's too enamored with the Beanstalker for her own good. His eyes don't dart around, his grin isn't forced. Yet something has to be amiss. *How is* this *the Beanstalker?* My hands tighten into fists, my knuckles accidentally cracking. *This is a trick. It* has *to be a trick.*

The Beanstalker looks down at my knuckles, then up at me. His eyebrows knit together as he asks, "Something wrong, Ben?"

"Thinking of Aurelia," I lie, stunting my words and grunting them to diminish my accent.

"Remind me never to get on your bad side," the Beanstalker jokes. I offer a small smile, but only because I imagine popping his head like a pumpkin. *Have to figure out how to get Jess out of here safely before I kill him. Want to take my time killing him.* "Please sit. I've seen how tall you are, so I don't need to keep you standing. These chairs are quite comfortable, I'll have you know. My mother approves."

If I sit, it will be harder to attack him. I should just attack him now. I hesitate, looking back at the guards behind me and the captain on the opposite side of the desk beside Jack. *Jess will die if I try. Am I willing to get her killed?* I glance over at her, and she looks back at me, waiting to see what I do. *Too trusting… and Mother said giants were. Humans aren't so different. Some of them, at least.*

I sit down. Jess follows suit. The Beanstalker leans back in his ornate chair, interlacing his jeweled fingers behind his head. "Allow me to get to the heart of our discussion. I have a big problem, Ben. Well, I guess you could say, a *giant* problem." Jack waits for us to laugh and genuinely looks disappointed when we don't. "I try to be a forward-thinker, wondering what the future holds for my family and the town at large. Before the beanstalk, Hawkins was *nothing*. Now? Sprigginsville is a place of wonder, where myth and legend become real. Where peasants can become *lords*. But the glamor is starting to wear off. We need more excitement."

"Why not create another beanstalk?" Jess asks.

The Beanstalker keeps the smile on his face, but his eyes are hard. "I would, dear, but I have no more magic beans. Nor can I find the mage. So, I doubt there is any way to travel back to the land of giants ever again."

As he sighs, a cold chill tingles down my back. *No more magic beans... How am I getting home? Am I getting home?* My gut sinks, offering a single word. *No.*

When I grimace, the Beanstalker asks, "Is everything all right?" When I nod, he continues, "As for excitement, I'm hoping you can provide it. In fact, I would like to offer you a job, Ben. I want you to be my giant. Your baby face might work to our advantage, actually. We could say you were a *young* giant who fell from those clouds but somehow survived the landing. You would be the face of our town. A mascot, I suppose."

What? I sit forward, causing the captain to react by putting a hand on the hilt of his sword. However, the Beanstalker is so carried away by his schemes and plans that he doesn't seem to notice. *How could he possibly know?*

"No... That idea is too far-fetched even for my liking." The Beanstalker snaps his fingers, and I lean back, trying to relax. "I've got it! Let's forget the young giant idea. Let's say that you are a *half*-giant. A giant, perhaps the king I killed, took a human as his bride and impregnated her, resulting in you. And now you *hate* giants." A wild smile overcomes the Beanstalker's face. "Yes. *Yes!* This is perfect. You'll be Sprigginsville's famed giant-killer: Big Ben! You'll be our sable knight. We'll give you plate armor, a caparisoned destrier, and knighthood." Jess gasps, and Jack winks with a glimmer of excitement in his eyes. "I can do that, you know. Because I'm Lord Jack Spriggins the First, slayer of giants, protector of peasants, governor of Sprigginsville, blah, blah, blah."

"You want *me* to work for *you*," I say as Jess shifts anxiously from foot to foot.

"Both of you! I'm happy to hire your friend as well," the Beanstalker replies. "I have no shortage of funds." He rubs his chin, looking at her. "Come to think of it, it would be even more interesting and outlandish for someone of your stature to be paired with her. She can be your Lady Knight." Jess straightens, looking as if she's about to cry tears of joy, but Jack doesn't see it. He's too busy staring at me. "Come to think of it, the Lady Knight idea might be difficult. Perhaps she'll be your damsel in distress, and you'll have to save her from the clutches of your neme-sis—whoever that might be—and you'll joust with him and save her for the delight of our tourists."

Jess's excitement has already evaporated by the time the Beanstalker turns his head back toward her. Reading her like a page of parchment and noticing how I watch her, he says, "I can see how much you mean to Ben, my dear. So if it means Ben accepting my proposal, I'm happy to oblige you in any manner I can. Perhaps making you a lady in your own right. Your family would never need to worry. Neither would your children. They, too, could be nobility."

"A lady," Jess whispers excitedly, seeming not to have heard anything else he'd said after that word. "Yes… I'd love that."

"Before I agree, I'd like to know more about you," I say in that same halting style of speech. Jess is crestfallen. She pleads with me using her eyes, but I look away. *So close to her dream only for it to be ripped away. I understand that pain, but it doesn't mean I'll give up my quest for her.*

"And you said he didn't speak often," the Beanstalker says to Jess, who smiles demurely. "Very well, Big Ben. Or should I say, soon-to-be *Sir* Big Ben. Ask your questions."

"Why was that farmer crying when he left?" I ask.

"Who?" Lord Spriggins asks, genuinely confused. Then he hides it with a smile. "Oh, right. Sam Horath. That old man always helped my mother when he could, and I haven't forgotten that. *Won't* forget it. So I paid him twice what his farmland was worth. Now he has the funds to be a merchant." He turns his head to Jess. "As I told you, I'm quite nice to my friends."

Because you have unlimited funds, Father's shadow says from the fireplace. *What happens to your enemies?*

"How did you get your funds?" I ask, watching him. I hate him, yet everything about him shows that he's supposedly a good man. And yet, there's something I can't quite figure out. Something *wrong*.

"My funds? I got them in exchange for the princess I rescued," the Beanstalker replies, smiling. "Quite beautiful. If I didn't believe in chivalry, I'd have kept her for myself. But she's safe at home now. And her father's reward is safe with me."

During all that time, Jack's eyes never left mine. The smile never changed. Either he was telling the truth about everything or lying about it all. It has to be the latter.

"How did you *really* get your funds?" I ask, too angry to speak slowly. My voice comes out full clip, as does my accent.

The Beanstalker blinks, tilting his head. "You know, there is something *quite* familiar about you, Ben. Where did you say you were from again?"

"I didn't," I reply.

"Wilmont," adds Jess, another lie. She hailed from Newshire. "Our entire family—"

"Pardon me, Jess, but I'd like to hear it from Ben here," Jack replies, standing from his chair.

"You visited my home once. Funny. I thought'd you remember," I say, also rising. Behind me, I hear ringing sheathes as swords are drawn. Jack doesn't tell them to put away their weapons, nor do I sit down.

I'll be across the table before they can stop me, I think, eyeing the captain. He expects me to lunge at the Beanstalker. I don't. I feint for Jack and dive on the captain. As big as I am, I topple him with my shoulder and kick

Jack's legs out before he can duck away. My left hand grabs his hair while my right wraps around his neck.

As I rise to my feet and pull the Beanstalker to his, Jess dives over the table, struggling for the captain's sword. Yet he pulls a dagger from his belt and holds it to her throat. We eye each other with our hostages.

"Tell your guards to drop their weapons, or you die," I spit. While I am only a couple feet taller than these men, I'm immensely stronger and could kill the Beanstalker with just a single squeeze of my fingers. He knows it, too, as I tighten my hand around his throat.

Jack licks his chapped lips and, in a half-strangled voice, replies, "No. I think you like your girl too much to—*agh!*" He thrashes as I squeeze my fingers and then loosen them enough to breathe. *"Guards! Drop your weapons!"*

The captain drops the dagger, but Jess doesn't immediately pick it up. "You... would've sacrificed me?" she asks, and her face breaks my heart.

"No," I lie, "but I know the Beanstalker cares more about living than killing you."

Maybe it's Spriggins's influence on me, but this lie passes her detection. Looking relieved, Jess picks up the knife and puts it to the captain's throat once she forces him to his knees. The rest of the guards—now four, because the other two guards waiting in the antechamber rushed in at the Beanstalker's scream—toss their swords and knives down, kicking them to one side and stepping to the opposite after I order them to.

"Who are you?" Jack rasps, still slapping my arms ineffectively.

I grin, though he cannot see it from his angle. *Three years I've waited for this.* "Where's my goose, Beanstalker?"

"*Your* goose?" Jack stills. Then he laughs mirthlessly. I squeeze him again so he can't breathe. The chuckling turns to choking.

After I repeat my question, I release his throat just enough to let him speak. "You're from the clouds, aren't you? Don't tell me... You really *are* the child of giants? Yes, you must be, because I know whose face yours reminds me of. I saw it hurtling toward the ground just after I cut down the beanstalk. I watched your father's face smash into the ground—"

With my freehand, I grab the quill on his desk and stab him on the arm with it. If I hadn't been holding him so tightly, he might've screamed. "I want you to tell them the truth. How many giants did you kill?"

"Four—*wait!*" he says just before I stab him again. Lower on the arm this time. "One, all right? It was one!"

"Yes. Only my father." I glare at the guards, who stare back at me with wide eyes. Then I rip the quill from the lord's flesh, tempted to write in blood with the blank parchment on his desk. I ask, "Was there a princess in the giant palace?"

"Yes—*no!*" he replies, just before I stab him again. "There wasn't a princess, all right? I made it up! Is that what you want to hear, you giant bastard?"

"It's time your people hear the truth," I reply. "How did you get into the palace?"

"I slid between the bars of the gate, all right?" the Beanstalker snaps. "Then I ran inside. I hid from the servants and searched the rooms to find valuables. I found those gold coins, your goose, and that harp, but the damned thing started screeching when I stole it. So I ran. Your father followed me, but I beat him to the ground. Then I cut down that beanstalk with an axe. He fell and died. I lived and celebrated." The Beanstalker looks over at me, his eyes bloodshot. "And you know what? I'm not even sorry! I did what I had to because I was starving. So was my mother. You had an entire palace, and I had nothing! What would you have done?"

"I would have just asked for food," I say. "My father would have given it to you, even a place to stay, had you asked for it. That's all you had to do. Instead, you stole from him. Then you killed him. And now you use his corpse for *tourism*."

"And?" the Beanstalker asks, frothing at the mouth. "What would you have done with it?"

"Burned it to free his soul," I say, sniffing as a tear drops from my eye. "Instead, you took the bones... What'd you do with his flesh?"

"Fed it to the hogs." When I freeze, he asks, "What? Would you have preferred it go to waste?"

I don't reply, but my resolve hardens. *I'm going to kill you before the day's over.* "Where's the goose?"

"I told you, oaf. The damned bird is dead—*agh!*" I stab him again, leaving the quill in his arm and twisting it. As his eyes water, Jack hisses, "It's dead, all right? Three weeks ago. You're too late."

"You're lying, Beanstalker," I say, tightening my hand. "There's no way you'd let that bird die. Not when it's giving you golden eggs."

"Ben?" Jess asks, interrupting the conversation while still holding a knife to the captain's throat. "We're running out of time." She gestures to the window. Somebody, somehow, must have seen the struggle in Jack's ornate window, because more guards are sprinting toward the keep along the ramparts and through the inner courtyard. "What are we going to do?"

"We're getting what we came here for," I say to her. To the captain of the guards, I say, "You might be paid by the Beanstalker, but you won't die for him. So where's the goose? Surely Jack's told you. *Someone* has to guard her."

"Fourth floor," replies the captain, hanging his head. "In a private room beside milord's quarters."

"You *fool!*" the Beanstalker shouts, color flushing his cheeks as he again tries to wriggle from my grasp. "That bird is the only thing paying your salary!"

"The fourth floor," I echo, trying to imagine my dear Helen stuck inside for three years. Even with light and an open window, she must be miserable. *Probably is on the verge of death.* "Why?"

"It was the only place we could ensure the bird wasn't stolen," the captain replies. "We kept her in the dungeon while the keep was being built, but she didn't do well in there."

As my throat dries, I ask, "And my mother's harp?"

"Given to the queen in exchange for lands and titles," the captain replies, wincing as Jess presses the knife closer against his throat.

"And the sack of coins?" I ask, though a weight settles in my stomach. I can already guess what happened.

"Melted down into normal coins and spent to build the castle and rebuild the town," the captain admits. "The goose doesn't lay eggs all year round, which we hadn't realized until we ran out of eggs."

The coins spent, and the harp sold. Only Helen is left... And I didn't even get any beans. The failure weighs heavier than the Beanstalker, and it takes all of my willpower to keep my hands from throwing him through the window. *Still need him to get out of the city.*

"We're going to the fourth floor for my goose, then we're leaving," I tell Jess, and she pulls the captain to his feet but is shorter, making it difficult to keep the knife at his throat. Instead, I grab him by the neck, pushing both men in front of me. "Bring three swords. Bar the door with one."

"Got it," Jess says, scrambling to follow my directions as we exit the room and step into the hallway. Behind me, Jess bars the double-door by sliding a sword through the handles. Then she grabs her bow and quivers left beside the door. Far away but approaching, I hear the clanging of armed guards running up the stairs and searching the keep, floor by floor.

"What are you going to do?" the Beanstalker asks in a raspy voice. "You think you're just going to *walk* out of the castle? Out of my town? No. You're going to die here. The truth will die with you. Or maybe, I'll let you live, to be in my zoo. Yes. *That.* You'll keep people coming here for decades. Then it won't matter how many eggs that goose lays. You'll turn Sprigginsville into a national attraction."

"Save your breath," I tell him. Lord Spriggins shuts up, if only because of my constricting hand.

Returning through halls to one staircase, we ascend two flights to the top floor, with the captain guiding me toward my goose. We run into two more guards outside of Helen's chamber, but they are quick to drop their weapons. The captain says, "Jack wears a key around his throat. You'll need it to get—"

I kick the door hard enough to rip it from its hinges. The wood falls in, clattering to the floor. Ushering the two guards inside first, I follow with the Beanstalker and his captain. The place is a pigsty. Sunlight from large, albeit barred, windows streams into the room. Bird feces litters the stone floor, as does hay, feathers, and a single golden egg. Jess gasps, seeing it. She picks it up and taps it against the ground, creating a dull thud.

"Solid gold. It's more money than we'd made in a decade," Jess says, in hushed awe. "My God. With that goose, we don't have to be knights or ladies. You could be a king. I could be a *queen*."

Before I can answer, I'm greeted by a surprised honk. A golden-feathered goose peeks her head up from a pile of hay in the corner. Honking incessantly, she flies straight at me. She quiets only when I shush her. Hopping on to my shoulder, she nuzzles my cheek and nips at my ear, just as she used to when I was a child.

I have Helen. I should just kill Jack while I have the chance... The clanging armor echoing over the stones is closer now. *But then I have no leverage against the knights.*

Perhaps, but you don't need the captain, Father's voice whispers. *If you let him go, what guarantee do you have he won't turn around and kill you? Better that your enemies don't have a leader.*

It's hard to question the logic, especially when Mother's voice offers no arguments.

"Does Jack have any magic beans?" I ask the captain as I decide his fate.

"Yes. Around his neck. In a leather pouch." He looks over at Jack, who would scream curses if I wasn't strangling him.

Because my hands are full, Jess is the one to pull out the pouch. She looks into it and shows me a solitary black bean still around Lord Spriggins's neck. *My way out.* I almost throw the bean out the window, hoping for a beanstalk to immediately rise from the dirt and reach the clouds. But if Jack was telling the truth, the beanstalk needed a full night to grow. That's time I don't have, and I don't dare waste my one chance. *I'll use the bean later.*

After Jess wraps the necklace around my thick neck, I ask the captain, "How many guards does the Beanstalker have?"

"Twenty in the castle," the captain says, sagging forward as if answering the question is costing him his soul. "Twenty more in the town."

I stiffen at his words. *Forty?* Maybe if I could kill all of them in a hallway, but out in the town? I need an escape route. "Where are the secret exits?"

"Milord knows if there are any. He hasn't shared." The captain looks over at Jack, who still can't speak. Then he looks at me. "Please. I just want to go home to my family, giant. If you let me go, I'll trouble you no longer. You have my word as a man and father."

He's lying. He'll turn on you. You can't let him go. Listening to Father, I close my fist and crush the captain's throat. Choking in vain as I release him, the captain falls to the floor and dies as I throw the Beanstalker into the adjacent wall. Helen honks, flying from my shoulder as I charge at the two defenseless guards and smash them with my sledgehammer fists. Their corpses turn the hay red.

Before Jack can recover his senses, I pick him up and grab him by the neck again. He flinches away, as if he realizes how close I am to killing him. I grab his right arm with my hand, the threat clear. "Are you going to tell me how to get out of here?"

When Jack hesitates, I snap his wrist. He can't scream. "The dungeon," Jack says eventually after I loosen my hold on him. "There's a secret passage down there. It leads out to the town."

"Perfect." Releasing the Beanstalker's mangled arm, I take a moment to pet Helen with my now-empty hand as she flies back up to my shoulder. Unaware or uncaring of the dead captain, she nuzzles me harder. Jess, however, is very aware. She stares down at him, then back up at me. I can't read her expression.

"Put on his uniform," I tell her, pointing at the captain's corpse. "Grab a helmet too. Maybe we can trick the others."

"Should've had the captain bring his helm instead of leaving it in the office," Jess says while sifting through the pockets of the three corpses. With a quick glance, I notice the bulge of the golden egg in her pocket but say nothing of it.

After she dons the guard's helm, we leave, traveling toward the same staircase we ascended earlier. With the circular stairs revolving clockwise, I have the advantage in descending—my right hand is free to swing my sword while the guards' swords will be scraping the innerwall of stone. Unless they are left-handed. Or they're following me down the stairs.

"Just go quick," I tell myself. With Jess watching my back and holding Helen, I clamber down the uneven stairs, keeping the Beanstalker in front of me as a human shield.

I encounter the first two guards on the third-floor landing. I expect them to lower their weapons, but they don't. Perhaps it's because Jack mouths something. Maybe because I'm already bloody. I don't know. I can only respond with steel. So afraid of hitting the Beanstalker, the guards can only parry my attacks as I hack at them and turn their wooden shields to ribbons. I push them back down the stairs with each thrust and slash until I break one guard's sword and stab through his leather armor. The other guard lunges forward, but I let go of my sword and smash his head into the wall hard enough to hear something crack.

Both guards fall on the stairs and block my path, but their screams draw attention. More guards come as I retrieve my sword. I hack through them, too, separating limbs as I become death's scythe. Jack shields me, slapping at swords and clawing at faces as he tries to pull away from me. He doesn't, though I bathe in his misery.

Blood spatters across the clothes Jess's mother made for me. It pools around my bare feet, almost causing me to slip. Jack is more affected. His clothes are ruined, and in using him as my shield, he's been cut numerous times. Most are shallow, but one is deep and cuts close to his stomach. Gone is the proud, cunning man. The Beanstalker has been replaced with a sniveling child wearing shoes too big for him to fill. Sadly, they aren't big enough for my giant feet either.

The blood should bother me. So should the screams and clamor. They don't. Father's hateful voice gives me the encouragement I need to continue my blistering assault. It thirsts for blood. No matter how much I give—with crimson pools cascading down the steps behind me—it is never enough. I wade through a dozen bodies as I lumber down the rest of the stairs and arrive in the decorated foyer, only to find it deserted. The other guards must be up on the higher floors.

"The dungeon is that way," the Beanstalker snivels, first trying to point with his broken wrist before using his left hand. I start walking in the direction he points but stop as Jess grabs me and shakes her head.

"What is it?" I ask, looking for hiding guards until Jess shakes her head.

"Why would he be telling you where the dungeon is?" she asks. "Why would he tell you anything?"

My head whips around to find the Beanstalker staring at the ground. "You're lying to me. You were going to trap me in the dungeon. What was you plan? For both of us to die?"

"You want to get out, right?" he asks, still too afraid to look at me. "And I don't want to die. If you die, I do too. I know it. So let's just go before the others get here."

Ignoring him, I command Jess to look outside. From her perspective, the portcullis is down and the drawbridge is up. The peasants and aristocrats are trying to leave but are being stopped by guards at the gates and searched. That's why the foyer is empty. The guards have barred the castle's exits.

We're not getting out of here, I think.

Dig a mass grave, growls Father. *That's what you said, isn't it? Now's the time to keep your word.*

If Jess wasn't with me, maybe. But I don't have that option. "No more lies, Beanstalker. Where is the escape tunnel? Tell me. Otherwise, I'll kill you. Right here. Right now."

Jack looks up at me, and I see what he's been hiding by avoiding my gaze: hatred. It's like the eyes I saw only in a mirror for three years. He isn't crying but stands straight, as if his fear had been a charade. Only now does he look like the Beanstalker I always envisioned.

Cunning.

The Beanstalker licks his lips. "In my private chambers. On the fourth floor. Trap door under the bookshelf." I stare at him. I don't know if he's telling the truth, so I break his other arm. When he replies with the same answer, I trust him even less. That's the problem with all his lies. I can't divine the truth.

Even if he were being honest, I'd have to go back up to the fourth floor. How many more guards are that way? How many will meet me in the staircase and have the advantage? These are risks I cannot make. Yet what is my other option? To run outside with archers on the ramparts and guards in my way? Then somehow raise the portcullis and lower the drawbridge? Perhaps if I was a full-grown giant, but not at my size.

I'm doomed, I think, closing my eyes. *But so is Jack.*

"I wanted more time to kill you... I guess we don't always get what we want, do we?" Turning the Beanstalker around in my grasp so I can see his face, I close my hand incrementally. "You took everything from me. My father. My goose. My happiness. Was it worth it?" As his throat collapses, Jack fights with his meager might and strains as I slowly suffocate him. "What was that? I can't hear you, Beanstalker. Nobody ever will. Never again." His broken hands beat at my chest, but I remain stoic, looking into his eyes as the light fades from them. When he stops fighting, I snap his neck to be sure of his death. I'm no idiot, but I know he's craftier than me.

When the Beanstalker falls, so does my anger. It dies with him, but the sorrow remains, weighing more now to fill up the vacated space. With that added weight, I crush Jack's head under my barefoot and grind his brains across the stone. Shards of bone spike my heel, but I relish that pain. *I fulfilled the first oath.*

With the broken hands and skull, I imagine this is exactly what it looked like when Father fell to the surface. *Their skeletons are identical now.*

"Titus," Jess says after finishing throwing up and wiping spittle from her lips. "How are we getting out of here? More guards are coming!"

The Beanstalker's corpse gives me the idea. Stabbing him in the chest with my sword, I rub his blood across my face and chest, soaking my shirt in the wound. Admittedly, it's already far bloodier than I expected, compliments of the guards in the stairwell.

"What are you doing?" Jess asks as I pull the rings, coronet, and robe from Jack's body so others won't realize it's his body. I pocket the rings but toss the robe and coronet into a random room near the staircase.

"Dying." Laying on the ground and holding my eyes shut, I ask, "You're a guard, right? Well, you just killed me. And now you've got instructions to pull my corpse to the museum and put it with the other giant. Lord Spriggins's orders."

"And if it *doesn't* work?" Jess asks.

"Then I'll really be dead," I say. "I trust you, Jess. You can do this."

"Easy to say when all you have to do is play *dead*," she grumbles, trying to drag me to the entrance. Considering my size, she struggles. When more sets of feet come trampling down the stairs, she shouts in a low grumble, "You three! Help me get this oaf out of the castle. Our lord wants him in the museum. We'll cut him up there."

"What happened?"

"No clue. Captain pulled the bastard down the stairs, now he's looking for the oaf's accomplice," Jess snaps with enough anger that even I believe her. "The rest of you should help search. She's still here. Might be pretending to be a servant." Without waiting to see if they follow her orders, Jess begins dragging me toward the entrance again.

Holding my breath and expecting trouble, I tense. *If I hear blades, I'll attack.* The attack never comes. Instead, I feel hands grab me around my shoulders and legs. They lift together, pulling me into the air and groaning with the effort. They curse me and complain, but none dare speak back to Jess. Especially not after having seen the devastation in the staircase. By the echoes of their footsteps and the heat of the sunlight on my skin, I feel the exact moment we exit the keep and enter the inner courtyard. I can't hear that annoying kid or her mother, but I assume they've already left. The only sounds I can hear are servants and guards running about, along with the sounds of animals from the nearby stables. For the goose's part, Helen lies on my chest to protect me, which also helps to hide the rise and fall as I breathe shallowly.

I hear the creaking sound of a door, and I imagine the guards carrying me through the small inner wall toward the outer courtyard. The sounds of baying animals intensifies as we pass the stable, and the guards drop me, convincing Jess to get a wagon to carry me the rest of the way. One guard kicks me in the chest out of spite, and I clamp down on the grunt in my throat. With little care, the three men heft me into a wagon and tether it to a horse. However, they don't leave as I'd hoped. They stay to escort the horse toward the museum, discussing how they'll cut me apart at the museum.

As the horse plods toward the gate, I hear clanking chains winding and unwinding around their winches as the portcullis rises and the drawbridge falls. The sharp echo of the horse's feet slap against the wood, but as we rumble onto the grass, that sound dulls.

When the horses stop, I hear voices. Lots of them. *The museum. We're here.*

My heart pounds heavier, and I can only pray that the guards are not watching me closely. As the people crowd around my wagon, clamoring like animals, I struggle to keep my eyes closed. Especially when one human touches my hand and another jumps onto the wagon. I imagine it's a guard who's about to stab me. Helen honks from atop my chest, and Jess tells the people to get away, but they don't listen. When I hear Helen's strangled cry, I know somebody has grabbed her by the neck.

No. My eyes blaze open.

The first thing I see is a boy in a light-blue suit standing between my legs and strangling Helen. The *same* boy who threw dust in my face. Terrified, he instinctively lets go of Helen and steps back, but not fast enough. I kick him in the chest. He flies backward and lands in the dirt hard enough to knock the breath from his lungs, even as others scream. Seeking vengeance, Helen flies at him, ripping out tufts of his hair before he can get back to his feet. She then assaults the boy's mother and shoves her into a dung pile. I'd laugh, but I don't have time.

As a guard reaches for his sword, I sit up, grab him by the helmet, and slam his head into the wagon's railing twice. As he falls, I pull his sword from its sheath and leap from the wagon onto my feet. The chaos of fleeing peasants spooks the horse, who tramples a few humans as they scatter in all directions. Some run toward the castle. Others to the museum. Most run down the hill toward the town. Jess isn't among them, but I can't see where she is because she's dressed as a guard.

A glint of metal moves in my periphery, and I somersault forward, narrowly missing the blade intended for my head. That guard and two of his friends charge at me, but he is faster than the other two. He reaches me first, and I bat his sword aside and punch him in the chest with my freehand. Even with his leather armor, I hear bones crack. He falls like dung from a horse's ass, and I take his sword as I stomp on his helmet.

The other two guards take a smarter tactic, approaching as a pair. Until one stabs the other in the neck. Jess pulls off her helmet, her hair matted on her face and neck with sweat. Despite the fear, she grins broadly. Yet the expression falters as two more guards from the museum charge toward us. Smartly, Jess takes refuge behind me as I await my enemies.

They attack simultaneously, and I parry their blades rather than overextend. Breaking from them and creating a foot of distance between us, I circle to the left, but they match me, going right. Then I feint to test their weaknesses. The right guard is slower to react and slashes with his blade, which misses me completely as I jump backward. With his blade down, I stab at the left guard with one sword as I cut off the right guard's sword-hand with the other. As that man falls, I turn my full attention to the remaining guard and break through his defenses with a fury of blows from both blades. After his head falls from his shoulders, I turn back toward the other guard, but Jess has already skewered him through the back.

Beaming at me, she says, "I can't believe it... We actually survived!"

"Yeah," I reply, but I'm not in the mood to celebrate. I spy the grass for more enemies, but these six slain guards are the only ones nearby. There might be more in the town, but they aren't here yet. The only humans left are the noblewoman and her child, who Helen keeps attacking, shoving, and tripping. I trudge through the grass toward the noblewoman and her child. Helen honks at me, but the woman only screams. Rightfully so, considering she's just seen me kill three guards. I look at my sword, then sigh. Part of me wants to kill them, but that'd be too merciful. These two need a lasting lesson to be kinder to others.

"Stand up," I say, but the woman recoils. "You're going to stand up, or I'm going to cut off your head. Your choice."

When she stands, I stomp on her foot hard enough to break all her toes. Without magic, they won't heal right, and she'll hobble for the rest of her life. I do the same to the boy, who holds a hand to his chest, probably having broken a rib or two when I kicked him. I feel no empathy for them as they limp away and disappear over the hill.

"We need to get out of here," Jess says as Helen flies to my shoulder again. "The guards in the castle are going to know we've escaped. So will the ones in town." As if by magical premonition, I hear a horn trumpeted by guards still in the castle. "See?"

"Not yet," I say, handing Helen to her and walking back toward the wooden museum, whose front door is now locked. It crashes to the ground after three kicks, and inside, the people cry out in fear.

"Get out," I say, and the humans sprint by me. The last one through the door is the ticket collector, but he doesn't get far. I grab him and pluck the cigar from his mouth. "Not you. Where's your ticket?"

"What ticket?" His mouth opens in horror as his jowls quiver.

"Two tickets actually. You're as fat as two men." My lips curve into a malicious smile.

"But I don't have any tickets!" he shouts, wriggling.

"No? Then I guess you won't be leaving. Too bad." I snap his neck. Though he falls onto his stomach, the ticket collector's head is twisted so he's still looking up at me.

With barely a thought, I flick the cigar at him and walk over to the glass coffin containing my father's bones. "You're going home, Father. I'm bringing you home." I smash open the glass and begin pulling out my father's bones, putting them in an impromptu sack fashioned from a tapestry I steal from the wall.

"What are you doing?" Jess asks, coming into the room with Helen in her arms. "We need to leave, Titus."

"I'm taking my father's bones. Then we'll leave. Then I'll make my beanstalk and return the bones and Helen to Mother. Then..." I don't know what comes after that, but I don't care. I'll have fulfilled my vows. Perhaps I'll go search for the harp. *Stealing from the Queen will take time.* Doesn't matter right now. Once I've delivered the bones, I'll have plenty of time to think.

"You're taking Helen back to the clouds?" Jess asks, petting Helen's head. When I nod, she adds, "But what about me?"

"I'll take you home," I say, still stuffing bones into the knapsack without looking at her.

"And if I don't want to go home?" Jess asks. "Could I go to the clouds too?"

I pause, thinking about it before realizing just how bad of an idea it is. *She'll corrupt them.*

"No," I tell her, finally looking at her. She looks angrier than I've ever seen her. Not that I've known her very long. Helen looks between us in confusion. Raising my hands in a placating gesture, I add, "Once I return Helen and the bones to the clouds, you can join me for whatever comes next. I'm not going to just abandon you, Jess."

"But we'll be poor alone. We can't be knights now that we're outlaws," Jess replies, stroking the golden goose's feathers. "But with Helen, we could be royalty. Build a new kingdom! Why give her back? She wants to be with you."

"I made a vow," I say, looking back down at the bones, "and now I have to fulfill it. Even if the clouds consider me Forsworn, I don't. I'm still a giant, and a giant doesn't break an oath."

Jess doesn't reply—not that I expect her to. I know things would be easier keeping Helen, but I've never taken the easy path.

As I'm pulling the last of the bones into the sack, Helen cries out a warning, but I'm too slow to turn. A sharp pain fills me with more agony than I've ever felt, a hundred times worse than the dagger in my side. With a grunt, I slump forward onto the coffin. I can't speak, I can't even move. My mind is engulfed in a flood of pain, and I'm drowning in it. All I do is stare down at the tip of a sword protruding through my chest. I try to reach back for Jess, but she twists the blade, ensuring my wound won't close. That seals my fate. I whimper, slumping to the ground as a tear falls onto my cheek.

"I'm sorry, but I won't do it," Jess whispers from somewhere behind me even as Helen chokes. She drops the sword with a clatter and adds, "I came with you to find a better life for myself—and I did. I've learned that I need to take what I want. You taught me that, Titus." I flick my eyes toward Jess and see Helen flapping frantically but held by the throat. "I'll take good care of the goose. I promise. And that's an oath I won't break."

Jess begins walking away. With the last of my power, I reach out and grab her foot. There's not enough strength left to break her ankle or even hold her in place—only enough to trip her. Jess falls and instinctively lets go of Helen to break her fall using her arms. With that, the golden goose escapes through the doorway.

"Go home!" I wheeze as my childhood friend honks back at me desperately. "Please."

Helen does. She honks a sad goodbye before unfurling her wings and climbing into the sky—back to the Kingdom in the Clouds.

"No!" Jess shouts, scrambling to her feet and running out into the grass, but Helen's far out of reach.

If I could laugh, I would, but it hurts too much. *You broke your oath as fast as I did,* I think, because there's too much blood in my mouth to speak. *But Helen's going home... I fulfilled my second vow.*

Jess turns back toward me. I see that same menace in her eyes that dwelled on Jack's face. In a way, she's far more cunning than he ever was. Jess takes a step toward me, but behind her, the horn of the guards rings out. Closer this time. With a choice between killing me and being caught or fleeing and leaving me to die, she chooses the latter. She retrieves Harry from the stable post and rides away. Considering the guards have faster destriers, she'll be caught quickly.

But they'll catch me first.

Lying on the ground of the museum, I exhale, and the breath causes the embers of the ticket collector's cigar to flare to life. Staring at it, I have an idea. *I can still fulfill my last oath.*

Grabbing the cigar, I crawl over to the closest banner of House Spriggins on the wooden wall and set it alight with the embers. Fire roars upward, consuming the cloth and spreading across the room. Smoke and ash fill the museum as I crawl back over to my father's bones, cradling them close to my chest.

Smoke rises just like souls, Father, I think, hugging him. *We'll return to the clouds, to Mother, before we go back to the sun and are reborn.*

And with that thought, I know I've fulfilled my third vow. My soul feels light, as if the clouds accept me again. Like my father, I know I'm saved. My soul will return to the giants in one body or another. Perhaps even as a goose.

Smiling, I close my eyes and burn.

Enjoyed the Book?

Please leave a review. We read each one and use your input to make our stories better. Not sure how to leave a review? Just scan the QR code or click the link to be taken directly to the *Crimson Ink* review page.

http://www.amazon.com/review/create-review?&asin=B0DPLN4RQ6

Tristan here. Being a family-operated publishing house, MW Press relies on reviews to gauge reader interest. If we don't receive reviews, we're forced to assume that readers aren't interested in the story and must abandon our other planned short story collections to work on other projects. We want to write more stories like *Crimson Ink*, but without your help, we can't.

This is Blaise. It's not often that a father and son get to work together as co-authors, and I've enjoyed every minute of it. We both have. Tristan and I have been working on stories together for years, but thankfully, reviews only take a minute of your time. They mean a lot more than you think. Your review means I get to spend more time with my son.

Want More?

You can read more of our stories for FREE by joining our mailing list. Just scan the QR code or click the link to be taken directly to our landing page.

https://mwpressbooks.com/crimson-ink-mailing-list

Acknowledgements

Another special thank you to our family for supporting our dreams: to Kathy Miranda, amazing mother and wife, for inspiring us to continue even when the way forward was arduous; to Jake Miranda, adequate brother and son, for distracting us as much as possible; to Jeanamarie Miranda, cherished sister- and daughter-in-law, for listening and sharing our enthusiasm; to Cecilia Miranda, adorable niece and granddaughter, for staring at us with uncomprehending awe while drooling.

Thank you to Katerina Krizner and Liam Betts who have read these stories before they were ready.

Lastly, thank *you,* dear reader. Without your support and interest in our book, none of this would be possible.

About Us

Blaise Miranda (right) and Tristan Miranda (left) are a father-and-son writing team. Whether it's writing, working out, or riding motorcycles, they do everything together. Both are engineers by trade and storytellers by craft. They live in California, where the weather is good and the memories are better.

Crimson Ink is their first short story collection. Their other works include *Drowned Sea* and *Tooth and Nail.*